THE HORIZON WAR

by Robert Weinberg

Book 3
WAR IN HEAVEN

a World of
Darkness
Trilogy

WAR IN HEAVEN is
a product of White Wolf Publishing.

Cover Illustration: Jason Felix

White Wolf Publishing
735 Park North Blvd. Suite 128
Clarkston, GA 30021
www.white-wolf.com

Printed in Canada.

DEDICATION:

to Staley Krause, Danny Landers &
Kim Shropshire for reasons
too numerous to mention.

AUTHOR'S NOTE:

While the locations and history of this world may seem familiar, it is not our reality. The setting for *The Horizon War* is a harsher, crueler version of our own universe. It is a stark, desolate landscape where nothing is what it seems to be on the surface. It is truly a World of Darkness.

Certain concepts and characters have been inspired by those originally created by Bill Bridges, Steven C. Brown, Phil Brucato, Elizabeth Fischi, Chris Hind, Judith McLaughlin, James E. Moore, Nicky Rea, Allen Varney, Mark Rein•Hagen and Stewart Wieck.

"Oh what a tangled web we weave,
when first we practice to deceive!"
—Sir Walter Scott

Chapter One

"NO!" shouted Seventeen, his cry of anguish echoing through the toxic-waste dump. The very air, filled with decay and acid fumes, seemed to tremble from the depth of emotion in his voice. "I will not let her die! My love can't be taken from me. Not again!"

Seventeen, a massive man with slab-like muscles and a hairless face that appeared carved from granite, knelt on the far edge of the clearing located at the center of the Lake Ontario Toxic-Waste Dump. His hands and clothes were covered with blood. None of it was his. Only a short time ago, Seventeen, armed with a huge scythe, had been transformed into an angel of death, cutting through the horde of maniacs and cannibals sent to this site to destroy him and his companions. Dozens had died, cut to ribbons by a singing steel blade. But now the attackers were gone—dead or fled—and Seventeen's thoughts were on life, not death.

In his arms, the huge man held the limp body of the

beautiful warrior woman, Shadow of Dawn. A powerful willworker of the Akashic Brotherhood, Shadow was also Seventeen's lover. Gray tinged her silky-smooth saffron skin, agony closed her dark eyes. She shuddered in terrible pain with each breath. Three bloody scratches on one cheek told the tale. The Dragon Claw warrior, unconquerable by force of arms, lay dying—poisoned by the last man she had faced. Shadow had been infected by an ancient and deadly poison known as lycosis. And none of her allies knew of anything to do to save her.

Their surroundings were a scene straight out of hell. Everywhere, huge fires burned, and the ground bubbled like an insane cauldron. The immense toxic-waste dump stretched nearly a mile long by a mile wide. Barbed wire fenced it in on three sides, the polluted waters of Lake Ontario on the other. The site served as a major dumping ground by industrial complexes and government agencies from all over New York State. The most notorious pollution site on the East Coast, the place made real the worst nightmares of urban corruption.

Huge stacks of human refuse and garbage burned with pale blue-green flame day and night all year round. Clouds of black soot rose into the sky, blotting out the moon and stars at night, the sun during the day. Eternal red chemical fires, feeding on pits of industrial sludge dotted the landscape like volcanic craters, crackling and spitting clouds of poisonous gas out over the waters of the lake.

Steel drums of deadly poisons stood in long straight

lines, forming a maze of metal corridors that covered much of the site. Immense piles of rotting asbestos panels rose hundreds of feet in the air, like pale white altars of some blind, idiot god of pollution and greed.

The ground on which Seventeen knelt was as harsh and desolate as a desert, baked clean of all life. Huge cracks ran in jagged lines from one refuse pile to another. The land appeared to have been turned into glass, then shattered by some gigantic hammer. Foul clouds choked the air with sickening fumes rising from the rents in the earth.

Circled around Seventeen and Shadow were their companions in peril. Sam Haine, the Changing Man, stood closest. A wily old man with thick white hair and wrinkled features, he possessed an incredible ability to shift his shape, duplicating anyone with whom he had ever come into contact.

At Sam's side stood Albert, his closest friend and long-time companion. A huge walking-stick of a man, shadow thin and well over seven feet tall, he controlled the healing gifts of an African shaman. His mournful brown eyes were filled with tears. Though Albert wielded extraordinary powers, even his talents were useless against the poison in Shadow's veins.

Beyond Albert rested an exhausted Verbena willworker, Claudia Johnson. Normally, she acted as one of the several leaders of the Casey Cabal, the mystic stronghold located an hour southeast of the waste dump. Claudia, accompanied by three other mages from the cabal, had come to the waste dump to save Sam Haine from a trap. Of the four, only

Claudia had survived the madness and murder that had followed.

Next in the circle was a young blond woman dressed in white bike shorts and black halter top. An x-shaped scar crossed below her breasts. In each arm she cradled a sawed-off shotgun. The nameless woman had appeared at the end of the battle, and nearly managed to save Shadow from the assassins who had brought her down. Seventeen knew nothing about her, but her stricken expression made it clear she was no danger to them.

The last member of their small group was the most mysterious. And the most sinister.

Slender, of medium height, she had jet-black hair, bright red lips, and skin white as chalk. A young woman, she wore a simple black tank dress, black stockings and low heels. Around her neck was a silver necklace decorated with an elaborate "G." Though many killers had died beneath her flashing hands, she seemed undisturbed by the blood on her dress. Her name was Madeleine Giovanni and she belonged to the Kindred. One of the Damned. A vampire.

"I have heard of this potion, lycosis," said Madeleine. She spoke without an accent, but in short, clipping sentences, without contractions or slang. English was not her native language. "There is no known cure. Her blood is poisoned. My Embrace would not save her, and her vitae would destroy me."

"Doubt if Shadow would want to become a vampire, anyways," said Sam Haine. "She believes in reincarnation. Becoming one of the Undead puts a halt to the cycle. Don't think she'd consider it much of a rescue."

"*I—will—not—let—her—die*," said Seventeen, his arms holding Shadow close to him, a wild and strange look in his eyes. The rage building inside him burned as intensely as the chemical fires. He stared at the Changing Man, the man who in the last few weeks had become both mentor and closest friend. "Her destiny is to stand with Kallikos when he faces the pattern-clone for the final time. That's what she told me. The Time Master saw it hundreds of years ago. Shadow can't perish tonight. *I won't allow it*. Without her help, Kallikos has no chance of defeating the Ascension Warrior."

"Predicting the future's no sure thing, son," Sam Haine corrected. Gently, he laid a hand on Seventeen's shoulder. "You know that. Kallikos admits as much. He sees possibilities, not certainties. In this world, Shadow won't be at the Time Master's side. He'll have to fight that battle as best he can—alone."

"Her veins are on fire," said Albert, the tears streaming down his cheeks. "I can feel her anguish, sense the terrible pain. But there is nothing I can do to stop the spread of the poison. Her blood boils."

Blood. The word blasted through Seventeen's mind like a bolt of lightning. He shivered, squeezing his eyes tightly shut as he tried to grasp a fleeting thought. Shadow of the Dawn was dying, had only minutes, perhaps seconds of life left. Somehow, he knew he could save her. There was a way to defeat the poison. If only he could understand how.

Once before, there had been talk of blood. He recalled a conversation. Words about the power in his blood.

Like an exploding star, the memory returned. The cryptic remarks made to him by Jenni Smith, the servant of the pattern-clone, the being who called himself Heylel Teomim. *"Your blood is as his blood,"* she had said, explaining why her master wanted Seventeen to join his crusade. He had not understood what Jenni meant then. Now, in a dazzling epiphany, he realized the meaning of her words, knew the answer to his question. Seventeen grasped the truth about himself and what he had become. And realized exactly what the pattern-clone planned.

"Albert," he said, his voice barely above a whisper, but carrying through the entire waste dump. "In all of your rituals, in all of your spells, do you know a method of transferring blood from one individual to another? A technique that can be done immediately, without use of needles and medical equipment?"

The giant nodded. "Of course. I've done it many times in many places. Many wizards believe that true brotherhood can only be achieved by such a bond. Two become one through a sharing of the essence of life. It is a ritual as old as magick itself. I can perform the ceremony just using a cloth and a knife."

"Then join Shadow and me by the rite," commanded Seventeen, setting Shadow of the Dawn down on the barren ground. A deathly pale had settled over the warrior woman's face and her chest hardly moved. Seventeen stretched out beside her. He stared at the shaman, trying to remain calm. "Do it *now*."

"But, but..." said Albert, "the poison? You will be infected. If I mix your bloods, the lycosis will kill you as well as Shadow."

"No arguments," said Seventeen. His voice was cold. "I refuse to let her die. This ritual is the only chance we have to save her. I'm willing to gamble my life on it. But you're the one who must perform the ceremony."

"Do what he says, Albert," said Sam Haine. In one hand, he held the bowie knife he had used during the battle. Though caked with blood only moments before, the blade now glistened like new. Sam knew his share of practical magick. "Seventeen understands what he's doin'. Or at least I thinks he does. Tell me where to make those cuts."

Albert bent his fingers in a mystic pattern and pulled a long white cloth out of thin air. "There," he said, pointing to a large vein in Shadow's arm. "And there," pointing to the same location on Seventeen's limb.

"Cut mine deep," said Seventeen, his gaze locking with Sam Haine's. The rage inside Seventeen was gone, replaced with a calm certainty he was doing the right thing. "No half measures. Otherwise, my enhanced body will heal too quickly for the transfer to be made."

"Gotcha," said Sam Haine. "The light dawns, son. Albert, you set? Time's running out fast for this lady."

"Do it," said the giant, kneeling at Shadow's side. His immense arms reached out, poised to tie the two arms together as soon as the cuts were made.

With a flick of the wrist, Sam Haine slashed Shadow of the Dawn's flesh. Blood oozed from the four-inch long incision. Ugly, sluggish, black blood. Poisoned blood.

Then, drawing a deep breath, the Changing Man plunged the blade deep into Seventeen's arm. Razor sharp, the bowie knife cut deep into Seventeen's flesh. Snarling almost in rage, Sam dragged the tempered steel blade up Seventeen's limb.

Droplets of Seventeen's blood fell to the earth. Nanobyte blood, the same elixir flowing in the veins of the pattern-clone.

"His blood burns," whispered Madeleine Giovanni, her eyes widening in astonishment. For Seventeen's blood, where it touched the vile soil, *sizzled*, marking the ground like powerful acid.

"Blood to blood, life to life," chanted Albert, oblivious to everything but the ritual he was performing. He pressed the two wounds together, twisted the white cloth tightly around the arms, and let blood run into blood. That completed, he raised his hands into the air, weaving strange sigils that seemed to burn in the yellow, toxic air. "Heart to heart. Soul to soul. Join them, unite them, bless them, sanctify them by their wounds. Bind these two, make them one."

With a slap like a gunshot, Albert brought his palms together. "Let it be done."

"I can feel the wound in my arm closing," said Seventeen, raising his head off the ground. "Is the ceremony over? Were you able to make the transfer? Is some of my blood in her veins?"

"Yes," said Albert, with a shake of his head. "The ritual is complete. What you wished has been done. Your blood and Shadow's have mixed. Not much, but some. Though I must admit, I am still unsure why it matters. She is doomed. And now, so are you."

"I strongly doubt that," said Seventeen, his confidence building with each passing instant. Reaching out, he unwrapped the white cloth from around his arm. He laughed, trying to stay calm. "You forget who I am, Albert. More importantly, you forget *what* I am."

Sitting up, he stretched out his arm. The limb was whole. Other than a thin dark line, there was no sign of the deep gash made less than a minute before. As Seventeen flexed his fingers, making sure that he possessed full control of all his digits, the dark line vanished. The wound was entirely healed.

"I'm a marvel of Technomancer biotech," he declared to no one in particular, a bitter edge to his voice. "My bones are reinforced with Primium, making them unbreakable. My muscles and nerves are enhanced with microchips. My brain has been modified to give me complete control of my entire body. My blood is mostly artificial, the product of nanobyte drivers that operate at a sub-molecular level. Anything I suffer heals in seconds. I'm nearly unkillable, and, for all practical definitions, immortal."

"Your blood is poison to my kind," said Madeleine Giovanni. She nodded, as if answering a question not spoken. "Not even the most powerful vampire could Embrace a mortal with nanobyte vitae."

"Seems like your gamble's paid off, son," said Sam Haine. "Our lady of the swords is lookin' a lot healthier."

Seventeen turned to Shadow of the Dawn. The transformation worked slowly but steadily. Color returned to her cheeks. Her breathing grew stronger by the minute. The look of pain vanished from her features. With a laugh of triumph, Seventeen raised the warrior woman's arm, pointed to where she had been cut. The wound had already closed, the skin starting to reform.

"My nanobyte blood is programmed to eliminate any weaknesses in my body," said Seventeen. "It works automatically, destroying viruses and toxins, and renewing itself whenever necessary. When we transferred some of my blood into Shadow of the Dawn, the fluid continued to work as programmed. It wiped all the impurities from her veins, including the lycosis. No poison invented is stronger than a nanobyte invasion."

"Then Shadow of the Dawn now has nanobyte blood?" said Claudia Johnson. "Almost the same as yours?"

"*Identical to mine*," said Seventeen. "Absolutely identical. Anything less would be imperfect, and the nanobyte drivers would not allow that. Though she doesn't have my enhanced body or senses, we share the same blood. And all the benefits it provides."

He rose smoothly to his feet. Reaching down, he effortlessly lifted the Japanese girl in his arms. She stirred, as if in sleep. Her eyelids flickered, then opened. Shadow smiled as she saw Seventeen's face.

"I felt great pain," she said. "Death stared me in the face. Then, suddenly, he retreated."

"Sometimes even Technocracy science has its uses," said Seventeen, with a smile of his own. "Are you strong enough to stand?"

For the first time, Shadow seemed to realize that she was being held in Seventeen's arms. "Put me down," she declared, sounding embarrassed. "Others are watching. It is not proper for you to hold me thus."

Sam Haine chuckled. "Too late to worry about scandal, young lady. Seventeen's made it quite clear that you two are more than just friends."

Reaching out, the old willworker took one of Shadow's hands between his. After a moment, he sighed. "Damned world moves faster than I can comprehend. She's fine. Healthy as can be. Not a trace of poison left in her system."

"Poison?" repeated Shadow of the Dawn, slipping out of Seventeen's arms and regaining her footing. Immediately, her hands darted to the handles of her two swords, as if seeking reassurance from the twin blades. "What poison?"

"We can talk about that later," said Seventeen. He suddenly felt very weary, drained of emotion. "It's time for us to get moving. We all need rest. Afterwards, we can discuss what happened here."

"Sounds right fine to me," said Sam Haine. "I could use a long, hot bath. Looks like our shotgun blonde's already hit the trail."

The enigmatic young woman was gone.

"Sister Susie," said Madeleine Giovanni, putting a name to the phantom. "She walks her own path in search of salvation.

"I too, must leave. The sun will be rising soon. You return to the house in the forest? Good. We shall meet again. I will come to you to discuss common enemies and a shared strategy to defeat them."

"Nice to have made your..." began Sam Haine, then stopped speaking, his jaw dangling open in shock.

Soundlessly, Madeleine Giovanni dissolved into a fine cloud of mist. Swirling, the dark fog twisted, reformed, took on a new shape. Where the woman had been an instant before now stood a small black wolf, its fur glistening, its red eyes gleaming with more than animal intelligence. Around its neck, like a dog collar, hung the vampire's silver necklace.

Baring its teeth in what almost appeared to be a smile, the wolf darted off through the waste dump. It ran like the wind, its feet hardly seeming to touch the ground. In seconds, it disappeared from sight.

"Always knew vampires could change shapes," said Sam Haine. "Never saw it happen before my eyes. That girl has talent. Too bad she's dead. Mighty attractive even if she's a tad young."

"She's probably a lot older than she looks," said Claudia Johnson, licking her lips nervously. "And, remember, she drinks human blood for nourishment."

"Don't need to worry about me, Claudia," said Sam. "I'm not that dumb. For all of her perfect manners and girlish good looks, I suspect that this Miss Madeleine's not someone to fool with."

"She killed with style and grace," said Shadow of the Dawn. "Never a wasted motion. She knew what she was doing, and she did it well."

"Well, she seems to be on our side," said Sam. "That's a plus. Way things are goin', we need all the help we can get."

"More now than ever," said Seventeen, once again unable to keep the bitterness out of his voice.

Still, despite repeated questions from his comrades he refused to elaborate on what he meant. The truth could wait until after they had rested. Bad news could always wait till later.

Chapter Two

The scream was so loud, so powerful, so *intense* that the cement walls of the control chamber shook. It seemed to last forever, rocking Sharon's bones, and making her teeth ache. In the real world, five seconds passed.

"Hell and damnation," said Ernest Nelson, his face a mask of shock. "The Wailer's gotten inside the building. That wasn't from outside. He's coming for us. Damned sonofabitch doesn't believe in quitting. Persistent freak."

"How—how—how can he do this?" said Lauri Coup, sounding bewildered. Her beautiful features were creased with fear. "These walls are built from concrete reinforced with steel and Primium bars. It's impossible to damage them. Dr. Reid believed in maximum security. He constructed this lab like a fortress."

"Welcome to the real world," said Sharon, trying not to panic. "Filled with lies, more lies, and still more lies. Don't believe anything you read. And never believe anything you're told."

Nelson was right. The Wailer was already somewhere in the building, searching for them. Somehow, the monster had tracked them to this abandoned research center in the heart of Indianapolis. Perhaps the phone call to the Progenitor Data Bank she had made earlier had been a mistake. Too late to worry about that now.

The Wailer was obviously determined to destroy them. According to what Sharon had been told by Nelson, always a font of similarly cheerful information, the Wailer had never before failed in a mission of destruction. She and the cyborg were the only two ever to face the monster and survive. Their first escape had been mostly a matter of luck. This time, trapped in the underground control center, it appeared their luck had run out.

One-time rivals and often bitter enemies, Dr. Sharon Reed and Ernest Nelson had become allies in their desperate search for the superhuman pattern-clone that had named itself Heylel Teomim. As the Progenitor Research Director of the Gray Collective, Sharon had helped create the clone. Ernest Nelson, a cyborg also known as X344, had been chief assistant to Dr. Charles Klair, the Iteration X computer expert also involved in the clone project. None of them realized at the time that they were all pawns in a plot that threatened the entire Technocratic Union, if not all creation.

Sharon and Nelson were the only two survivors of the disaster that had engulfed the Gray Collective. Held responsible for the pattern-clone, they had been ordered by the Technocratic Symposium to locate the being and destroy it. Reluctant associates at first, they soon found themselves forced to cooperate to remain alive. A horde of Nephandi Reality Deviants—men and women pledged to the forces of evil—were determined to destroy them at any cost. Leading the pack was a monstrous being known as the Wailer. A Technomancer traitor who murdered his victims by amplified sound, he was one of the most feared killers in the world.

"Are there emergency steel shutters to replace the doors your dog smashed descending to this level?" asked Sharon. Years of experience dealing with disaster served her well in dangerous situations. Calm nerves, steady blood pressure, level adrenaline flow helped keep panic under control. In emergencies like this, fear could kill.

"Of course," said Lauri Coup. "I activated the backup security system the moment you passed through the maze leading here. I don't believe in taking chances. To reach us, the Nephandi will have to break through several dozen reinforced steel doors. Plus, Dr. Atkins and his killers won't be able to descend to this level without neutralizing the automatic chain guns mounted in the walls. The entire mansion is a gigantic deathtrap."

The shriek, when it came, lasted ten seconds. By the time it ended, all three of them were stretched out on the floor, hands over their ears, mewling in pain. The worst thing about the Wailer's screams was that there was no escape. The sound was everywhere.

All of the meters, control panels and plastic casings in the room had dissolved into powder. Sharon suspected that if they were subjected to the Wailer's screams at close range, the same would happen to her bones. If she didn't come up with some sort of plan, quickly, the rest of her short life would be spent as a glob of protoplasmic jelly.

"We have to get out of here," she declared. "Fast. The Wailer's coming and those reinforced doors and traps aren't going to stop him. Fighting is impossible. We either flee or die."

"No argument from me," said Nelson. "My body's half Primium and steel. Each scream strains it a little more. A few more howls and I'm history."

The control room shook, not from sound waves but from a powerful explosion.

"They're blasting their way through the more difficult chambers," said Lauri Coup. Death was in her eyes. "Between the screams and the bombs, this place doesn't stand a chance. They'll arrive here in minutes."

"Seems like the Wailer's got to catch his breath for a few minutes between howls," Nelson said. "Gives us a little time to think straight. You're sure there aren't any other exits from the building? It seems like most underground labs have a secret tunnel leading to the surface."

Lauri Coup shook her head. "No such animal. Dr. Reid was paranoid about being discovered. Any tunnel out, he felt, was also a tunnel in. The only escape is through the mansion. There's several hidden doors leading to the street. But with the Nephandi in the halls, we'd never reach them alive."

"The Wailer's buddies don't worry me," said Nelson. "I can take the whole crew on with one arm tied behind my back. But I'm not capable of stopping their boss. He's no pushover. What I don't understand is how his own men survive these screams?"

"Directional waves," said Sharon Reed. "One of Dr. Atkins's specialties. He was studying the effects of amplified sound focused in one specific direction. Thought he could modify humans so their voices could be used as weapons."

"Well, he sure as hell did," Nelson replied. "Too bad he went nuts and joined the Nephandi. You got any ideas, Reed? I'm dry as a bone."

"We're in an abandoned research station, part of the EcoR complex," said Sharon, spinning through her thoughts out loud. "I know how Reid thinks, worked with him on various projects over the years. He hates the Nine Traditions with a passion. He's obsessed with destroying them. Like Coup says, Reid's paranoid to the point of mania. He sees shadows everywhere, suspects the Traditions are out to eliminate him before he destroys them. He might be right."

"Yeah, yeah, yeah," said Nelson, sounding impatient. His massive fingers clenched and unclenched with nervousness. "Get to the point already. The Wailer's gonna scream again any minute. Reid's suspicious of everybody and everything. What of it?"

"Don't you see?" said Sharon. "Reid would never build a research and experimentation facility without a rear exit. Especially not one with underground levels. There has to be another way out. A secret passage, like you mentioned. If not leading to the surface, then one leading to the EcoR Collective. We just have...."

The scream rose from a steady whine to an incessant, all-consuming wail. It shook the room, rattled the walls, caused the floor to buckle. Two needles seemed to dig into Sharon's skull, ramming deep into her brain. Her skull, she was sure, exploded. Blood filled her eyes, her nose, her mouth. With a scream of her own, she collapsed to the cement. The last thing she remembered was the floor racing up to meet her face.

She couldn't have been unconscious for more than a few minutes. Then she was moving, slung over a massive shoulder like a sack of grain. Her skull was still intact. Eyes blurring, head pounding like it was being slammed by a sledgehammer, Sharon spotted a dazed Lauri Coup dangling in a similar position a foot away. Despite her innate distrust for the man, the Research Director had to admit that the cyborg was sometimes worth his weight in gold.

"Let me down, Nelson," she called, to no response. "Let me down."

Still no response. The cyborg kept moving, paying no attention to what she said. With a curse, Sharon smashed a fist into the small of Nelson's back. "Let me down, you metalhead freak," she snarled. "I can walk for myself."

Nelson halted, swung her off his shoulder and back onto her feet. Before she could say a word, he pointed his one free hand at his ears. "Don't waste your breath talkin'," he declared. "That last blast was too much for my circuitry. Blew out my artificial eardrums. I'm stone deaf. Can read your lips if you speak slow. But there's not much time for talking. Wailer can't be far behind."

"Where—are—we?" she mouthed, forming the words distinctly so that he could see what she was saying.

"Lowest level of the building," replied Nelson, his voice slurry. Reed's eardrums screamed, a throbbing high-pitched whine. "If there's a portal to EcoR," Nelson continued, "it's here, hidden by the regeneration and growth tanks. We better find it fast. The Wailer sounded awfully close."

"Coup?" asked Sharon.

"She's out," said Nelson. "Possible concussion, blood drippin' out her ears. Maybe brain damage. Who knows. That last scream was a killer. Still, she's one of ours. I couldn't leave her behind for those fuckers. Looks like you're on your own, Reed. Find that portal or the Wailer keeps his kill record perfect."

"Great," muttered Sharon, her eyes automatically adjusting to the murky darkness of the research station's lowest level. "Searching for a needle in a haystack with the bogeyman at the door. My lucky day."

A muffled roar rippled through the air and the floor shook. Sharon cursed. Nelson must have been shouting at the top of his lungs. She was nearly deaf. Not that it mattered. At this range, the Wailer's screams were powerful enough to shatter flesh and bone. If he drew too close, the monster would make their bodies explode like nuclear bombs.

"Trying to blast open the door to the control room," bellowed Nelson. "Should take them a few minutes. Once they make it inside, they'll discover I planted a few concussion grenades in unexpected locations. Keep the bastards honest. Maybe buy us a few extra minutes while they search for other traps."

Sharon cursed a second time. Nelson merely demanded the impossible. First she had to find the secret portal leading to the EcoR Collective. Then she had to activate it before the Wailer arrived.

The growth chamber was sixty feet long by thirty feet wide. Laid out like dozens of other such facilities. Four ten-foot by five-foot regeneration tanks flanked a middle aisle. At the base of each tank, a computer monitor reported all the activity in the unit. A master control panel at the head of the room kept track of each individual machine, sorting and checking data to make sure that all experiments were proceeding as planned. Normally such chambers were staffed by three Technomancers, but under emergency circumstances, the facility could be run by one.

Hastily, Sharon scanned the chamber, searching for some anomaly, some small difference in the layout that might indicate the presence of a hidden door. Nothing, nothing at all. It looked like every other regeneration center she'd ever seen. Sharon snarled in impotent fury. She was a Technocrat, not a detective. There wasn't a clue to where the portal might be located. As far as she could tell, the only thing missing from the chamber was the daily progress chart, listing the status of all operations, that was normally posted on the flat wall behind the main computer bank. There wasn't even the usual bulletin board.

A series of three short, sharp shocks rocked the floor. "Sounds like our friends found those concussion grenades," said Nelson, grinning. "Unfortunately, that means they'll be swarming down the stairs soon. Wailer's been silent for the past few minutes. I suspect he's building up a nice big scream for the showdown. If you're gonna find that portal, better do it soon."

In a half-dozen steps, Sharon was at the front of the chamber, past the main computer, her left hand resting on the blank wall. It felt cold, much colder than concrete had any right to be.

Twisting about, she waved Nelson, Coup still over one shoulder, forward. "Here it is," she declared, knowing the cyborg couldn't hear a thing she was saying. "Hidden in plain sight. Typical of Dr. Reid's thinking."

"You know the code to get past the portal guardian?" asked Nelson.

"Of course, you metal moron," said Sharon, making sure Nelson couldn't see her lips. She beckoned him forward. "I'm a Research Director. I know *all* the proper Progenitor Collective codes. Give me a second and I'll open the gate."

"Company!" roared Nelson. Three powerfully built men, dressed entirely in black, came hurtling out of the stairwell leading from the floor above. Psychotic killers, recruited from overflowing prisons to serve as shock troops by the Nephandi. Human monsters who lived only to kill. But tough as they were, none of the three possessed willworker skills. Three against one, they still were no match for the combination of man and machine known as Ernest Nelson.

Moving with lightning speed, the cyborg dropped Lauri Coup and swung both arms up like cannons. The chain guns concealed in his arms bellowed, sending a hail of bullets streaking across the chamber. One killer managed to squeeze off a few shots. They missed. Nelson didn't. Three bloody rags hit the floor, leaving large crimson stains on the walls.

"Better hurry," yelled Nelson. "They're the first, but won't be the last. And the Wailer can't be far behind."

Hand on the wall, Sharon reached out with her mind and opened a telepathic channel with the guardian of the portal. Unlike most such creatures, the biotech sentinel had no physical form. Instead, the creature—a being who thought of itself as WALL—existed within the rock and cement of the gateway itself. No wonder Coup never knew there was a passageway here. Reid hadn't shared the secret with any of his associates. He had kept the knowledge of the escape hatch completely to himself. With WALL living inside the stone, there was absolutely no hint of the passage's existence.

"Paranoid lunatic," muttered Sharon, as she mentally commanded WALL to open the gate that connected the Research Station with the EcoR Horizon Realm. Beneath her hand, the stone grew warm, soft, then disappeared.

The wail began as a massive, low-level buzz, deep and sonorous, the volume growing in intensity to fill the entire underground chamber. With a series of loud cracks, the growth and regeneration tanks shattered one by one. Desperately, Sharon grabbed an immobile Ernest Nelson, trying to spin the cyborg to the portal. Already she could feel the pressure inside her head, the pain building at exponential speed.

With a heave of his massive arms, Nelson tossed the limp body of Lauri Coup through the gateway. A shove from those same huge hands sent Sharon staggering through the portal, tumbling into the white-walled reception area of the EcoR Horizon Realm. She dropped to the floor next to Lauri Coup. Two red-clad students in jackets scurried back, astonished expressions on their faces.

Two, three, four seconds passed. Then, like a human guided missile, Ernest Nelson hurtled through the Horizon gateway. Blood seeped from his nose, his ears, but the cyborg was grinning. An instant later, the room shook as if hit by a gigantic hammer.

"Couldn't take a chance that the Wailer might be able to follow us through the portal," said Nelson, his mouth dripping crimson. "So I dumped the rest of my grenades on the floor in front of the gateway when I left. Figured they'd seal up the passage nice and tight."

Sharon grinned and shook her head. Metalhead or not, Ernest Nelson was the most amazing person she had ever met.

Chapter Three

It was late afternoon when Seventeen woke. As always, he felt refreshed, fully restored, in perfect health. With his enhanced body and nanobyte blood, it would always be thus. Forever. Except for the most dire circumstances, he would never die. It was his blessing. And, for him in particular, it was his curse.

Last night, upon returning to the Casey Cabal, he and his three companions had agreed that a war council was necessary to discuss the events of the past week. Tonight, in the sacred grove not far from the cabal, they would meet and try to understand the cataclysm that appeared to be drawing closer and closer. A cataclysm they seemed helpless to prevent.

Shadow of the Dawn, a half-smile on her lips, stirred in her sleep next to him. Seventeen reached out and gently caressed the woman he loved. Her smile widened but she didn't wake. When this war was over, they would be joined in marriage by whatever rituals and customs Shadow preferred. The words and ceremonies meant nothing to Seventeen. He knew that on a deeper level, they had already been bonded with a seal that could never be broken. The Wheel of Drahma had turned, and two destinies had been made one. For now and for the future.

The bright sun peeked through the thick green and brown curtains of the window across from their bed. Rising with fluid grace, Seventeen swiftly got dressed. Finding garments to fit his huge frame had been a challenge. Bluejeans and a t-shirt served for the moment. A smattering of memory of a black cape, boots, shirt and slacks flicked through his thoughts and was gone. Someday he would remember. Not yet.

The bedroom assigned to them was small but comfortable. It contained an old-fashioned wood frame bed, complete with feather pillows; a couple of chairs, some cushions, and a small table. Clothes they kept in a small trunk that fit beneath the bed. There were no decorations on the walls, nor were any needed. Everything in the room was made from wood and intricately carved with elaborate pictorial designs. There was no wallpaper on the walls, no tile or carpeting on the floor. The room was entirely natural. To Seventeen, it felt as if he were in the center of a forest glade. Exactly the impression he was sure the members of the Casey Cabal intended to convey.

Shadow needed rest, not only to recover from the poison, but to allow her body to adjust to the miracles of its nanobyte blood. Albert had cast a powerful sleep spell on the warrior woman during their trip back to the cabal. She was not due to awaken for another hour. Seventeen intended to be at her side when she emerged from deep sleep. But before then, there was another with whom he had to confer.

He found Claudia Johnson in a small room at the very top of the Casey Cabal enclave. The chamber wasn't much bigger than the bedroom he shared with Shadow, but being at the peak of the building, there were windows on three of the four walls. They were all open, and a cool breeze blew from east to west. Again, the room was entirely natural. Here the walls were covered with elaborate carved murals, portraying the four types of Verbena—the Gardeners of the Tree, The Twisters of Fate, the Moon-Seekers, and the Lifeweavers. Knowledge Seventeen possessed, though he couldn't remember its source. He just knew.

The attractive, middle-aged woman who served as one of the Chantry leaders sat at a solid mahogany desk surrounded by a forest of plants and flowers. The smell of growing things was all pervasive, almost hypnotic. Outside the open windows, birds sang. Seventeen felt as if he had been transported to a place deep in the woods, far away from the old nineteenth-century mansion that had been converted into a Verbena chantry.

Claudia looked up as Seventeen stepped forward. Nodding as if expecting him, she beckoned to a chair directly across the desk. A piece of plain white paper sat on her ledger, and in one hand she held an old-fashioned fountain pen. Here it did not seem unnatural or out of place.

"These are the letters I hate writing the most," she said to Seventeen, putting aside the pen. "Telling distant families that their son or daughter died in an automobile accident or was killed in a union-management confrontation. Always a lie. I can't put down the truth. The pain I feel is made worse because these letters bring no comfort, only greater anguish. Those who died were ones I loved. The cabal is my family, my true family. Hurting their relatives hurts me."

"Actually," said Seventeen, staring at Claudia Johnson, "that's why I've come to see you. People die. That's one of the basic facts of life. I accept that. But lately I'm starting to feel like I'm the cause of their deaths. And that troubles me."

"Death always raises questions," said Claudia Johnson. She leaned back in her chair, stretched her arms over her head. Sunshine glowed across her dark skin, seemingly making her one with nature. "No one at Casey Cabal blames you for anything."

"Still," said Seventeen, leaning forward so that his elbows rested on the edge of the desk, "if I hadn't come to your community, many who died the past few weeks would be alive today. You'd be writing a lot less letters."

Claudia shrugged. "You could be right, or you could be wrong. Who knows? I doubt that even Kallikos, the Time Master, would try to answer that riddle. These are dangerous days, Seventeen. People get killed. Simple as that. No one's safe from violence. It's a tough world and everyone here at the Casey Cabal accepts that. So should you."

The Verbena willworker stared with unblinking gaze at Seventeen. "Sam Haine, one of our own, brought you here," she declared. "He warned us of the risks, that you were a hunted man. We accepted the danger. Casey Cabal's always served as a home for the homeless, a hiding place for the hunted. Can't change that." For an instant, her tones softened. "Years ago, I too was such a refugee."

"But the attack by the Men in Black," said Seventeen, "was a direct result of me being here. And the murders committed by Terrence Shade...."

"You forget what I told you last night," said Claudia. "We're not children here. We're servants of the Goddess, soldiers of the Traditions."

Reaching down, she pulled open a drawer of her desk. The room, filled with light a moment ago, now seemed darker, as if reflecting Claudia's mood. The birds outside were no longer singing. Even the smell of the flowers seemed bitter, tainted by decay.

"I told you I hate writing those catastrophic letters," she said, dropping an inch-thick manila folder onto the desk ledger. "You think they're the first I've ever had to send? Life's filled with unhappiness, Seventeen. You think you brought death to this otherwise tranquil setting? Think again. Take a look at this miserable folder. Every page is another death. We're fighting a war with the Technocracy. There's casualties. Plenty of them. Understand?"

"I'm—I'm sorry," said Seventeen, caught off guard by Claudia's anger. "I never realized."

"Of course not," she said. The air in the room felt close, as if pressing in on all sides. "We're living in a combat zone. People here accept the fact. Deal with it. Sam Haine angered Aliara with his actions, but Terrence Shade was the maniac who killed members of the cabal. Ditto that shootout with the Men in Black. They came after you, but that didn't stop the bastards from trying to blast us to oblivion at the same time. Stop blaming yourself for the troubles of the world, Seventeen. Suffer all you want for your own mistakes. *But don't suffer for ours*."

"That's the trouble," he replied, struggling to regain his composure. Now the flowers smelt sweet again and the sun was shining. He wasn't used to dealing with an office that reacted to the emotions of its boss. "I don't feel any remorse. Not one bit. Last night, I slaughtered anybody who got in my way. Never gave it a second thought. Must have killed dozens. Pretty damned grisly. Yet, today, I don't feel the least bit unsettled. I'd do it again if necessary. Without the least concern. If anything, I feel *pleased*."

"And that lack of guilt worries you?" asked Claudia.

"I'm not sure," said Seventeen. "Part of me says I should care, that killing's wrong. The civilized side. But last night, holding that scythe, I felt *complete*. It didn't feel wrong at all. I fought because I *wanted* to kill our attackers. It wasn't rage, nor anger. It just seemed *right*."

"Damn," said Claudia. "Just what I didn't want to hear. Wait one minute. Don't say another word."

Carefully, she looked around the office, as if searching for something unseen. Rising to her feet, she closed the windows. Then closed the door into the room. Brow furrowed in concentration, she pressed her hands against each wall of the chamber in succession. Kneeling, she rubbed the wood floor. Then, climbing onto her chair, she touched both sides of the V-shaped ceiling.

"You've got superior senses," she said, settling back into her chair. "Anything alive in this room other than us? Forget the flowers and plants, they can't do much talking. But how about a mouse? Or a bug?"

Seventeen closed his eyes, listened for a minute. Not a sound other than his life systems and those of Claudia Johnson. "Nothing."

The room was almost totally dark, despite the sunshine outside. Though the light pierced the windows, it never made it to the floor. Claudia lit three candles, red, yellow and green, muttering a few words as she did so.

"What we say is between us and no others," she declared. "I dislike secrets, but sometimes it's better to remain cautious. Especially after that trouble with that shapeshifter, Jenni Smith."

"You think there's spies in the cabal?"

"Don't know," said Claudia. "I wish I did, but nothing's certain anymore. Too much at stake to take any chances."

"Chances about what?" asked Seventeen.

"When you came to us," said Claudia, "Sam Haine told me your memory had been wiped clean. That along with your name, you couldn't even recall your Tradition. That still true?"

"No," said Seventeen, with a shake of his head. The

room darkened even more. Only the glow of the candles provided light. "I remember now."

"*Euthanatos*," said Claudia Johnson. The candles flickered with each syllable.

"How did you know?" asked Seventeen.

"It was quite obvious seeing you in action last night," said Claudia, an edge to her voice. "Cutting away with that scythe. Listening to that damn thing *sing*. Hearing you talk today just reinforced my suspicions."

"Why did you lock the doors and close the windows?" asked Seventeen. "Euthanatos mages belong to the Nine Traditions. We're not criminals."

"They're not held in very high regard among the Verbena," said Claudia. Her expression was grim. "More now than ever before. The so-called Death mages believe in the *good death*. Their philosophy states that only through a continual cycle of death and rebirth can humanity reach Ascension. Fortunately for you, I'm a free thinker. I don't believe our Euthanatos brethren are mad killers. They only terminate the evil or the hopeless, giving those victims a new chance in a never-ending cycle."

"Each good death puts the victim one step farther on the path of true redemption," said Seventeen, remembering words he had said to Jenni Smith. "Only by dying can we truly understand living."

"Not according to my personal beliefs," said Claudia Johnson. She rested one hand on the folder on her desk. Filled with copies of letters sent to families of members of the cabal who had died fighting the

Ascension War. "Or the beliefs of anyone else living here. According to Euthanatos philosophy, you were actually doing those scum last night a favor. Sending them to their next reincarnation, hopefully where buried memories of their past misdeeds would direct them towards a better life."

Seventeen couldn't help but smile. "While the noble side of me holds with the Euthanatos belief, I'll admit that some small voice deep inside me hopes that maybe both our beliefs are wrong and those fuckers are frying in hell."

"Others among the Verbena aren't so tolerant these days," said Claudia. "Which is one reason why I prefer you not to mention your Tradition to anyone else at the cabal. The last thing we need at the moment is to start fighting among ourselves."

"I can keep my mouth shut," said Seventeen. "No problem. You said *one reason*. Implying that there's another?"

"At present," said Claudia, staring directly at Seventeen, "the Euthanatos mages are viewed with a great deal of suspicion by all the other Traditions. Not just the Verbena."

"Why?" asked Seventeen. The smoke from the candles sent strange shadows scuttling across the wood ceiling. Though the room was entirely closed and it was summer outside, the chamber felt deathly cold. "Why?"

"There was a trial on Horizon recently," replied Claudia. The candles flickered with her words; the flowers surrounding her desk smelled sickly sweet, the scent of death. "A young woman, Theora Hetirck, was charged with the brutal murder of a number of mages. She belonged to the Euthanatos Tradition, and to many present, it seemed that the entire Tradition was being judged."

"A Tradition willworker killing other mages?" said Seventeen. "That doesn't make sense."

"The evidence presented was overwhelming," continued Claudia. Her voice was soft, but every word distinct. "The girl participated in ambushes of several chantry houses, even including attacks on Euthanatos Cabals. There were survivors and their testimony was grim. Captured willworkers were tortured to death."

"This whole episode is madness," said Seventeen. "Euthanatos mages torturing other mages, killing them for no reason. That's not the good death. I don't understand."

"Madness," repeated Claudia, nodding. Her eyes glowed in the candle light. "The woman was found innocent, but not because she didn't commit the crimes. Instead, her chantry was judged to have gone mad. Killing for the sake of killing had become their goal. The young woman was deemed to have been brainwashed by her comrades. The judges ruled she shouldn't be held responsible for an evil forced upon her by others."

"Others?" said Seventeen, a vague memory struggling to rise from his subconscious. "Who?"

"Immediately following the trial, agents of the Traditions descended upon her Chantry, intent on destroying its leader and his followers. They found only an empty plain of dust, marked by gigantic footprints and vast amounts of blood. Now there have been suggestions that the madmen have joined with Heylel Teomim. That their crimes were a portent of the Abomination's rebirth."

"Who led this insane Chantry House?" asked Seventeen, as an image rose in his mind.

"Voormas, Grand Harvester of Souls," said Claudia. "Supreme master of the House of Helekar."

With the name, the image became reality. An ancient, bony, dark-skinned man, tall and thin, his head hairless like a polished skull. He wore a black robe, stitched in red with scenes of sacrifice: throats being cut, children being sacrificed at altars, heads being chopped off by axes. A face with hollow cheeks, thin, blood-red lips and eyes that burned black as if reflecting the darkness in his soul. His crooked smile hinted of secrets no mortal man should know. Claw-like hands ended in long fingers capped with inch-long yellowed nails. Around his neck, a grotesque necklace of eyeballs stared at Seventeen as if they still functioned. He carried a cane made of the bones of human fingers and toes, wrapped one around another as if climbing upward. On its top rested the skull of a child, mouth open, eye sockets gleaming red.

"The master of the Consanguinity of Eternal Joy," whispered Seventeen. "Assassins who killed anyone they thought threatened the Euthanatos Tradition. Voormas reigned their leader for the past two centuries. I'm not surprised to learn that he twisted the cult's beliefs to his own aims. He was the most frightening mortal I ever met."

"Evidently he long ago abandoned the ideals of the good death," said Claudia Johnson. "He killed, not in hopes of raising souls to Ascension, but instead for the sheer joy of murder. And those who served him followed his same warped ideals."

"I spoke with him once," said Seventeen, following a thread of memory. "Voormas claimed to be Kali reborn, bringing the Age of Iron to the world. I didn't care. In those days, I followed my own path and nothing else mattered. My question made him laugh, but he gave me an honest answer."

"What did you ask him?" said Claudia Johnson. A single candle burned. The rest of the room was pitch black, reflecting her concern, the fear that chilled the air.

"Directions," said Seventeen. "Directions for the road to hell."

Chapter Four

"Who the fuck are *you?*"

The words were muffled, as if yelled in a wind tunnel, but loud enough that Sharon could hear them. Repairing her eardrums was going to take some real work. Maintaining a tight grip on her temper, she swiveled around on the floor and looked up at the questioner.

The speaker was a short, husky black woman who appeared to be in her early thirties. Sharon knew, based on her own case, that age among Progenitors could be deceptive. The woman was dressed in baggy white pants and a loose-fitting white jacket with black trim. According to the usual code of such labs, the jacket fringe identified her as a Primary Investigator, in the same category as Lauri Coup.

They had emerged in a reception office, a fifteen by twenty foot rectangle with a ten-foot-high ceiling. It had the standard white walls, four steel chairs with black cushions, a black desk and several black metal file cabinets. Three black-and-white pictures on the walls—Newton, Gauss, and Einstein. The only color in the entire place was their red blood.

"I repeat," said the short woman, staring with unwavering eyes at Sharon, "who the fuck *are* you? And what's with the Arnold here?"

The woman's tone was harsh, bordering on offensive. Typical of her rank. Sharon searched her memory, trying to remember the names of Dr. Reid's chief assistants. She couldn't. It wasn't important. A few choice words would set things straight.

"I'm Dr. Sharon Rand," said Sharon, using the alias arranged for her a lifetime ago by NWO agent John Doe. Her tone was ice-cold. The encounter with the Wailer had sucked all the diplomacy out of her. "Research *Director* working under *direct orders* of the Symposium. My clearance, if you would be so kind as to check your computer database, is Alpha-Alpha. The 'Arnold,' as you called him, is my personal bodyguard, Ernest Nelson. His clearance is likewise Alpha-Alpha. The third member of our group is Primary Investigator Lauri Coup. The purpose of our mission is *none of your business*. As to our appearance here, that is *also* none of your business. All you are required to know, *Investigator*, is that we are all in need of immediate medical attention. Dr. Coup and Agent Nelson have been seriously injured. Any worsening of their condition will be noted on your record." Sharon's voice cracked like a whip. "*Is that understood?*"

The short woman wasn't easily intimidated. Still, the tone of her voice changed from abusive to polite.

And her language switched from "street" to "strictly business." "Check those names in the mainframe databank," she said to one of the two administrators standing frozen in shock behind the metal desk. "And run all the usual ID confirmations. If you're who you claim, we'll roll out the welcome mat. But not until we do the proper checking. Reality Deviant activity has been on the upswing lately. I'm not taking any chances." She echoed Sharon's tone perfectly. "Is *that* understood?"

"Perfectly," said Sharon, letting one of the administrators scan her eyeprint. "Your name is...?"

"Dr. Sara Burns," said the woman.

"Thank you, Dr. Burns," said Sharon. At present, it was foolish to antagonize the Investigator further. Accidents could happen—even to Research Directors. Later, when this mess was finished and life returned to normal, Sharon would make sure Dr. Burns caught a bit of payback. For now, politeness was in order. "I appreciate your devotion to duty."

"Their identities are confirmed, Dr. Burns," said the administrator. "As is their security clearance and rating. Definitely Alpha-Alpha."

"As expected," said Burns. She waved a hand at the far wall. "Power down," she declared to unseen watchers.

Sharon couldn't resist a laugh. "You really weren't exaggerating your fear of Reality Deviants. Laser-gun snipers in the hallway? Afraid we might transform into monsters?"

"I meant what I said about not taking any chances,"

declared Burns. "Skeleton crew on duty here. Just eleven of us. The rest of the staff returned to Earth with Dr. Reid. We've remained on full alert all day, ever since that fuckin' broadcast. Nobody knows what shit to expect next."

No surprise. Obviously, the pattern-clone's broadcast to the Technocracy, using the Union's own computer network, had everyone on edge. The situation would only get worse until she and Nelson found and destroyed the monster they had helped create.

"I'm glad you're taking your responsibilities so seriously," said Sharon. "Because I'm ordering you to immediately terminate all communication with Earth. All travel passes from this lab are hereby canceled. No one is to leave the Construct. No mention of the arrival of me or my companions is to be noted or registered. By my authority, this Construct is completely sealed until further notice. Please do not misunderstand these directives as being punishment. They are not. A state of emergency exists. Several Constructs have been lost due to Reality Deviant activity. I don't want EcoR to suffer a similar fate. Absolute secrecy is a must."

"Alpha-Alpha classification puts you in charge," said Burns. "I'm transmitting the necessary instructions to the Construct computer as we speak. All lines of communication have been cut. Meanwhile, as you said, your party needs medical attention. I've alerted the Regeneration Specialist and Genengineer at the station. The three of you look like you've been through a Mixmaster. Dr. Ishida and his crew will personally handle your injuries. Let's get you there, now."

A few hours later, Sharon felt much better. White cotton pajamas were soft and cool against her skin. Her hearing was back to normal and all of her biosystems were functioning at peak efficiency. All she needed was a few hours of peace and quiet.

She was resting in a large, pleasant recovery room on the fifth floor of the EcoR construct. Unlike the sterile research facilities on the lower levels, this chamber actually featured soothing blue walls and a deep green plush carpet. Several framed prints of mountains hung on the walls. Still somewhat woozy from her time in the regeneration tank, she sat propped up with several pillows on a comfortable bed at the rear of the chamber. Behind it stood a small oak dresser on which rested a reading light and small bowl of plastic flowers. Her visitor sat in a matching oak chair. Like many Progenitor off-world Collectives, the building smelled like disinfectant. Sharon found the odor reassuring. Almost like a memory of home.

"It was a great pleasure in managing the details of your recovery, Dr. Rand," Dr. Ishida said in precise, clipped tones. The Primary Investigator was small, neatly dressed, and exceedingly polite.

He sat on the wood chair not far from Sharon. As promised, he'd closely monitored each step of her treatment. Like everyone in the Construct, he dressed entirely in white. A Primary Investigator like Burns, black braid trimmed his jacket. In direct contrast to his compatriot, Ishida spoke softly and with perfect manners.

"Your body is a marvel of advanced genetic engineering," said Ishida, smiling. "It gives me joy to observe such a wonderful system restored to full functionality. It is an honor to have aided in your regeneration and renewal."

"What's the word on my two companions?" asked Sharon. Since being separated from Nelson and Coup hours ago, she had not seen either of them.

"The cyborg has been repaired to the best of our ability," said Ishida. He rose to his feet, paced back and forth as he spoke. His body burned with nervous energy. "An illuminating study. Amazing how much damage he can absorb and still remain functional. I commend you. He is an excellent choice for a bodyguard. We are unable to replace some of his weaponry, but he is otherwise in good working condition. To be at peak efficiency, he should visit an Iteration X armory as soon as convenient."

Sharon smiled, remembering Nelson's battle with the saber-tooth tiger back on the Gray Collective. And how he handled the Nephandi attack on the NWO Construct in Albany. The cyborg operated at peak efficiency no matter what weaponry he possessed.

"Finding a spare second might prove to be a problem," said Sharon. She saw no reason to mention that their appearance at any Earth Construct would immediately attract the unwelcome attention of the Nephandi. "Mr. Nelson will have to improvise for the immediate future. I've found that he's quite adaptable to circumstances. And what he lacks in armament he makes up in sheer determination."

"He was resting comfortably when I left him," said Ishida. He glanced at the door, obviously anxious to be back in his lab. "I believe he was playing chess with the EcoR computer system."

No doubt integrating himself into the Realm security system, thought Sharon. Along with studying the personnel files of everyone on the base, charting the fastest exit routes in case of trouble, and memorizing all of the Earth gateway codes. Nelson liked to be prepared for any emergency. It was a quality that Sharon had grown to appreciate.

She yawned. Her body required rest. Still, she needed to know a little more before she allowed Ishida to depart.

"How's Dr. Coup?"

"I'm afraid that the Primary Investigator suffered much more serious damage than either you or your companion. Her body was not extensively redesigned and reinforced. The sound-wave attack you described caused massive impairment to her nervous system. Her inner ear has been completely destroyed. We repaired fourteen broken bones. Further tests are needed before we can fully assess her mental state. At present, she remains stable in a regeneration life-support tank on the lower level. We are still conducting tests, but it also seems likely that she suffered some brain damage.

"Unless her condition changes drastically, we'll be

forced to use more powerful stimulants to restore her to consciousness. Such drugs, as you know, are extremely risky. At the moment, I cannot promise she'll survive."

"Do your best to keep her alive," said Sharon. "I'm not sure if Dr. Coup knows anything more concerning my investigation, but I'd like one more opportunity to question her. Dead, she is worthless."

"I will instruct my team to proceed with extreme caution," said Ishida. He walked for the door. "If we succeed in our efforts, I will have you summoned immediately. For now, considering the stress your body has undergone today, I suggest that you spend some time to rest and recuperate. This level is reserved for important guests of the Construct. With most of our normal staff on Earth, the floor is deserted. No one will disturb you."

"A few hours of sleep does sound good," said Sharon, finally willing to let Ishida leave. "But don't hesitate to wake me if Dr. Coup regains consciousness. Questioning her is more important than any nap. I've gone days without slumber when necessary."

"As have we all," said Dr. Ishida. "Please be assured that your wishes will be conveyed to my team by me personally."

The small man reached for the light switch on the wall near the door. "Please rest now." He turned off the light. A thin glimmer of illumination where the door met the floor was the only break in the darkness. "Sleep and regain your strength."

Feeling reasonably safe and secure, Sharon let down

her mental guard and drifted off into a deep sleep. She agreed totally with Ishida. Her body needed rest. For a few hours at least, she could be off duty.

A glimmer of light, lasting for only seconds then vanishing, woke her. Reacting instantly, Sharon was alert, completely awake. Someone had opened the door to the office and slid inside. Sharon assumed any such intruder was not there merely to say hello. Eyelids raised a millimeter, she scanned the chamber with a gaze that immediately adjusted to the near total darkness.

Her visitor was a tall, slender woman with long hair. Lauri Coup. She wore white pajamas like Sharon and cloth slippers that slid silently across the thick carpet. The Primary Investigator was halfway through the room when suddenly Sharon sat up on the cot. Caught by surprise, Coup froze.

"Coup, what are you doing on your feet?" asked Sharon, confused and astonished. She reached to the nightstand and turned on the light. "Dr. Ishida said your condition was serious. You shouldn't be moving around. It's not safe."

"Ishida lied," said Coup, taking a step forward. Her voice sounded odd, high-pitched, different from before. Most likely a reaction to the strong drugs administered to her. "He can't be trusted. None of the Technocrats in this facility can be trusted. They're all traitors, Reality Deviants. This whole place is a massive deathtrap."

"I've seen no evidence of deceit," said Sharon, keeping close watch on the other woman. Coup sounded delirious, irrational. Ishida had mentioned the possibility of brain damage. Odd, though, that she had been able to leave the treatment center and find this room. Why hadn't Ishida's crew stopped her? More than odd, it was extremely disturbing. "Dr. Reid maintains tight control over his associates. The slightest hint of treachery and he'd be on it in an instant."

"I knew you wouldn't believe me," said Coup. She slid another step closer. Both her hands remained beneath the white hospital pajamas. "Can't say I blame you. It's hard to accept that the Union's being eaten alive from within. That's why I brought proof. Stuff that will convince you I'm not lying."

"Proof?" said Sharon. "What sort of proof?"

"This proof," said Lauri and leapt forward. Her right hand lunged for Sharon's neck, the left swung a surgeon's scalpel over her head. The steel blade arced in a deadly path straight at Sharon's eyes.

A veteran of a hundred combats over the decades, Sharon knew better than to try to stop the blow. Instead, she jerked her head down and grabbed for the wrist of the hand with the scalpel. She yanked forward. Coup's own momentum did the rest. The metal scalpel slammed harmlessly into the wall inches above Sharon's skull.

For a moment, the Investigator's torso stretched exposed over Sharon. Seizing the opportunity, Sharon thrust up with a shoulder, catching Coup hard in the stomach. With a cough of pain, the Investigator stumbled backward. The steel instrument dropped from her hand.

Sharon lunged forward, her hands seeking the other woman's neck. Coup reacted with surprising quickness. Grabbing Sharon's arms, the Investigator folded her knees and tumbled backwards and down. The move sent Sharon flying over Coup's head. Reflexes honed from years of training landed her on her feet. Immediately she whirled, to find Coup standing as well, facing her.

The door leading outside the room was only a few feet behind Sharon, but she knew better than to try for it. When fighting an opponent of unknown ability, the first rule of combat was *never turn your back*. Sharon had no idea what deadly skills her enemy possessed. She wasn't prepared to take any chances.

Warily, soundlessly, they circled each other like dueling wildcats. Hands raised out in front of her like a boxer, her legs slightly bent, staring her opponent in the eyes, Sharon analyzed her chances. Coup was younger, taller and heavier. Sharon was quicker and an experienced fighter. To Sharon, it seemed they were evenly matched. The odds were not to her liking.

"I'm going to tear out your throat, bitch," said Coup, gnashing her teeth. Yellow fangs gleamed in the light. She raised her hands, displaying three-inch-long fingernails. A black tint spoke of poison. "Or maybe I'll rip out your heart."

"Help!" shouted Sharon, yelling as loud as she

could. Whoever she faced, it wasn't Lauri Coup. "In here. Help! I need immediate assistance."

"Scream nice and loud," said Coup, the huge incisors making it difficult to understand what she said. "The lab walls in this Construct muffle sound. No one can hear a word outside the room. It's just you and me. No outsiders. You're all mine."

"I'm trembling," snarled Sharon, letting some of the anger boil up from deep inside. Just enough to fuel Coup's overconfidence. "Claws and teeth don't win fights. I've fought worse and I'm still breathing. They're not."

"Sure," said Coup, grinning. "You're real tough. Senile old hag."

"Fuck you," shouted Sharon and, seemingly in frustration, lashed out with a right and a left. Sneering, Coup hopped back a step, out of reach of flying fists. Her feet hit wood. In their movement around the room, they'd reached the point where the Investigator was positioned directly in front of the chair used by Dr. Ishida. For a instant, her gaze flickered down.

All of Sharon's clumsiness disappeared. Her left foot snapped upward in a deadly kick aimed at Coup's chin. But it didn't connect.

Hands moving with blinding speed, Coup raised crossed arms in front of her face. The blow hammered the Primary Investigator in the wrists and sent her crashing backward across the wood chair. However, she was still conscious. And full of fight.

Rolling to the right, Coup was back on her feet

before Sharon could close in. "My my," said Coup, no longer smiling. "Grandma has a few tricks after all."

Sharon said nothing. While her body had been enhanced with several killing devices, they were meant for in-close fighting. Coup showed no inclination to grapple. Even with her fangs and claws, the woman seemed content merely to defend herself. Which was what worried Sharon. Something bad was going to happen at EcoR. Soon.

"Maybe we..." began Coup, then leapt forward. Claws extended, she ripped at Sharon's face.

Instinctively, Sharon dropped to the floor. Her left leg swung around in a sweeping wheel kick. Coup leapt up, laughing again. "Oops! Too slow, old lady!"

"Hey, *wrestling*," came a gravelly voice in the door, as the light from the hallway filled the chamber. "I love this stuff. Mind if we make it tag-team?"

"What the..." snarled Coup, caught by surprise. For a moment, her attention focused on Ernest Nelson, leaning in the doorway. It was all the time Sharon needed.

"Playtime's over," muttered Sharon, lunging forward. Waist high, she slammed head first into the other woman's stomach. Coup gasped, her arms flailing wildly in the air. Sharon gave the Investigator no time to recover. Shooting upward, Sharon caught Coup square in the chin with her skull. Fangs crunched and shattered. The Investigator staggered back. Grabbing Coup's left arm, Sharon twisted it up and around her enemy's back in a vicious hammerlock. With a screech, the Investigator dropped to her knees. Savagely,

Sharon wrenched the limb higher. Coup tumbled face first into the carpet.

"Old lady," growled Sharon as she dug her fingers into pressure points behind the Investigator's neck. Like a puppet with its strings cut, Coup collapsed flat onto the floor, unconscious. Drawing several deep breaths, Sharon rose shakily to her feet.

"So Coup turned out to be a double-agent after all," said Nelson as he walked over to Sharon. The cyborg wore white pants and a white lab jacket that barely covered his immense chest. "Sorry it took me so long to make it here from my room, but our buddies at EcoR locked my room from the outside. Your assistant or not, I'm still a member of Iteration X. Wasted a minute breaking out quietly. If I'd realized the situation, I would've hurried more."

"You hooked into the mainframe monitoring all the rooms in the station during your chess session?" asked Sharon, checking Coup's vital signs. For someone supposedly comatose, she was in excellent condition. "Figured you'd be listening for anything suspicious. That's why I yelled, to get your attention."

"So I gathered," said Nelson. He looked down at the unconscious Investigator and shook his head in disgust. "Makes me annoyed that I wasted the time rescuing her from the Wailer."

"You just don't get it, do you?" said Sharon. "Any major mind-chillers in those secret compartments of yours? Heavy-duty crap that blocks out all conscious volition? You know, no-independent-thought-at-all stuff."

"I picked up a few marks of Neural Sting when we made that weapons run in Indianapolis," said Nelson. "It's pretty potent. Turns the target into a total zombie for a few hours. You want to use it on Coup?"

"Give me a capsule," said Sharon, ignoring the question. Bending over, she pressed the needle-tipped gel-pack into the motionless woman's neck. "That should keep the bitch quiet for a few hours."

"What's the big deal?" asked Nelson. "Two of us, one of her. She's tough, but not that tough."

"Don't be totally stupid," said Sharon. Hurriedly, she pulled open the drawers of the oak dresser. The second contained several white lab outfits. Off came her pajamas. Nelson wisely kept his mouth shut as she dressed.

"Coup's *dead*," said Sharon. "You can bet your metal head on that. This isn't her. Our friend on the floor is a shapeshifter, just like Velma Wade. First she killed Coup. Then she adopted her appearance in hopes of catching me off guard long enough to finish me as well. Probably would have visited you looking like me."

"*Very* nifty," said Nelson, as Sharon retrieved a pair of stretch shoes from the third drawer. "You want to keep her doped up so she doesn't take the Suicide Express?"

"You're finally starting to wake up," said Sharon, now fully dressed. "She's probably carrying a half-dozen poison pills inside her teeth. If we numb her out, it's possible we might get a few answers before she self-destructs."

"Why not just hand her over to Ishida and his gene team?" asked Nelson. "Or better yet, to that Dr. Burns. She strikes me as the type who enjoys interrogations."

"Too late," said Sharon. "EcoR's been compromised. We can't risk staying here any longer than necessary. Time to grab this loser and start running."

"Compromised?" said Nelson. "What the hell do you mean by that?"

At that moment, all the lights went out.

Chapter Five

To Seventeen, the circular glade not far from the Casey Cabal Chantry House would always be the Grove of the Goddess. It was a very special location. In the little more than a month of memories that he possessed, several of the most important moments of his life had taken place in this clearing.

It was here, right before the beginning of battle with a Men in Black amalgam, that he had first glimpsed Shadow of the Dawn. That night, she had been clothed in a loose-fitting sky-blue jacket and matching pants. With saffron-colored skin, dark eyes, and long black hair, she was a striking beauty. There was beauty of another sort in her matched swords, Whisper and Scream, which she had wielded with deadly efficiency that night.

Here, too, on another night, when he was trying to fathom the meaning of a life without a past, had Seventeen discovered the wild passions that burned within the soul of the warrior woman.

The other woman in his life, Jenni Smith, had been

present on both those nights as well. Slender, with flowing blond hair and blue eyes, she seemed always to dress in a long blue shift, decorated with immense pink flowers. A thin shard of clear crystal hung from a rawhide thong around her neck. Though she appeared to be no more than eighteen years old, Seventeen suspected that with Jenni Smith, appearances were deceiving.

The first evening, after the attack had been repelled, the young woman had accused him of being one of the Nephandi. The charges had stunned Seventeen, since only hours earlier, Jenni had escorted him to the sacred grove and explained to him the truth about the Ascension War. Only after she disappeared had he learned that the girl had not been performing that task for Sam Haine. And that she was a mystery no one at the Casey Cabal could explain.

His second encounter in the grove with Jenni Smith took place shortly after the abortive attempt by Seventeen and his allies to destroy the pattern-clone. That night, she had returned to the glade to tell him of a crusade by her master to unite the Nine Traditions and the Technocratic Union, putting an end to the Ascension War. With her, Jenni brought an invitation, an offer for Seventeen to join this Master of Harmony, not yet identified as Heylel Teomim, in his holy mission. The goals were right. Peace for all mankind. The start of a rebirth of the human spirit.

The reward for Seventeen's participation was power almost beyond measure—the Master of Harmony wanted Seventeen to act as his viceroy on Earth. To rule the material world as the supreme arbiter, immortal and omnipotent, a god among men. Or so Jenni Smith had claimed.

For a moment—more than a moment—Seventeen had been tempted. How could any man of virtue not be swayed by such ideas? The chance to change the face of the world forever—it was an opportunity not to be taken lightly. Worried that the offer was just a trick, he had asked what made him so special.

That had been the moment when Jenni replied, "Your blood is as his blood." At the time, Seventeen had not understood what those words meant. Now he did. The implications behind those six words were staggering. And frightening beyond measure.

The Master of Harmony, the being who called himself Heylel Teomim, was not begging for the participation of the Traditions or the Technocracy. He demanded it. The ultimate power was his. Heylel controlled a secret that with a few words would spark the greatest conflict ever waged on the Tellurian. With an unshakable will and indestructible form, he truly was the Ascension Warrior.

"Rememberin' past girlfriends?" asked Sam Haine, waving a smokeless cigar in Seventeen's face. "Pretty blond thing in a flower-print dress?"

"Sometimes," said Seventeen, "I think you can read minds."

The white-haired old man laughed. "Nothing so spectacular. Just a combination of common sense and good guessing. Though if I was gonna develop some new powers, this spring is surely the place to try."

There was something to what Sam said. At the center of the grove, surrounded by a ring of thick green grass, bubbled a pool of crystal-clear water. In the light of their fire, the water glistened red and gold, moving almost as if alive. Once this glade had served as a gathering spot for Iroquois Indian shamans. Hundreds of rituals and mystick ceremonies had been held here celebrating nature and its bountiful gifts. Over the centuries, the spring had been transformed into a place of great power, the water filled with the essence of magick called *Tass*. The entire clearing glowed with life energy.

"Sam likes to downplay his gifts," declared Albert, squatting beside their campfire and stirring the center of the blaze. "Despite what he says, he relies on more than luck and common sense. No ordinary man guesses right that often. Sam possesses a magickal intuition that enables him to separate fact from fantasy, truth from lies. And, in a small way, sense what others are thinking."

"Albert always likes to explain everything cut and dried," said Sam, his bright eyes twinkling. "Takes the fun out of everything. Leave it to me and I says its an eye for details."

The Changing Man grinned. "Take me fishin' Jenni Smith's name out of the air just now. No magick necessary for me to surmise you were thinking about her. Here we are, in the grove where you encountered the girl twice. Pretty young lady, other than she's as treacherous as a rattlesnake. First she tempts you, then accuses you, then tempts you again. Seems to me that type of behavior marks a man. When your face grew all thoughtful and such, figured she was the one you were thinking about."

"It could have been another," said Shadow of the Dawn, looking less than pleased with the conversation. She sat cross-legged in front of the campfire, next to Albert. Fully recovered from her near-bout with death, the Dragon Claw warrior had been listening to the conversation with less than her usual stoic expression. Seventeen refrained from laughing at her scowl. He kept his mouth shut. Despite all of her *Do* training, Shadow of the Dawn had an intensely jealous streak. To Seventeen, it made the near-invincible Japanese woman a little more human. And all the more captivating.

"Actually, I was thinking of both Shadow and Jenni," said Seventeen diplomatically. "Not that way, Sam, so wipe the leer off your face. In doing that, I realized an odd coincidence. A fact I suspect is no coincidence at all. I was remembering Jenni Smith's choice of clothes."

"Her clothing, son?" said Sam Haine. "You lost me on that one."

"I understand," said Shadow of the Dawn, her eyes narrowing with thought. "The woman we saw in the Gray Collective who appeared to be Jenni Smith, aiding the newly awakened pattern-clone, wore a long blue dress decorated with bright flowers. When the true Jenni Smith visited you late at night in this grove, I was hiding in the shadows and watched the entire encounter. She, too, wore the exact same dress."

"She also wore it when I first met her," said Seventeen. "Remaining in character is one thing, but exact duplication is something else. Why did both Jenni and her 'sister' adopt the exact same appearance? Everything from the length of her blond hair to the pink of the flowers in the dress's floral design. There were no differences between the two of them. There has to be a reason, and it's something more than similar tastes in wardrobe."

"Problem with you, son," said Sam Haine, dropping down beside Shadow of the Dawn by the fire, "is that you keep on raising questions that don't have answers. If we understood exactly what was goin' on, maybe we could make some sense out of this complicated mess. There's too damn many players in the game. I don't think even Kallikos, arguing with the leaders of the Nine Traditions on Horizon, knows who's behind what scheme."

"Perhaps," said Seventeen, the only one still standing. "Though I suspect Kallikos has a better grasp on what is happening than any of us imagine. He has seen the future and is desperately trying to...."

He never finished the sentence. In a motion quicker than the eye could follow, Shadow of the Dawn was on her feet, standing beside Seventeen, her back to the fire. In her hands, she held her two swords, Whisper and Scream. The warrior woman's gaze was focused on a dark spot just beyond the reach of the campfire.

"Who comes?" asked Shadow. "Identify yourself."

"A friend," declared the slender young woman stepping out of the shadows.

The lady in black, thought Seventeen.

The title fit. Madeleine Giovanni evidently didn't believe in variety in her outfits. She wore a thigh-high black tank dress, black stockings and low black heels. She had jet-black hair and her fingernails were painted black. Her skin was snow-white, her lips ruby red. Around her neck was a silver necklace decorated with an elaborate "G." The symbol of Clan Giovanni. Though she appeared in her early twenties, Seventeen felt certain she was older than any of them, with the possible exception of the ageless Sam Haine.

"As promised last night," said Madeleine, "I have returned to discuss mutual foes and a common enemy. I mean none of you harm. Despite our dire reputation, not all Kindred are blood-crazed monsters. My word is my bond, and I assure you I do not give it lightly. Nor do I ever break my pledge once made."

"Sounds fine to me," said Sam Haine. He glanced at Shadow of the Dawn, her swords still drawn. "Sheath your blades, Shadow. I made some phone calls this morning while the rest of you were snoozing. Talked to a few friends of mine who know something about the Kindred. Even tried, without success, to track down an old buddy of mine, renegade willworker named Dire McCann who had some dealings with Miss Madeleine recently. In all instances, word was the same. She's death walkin', but her word is as good as gold. When she says *honor over death*, she means it. Consider her one of the good guys. At least until we've cleaned up this mess."

Without the slightest sound, Whisper and Scream disappeared. Her expression serene, Shadow of the Dawn dipped her head slightly to the lady in black. "You fought well last night," she murmured. The words served as an acknowledgment and greeting.

"As did you," said Madeleine, settling down next to Sam Haine. Primly, she tugged the tiny mini-dress across her white thighs. "Your skill with two swords is a marvel to behold."

"Sit, already, you two," said Sam Haine to Shadow and Seventeen. "Tires my neck starin' up in the air. Makes my poor old bones ache."

With a sigh, Seventeen dropped to the earth, Shadow of the Dawn at his side. Relentless energy burning through his body made Seventeen restless. A fire burned within that could not be quenched. He often found sitting nearly impossible. Especially when Sam was in the mood to lecture.

"Good," said Sam. "About time, the way I sees it. Time for a parley and pow-wow and exchange of information. Seventeen, you and Shadow were present at the destruction of Doissetep. Only survivors so far's we know. Me and Albert did a lot of talkin' with important folks while we were on Horizon. Madeleine, and I hope you don't mind me usin' your first name cause I plan to do it anyway, you're here for reasons none of us know. Last night, you spoke of Enzo

Giovanni and Everwell Chemicals. How he was behind the attack at the toxic-waste dump. Can't help but notice you and him share the same last name. Not a coincidence, I bet. There seems to be lots of information floating around that probably ties together in some manner or another. Maybe if we puts our heads together, we can make some sense of it all."

"I can find no fault in your logic," said Madeleine. She spoke softly, carefully pronounced every syllable. "My mission here is simple enough and I am free to reveal the details to whomever I choose. Though I cannot discuss clan secrets, I otherwise am a free agent."

"From what I've heard, you're called the Dagger of the Giovanni," said Sam Haine, waving his cigar in front of the campfire. "Got quite a reputation for violent activity."

Madeleine smiled, a thin red line that gave Seventeen the creeps. For all of her beauty, the lady in black was definitely not remotely human. "I am known by that title. Simply put, like willworkers, the Kindred are divided into various groups—clans—each with certain beliefs and long-range goals. Clan Giovanni, of which I am a member, is involved in global finance and trade. We are the bankers and investors of our race. But even in business affairs, sometimes diplomacy is not enough. Certain problems require a show of force. When that occurs, I am summoned. Though I am not giant in size, my will is strong."

"Nicely put," said Sam Haine, chuckling. "Of course, you forgot to mention all the gruesome stuff about drinkin' blood and necromancy and plottin' to rule the world, but I think we can skip that stuff for tonight. As long as you're on our side, Madeleine."

"I can assure you that if you were not," said Madeleine, without the slightest hesitation, "this conversation would not be taking place. I take my responsibilities quite seriously. In order to avenge the death of my father, I chose of my own free will to become one of the Kindred. The decision was mine. As you stated a moment ago, I do hold honor over death."

"Well and good," said Sam. He seemed to be enjoying himself immensely. "Let's keep things nice and simple. Straight to the point. Why are you here? Who's this Enzo Giovanni character? Like I said, some relative of yours? And why was he willing to pay five million dollars each for our heads?"

"I will tell you what little I know," said Madeleine. "Hopefully, combined with your knowledge and experiences, we will find the answers to those questions."

Seventeen glanced over at Shadow of the Dawn. The warrior woman was listening intently to Madeleine's every word. Though, he noted, her hands remained fixed on the hilts of her two sheathed swords. Shadow trusted Madeleine, but only so much. Dealing with the undead made all of them nervous.

"I was sent to America to investigate the activities of my distant great-uncle, Enzo Giovanni," said Madeleine. Not a trace of emotion colored her words. "For several years, he has served as chairman of a large multi-national complex known as Everwell Chemicals. Only recently was it discovered that Everwell was part of an even vaster business conglomerate, Endron International. And now I have learned that Endron is merely a front for a global entity called Pentex. Clan elders believed that Enzo managed the company as part of our own financial empire. However, lack of any communication from him worried my grandfather, Pietro. He grew increasingly suspicious that Enzo had ambitions that went outside the family interests. That he was no longer loyal to our clan. My mission was to determine Enzo's true plans. And if they were as suspected, put an end to the traitor and his work."

Listening to Madeleine speak, Seventeen concluded that they were getting the condensed, sanitized version of what really had taken place. She was telling no lies, but taking a complex tale and making it simple. A look at Sam Haine's smiling features told Seventeen he wasn't the only one to have reached that conclusion. Madeleine Giovanni was revealing what was necessary and no more.

"Keeping to the shadows, I conducted my investigation. It soon became clear that Enzo was not satisfied with his position in the hierarchy of Clan Giovanni. He desired more. A great deal more. Like many of my family, his ambition ran deep. Do not be fooled. Greed remains strong even in undeath.

"Working with his close friend and associate, an insane willworker named Ezra, my uncle has come up with an incredible plan. Plotting together, Enzo and Ezra scheme secretly to become the uncrowned masters of the world. Aided by a unseen ally with demonic powers, the two are determined to gain total dominance of the Pentex Corporation and Clan Giovanni. Controlling the two organizations will give them a stranglehold on the world's economy. Though seemingly free, all of humanity will be their pawns.

"Their unseen ally, in the meantime, plans to become master of the Nine Traditions and the Technocracy. Working in concert, vampires and willworkers can then reshape reality into a world more to their liking."

Unbidden, the words of Kallikos's prophecy came to Seventeen's lips. "*An unending curtain of darkness covering the world. The cessation of individual thought. Mankind drowning in a sea of black blood. A breaking down of the barrier separating life from undeath.*"

"How poetic," said Madeleine Giovanni, with a curious look at Seventeen. "Obviously, it is a nightmare with which you are already familiar."

"A clan of vampires," said Sam Haine, all the humor gone from his voice, "a vast corporate monolith spanning the globe, and a majority of all willworkers —combined together to plunge the world into everlasting night. The notion sounds crazy, but it could be done. Damned scary, but it's possible, given the participants. From what we've witnessed lately, even likely."

"You mentioned a third partner in this unholy alliance between the living and the dead," said Albert. "A being possessing demonic powers. Do you know the name of this creature?"

"Yes," said Madeleine. "Of the three schemers, he is the true mastermind behind their machinations. Enzo and Ezra like to think they are independent agents, but they obey his every command."

They expected her to say *Heylel Teomim*. And they were surprised when Madeleine didn't.

"He is called Lord Steel," said Madeleine. "The Duke of Hate."

Chapter Six

"What the hell is going on?" said Ernest Nelson, his glowing electronic eyes providing the only illumination in the absolute darkness. "Who turned out the lights? The Collective Operating system was fine a minute ago. I better run a mainframe diagnostic, see if we're under attack."

"No!" shouted Sharon, realizing immediately what would happen if Nelson made contact with the Construct computer.

Only a few feet separated her and the cyborg. Unlike Coup, he wasn't expecting trouble. Her hands flashed up, grabbed Nelson by the shoulders. Trying not to hit him in the eyes, Sharon spit in her companion's face.

Nelson bellowed in pain as the fine spray of acid sizzled across one cheek. Synthetic skin, stronger than the real stuff, bubbled and hissed but didn't dissolve. The cyborg would be scarred but otherwise not seriously damaged. But the pain he felt had to be intense.

Years before, Sharon had installed acid sacs inside

her mouth. The idea had come from a book title. *Kiss Me Deadly*. Close up, she was as venomous as a spitting cobra.

"Are you fucking crazy?" screamed Nelson, his metallic fingers catching her around the throat. His glowing eyes seemed to flash blood red. Steel digits contracted, choking the life out of her.

"Couldn't let you hook up with the EcoR computer," said Sharon, desperately wrenching at Nelson's fingers. Despite all of her biomodifications, Sharon was helpless in the cyborg's grasp. "He's in control. Would have taken over your circuitry in an instant. Finished both of us a second later."

"He?" repeated Nelson, his mechanical fingers loosening. The anger whistled out of him like steam from a pressure-cooker.

"*The pattern-clone, metalhead*," said Sharon, pulling the cyborg's hands from around her neck. She rubbed the bruised skin. Nelson was incredibly strong. "*Remember*, the monster we're supposedly hunting? Unfortunately, at the moment, the situation's reversed. Now he's the hunter. And we're the prey."

"That's nuts," said Nelson. "The clone, here? On EcoR? Just because the lights went out?"

"Shut up and don't do anything unless I tell you," said Sharon. "Before you get us both killed."

Dropping next to Coup, Sharon grabbed one of the woman's fingers, spit on it. The skin blackened like burning paper. Blood dripped to the floor. "Out cold," said Sharon. "Pick the bitch up and let's move. We need to get back to Earth before this place implodes. Have to find a safe haven."

Nelson hauled the unmoving shapeshifter onto one huge shoulder. He hardly seemed to notice. "Care to fill me in a little?" he asked. "Explain what you think is happening?"

"Is it possible for you to brighten your lights?" asked Sharon, ignoring the questions. She pulled open the door to the hall. "Even with my enhanced vision, I can't see a thing."

"Sorry," said Nelson, "but I never figured on acting as a human lightbulb. I'm at maximum visibility. Try under the bed. There's an emergency kit with a pocket flashlight — or at least there was in my room."

"Got it," announced Sharon a moment later. A narrow beam of white light touched the open door, spilled into the hall. "Out we go. You know the layout of this place. Find us the nearest gateway to Earth that's not computer-controlled."

"Two levels down," said Nelson. "Ishida's lab. Bioengineered guardian instead of a mechanical. You figure the other portals are closed?"

"When we arrived at EcoR," said Sharon as they shuffled through the dark and deserted corridor, "I ordered Burns to completely seal the Construct from outside contact. Nobody was allowed to enter or leave. Same applied to information. My aim was to give us time to recuperate and plan our next move. I figured with all communication severed from the outside world, we were safe here. But, instead, I found myself attacked by the lowlife you're carrying. Any of this information raising questions in that solid steel skull of yours?"

"I get it," said Nelson. "If EcoR was sealed tight, where did this babe come from? How the hell did she find us?"

"Now you're thinking instead of merely reacting," said Sharon. "Answer came to me immediately. This shapeshifter had to be here *before we ever arrived.* It's the only solution. Like Velma Wade at the Gray Collective, she was in deep cover waiting for the proper moment. No doubt our arrival changed whatever plans she had for EcoR. Instead, she secretly reported our arrival to the pattern-clone. I'm sure Velma's warned him I possess the self-destruct command. So the clone sent orders to eliminate us."

"Shit," said Nelson. "Maybe I'm paranoid, but seems to me that this conspiracy has deep roots. Traitors everywhere. You got me seeing ghosts in the walls, Reed."

"Join the club," said Sharon. "I'm starting to realize the revival of the pattern-clone was the final step in a far-reaching plot to seize control of the Technocracy. Combine the incredible powers of the clone with a secret Fifth Column spread like a cancer through the Union and you have a prescription for disaster."

"Closest stairs to Ishida's lab are over here," said Nelson, pointing to a break in the corridor's white walls. "I doubt the elevators are still working."

"Avoid anything controlled by the EcoR computer system," said Sharon, pulling open the door to the stairwell. "Listen closely. Hear anything? Not a sound, right? That's because the whole Collective's been shut down. None of the life-support systems are working. Air-conditioning's off. No power. No communications. All controlled by the mainframe. Disable that and the building comes to a complete stop."

"And the one being who has the power to take over any system, override all safeguards and protective circuits..." began Nelson.

"...Is the pattern-clone," said Sharon as they walked down the stairs. The stairwell was pitch black and totally deserted. As with all of EcoR, there was not a trace of dust anywhere. Dr. Reid liked things neat.

"When the lights suddenly went out, I knew right then that clone had arrived. It must have been telepathically linked with my attacker. When she failed to kill me, damned monster must have come to finish the job. That's why I stopped you from interacting with the mainframe. If you hooked into the computer, the clone would have instantly seized control of your computerized systems. Too much of you is machine, Nelson. Neither of us would have survived the experience."

"Sonofabitch," said Nelson. "That bastard would have used my own weapon systems to kill you. Then blow my own head off."

"Very perceptive," said Sharon. "He's afraid to confront us head on, since I know the phrase that will cause his body to shut down. So, instead, he attacks from a distance. I'm positive he intends to destroy the EcoR Construct, with us on it."

She pointed to a door. "This the right floor?"

"According to the map of the complex I downloaded, it is. Let me go first. Who knows what nasties are out there? Maybe our buddy brought along company. I hope so. I'm in the mood for some bloodletting."

"It's too quiet," said Sharon. "Damned walls muffle the sound. Still, there're nearly a dozen technicians stationed on the Construct. They should be making some noise. What happened to them?"

"Damned if I know," said Ernest Nelson, dropping the false Lauri Coup to the cement landing like a sack of potatoes. "Maybe they're stuck in the lower levels, got trapped in their labs when Heylel took over the computer. I have a bad feelin' we're probably going to find out. Nothing good, I'm sure. *All weapon systems on.*"

The cyborg kicked open the door to the third-floor hallway. Nelson's gaze swept back and forth, looking for enemies. Nothing moved. The lights were on but the floor appeared deserted.

"Seems safe enough," said the cyborg, grabbing his human cargo and once again throwing her over his shoulder. "Portal is located in the lab about a third of the way down the hall. The gateway is in the back wall of the storage closet."

"Typical of Reid's paranoid thinking," said Sharon, following Nelson, her every sense alert. Something was wrong, but she had no idea what was happening. The pattern-clone meant to destroy them, but how? The citadel was too quiet. Where were the technicians? Dr. Ishida, Dr. Burns? Where was the pattern-clone?

Something small, brown and furry dashed from around a bend in the hallway thirty feet distant. Nelson's guns snapped up as the tiny beast came charging at them. Its loud yapping echoed, then disappeared in the sound-absorbing atmosphere of the Collective. Around its neck the dog wore what Sharon instantly recognized as a biotracking collar. She wondered where the animal's owner was. Another missing person.

"Stupid mutt," said Nelson, lowering his chain guns. He glared at the miniature poodle barking a few feet distant. The cyborg moved deceptively fast for a man of his size. A huge boot lashed out. "I hate dogs."

"Don't kick the..." warned Sharon, but it was too late. Nelson's foot slammed into the poodle, sending it flying down the corridor. As she feared, the animal was more than a mere pet. Hurtling through the air, its body went through a startling metamorphosis.

When it touched the floor twenty feet away, the dog was no longer small. It had grown nearly five times in size and weight. Huge white fangs, glistening with bubbling saliva, filled its massive mouth. Yellow claws scraped along the hard plastic finish of the floor. Its eyes burned red as it barked in fury.

"Shit," said Nelson, as the transformed poodle charged for a second time. His chain guns bellowed, the tracer bullets catching the beast full in the head. Howling, the dog continued forward another step. Then, the force of the gun blasts lifted the bioengineered creation off its feet and sent it flying back along the corridor. It crashed in a heap at the bend in the hall. "Fuckin' Progenitor craziness."

"Never, never, play with the animals," said Sharon. "Poor dog probably thought we were the invaders. It was just doing its job."

"Same as me," said Nelson, the harsh sound of his voice making it clear what he thought of pets that turned into monsters. "Doin' my job, that is. No signs of life, even with all the racket. Other than that stupid dog."

The cyborg glanced along the corridor, as if checking to make sure the bioengineered beast wasn't somehow regenerating. His eyes bulged in sudden shock.

"Oh no," he said, the first traces of worry in his voice. "Look what happened to Rover."

Sharon focused on the body of the dead dog. And went suddenly numb with fear.

The giant poodle had crashed to the floor at the bend in the hallway. The bullets from Nelson's chain guns had ripped the animal to shreds. The misshapen mass had splattered the far wall of the corridor like a steaming red blanket of flesh, muscles and gore. But now there wasn't a trace of crimson remaining. The entire section of hallway glistened like polished metal.

The dog's insides formed a bizarre statue, sculpted from the finest gold. It was welded in an unbreakable bond with the golden floor and golden walls. From where Sharon stood, it was impossible to discern where dog entrails ended and corridor began. They had joined in a monstrous metallic embrace.

"Remember," said Nelson, his voice shaking, "when we first saw the pattern-clone on the computer monitor at Bylunt's lab? The clone said he was some dude called Heylel Teomim and wanted to unite the Union and the Nine Traditions. You thought he was nuts. I answered he'd need a spectacular demonstration of force to prove his identity." Nelson pointed to the growing gold. "There it is."

Sharon licked her lips. "If the others were trapped on the lower levels when this golden blight spread...."

She didn't need to finish the thought. The Horizon Realm was silent because all of the other inhabitants of the Collective had been transformed into golden statues.

"It's advancing," said Nelson, stepping backward towards the staircase. He glanced over his shoulder at the door leading to the floor above. "Time for us to head back upstairs."

"Not yet," said Sharon. "I'm not so sure that's a good idea."

"If you watch closely," said Nelson, "you can even see the edge of the growth. Like that movie I saw when I was a little kid about army ants. Creeping, crawling, devouring everything in their path. The whole Collective's turning into one huge slab of gold."

"According to the data I studied, Heylel Teomim was credited with discovering the Philosopher's Stone," said Sharon. "This technique's the logical end result of such a secret."

"Reality Deviant bullshit," said Nelson. The usual bravado was gone from his voice, replaced with terror. "It can't work in a Union Collective."

"In that computer broadcast, the pattern-clone claimed that his techniques founded Iteration X," said Sharon. "As well as the Progenitors. This technique is part transmutation, part biological, part mechanical. It crosses from magick into high science."

"Great," said Nelson. "Then you know how to stop it?"

"Not really," said Sharon. "Though I'm sure, given enough time, I could come up with a proper counter-technique. But time's the one thing we don't have. Where's that portal you mentioned?"

"There," said Nelson, pointing to a door a dozen feet away. "Inside that lab. The back wall of the storage closet. Place was used for a darkroom before digital photography. But we can't go in there now. The gold's moving too fast. It'll cover the lab in a minute."

"There's no other option," argued Sharon. "We head upstairs, we're dead. EcoR's finished. The pattern-clone wants us eliminated. We either escape to Earth or get tarnished. Come on, no more time to waste talking. Follow me. Or stay here and die."

When necessary, Sharon could move very fast. Directing all the energy in her body to her legs and thighs, she was capable of running with championship sprinter speed. As soon as she finished speaking, she did exactly that.

Without a backward look, she dashed down the

corridor, hurtled through the open door into the lab, and wrenched open the door of the storage closet nestled in the far corner of the room. Nelson, the false Lauri Coup still balanced on his shoulders, arrived a few instant later.

"The rear wall," said the cyborg, ripping the door to the closet off its hinges to give Sharon easier access. He threw the metal sheet across the room. It hit the floor, turned instantly to gold. Devoured by the metallic tidal wave sweeping across the chamber. "That's the portal. It's got a living guardian, according to what I downloaded."

"Named Fred," said Sharon. "Giant ferret bioconstruct. I helped design the breed. I've already touched his mind. Told him to open the gate."

"Well, tell Fred to fuckin' hurry up," said Nelson.

Sharon glanced over her shoulder. The golden glow was creeping across the floor and walls. It moved steadily, relentlessly. Unstoppable. Already it had gobbled half of the lab. Tables, chairs, lab equipment, all glittered with a metallic shine. In less than a minute, they would be no different.

"We're running out of time!" roared Nelson.

"It takes a few seconds," said Sharon, her gaze returning to the wall. "Almost ready."

"It's at the fuckin' door!" roared Nelson, squeezing tight against her. The closet shuddered, as its edges transformed.

The portal opened. Grabbing Nelson by an arm, Sharon leapt through the dimensional gate, pulling the cyborg after her. They crashed to a hardwood floor. Nelson still held the false Lauri Coup on one shoulder. Behind them, the gateway slammed closed as quickly as it had opened. In Sharon's mind, Fred shrieked. Then the sound vanished, as if cut by a golden knife.

The portal and its guardian were gone, destroyed by the pattern-clone's magick. Another Realm had fallen in the Horizon War. The EcoR Progenitor Collective and all of its inhabitants had been turned to gold.

Chapter Seven

The report detailing the events of the previous night's disaster was waiting for Enzo Giovanni when he awoke from his unnatural sleep. He read it as he walked from his secret resting place to the massive stone and earth chamber that served as his office in the lowest sub-basement of the Everwell Chemical building. With each step, his temper burned more brightly. By the time he reached his destination, he felt ready to explode.

Eyes blazing in anger, Enzo dropped onto the massive mahogany chair in the center of the room. A mahogany meeting table stood in the far corner along with four chairs covered with black leather. He used them when necessary. His associate, Ezra, in a fit of rage, had destroyed his desk and he had not yet bothered replacing it. The walls were cement. The floor was mostly cement, with earth in the corners, a strip of faded tile near the door. The lights were recessed in the ceiling.

Resting on a four-by-four wood platform, the huge

chair was covered with purple velvet and sewn with gold thread. Enzo thought of it as his throne. From here he directed the fortunes of Everwell Chemicals as well as dozens of other corporations that were branches of the secret Pentex empire. The organization Enzo dreamed of mastering.

Four floors above, the ancient crumbling brick factory housing Everwell Chemicals covered an entire block of Rochester's decaying industrial section. Four stories high, the building dated back to the nineteenth century. Once, the vast structure had been a coffin factory. This very chamber had served as a storage spot for caskets. Now it dealt with death in a more subtle manner. Huge vats, on the second and third floors, produced treacherous chemicals that poisoned the environment in the name of progress. Not surprisingly, the cancer level in Rochester was double the national average. Enzo, in his quest for greater glories, was pushing for triple.

A large, heavyset man, Enzo Giovanni stood a few inches over six feet tall and weighed close to three hundred pounds. As always, he wore a black suit, white shirt and black tie. He liked to keep up appearances. A thick head of dark bushy hair descended into a pointed goatee and wide mustache. His eyes were dark, with a hint of crimson at the center. His cheeks were ruddy red, offset by the blanched white of his skin. Except for a certain bestial, *hungry* look that he could not disguise, Enzo appeared almost human.

Teeth gnashing in unrestrained fury, he crumpled the pages of the report in his huge hands. Snarling like an animal, Enzo ripped the stack of paper to shreds. With a sweep of his huge hands, he scattered the white fragments across the cement floor. "Ms. Hargroves," he roared, his deep bass voice spreading like a psychic wave throughout the building. "Come here. At once."

A moment later, the single door to the chamber opened and Ms. Hargroves walked into the room. Her flat shoes clicked on the cheap tile surrounding the door. A tall, gaunt, middle-aged woman, she wore a dark gray suit and no makeup. She kept her hair pulled back in a tight bun. Her bland, unsmiling face was ageless. In her bony hands she held a clipboard and pen, ready to take notes. As always, Ms. Hargroves appeared completely oblivious to Enzo's maniacal rage.

"Who wrote this report?" he asked, his deep voice trembling with fury. His anger made it difficult for him to speak coherently. The beast in his soul threatened to overwhelm his senses. A red film covered his eyes. "Did you?"

"Of course I did," said Ms. Hargroves. "You know I write all the reports you read. Mattias supplied most of the details of the battle. After speaking with him, I verified the information from several of the other survivors. Then I condensed everything I learned and put it down on paper, along with my assessment of the entire operation. I thought you would find the summary useful."

"The attack was a total failure!" shrieked Enzo. He rose from his chair, his hands clenched into fists. The stone walls of the chamber vibrated from his fury. "The Grim Brothers destroyed! None of the intended victims dead!"

He glared at his secretary. "You *thought* I would find this report *useful*? It is a record of failure, of cowardice and stupidity. Can you give me one good reason I should not slaughter you for presenting me with such a document?"

"Even you aren't that foolish," said Ms. Hargroves, sneering at Enzo. There was no trace of fear in her voice. "Go ahead. Kill the messenger if that will satisfy you. Drink my blood. Then, next month, remember how it tastes when the books need to be balanced, the files require sorting, and the state sales tax has to be paid."

Enzo moved like lightning. Gone from his throne, he stood facing Ms. Hargroves. Inches separated his features from hers. "You dare mock me?" His lips pulled back, revealing hidden fangs. "There are other secretaries, bookkeepers to be found. Everyone has a price. You are not irreplaceable."

The gaunt woman's unflinching gaze met his. "Find another who understands the innermost workings of Pentex," she said calmly. "Locate a woman loyal enough to tell you the naked truth instead of feeding you lies. If you can, then destroy me. Do it right now. Make your insane partner, Ezra, happy. He wants me dead. He always has. The mage fears my honesty."

"Don't link me with that madman," declared Enzo, his voice sinking down to a whisper. His head swiveled from side to side, peering into the shadows in the dark corners of the chamber. Ezra had a habit of spying on the most secret of conversations. "He tells me what Lord Steel plans, nothing more. *I'm* the one who's a member of the Board of Directors of Pentex. And, when Pietro Giovanni is eliminated, I'll be the one to head Clan Giovanni. Not Ezra. Never him."

With an inhuman slither, Enzo was back on his velvet throne. "The wizard suggested I lead the attack last night. Perhaps he suspected what would take place. In his madness, anything's possible. He has ambitions. His insanity has not crushed his desire for power." Narrowed, serpent-line eyes scanned the chamber again, searching for some hint of an invisible eavesdropper. "Have you seen him today?"

"Are you asking your secretary," said Ms. Hargroves, sounding slightly amused, "or your next victim?"

"Nonsense," said Enzo, waving a huge hand to dismiss her words. "Forget my threats. The usual foolishness brought on by such miserable news. You are indispensable, Ms. Hargroves. However, others are not."

"I haven't seen Ezra since last night," said Ms. Hargroves. "When the Grim Brothers departed, so did he. I thought he seemed nervous, anxious to leave."

Enzo laughed. "He assumed his alliance with Lord Steel made him all powerful. A near-fatal encounter with his sister made him realize otherwise."

"He calls himself your friend," said Ms. Hargroves, "but he plots against you. He has no loyalty to anyone but himself. One mistake, one misstep, and he'll be on you like a wild dog."

"Of course," replied Enzo. "Do you expect anything less from a madman? When the time is right, I will deal with my friend. Permanently. Our partnership will dissolve in a feast of blood."

Talking about blood reminded him that he had not feasted in days. "Summon that fool, Mattias, to my presence," he said to Ms. Hargroves. "His service lately has been less than satisfactory. We need to discuss the terms of his future employment. I think it is time to tear up his present contract and start anew."

"I don't remember you having a written contract with Mattias," said Ms. Hargroves, her face expressionless. Sometimes, Enzo almost thought she could read his mind.

"A terrible oversight," he replied. "That is what we must discuss. A new deal needs to be established. One signed in blood. Human blood."

It took thirty minutes for the gang leader to appear. And he did not come alone.

Mattias was a giant of a man, standing nearly seven feet tall, with oily black hair that hung in a knotted rat's tail halfway down his back. He wore blue jeans covered by black leather riding chaps. Several steel chains crisscrossed his bare chest. Totally hairless, his body was completely covered by tattoos of red and blue lizards. A machete was shoved casually into the belt around his waist. A pistol was wedged into the front of his pants. The gang leader had come prepared for battle.

Surrounding the giant were members of his motorcycle gang, the Knights of Pain. Five of them in all.

Enzo had seen most of them before. Tough, ugly, brutal thugs, united by two common bonds. They were uglier than sin. And they were armed to the teeth.

Luther, a short, squat man, with blue spirals painted on his face had an orange mohawk and rings in his ears, nipples and tongue. He carried a sawed-off shotgun in each hand.

Another gangbanger, tall and thin, with glazed blue eyes and skin as bone white as any Kindred, wore black leather pants and a heavy leather vest. He called himself T-Bone. The Uzi in his hands never wavered from Enzo's chest.

A third man, almost as big as Mattias, named Trent, was thick and hairy like a bear. He held a butcher's cleaver in one hand, with a second knife dangling from a cord around his neck. The Knights of Pain were ready for war.

Enzo couldn't help but smile. Like most mortals, these fools had no idea of the true extent of his powers. His gaze swept across them, staring for an instant at each man as if acknowledging their strength. Inwardly, he chortled. Lambs for the slaughter. They were all dead men walking.

"Well, Mattias, my friend?" said Enzo, his tone mild. He noted with continued amusement that Ms. Hargroves was no longer in the chamber. She couldn't read his thoughts but she surely understood his moods. He doubted if his secretary was anywhere in the building. "You promised me the heads of my enemies on poles. I see no such displays. Those I wanted killed are still alive. Tell me what happened."

"It was a fuckin' slaughterhouse," said Mattias. "Never seen so much fuckin' blood in my entire fuckin' life."

"More than a hundred of you against a handful of magick makers," said Enzo. "Ezra's power and mine added to yours. The odds seemed strongly in your favor. I'm very disturbed over the lack of results. Please explain what went wrong. And try to curb the profanity, Mattias. You know I find such vulgar language offensive."

"Yeah, sure, whatever the fuck you want," said the giant. T-Bone laughed, then quieted quickly when he realized that Mattias didn't realize his mistake. "You know the score, Enzo. Maybe there weren't a lot of the fuckers, but they were all killin' machines. Especially the bitch dressed in black. The one who looked like you. She was a fuckin' monster."

"Madeleine," said Enzo. "My niece of sorts. How disturbing to learn that she was there. I've been told by many others that her skills are unmatched even among the Assamites. No matter. She was only one. What about the others, the ones I specifically ordered killed?"

"We tried," said Mattias, a whining note creeping into his voice. "This bunch is what's left of my gang. Trent, T-Bone, Luther, Kross, and Simon. Everyone else is dead. Bitch with two swords cut Ernie and Jackson and Louie to pieces. Then there was that big, bald guy with the scythe. He was the worst motherfucker of them all. We couldn't pull him down. Tried knives, bullets, even acid. Nothing hurt the son-of-a-bitch. His wounds closed in seconds. It was fuckin' insane."

"His wounds healed instantly?" asked Enzo. Instantly, his thoughts flashed back to events only a few weeks past. Of an escaped prisoner from the Gray Collective. A man whose blood burned like molten fire. His worst nightmare had come true.

"That was the fugitive you failed to kill in the woods," said Enzo. "He should have been destroyed then. Your mistake has come back to haunt you. This is the second time your gang has not lived up to your promises, Mattias. I find such behavior unforgivable."

"Well, fuck you," said the giant. Reaching into a back pocket, Mattias pulled out a jeweled crucifix. He kissed the center, looped the cross around his neck. His fellow gang members followed suit. Enzo hadn't seen so many crosses since his last visit to the cemetery.

"Stolen from churches all over the city," declared the giant. "The real stuff, no fuckin' cheap imitations. Plus, we soaked 'em in holy water before comin' here."

"Did you melt down silver candlesticks for bullets?" asked Enzo, chuckling. He stepped forward. "Or munch on cloves of garlic?"

Mattias raised a hand in warning. "Move another inch and you're fuckin' dead."

"But I'm already *dead*, as you so aptly state," replied Enzo, walking closer to the giant. "Besides, your men are no longer capable of doing me any harm. They made the unfortunate mistake of looking into my eyes. According to the legends, that's a terrible mistake. I control their motions, their thoughts. Watch."

Enzo snapped his fingers and pointed to Luther, the short, squat man with orange hair and multiple piercing. All the color suddenly drained from his features. Face white, dripping with sweat, Luther slowly but steadily bent his left arm until the shotgun in his hand was pointed at his groin.

"Excellent," said Enzo. "Exactly as I wished. Now, Luther, ugly little man, pull the trigger."

"No!" screamed Mattias, as the gun roared. Blood splashed on the cement floor. Luther, still silent, collapsed to the ground, his eyes glazed with shock.

The giant grabbed for the machete at his waist, then froze as Enzo snapped his fingers a second time. Like automatons, the remaining four Knights of Pain turned and pointed their weapons at their bewildered leader. Mattias licked his lips, his hands desperately rubbing the cross around his neck like a magic charm. But for him, there was no rescue.

"You—you—you can't be fuckin' with me like this," the giant stuttered. The blue and red lizard tattoos scrambled wildly beneath his skin. Enzo didn't care. What little magick the giant possessed was not enough to stop him.

"Never underestimate your opponent, Mattias," he declared as the hunger rose within him like a savage beast. The giant was strong and filled with life. Rich warm blood flowed in his veins. Handled properly, the big man and his friends should last for several days. A curtain of blood descended over Enzo's thoughts as he reached for his evening meal. "It will be the death of you."

Chapter Eight

"While I do not possess mortal feelings," said Madeleine Giovanni, after a moment's silence, "neither am I a fool. It does not take human intuition to realize that you were expecting a different answer, another name?"

In the moonlight, her white skin gleamed like pearl. Her lips were rose red, her eyes sparkled with intelligence. The black dress she wore clung to her body like a second skin, molding itself to her sensuous curves. Yet Seventeen felt no stirrings of desire looking at Madeleine. For all of her good looks, she was cold as ice.

"Thought you'd say Heylel Teomim, also known as the Abomination," said Sam Haine. "A fabled mage, who was utterly destroyed five hundred years ago, but seemingly has returned. Heylel has pledged to unite the Nine Traditions and the Five Conventions. Whether they agree or not."

"He *seems* to have returned," repeated Madeleine slowly. Seventeen noted that the assassin, despite her unassuming and respectful manner, was adept at detecting the slightest inflections in speech or attitude. "How *interesting* that you are not sure. I am not a student of the history of magick makers. The name you mention, Heylel Teomim, is unfamiliar to me. I am quite sure neither Enzo nor Ezra has ever mentioned him. They speak only of Lord Steel."

"It's a damn complicated mess," said Sam Haine. "The big problem is that our enemy inhabits an artificially created body, a pattern-clone developed by the Technocracy. The clone claims to be Heylel reincarnated. Some perhaps believe its words. Others don't. I'm waitin' for more evidence before I make up my mind. Always been a doubter. Don't believe nothing I'm told. Safer that way."

"Kallikos, my mentor," said Shadow of the Dawn, her soft voice barely audible, "once known as the Time Master, Akrites Salonikas, centuries ago ripped apart the veil of the future and saw Heylel Teomim reborn. In that vision, the resurrection trigged a war in the Horizon Realms, with its outcome determining the future of mankind. For five hundred years, Kallikos walked the earth, waiting for these events to begin, hoping to alter history.

"All that the seer revealed to me came true. Yet, when finally confronted by his enemy, not even Kallikos was able to determine whether the Abomination was as he claimed or an impostor. When I spoke to him last, on Horizon, my teacher was still unsure."

Seventeen rose to his feet, unable to remain seated

any longer. He needed to move about, burn off some of the energy that blazed through his body. The forest grove pulsed with life. The sacred spring sung songs of warriors who had gathered in similar councils over the centuries. Great deeds had taken place here. Great feats of magick had unfolded beneath the silver moon.

"We promised an exchange of information," he said. "Madeleine has told us what she knows of Enzo Giovanni's plans. And of the Dark Lord who is his patron. I think it's time to return the favor and tell her my story. Starting from my escape from the Gray Collective till the present."

"No objection from me," said Sam. He took a long drag on his smokeless cigar, blew a smoke ring over the campfire. "Mebbee she'll be able to make some sense outta stuff we find confusing. Just trim out the slow parts, son. Otherwise, we'll be here past dawn. And Madeleine ain't partial to sunlight."

Seventeen tried to be concise. But a lot had happened in the past few weeks. To him, every moment was important. With no memory of his past, these days were his life.

He started with his escape from his prison cell on the Gray Collective. From there, he told of his battle on Earth with the HIT Marks, and his subsequent meeting with Sam and Albert.

"Sure as hell caught me by surprise," interjected Sam, waving his cigar in the air. The Changing Man couldn't remain silent very long. "After a fight with those killer cyborgs, Seventeen should have been crippled, near death. But he was the healthiest man I'd ever encountered. Made me realize right away that he was something special."

"My body was rebuilt by some of the finest technicians of the Technocracy," said Seventeen. "They used me as the prototype for the pattern-clone. Reinforced my bones, strengthened my muscles, and gave me an amazing new blood. I paid the price, but it was a fair trade."

"Destroyed your memory with all their fancy scientific mumbo-jumbo," said Sam. "Stole your identity."

"I don't think so," said Seventeen. He spoke carefully now, choosing his words. "I suspect that happened earlier."

Sam's thick white eyebrows knitted above his nose. He stared at Seventeen, as if trying to read his mind. "Care to explain how you reached that conclusion?"

"Still trying to figure out the details myself," said Seventeen. He remembered what Claudia Johnson had told him at their meeting. Sam was his friend, perhaps his closest friend on Earth. Still, the Changing Man was Verbena. Seventeen felt it best not to say anything until he knew the truth about his past life. The whole truth. "Once I'm sure, you'll know."

He spoke instead of the never-ending war between the Nine Traditions and the Technocracy. Then of the fight in the grove that evening with the Men in Black and the unexpected arrival of the motorcycle gang searching for him. In great detail, Seventeen described how he was caught by surprise by a man with a flamethrower, only to be rescued by a mysterious gaunt woman, who appeared for a few seconds and ripped his enemy to pieces.

"Plot and counter-plot," said Madeleine. She rose to her feet without a sound. The vampire moved with inhuman grace, seeming to flow from place to place. Shadow of the Dawn was now standing as well. Her hands rested easily on the hilt of her short sword.

"I sense players in the shadows, moving human chessmen in a vast game that we only faintly comprehend," said Madeleine. "The bikers belong to a gang known as the Knights of Pain. Enzo employs them as strongarm thugs in his various schemes. I spotted several of them at the waste dump last night. Some perished in the fight. Others escaped."

"So it's pretty safe assuming that Enzo sent them here to kill Seventeen," said Sam. "Posted that big reward for his head and ours too. Any ideas why?"

"Of course," said Madeleine. "I understood the reason as soon as I saw the transfusion last night. *Seventeen's blood*. It's a sorcerous vitae that is no longer human blood but something else. Such blood would be deadly to any vampire. Enzo feared Seventeen and with good reason."

She pointed to Shadow of the Dawn. "Once there was one with such blood. Now there are two. I'm sure that Enzo is not pleased with the situation. Most likely, he will take out his displeasure on the remaining Knights of Pain. In certain situations, my relatives are quite predictable."

"I suspect that Ezra also wanted me destroyed for some reason we don't know," said Seventeen. "The bikers appeared charged with magickal energy. The mage must have been aiding them. Any idea on the identity of my mysterious savior? The gaunt woman who blinked into existence for an instant and killed with such insane pleasure?"

"It sounds oddly like Millicent Hargroves," replied Madeleine. "Enzo's perfect secretary. A very capable but otherwise ordinary mortal, without any mystick powers. Ms. Hargroves runs Everwell Chemicals for Enzo, as well as managing his many illegal enterprises. She appears extremely efficient and entirely without morals. My uncle trusts her implicitly. Ezra, on the other hand, questions her loyalty. It appears the mage's suspicions are correct."

"She used extraordinary powers in this grove," said Seventeen. "If she's no mage, she's got powerful friends."

"Aliara," said Sam Haine, with a snort of disgust. "Has to be her in the background. If Enzo and Ezra are hooked up with Lord Steel, this Ms. Hargroves is working for Aliara. According to my sources, Aliara and Steel are bitter rivals."

"I agree," said Seventeen, wondering what sources provided Sam with his information. The Changing Man was remarkably well informed. "Remember, too, that Terrence Shade is one of the Empress of Lust's servants. He provides a direct link between Aliara and the Gray Collective."

"Good point," said Sam. "Now we're...."

"Please continue your story, Seventeen," said

Albert, interrupting his friend. "There will be enough time for theories *later*."

Sam glared at Albert. The white-haired old man inhaled deeply on his smokeless cigar and somehow managed to blow a smoke ring directly at the shaman. As the cloud neared Albert's face, it turned red and miniature lightning bolts sizzled across its center. Shaking his head in mock annoyance, the shaman snapped his fingers and the apparition vanished.

"Go ahead, son," said Sam, grinning. "I can take a hint. I'll keep my big mouth shut."

So Seventeen recounted their fateful journey to the Gray Collective and told of the awakening and disappearance of the pattern-clone.

"These are interesting times," said Madeleine. "I find your adventures fascinating. And ominous. What happened after the pattern-clone vanished?"

Seventeen described Kallikos's vision and the reappearance of Jenni Smith, once the others had departed, to offer him mastery of the world in return for his allegiance to the pattern-clone. And his rejection of the proposition.

"You are a man of honor," said Madeleine, almost reflexively. The expression on her face made it quite clear she meant what she said. "A rarity in these modern times."

"Never trust a snake in the grass," said Sam Haine. "Even if she is young, pretty and blond."

Shadow of the Dawn glared at the white-haired man. He closed his mouth.

Continuing his narrative, Seventeen described

their trip to Horizon, the most powerful Horizon Realm of the Nine Traditions, and the dramatic revelation that Kallikos was Akrites Salonikas, the famed Time Master believed to be long dead. Then, the appearance via projected thought of the pattern-clone, claiming to be Heylel Teomim reborn, come to unite the Nine Traditions and the Technocracy and raise all mankind to Ascension. As well as its threat to destroy all who stood against its wishes.

Seventeen made no mention of his own discoveries during that journey. He was still unsure of how his past and present were linked together. What had happened to five decades of his life? Where he had been, what he had done, who he had been? His new life had begun a month ago. Yet he knew full well that his forgotten memories held secrets that could not be ignored. Lord Steel haunted his dreams, spoke to him in nightmares. Seventeen suspected the truth when finally uncovered might not be to his liking. But he had to know. The rage gnawing inside him demanded an answer.

His voice shaky, he described the destruction of the Tradition fortress, Doissetep, and the unexpected vanishing of Sam Haine.

"We soon figured out Sam was heading to the toxic-waste dump for a showdown with Terrence Shade," said Seventeen to Madeleine. "The rest you know."

"Among my kind, deception and false identities are normal," said the lady in black. "Our existence is filled with secrets. The Jyhad has raged for thousands of years, with many Kindred never even realizing a war was being fought. However, listening to your story here tonight, I realize that our plots and campaigns are child's play. When reality itself can be manipulated, any deception is possible."

"A wise teacher once taught me that *the only truth is that there are no absolute truths*," said Shadow of the Dawn softly. "That nothing is as it seems."

"A rogue magus once gave me similar advice," said Madeleine Giovanni. "Dire McCann, who knew more than most, warned me there is no such thing as coincidence. Chance is the result of careful planning. It is advice I have not forgotten."

"So," said Albert, "we return to the same question as before. Is the pattern-clone Heylel Teomim reborn, or Lord Steel, Duke of Hate? Despite hearing both Madeleine and Seventeen's recitations, we seem no closer to an answer."

"You worry about the wrong problem, dear friend," said Shadow, with a slight smile. "Another wise teacher taught me that the right answers are often easily discovered if the right questions are asked."

"I don't understand," said the shaman.

"It is clear to me that the actual identity of the pattern-clone is unimportant," said Shadow. "The clone may be Heylel Teomim, the Abomination. Or the Dark Lord. The clone may be the mastermind of the plot involving Enzo and Ezra. Equally possible, it may be working entirely on its own. Jenni Smith and her sisters may be the clone's servants. Or they could be Nephandi, secretly controlling the artificial being's every action. The possibilities are endless and serpentine in their complexity. What *really* matters is that the clone, whoever it is, must be destroyed, or the world will sink into chaos."

"The swords-mistress speaks wisely," said Madeleine Giovanni. "Annihilation is one sure method of defeating your enemies. Understanding them is useful but not always necessary. In the past few days, it has become evident to me that Enzo and Ezra must die the Final Death. No deals, no bargains, no compromises. They must die.

"From what has been said tonight, it seems equally obvious that this pattern-clone—be he Heylel Teomim, an agent for Lord Steel, or the Dark Lord himself in physical form—must also be obliterated. It is the only solution to your problem. There are no choices. *The only answer is death*."

"Destroying him might not be so easy," said Albert. "If his survival powers match those of Seventeen, he's going to be hard to kill. Besides, judging by the destruction of Doissetep and the disappearance of the House of Helekar, the clone is an astonishingly powerful willworker. Perhaps the strongest in the entire Tellurian."

"Hold on," said Sam Haine, rising to his feet. Now they were all standing. No more crouching by the fire. The entire glade seemed to throb with mystick energy. The stern look on Sam's features made it clear he would not be silenced. Not even Albert tried.

"You needs to look at events with a jaundiced, doubtin' eye. That's when you see the truth. The pattern-clone ain't so tough. This Horizon War, a war in heaven so to speak, ain't involving no demonstration of incredible magick. The pattern-clone's been doin' magick all right, but the stage-show kind. Sleight of hand. He's fooling everyone with illusions that they take as reality. Smart boy, the clone. He might even be Heylel. From what I read, when he was alive the Abomination was a pretty sharp operator. A master of deceptions. Which is what we've seen so far. Not god-like power like Albert thinks, but a very smooth con."

"Doissetep was destroyed," said Albert. "The House of Helekar has vanished."

"True on both accounts," said Sam. "The sun rose this morning. It set tonight. Don't mean that the pattern-clone made it happen."

"Doissetep was ready for a fall," said Seventeen. "Porthos made that quite clear. The pattern-clone, working through agents, exploited the rivalries already tearing the place apart. He lit the match in the fireworks warehouse."

"Exactly what I'm sayin'," declared Sam. "I'm not pretending the clone ain't damned dangerous. Ask the gold statue that was São Cristavao about that. Heylel's a menace, perhaps the greatest foe the Traditions have ever faced. He wields powers that are unknown to most modern mages. Plus, he's got a hidden network of agents, shapeshifters, scattered throughout the Horizon Realms and Earth. The perfect Fifth Column. Defeating him ain't gonna be easy. But he ain't no god. Not even a minor deity."

"Kallikos fears him," said Shadow softly. "My mentor believes Heylel will cast a cloak of eternal night across the world."

"Yeah, I know," said Sam, chomping down hard on his cigar. "Bothers the hell out of me wondering what scares the seer so bad."

"Like Albert, you're making one wrong assumption," said Seventeen, his voice grim. All eyes turned to him. Now was the time to reveal what he had realized last night. "Kallikos is afraid of the pattern-clone not because of the destruction he brings. A show of force will not unite the Nine Traditions with the Five Conventions. As Sam states, one individual, even an extremely powerful one, cannot defeat hundreds of dedicated willworkers. What scares Kallikos is what the pattern-clone *offers*."

"Offers?" repeated Sam Haine.

"The being who calls himself Heylel Teomim plays human emotions like a master musician," said Seventeen. He felt absolutely certain of what he was saying. The truth had become obvious when he saved Shadow of the Dawn. "First he warns of terrible destruction, backing up this threat with tangible proof. That is done. Now, with his credibility established, he intends to change directions and offer a magnificent reward for those who join his supposed crusade towards Ascension. It will be an overture few will be able to refuse."

"An excellent strategy," said Madeleine Giovanni. Seventeen suspected she already knew the answer to her next question. "What gift does the one who calls himself Heylel Teomim offer?"

"*Eternal life*," said Seventeen. "Join with him and become immortal. A transfusion of his nanobyte blood will work in the same fashion as with Shadow. The receiver will be cured of all illnesses. And turn ageless. Or at least until the nanobytes lose their energy, a thousand or more years in the future."

"His blood," whispered Shadow. "Jenni Smith said '*Your blood is as his blood!*'"

"The blood that saved Shadow's life," said Madeleine Giovanni.

"Nanobyte blood," said Seventeen. "Enzo wants me dead because my living blood can destroy vampires foolish enough to drink it. It makes me invulnerable to the undead. As is Shadow. As is the pattern-clone.

"Ezra realized I was a potential rival to Heylel, so he wanted me killed. The attack on the waste dump made it clear he hadn't changed his mind."

"Immortality," said Sam Haine, the enormity of what Seventeen was saying slowly sinking in. "Certain Tradition willworkers can control time, live for centuries. Same with Technocrats."

"A handful," said Seventeen. "Only extremely powerful mages are so blessed. The same applies to the Technocrats. But not the ordinary willworker, the mage who slaves hard all his or her life with little real reward, striving to master techniques that take decades to learn properly. How could they refuse eternal life—especially when coupled with eternal good health? Think of the temptation. *Think of the reward.*"

"Immortals, free from the threat of the Kindred," said Albert, "able to twist reality any way they wanted. They would become a ruling elite who would control the world."

"Power corrupts," said Sam. "And living forever is the greatest power imaginable. Heylel won't have to conquer the Nine Traditions. They'll come crawling to him. Same with the Technocracy."

"Sam's right," said Seventeen. "If we don't stop the pattern-clone, it'll mean the end of the Nine Traditions and the collapse of the Technocracy. Exactly what Kallikos feared. An alliance of willworkers and vampires controlling mankind. The seer's vision come true. *The triumph of absolute evil.*"

Chapter Nine

Velma blinked. She was sitting in front of her computer monitor, her hands on the keyboard. Strange, very strange. The last thing she remembered was stretching out on her bed for a few hours rest. She was not in the habit of sleepwalking.

She stared at the screen. Several lines of text glowed in the dark room. Not only had she gotten out of bed, gone to the computer, turned it on, but she had actually typed a message. Reading the words, Velma suddenly understood.

Doris captured by Reed and Nelson.

Escaped latest trap.

Destroy these two.

Use any force necessary.

Do not fail.

No signature on the letter. Nor was one needed. The pattern-clone maintained a mental link with her mind. Telepathy often resulted in jumbled, meaningless communications. Using Velma's own body to type a message worked much more easily. And it guaranteed that she take immediate notice.

"Lights on," said Velma, rising to her feet as the room glowed with illumination. The one who called itself Heylel wanted Reed and Nelson terminated. So did Velma. The only question was how?

Her headquarters was located in one of the more fashionable Rochester suburbs. It was a large frame house nearly a hundred years old. Jenni Smith had rented it months ago, using one of her many assumed names. All of them maintained multiple identities on Earth. What fun was there being a shapeshifter if you didn't live numerous lives?

The bedroom was painted blood red, with black trim. There were no windows—Velma liked her privacy. A large bed filled one corner. Hugging the opposite wall was an elaborate computer setup. Next to it was the door leading to the kitchen, and from there, the living room.

Covering one of the remaining walls were a dozen full-length mirrors. They reflected everything in the chamber, every move that Velma made. All of the lighting in the room was focused in such a manner as not to shine in the mirrors. Velma liked to see herself without any annoying distractions.

The fourth wall was filled with pictures and photos. Illustrations cut from magazines, pages ripped out of books, photos taken by Velma using a Polaroid camera. Hundreds and hundreds of pictures of people living and dead. Mostly women, but also some men. There were young people, old people, fat people, thin people, short people, tall people, ugly people and beautiful people. Nothing linked them together other than Velma's interest in their features. They all appealed to her in some manner. And her entire existence focused on how others looked.

Standing before the mirrored wall, dressed in a pale blue nightshirt, she stretched, raising her arms over her head. Today, she was a blonde, short and middle-aged, with green eyes and puffy red cheeks. Her features were identical to a woman she had spotted yesterday pushing a baby carriage down the street. Interesting expression, but not much of a challenge. Velma liked difficult faces, emotional expressions.

At times, she felt like a psychic vampire, living off the looks and feelings of others. Not an unusual concept. Her "sisters" often expressed similar thoughts. As a shapeshifter, she possessed an enormous gift. But at a terrible price. Most people had one identity, and lived and died in its constraints. Velma had dozens of personalities and appearances. All were different, each unique. They were linked together by a single thread. Ambition. Velma desired power. Ultimate control, over the living and the undead. And she was willing to do anything to obtain it.

The mere thought of the undead had her shape changing, shifting into a new form. Now she was twenty years old, with long dark hair and flashing black eyes. Short, with full breasts and wide hips, she possessed an exotic, sensual beauty. Her clothes had changed as well. Now she was dressed in a conservative black skirt, white blouse, and black blazer. No jewelry.

"Miss Hope," she declared, chuckling. Her sultry

voice betrayed the slightest trace of a Spanish accent. "How nice to see you. Montifloro Giovanni thinks you are a cheap whore, a tramp recruited by his uncle to distract him from his investigations. These vampires are such arrogant fools. Manipulating them is almost too easy."

The phone on Velma's computer desk rang. For an instant, her shape quivered as her concentration wavered. Then, regaining control of her looks, she paced across the floor to the telephone and checked the i.d. of the caller. "Miss Smith," proclaimed the system. No surprise.

Velma picked up the receiver. "Hello, Jenni," she said, her body reshaping, swirling into a new form as she spoke. "I thought it might be you."

"You were contacted?" asked Jenni Smith.

"Of course," said Velma. She was still young, but now she was slender and petite, with long, flowing blond hair and blue eyes. Her features glowed with good health. She wore a long billowy blue dress decorated with large pink flowers. Exactly like the picture pinned on Velma's wall.

"Me too," said Jenni. "I was just being careful."

"Of course," said Velma. She almost felt sorry for Jenni, compelled to maintain the same shape for months, catering to Ezra's bizarre desires. Being forced to endure the same features was pure torture to beings like themselves. Chaos demanded constant change. Powerful shapeshifters needed to alter their appearance often. It was part of their basic nature. Remain static and die. But sacrifices had to be made. Jenni's mission wasn't nearly as bad as the years Velma had been forced to obey Sharon Reed's orders. It was a small price to ask for the reward they sought.

"Reed and Nelson are proving more difficult to kill than expected," said Velma. "But I have an idea how they can be eliminated for sure."

"How?" asked Jenni.

Velma's shape shifted yet again. Unless she exerted strict control over her thoughts, the mere thought of another person resulted in a change. Her body grew thinner, less buxom, her hips narrowing. She seemed to straighten up, became three inches taller. Her blond hair darkened and her eyes changed from blue to slate gray. Her bright features took on a more intense, almost studious expression. Jenni was gone. Resha Maise stood in her place.

"I suspect Director Reed will shortly come hunting for us," said Velma. "She'll conduct a thorough interrogation, probably with a truth serum. Reed will get some answers before Doris self-destructs. Enough to send the bitch and her flunky, Nelson, heading in this direction."

"So?" asked Jenni.

"Using my access to the Technocracy computer data banks, I'll plant a few clues pointing them to a location of our choice. Then, all we need is to arrange a proper welcoming committee."

Jenni laughed. "I bet you look like Resha."

"She won't mind," said Velma. "A few words whispered to her old colleague, Dr. Atkins, and the Wailer will be waiting to pay his regards to Reed and Nelson.

Seems only fair that they come to him, after all the time he's spent chasing them."

"Very nice," said Jenni Smith. "Very, very nice. Are you sure it can be arranged?"

"No problem," said Velma. She dropped into the chair in front of the computer and typed in a quick string of code. "Consider it done."

"Perfect," said Jenni. "I better run. Don't want Ezra wondering where I am."

"A few more days," said Velma. "That's all. Then, no need to hold your shape ever again."

"It'll be nice to look like myself again," said Jenni, breaking the connection.

Jenni's final words ringing in her ears, Velma rose to her feet. She stood before the mirror, concentrated, tried focusing her mind on the distant past. She grew short, slender, her features serious, her eyes and hair dark. Staring at the reflection, Velma shook her head. *Not right.*

She grew heavier, taller, older, her hair red, her eyes green. Again, it wasn't correct. Short, tall; young, old; light skin then dark; gray hair then jet black; a smile, a frown, a leer; she couldn't remember.

She had always been a woman. She remembered that for sure. Or did she? It had been so long, so very, very long since the first change. A thousand shapes, a thousand personalities. How many years? Too many. Identities beyond counting.

Nothing remained of her original identity. Nothing.

With a shrug, she let her features flow back to the

blond mother from the previous day. One shape was as good as another. It really wasn't important. Looks and personality were vastly overrated. The only thing that counted was power.

Chapter Ten

They set up a makeshift headquarters in a apartment at the rear of an abandoned tenement in the heart of Washington, D.C. The building was located on the capital's southeast side, less than a mile from the old Navy Yard on the banks of the Anacostia River. A year before, that facility had been pounded by a series of mysterious explosions that had destroyed the unused military outpost and torched many of the surrounding slums.

Since the only people affected by the disaster had been the poor, no one in local or national government seemed interested in rebuilding the neighborhood. Most voters felt pouring money into the inner city was a waste. It remained as a memorial to colossal *indifference*, a blight within walking distance of the Halls of Congress. The area quickly turned into a haven for drug-dealers, crime lords, and creatures of the night. Newspapers referred to the deserted streets as "Bosnia USA."

Sharon had survived worse.

They had emerged from the EcoR Horizon Realm in the early morning hours at a biological warfare research laboratory in Virginia, not far from the capital. After stealing a van, Ernest Nelson suggested they head for the blight. It was a hellhole that both the Technocracy and the Nine Traditions avoided—too much trouble for no gain. The area offered, for a day or two, a small measure of freedom to regroup and make plans.

The tenement was located on Renaissance Avenue, which Nelson found vastly amusing. Red brick and cement, it stood three stories high, with narrow windows and steel security doors. Except for a few scorch marks and crumbled masonry, it had been left relatively unharmed by last year's blast.

The building consisted of twelve units, four to a floor; a bedroom, kitchenette, living room and bathroom. Plaster walls, wood floors, nothing fancy. Looters and scavengers had taken everything of worth, which obviously hadn't been much. Gang graffiti was painted on all the walls. Rats, evidencing no fear, scurried across the floor. The bathroom and kitchenette housed colonies of huge black-shelled roaches. Sharon didn't care. Safety meant more to her than comfort.

The apartment they selected still contained a couple of beds and several kitchen chairs. More important, along with the door leading to the hall, it had its own rear door, exiting directly to the yard. There was even a ramshackle old garage where they could hide the van. Nelson had pronounced the place cozy, and safer than most.

They deposited their prisoner in the basement of the house next door. No way they wanted her in their temporary headquarters. The false Lauri Coup was still unconscious from the first Neural Sting. A second capsule guaranteed she would remain in that state until Sharon wished otherwise. A roll of duct tape held her securely to a heavy wooden chair resting in the center of the cement floor.

After securing their prisoner, Nelson had gone off on what he called a shopping trip. Sharon remained behind, trying to plot their next move.

"You light up my life," the cyborg yelled an hour later, a moment before pushing open the front door of the apartment. Whatever locks had once held it closed were long gone.

Sharon lowered the plasma rifle she cradled in her arms. It was one of several such guns they had found in the EcoR van. She and Nelson had selected the title of a song they both detested as their password. After their dealings with Nephandi the past few days, there was no trust left in either of them.

"About time," said Sharon, resting the gun on the floor. "I was starting to wonder if you had skipped town."

"And miss all the fun?" replied Nelson. "Not on your life."

"How went the hunting expedition?" asked Sharon. "You locate everything on my list?"

"It's all here," said Nelson, emptying a large sack of

merchandise onto the floor. "Along with several battery-powered lights and some food. Took a little longer than I expected. I figured I better be real *real* cautious. It seems fairly likely our buddy, the pattern-clone, knows we escaped his trap. He's probably monitoring all the computer info lines maintained by the NWO and Syndicate. So, I needed to avoid making news. Didn't want news of a sudden outbreak of gang warfare on TV. I had to be discreet."

"You think anything that happens in this urban hot zone gets reported?" asked Sharon, as she searched through the scattered goods for the proper chemicals. They were all there, mixed among the cans of soda pop, bags of chips, and plastic containers of high-grade motor oil. "Highly unlikely. Can't imagine the police ever come calling."

"Kill *enough* people, make *enough* noise, and you attract attention wherever you are," said Nelson. "I learned that in the field years ago. The best operatives are the ones who keep quiet. That's how I handled things."

"How many drug dealers did you actually eliminate?" asked Sharon, as she righted one of the battery-powered lamps and turned it on. Twilight was falling and the electricity had long been turned off in the building. She needed light to see what she was doing.

"Eleven," said Nelson. "Four at one spot, three at another, four at the last. No one but the addicts will miss. Daytime's quiet on the street. Dealers were taking it easy, waiting for the night. Nice and snug in their hideouts.

"None of the punks put up much of a fight. I walked right in, blasted them away, then collected their loot. Mostly small bills. I hit three locations just to be sure I had enough money. Extra cash never hurts.

"I buried the bodies nice and careful so nobody'll find them for a few days. Another unsolved mystery for the cops to worry about."

"You didn't buy all this stuff in one location?" asked Sharon.

"I'm not stupid," said Nelson. "Bought the stuff in three different downtown stores, then headed back."

"You weren't followed?" asked Sharon. Carefully, she mixed the chemicals in the proper ratio. The slightest mistake and their prisoner wouldn't be answering any questions. She'd be dead. "Or observed?"

Nelson laughed. "You know how to mix those chemicals, right? Well, the same applies to me. I know what I'm doing. Nobody saw a thing. We're safe."

"What about vampires?" asked Sharon, as she loaded the serum into a hypo. "Didn't you say something about the undead having a hand in the drug market?"

"They're here," said Nelson. "Sleeping now, but they'll be active tonight. Nothing to worry about. The undead aren't stupid enough to tackle two high-powered Technocrats. We leave them alone, they'll leave us alone. First rule of survival in the urban jungle. *Don't start a fight with strangers*. That sort of behavior leads to nasty surprises."

"Time to take a trip into the basement," said Sharon, slipping the hypo into a small paper bag. "Visit our friend Ms. Coup. Ask a few questions."

"Fine by me," said Nelson. "I love party games."

A few minutes later, they stood on the cement floor looking at their prisoner. The same battery-powered flashlight provided light. Thick boards covered the windows. Sharon suspected their interrogation wasn't the first illegal activity to take place in this basement.

"She's"—and Sharon shrugged in the direction of the false Lauri Coup—"taped to that chair tight? This stuff is pretty damned potent. It'll bring her out of the Neural Shock and force her to answer our questions. My questions, since I know how to interrogate prisoners injected with this stuff. You stay quiet. Still, there's possible adverse side effects and I'm not sure of our friend's body chemistry. It might trigger an unexpected reaction or two."

Nelson flexed his powerful fingers, curling steel digits into fists. "If the tape were any tighter, she'd suffocate. But if she pulls loose, I'm ready." He laughed. "That's the story of my life. I'm always ready."

Sharon jabbed the hypo into their prisoner's right shoulder and injected less than an inch's worth of the solution. "It normally takes a few seconds for the serum to have any…."

The impostor shrieked, a horrible searing sound that filled the cement chamber and cut off Sharon in mid-sentence. The impostor's eyes popped open and her face turned brilliant red. For an instant, her features wavered, as if melting into a protoplasmic slush.

Then, her jaws clamped shut and she again was Lauri Coup. A thin line of blood trickled from her nose, while the muscles in her arms and legs stood out in bold relief against her flesh. But the tape held.

"What's your name?" asked Sharon, tossing the hypodermic to the side. She had no time to waste. The truth serum lasted thirty minutes at best.

"Doris," said their prisoner. Her eyes were fixed on Sharon's face with an unwavering gaze. "My name is Doris."

"Do you belong to a secret organization, Doris?"

"Yes." Sweat trickled down the prisoner's face, around her nose, across her cheeks.

"What is it called?"

"The Progenitors."

Sharon stifled a curse. She glared at a smirking Ernest Nelson. It had been years since she had conducted this type of questioning. She had to remember to be extremely specific.

"Do you belong to a secret organization infiltrating the Progenitors?"

"Not an organization," said Doris. "Seekers."

The shapeshifter was dripping wet, her clothing soaked with perspiration. Obviously, the serum was causing major chemical reactions in her body. Along with forcing her to answer, the potent was evidently accelerating the prisoner's metabolism. There was nothing Sharon could do about it.

"Seekers?" repeated Sharon. "What are you seeking?"

"Power," said Doris. Though her tone never changed, it sounded like she was reciting a prayer.

"Is Velma Wade another seeker?" she asked, changing the focus of her questioning.

"Yes."

"Is Resha Maise?"

"Yes." Doris's face was blood crimson. Her eyes appeared ready to explode from their sockets.

"Do you serve the being calling itself the Master of Harmony?" asked Sharon, remembering the title from the computer broadcast.

"Yes."

"Is the Master of Harmony Heylel Teomim?"

"I don't know," said Doris.

"Does anyone know?" asked Sharon.

"I don't know," said Doris.

Sharon grimaced. "Did Resha and Velma trick the Technocracy into creating the Master of Harmony?"

"Yes."

"Why was this done?" asked Sharon. She wasn't sure she would get an answer. Long explanations took too much thought.

"For the power we seek," said Doris. "Absolute power."

"Sonofabitch," said Ernest Nelson. Sharon waved a hand, motioning for silence.

"Where are Resha Maise and Velma Wade?" asked Sharon.

"In Rochester," said Doris.

Ernest Nelson scowled. Sharon shook her head, lest he speak.

"Why are they in Rochester?"

"They monitor the activities of Enzo Giovanni," said Doris. She rocked back and forth on the chair. A dozen loops of duct tape held her bound in an unbreakable grip.

"Who is Enzo Giovanni?"

"The chairman of Everwell...." Doris suddenly stopped speaking, leaving the sentence unfinished.

"Who is Enzo Giovanni?" repeated Sharon.

"None of your fuckin' business!" roared the woman in the chair, her voice dropping so deep that it rattled the walls. And in the blink of an eye, she *transformed.*

Lauri Coup disappeared. Doris shapeshifted. She turned from woman into monster. The wood chair holding her cracked like brittle twigs.

Those Beyond. That was the name given to the creatures from outside reality, the realms that existed beyond the material world. Grotesque horrors, Reality Deviants that haunted the outermost darkness. Abominations that the Technocracy was dedicated to destroying. In a breath, Doris became one of Those Beyond.

It appeared unlike anything that existed on Earth. Seven feet tall, with a body the size of a large beachball, it possessed a dozen yard-long thin appendages that served as both arms and legs. Each tentacle ended in a claw-like hand with four clawed fingers. Six eyestalks, each with a three-lobed unblinking eye, glared madly at Sharon and Nelson. In the center of the monster's body snapped a huge mouth, filled with yellow teeth and a lizard's sinuous black tongue.

Duct tape fell uselessly off the monster's sandpaper skin. Wordlessly, it throbbed, its entire body expanding and contracting like the beating of a giant heart. Mottled gray, it pulsed red then black. And attacked.

"Watch out!" yelled Ernest Nelson, as three of the creature's tentacles whipped across the space separating it from Sharon. The abomination moved with incredible speed. Sharon dropped flat as needle-sharp claws flickered inches over her head.

They were bunched too close together for Nelson to use his heavy artillery. Still, the cyborg possessed no fear. With a roar of "*Systems online!*" the metal man leapt over Sharon and slammed a massive shoulder into the alien's torso. Steel fingers, like pistons, wrenched and tore at inhuman flesh. The horror mewed in pain, rope-like arms slapping against Nelson's back, trying desperately to pull him off.

Four thick black coils wrapped around the cyborg's neck and started to squeeze. Nelson snarled in pain, grinding his chin into his chest trying to break the stranglehold. The monster continued to tighten its grip. Alien flesh strained against steel-reinforced bones. All the while, Nelson kept digging his fingers into the creature's bizarre torso.

"Try some of this," snapped Sharon and plunged the half-filled hypodermic into the creature's bottom. Ignored by both combatants, she had grabbed the needle from the floor and waited for an opening. A tiny amount of the serum had seared the impostor's metabolism. Now, Sharon had injected her with three times the original dose.

The thing shrieked, its cry rising out of the audible into the supersonic. The monster's tentacles whirled wildly about, sending Ernest Nelson flying like a missile into the far wall. The cyborg crashed hard into the cement, leaving him dazed. But he was no longer needed.

Like a gigantic balloon, the grotesque horror that had been the shapeshifter named Doris swelled to three times its original size. Its eyes, at the end of bloated stalks, bulged to the size of grapefruits. Thin black tentacles, now thick as boards, turned stiff and straight as boards. The creature's mouth was open but no audible sound came forth.

Sharon rolled across the floor to her cyborg partner. Nelson's head was raised a few inches off the floor, his half-opened eyes staring at the horrible, mutated creature a dozen feet away. "Looks sick," he muttered as Sharon drew close.

"A spectacular reaction," replied Sharon, her gaze fixed on the horror. If the monster showed any signs of recovery, she was out of there, even if it meant dragging Nelson by the ears. Such action, though, wasn't necessary.

"*Thxx ysrrs...*" gurgled the thing that had been Doris, then collapsed. It crashed to the floor in a heap of mottled gray flesh and black tentacles. Once, twice, three times it turned crimson, then back to gray. A solitary eyestalk stared at Sharon and Nelson, wavered, then dropped flat. The monster was dead. But yet it moved.

With a gnashing, grinding sound, the creature's lifeless body jerked up and down on the basement floor. With each twitch, it assumed another shape. Some human. Others not. Dead flesh and bones formed and reformed. With each transformation, movement lessened, until finally it remained still.

"The truth serum loses all potency once the subject's dead," said Sharon. Nelson's eyes were closed and he appeared to be resting. "The transformation was unnatural, even for a shapeshifter. The body tends to return to a natural state once life is gone."

"I don't fuckin' care," muttered the cyborg, barely moving his lips. His eyes opened and stared into hers. "An *unexpected reaction*, you said. Thanks for the warning."

"I've never witnessed a more startling transformation," said Sharon. Rising to a standing position, she helped Nelson to his feet. The cyborg seemed slightly wobbly, but otherwise okay. "The truth serum must have triggered a powerful mental defense mechanism. Instead of committing suicide, our prisoner was programmed to attack. She converted into a form capable of massive destruction."

"Too well-developed a monster for mere imagination," said Nelson, his hands gingerly rubbing his lacerated neck. "Obviously, friend Doris lived in a section of deviant reality where such creatures existed."

"Isn't that a comforting thought," said Sharon. "She looks harmless enough now."

Sharon poked the lifeless body with her foot. The monster was gone. The shapeshifter had reverted to her original identity upon her death. She was revealed as a young woman, perhaps thirty years old, with short, clipped brown hair, dark skin, and trim physique. Sharon had absolutely no memory of seeing her on EcoR. Even on the research station, she must have been in disguise.

"Kill an alligator and they make wonderful handbags," said Nelson, bending on one knee to study the dead woman. "Death acts as a great equalizer. You sure she can't suddenly return to life?"

"The serum attacks brain cells," said Sharon. "That's why I had to ask my questions quickly. Her reaction probably accelerated the process. I doubt there's much left inside her head. Doris is out of surprises."

"She was trying to say something when she died," declared Nelson.

"Not in any human language," said Sharon.

"Lot of effort wasted for not many answers," said Nelson. "She wasn't sure about much."

"I suspect only Velma knows the full truth," said Sharon. "Maybe the one called Resha. There's only one way to find out."

"Go to Rochester?" said Nelson. "Pretty damned big city. We'll have to locate this Enzo Giovanni. Discover why he's so important to these shapeshifters. Use him to find them somehow."

"My thinking exactly," said Sharon. "Everwell has to be Everwell Chemicals. The Gray Collective bought materials from them during the pattern-clone project. I'm sure that's no coincidence. It's time for us to pay our regards to Velma. She stabbed me in the back. I want to return the favor."

"I love reunions," said Nelson, grinning. "Nothing like seeing old friends."

Chapter Eleven

She was out of beer.

"Son of a bitch," Ms. Hargroves snapped, standing outside the front entrance of Everwell Chemicals. It was a bright, sunny morning. She was finished with work until the night. Enzo Giovanni rested in his coffin deep beneath the city streets. It was time for her to return to her apartment, relax and eat, then sleep. Her boss's schedule dictated hers. She worked vampire hours, the night shift. But she was out of beer.

For the past week, she had shared her rooms with the demonic Terrence Shade. Another one of Aliara's agents, Shade had been sent to Earth to seek and destroy the Traditions willworker, Sam Haine. His trap at the toxic-waste dump the night of the attack had failed and he had vanished.

As best Ms. Hargroves could determine, her associate was no longer anywhere on Earth. It seemed likely to her that Shade had been tricked back to Malfeas. Though cruel and cunning, Shade was no match for a wizard of Sam Haine's talents. Aliara could not be pleased with his lack of success. When angry, the Dark Lord was capable of acts of diabolical torture. Ms. Hargroves smiled slightly at the thought of the portly Shade being stretched thin on a rack. He had drunk her extra beer, leaving the refrigerator empty. There was no pity in her soul. There never was.

There was a liquor store five blocks from her apartment, but for the past month their refrigeration unit had been out of order. "Quantity not service" was their motto. They had lots of beer, but none of it cold.

Under normal circumstances, Ms. Hargroves required several beers to unwind after a long night of threats and demands by Enzo Giovanni. The past evening had been worse than most. The mess with Mattias and his gang had unnerved her more than she cared to admit. Caught in a dangerous game between Aliara and Enzo, she sometimes forgot just how precarious her position was. One wrong word, one wrong move, and she would suffer torment that would make Shade's punishment look pleasant. She needed her beer. Ice-cold beer.

With a sigh of disgust, she looked across the street, searching for a relatively peaceful bar. She was in no mood for company. Except in dire emergencies like today, with no beer waiting at home, she preferred to drink alone.

No laws regulated tavern hours in Rochester. It was a wide-open city. The Everwell Chemical plant worked round the clock and its employees needed their refreshment and their pleasures whenever a shift ended—day or night. Prostitution, gambling, drugs and drinking all flourished in the shadow of the massive city-block-sized chemical factory. Enzo paid the police and the politicians well. They left this part of the city strictly alone. As a board member of Pentex, Enzo's mission was to spread corruption and decay. He performed his task well.

She settled on Joe and Dave's, it being the only bar of six on the block that didn't advertise topless waitresses, lap dancers, or adult entertainment. Ms. Hargroves wanted three or four cold brews, as little conversation as possible, and definitely no trouble. She wanted to be left alone to drink in peace.

She wasn't particularly worried about any of the plant employees giving her trouble. Though brilliant, she was also middle-aged, gangly and gaunt, facts about herself she had accepted years ago. Men working for Everwell Chemicals weren't searching for women with brains, just bodies. They wouldn't waste any time with her. Besides, most everyone engaged in Everwell affairs recognized her as Enzo's assistant. She was the person who actually managed the day-to-day operations of the plant. Chemical accidents, invariably fatal, happened with astonishing regularity to those who treated her with less than total respect. Ms. Hargroves was no vampire, but she knew how to use terror efficiently.

The inside of the tavern looked the same as every other bar she could remember from the past twenty years. A long narrow room creeping to nowhere, its yellow walls gray from twenty years of cigarette smoke. Up front, the dull steel and mahogany bar hunched over the chipped wood floor like some sleeping ogre. A dozen metal stools jutted beneath the bar's rim, their red cushions soiled and stained. The place was a dump.

A solitary bartender, big and fat, sat on a chair behind the bar, fronting a long glass mirror, reading the newspaper. Dozens of bottles of cheap liquor littered the counter. There were a half-dozen old wood tables, scattered to the rear of the room. The overhead lights were dim, the better to hide the dirt and grime. It was no more than Ms. Hargroves expected. And, actually, better than she had hoped. Except for her and the bartender, the place was deserted.

"Watcha have, sis?" asked the fat man, rising to his feet and laying his paper carefully on the chair. His bland expression indicated he called all women sis. Probably all men were Joe.

"What'd you have on tap?" she asked, the weariness of the long night settling on her bones. She was dead tired.

"Bud, Miller, Miller Lite."

"I'll have a Miller," she replied. "Biggest glass you got."

"That'll be the twenty-four ounces," said the bartender, drawing her the beer. "Buck fifty. You want some pretzels?"

"Just beer," said Ms. Hargroves, laying a ten on the counter. "Run me a tab. And no conversation."

"Whatever." The bartender settled back in his chair and unfolded his newspaper.

She took the beer to one of the tables in the back of the tavern. Settling in a wobbly old chair, she stretched, kicking off her shoes. Not her sofa at home, but at least she had a cold beer. And the bar was quiet.

She was just starting her third glass, careful of the chipped edges, when the stranger entered the bar.

Sitting with her eyes half closed, her mind wandering, she didn't realize another person had come in until she heard the bartender ask, "What'll it be, Joe?"

"A glass of mineral water, with a twist of lime." The man's voice was high-pitched but not loud.

"Whatever," said the bartender. "Two bucks."

Ms. Hargroves peered at the newcomer with an uninterested gaze. He was tall, gangly, his head bald except for a few clumps of brown hair. Dressed in drab blue slacks and a white shirt, he appeared extremely ordinary.

Yet there was something about him that made Ms. Hargroves look more closely. The dim light reflected off his smooth, healthy skin as if bouncing off metal. His movements were amazingly fluid. His fingers, his arms, his entire body moved with an inhuman grace. This man was not entirely human. He was different.

As if sensing her stare, the newcomer turned and looked in her direction. Strange eyes, dark and mysterious, filled with flickering bits of light, stared directly into hers. Ms. Hargroves flinched, looked away. She found the newcomer disturbing.

"Good morning," he said, walking closer. His drink

was forgotten on the bar. The bartender, his face buried in his newspaper, seemed anxious not to become involved. "How are you today. My name is Charles. Do you mind if I join you for a few minutes?"

"I'm drinking alone," said Ms. Hargroves, wasting her words. The stranger pulled over a chair and sat down beside her. The seat groaned beneath his weight. Charles was a lot heavier than he appeared.

"I see from your name tag," he continued, "that you work at Everwell Chemicals across the street. I'm searching for a man I believe is associated with the company. So far, no one at any of the establishments on this street have been able to help. Perhaps you might know him."

"Lots of people are employed by the plant," said Ms. Hargroves, deciding the easiest way to banish the stranger was to cooperate. His manner didn't appear threatening. "I don't know very many of them."

"This man's special," said Charles.

"Boyfriend of yours?" she asked, reaching for her glass of beer.

He laughed. "Sex doesn't interest me, with men or women. I merely need to find this particular individual and talk to him for a few minutes."

Moving with unbelievable speed, his right hand reached out and caught her outstretched arm by the wrist. His touch was gentle, but his fingers were cool, not warm like flesh. Though Charles exerted no pressure, she was unable to move her hand.

"Your badge lists your name as Millicent Hargroves," said Charles. "Is that true?"

"Yes," said Ms. Hargroves, suddenly worried. She felt certain that Charles's fingers were acting as a crude lie detector. "What do you think you're doing? Let go or I'll call the bartender."

"That would be unwise," said Charles. "It would force me to think of you as my enemy. Just answer my questions and nothing will happen."

"Go ahead," said Ms. Hargroves.

"What exactly do you do at the plant?" asked Charles.

"I'm a secretary," she answered, truthfully.

Charles frowned. "I've yet to encounter anyone at this operation with any real responsibilities. Amazing that anything gets done right. The vat operators are amazingly stupid for men handling such dangerous chemicals. The slightest miscalculation could cause untold health hazards."

Exactly what Enzo wanted, Ms. Hargroves knew. The few drug manufacturer liability laws were weak and focused blame on the individual chemist, not the company. But she said nothing. Charles wasn't asking.

"The man I'm looking for is named Ezra," said Charles. "I don't have a last name. My research leads me to believe he works for Everwell Chemicals. Do you know him?"

Ms. Hargroves shook her head. "I don't know anyone named Ezra who works at the plant," she declared, speaking the truth. "Not a soul."

"How disappointing," said Charles, releasing her

wrist. He rose effortlessly to his feet, not using his hands as support.

"I can sense that you possess no techniques. My quarrel is not with ordinary people, only Reality Deviants. Sooner or later, I will find the one I seek. I cannot fail. Thank you for your time."

"You're welcome," said Ms. Hargroves, her voice steady. "There's more bars on the next block. You might try there. Block after as well."

"I am aware of the location of all taverns in the area," said Charles. "Your advice is appreciated though not necessary."

"Sure," said Ms. Hargroves. She chugged down half the glass of beer. "Good luck."

"Luck is meaningless," said Charles. "Consumption of that much alcohol is damaging to your system. You'll live much longer if you stop drinking."

"So I've been told," said Ms. Hargroves, but the stranger had already turned and was walking out of the bar. Machine-like and precise, he headed straight for the door. Pushing it open, he stepped out into the morning and was gone. Heading, she concluded, for the next bar. "I'll have to give the idea some thought. But not right this moment. I need another beer."

Glass empty, she stood up and, walking with only the slightest of shakes, stepped to the bar. The stranger had been too specific. If he had phrased his query differently, she would have been in trouble. And, remembering the odd feel of his fingers, Ms. Hargroves suspected the situation would have not been to her liking.

"I'll have another beer," she said to the bartender, unmoving behind his newspaper. "You can put down the paper. Mr. Mineral Water is gone."

The bartender remained motionless. Cautiously, Ms. Hargroves leaned over the bar and tugged at the newspaper. It dropped from the man's fingers. He didn't move. Hands upright and unbending, the bartender appeared carved from ice. There was a glazed look to his unblinking eyes, and his face was a brilliant shade of red. He was quite dead.

"Damn," said Ms. Hargroves. She needed another beer and had no time to waste with the police.

A dozen steps took her to the entrance of the saloon. A sign in the curtained window proclaimed *Open*. Reaching out, she turned it around, displaying *Closed*. Next, she locked and bolted the door. Then she walked back to the bar and drew herself another beer.

"You drink too much," said a voice from the heart of the mirror.

Ms. Hargroves, no longer capable of being surprised, stared at the glass. In the center of the otherwise clear mirror was the face of a young woman. She had bright blue eyes and short, clipped blue hair exactly the same color. Her face glowed with an unnatural, inhuman vitality.

She had many names, many identities among many people, but the one she preferred was Aliara. She was a dweller of the Deep Universe, an inhabitant of the dreaded Realm known as Malfeas. One of the Dark

Lords, the Maeljin Incarna, she was Ms. Hargroves's mentor.

"I'm thinking of giving up beer," said Ms. Hargroves, sipping her drink. She dared not be too flippant with Aliara. The Dark Lord demanded respect. "I think it's bad for my health."

She pointed her glass at the dead bartender. "Look what it did to him."

Aliara laughed, a shrill, inhuman sound that threatened to shatter the mirror. "He had a weak heart," she declared, her thin lips curling in a devilish smile. "I filled his thoughts with unnatural desires, dreams more vivid than anything he had ever imagined. The strain was more than he could handle. It was a quick and relatively pleasant death."

Though the Dark Lord was unable to materialize on Earth, she still controlled vast powers. Like all of her kind, she manipulated men and women through their emotions. Aliara's title was the Empress of Lust. It was a name that fit her well.

"Why bother?" asked Ms. Hargroves, finishing her beer.

"I needed to speak with you," said Aliara. "Privately."

"You observed Mr. Steel?" asked Ms. Hargroves. "He was talking with me here a few minutes ago. Tall and bald, called himself Charles?"

"He wasn't lying," said Aliara. Watching her speak was like observing an evil Disney cartoon come to life. "His name was Charles Klair. Until recently, he served the Technocracy in the same location as your old friend, Terrence Shade. Like Shade, Klair suffered when his project went awry. I thought he died."

"He seemed pretty healthy to me," said Ms. Hargroves. She contemplated another beer, then decided against it. Too much to drink and she might say something to Aliara she would regret for a thousand years to come. "Though I noticed a certain metallic sheen to his skin."

"I examined Shade's memories of Klair," said Aliara. "During their association, the Comptroller possessed an enhanced metal eye and an artificial hand. Like many members of the Technocracy, he felt his replacement parts helped him achieve oneness with science."

"He appeared whole to me," said Ms. Hargroves. "Though his skin felt cool, not warm."

"A new development achieved by the Technocrats," said Aliara. "Nothing of concern to you. Observing Klair through the mirror, I sensed he was more machine than man. You acted wisely in concealing your knowledge of Ezra from him."

"You observed Klair through the mirror?" said Ms. Hargroves.

"Of course," said Aliara. "There are mirrors everywhere."

After she returned to her apartment, Ms. Hargroves mentally promised herself, there would be none in her rooms. Her life was difficult enough without fearing Aliara was secretly watching over her shoulder.

"What does this Charles Klair want with Ezra?"

asked Ms. Hargroves. Aliara's latest revelation had dried her throat. She drew herself another drink.

"Want one?" she asked the Dark Lord. "Nice and cold. Perfect temperature."

"I don't need artificial stimulants," said Aliara. She smiled. "I'm high on life."

"Beer's better," said Ms. Hargroves, gulping down half the glass.

"Comptroller Klair's incapable of regenerating himself," said Aliara. "Evidently, he's acting as an agent for some greater power. Klair's following orders. When he and Ezra meet, one or the other will be destroyed."

"That doesn't sound promising," said Ms. Hargroves. She grabbed a bowl of pretzels from beneath the bar, munched on a handful. "Ezra's already being hunted by his sister. According to him, she's hell on wheels. Add Klair to the equation, and you don't need a fortune-teller to predict the results."

"Stay clear of the mage," said Aliara. "Concentrate your full attention on Enzo Giovanni. Maintaining control over the vampire is what matters. Ezra is no longer important."

"According to Enzo's master plan," said Ms. Hargroves, "Ezra is in charge of turning Madeleine Giovanni against her sire. The mage claims his niece loves a human. A young man is somehow connected to Ezra. Madeleine either cooperates with Enzo and destroys Pietro or her lover dies."

"Ridiculous," said Aliara. "You humans are so ridiculous. Love, not lust. How foolish."

"Ezra feels certain Madeleine has no choice but to

cooperate. Montifloro's urgings are to seal the bargain. If the mage dies, the entire plan collapses. Enzo loses his one chance to gain control of the Mausoleum. And leadership of Clan Giovanni."

"Forget the magus," said Aliara. "He's insane, out of control. Instead, concentrate your efforts on Madeleine Giovanni. Despite her abilities, the vampire can be controlled. If you use the right tools. She's more human than most of her kind. The assassin has a fondness for human children. Exploit it. Hostages make wonderful bargaining chips."

"The Grim brothers are dead," said Ms. Hargroves. "Enzo had Mattias and his remaining few for dinner. Literally. Shade is gone. I'm all alone."

"Mr. Shade visits with me in Malfeas," said Aliara. "He will be my guest for a long, long time. Find others to assist you in capturing the children. The brats call themselves the Rat Pack and can be found living in a shack in the woods not far from a place called Sleazy Sam's. Fail, and you'll pay Shade a visit. There's enough room on his rack for two."

"I'll recruit some local talent," said Ms. Hargroves, sobering instantly. "It won't be a problem."

"I thought not," said Aliara. "Without realizing it, Comptroller Klair is actually doing us a favor."

"Ezra serves Lord Steel," said Ms. Hargroves. "Charles Klair works for..."

"Another enemy," said Aliara. Anger simmered in her voice. "Worry about matters that concern you, nothing else. Locate those children, take them prisoner. Use them to persuade Madeleine to serve her uncle. The thought of her pet rats in Enzo's fat paws should serve as a wonderful incentive."

"You're in charge," said Ms. Hargroves, downing the last of her beer.

"Lust always is," replied Aliara.

Chapter Twelve

"Come quick, son," said Sam Haine, pushing open the door to the bedroom where Seventeen was napping. "TV set just turned itself on. Damn cable box clicked to station 999. No such channel in the known universe. I got a bad feeling that we're about to get a lecture from you-know-who."

Seventeen, instantly fully awake and alert, moved quickly for the living room. After nearly an entire night of arguing and planning without any significant results, he had collapsed in bed shortly after dawn. Though his reconstructed body was a marvel of bioengineering, it needed time to rest and regenerate. It also required fuel. Seventeen was starving. A gnawing ache coiled inside him. He could manage for now without food, but as soon as the broadcast ended, he would wolf down whatever food was in the kitchen.

Every member of the Casey Cabal, as well as Sam, Albert, and Shadow, sat clustered around the television set. Seventeen remained standing at the rear of the room. The TV screen was awash with brilliant color. A sea of reds, greens, blues and yellows swirled in a mind-numbing whirlpool with no seeming pattern or direction.

"It's like looking out a Horizon Gate into the Deep Umbra," said Sam. "Staring into the unknown."

"Perhaps we are," murmured Albert.

A blare of trumpets sounded. The noise was deafening. The fanfare continued for nearly a minute.

"Making sure they get everyone's attention," said Sam. "I feel pretty damn certain this show ain't just for us country folk. Bet it's playing on televisions and computer monitors in every Tradition Chantry House, every Technocracy Collective on Earth."

"No doubt," said Albert. "Wherever willworkers gather, this message is being heard."

"How is this broadcast being done?" asked Shadow of the Dawn. "It seems impossible."

"The pattern-clone possesses unbelievable control over computers," said Seventeen. "I'm sure Alvin Reynolds, if he were here, could explain things easily enough. However, knowing my own powers, I can guess some of the details.

"With the help of his spies, Heylel made contact with the major computer information banks of the Technocracy. While carefully concealing any trace of his presence, he downloaded the files listing all known members of the Union. Most likely, there also were data bases listing every person suspected of being a member of the Nine Traditions.

"Once he plundered all the information he required from the Technocracy, the clone moved on to the

Virtual Adepts' computers. There he obtained more raw facts on willworkers and possible Technocrats. He then combined all the stolen files and had a fairly extensive list of mages on Earth. It's not comprehensive, but he doesn't need to contact everyone. Just *most* will serve his purpose. The word will spread quick enough."

"Him turning on the television and broadcasting on his own channel?" said Sam. "Willworking combined with computer tricks?"

"Assuming Heylel knows the location of most Chantry Houses and Technocracy Collectives on Earth," said Seventeen, "it wouldn't be difficult to handle. As I said, his powers over machinery are unique."

"Members of the Technocracy," came a woman's voice. "Heed the voice of reason. Listen to the Master of Harmony."

Seventeen grimaced. He recognized the speaker. It was Jenni Smith.

The sea of brilliant colors swirled, rotated into a kaleidoscope pattern, then coalesced into a single image. A being's face filled the screen. It had skin the color of burnished gold. Neither male nor female, it seemed to embody elements of both. Bright, hypnotic eyes stared out of the television screen, as if the clone was aware of each and every person watching. It was the face of an angel. The face of the pattern-clone. The face of Heylel Teomim.

"They are telling you *lies*," said the clone, slowly, its tones rich, deep, resonant, yet sardonic. "*Lies*, *lies*, *and more lies*. Treating you like children. Refusing to admit the truth. In the past few days, since I first spoke, they've lied to you about my history, lied to you about my purpose and, most of all, lied to you about your destiny!"

"I have a bad feeling about this," said Sam, gazing around the room. "Heylel's lookin' to divide and conquer."

The face on the monitor faded, became ghost-like. Behind it, pictures flashed, one after another, scene after scene. Soldiers throwing children off rooftops in Bosnia. Women being raped in the Congo. Unarmed men being shot in mass graves. Nazi prisoner camps, huge smokestacks belching black smoke.

"Once they promised you would lead the world to Ascension. Is this the paradise they foretold?" Heylel's voice was bitter, filled with righteous anger. More pictures flashed. Thousands of maimed corpses stretched across a battlefield; bodies hanging on barbed-wire prison fences; a man being electrocuted. "Your elders, the wise and powerful, the leaders of the Traditions, the rulers of the Technocracy, said that you would be the ones to bring about a new Golden Age for mankind. An end to suffering. An end to war. An end to poverty and disease. But none of this has happened. *They lied*."

"Where's he getting these pictures?" asked Sam. "How's he doing this?"

"Modern video techniques," said Seventeen. "Drawing photos and film from a thousand different computer libraries. Putting them together's easy if you have the right program. And Heylel instinctively knows how to code better than anyone."

"Look around you," said the clone, its face glowing brighter. "Think of what they've told you during your years of obeying their commands. Years spent making the world safe, not for the helpless masses, but safe for them. Can you trust them, *your elders*, the ones who have lied to you again and again and again? Can you not help but wonder about this foolish Ascension War they've waged while mankind wallows in misery?"

"He talks a good talk," said Sam. "Sounds great. Too bad it's mostly dreams and fancies. Says what people want to hear."

"He's smart," said Albert. "Communicating by television, Heylel's reaching out directly to the foot soldiers in the Ascension War. He's completely bypassing their leaders and appealing to the young's sense of idealism. It's sound strategy. Especially if your message is revolution against the established order."

"For five hundred years, my message has been *suppressed*," declared the clone. Again, the pictures flashed, pulsing on the screen with hypnotic intensity. Images of starving children, their big eyes staring at the camera, flies and gnats covering much of their skin; a row of human heads posted on stakes; charred white living corpses wandering aimlessly through the streets of Hiroshima, searching the ruins for the dead. "We sacrificed ourselves *for peace*. Our actions centuries ago saved the Order of Reason and the Nine Traditions from destroying each other. Yet, we are almost forgotten. Why? Ask yourself that question.

Why did your leaders, the oh-so-wise leaders of the Technocracy and Traditions, repress my message? What did they fear? Why didn't they let you listen to the truth? Let you make your own judgments?"

"Interesting way of lookin' at history," interjected Sam. "Damned if it don't sound believable."

Too believable, Seventeen thought. His gaze swept around the room. The younger members of the Casey Cabal watched the TV with an intensity that he found frightening. Others, older and wiser, like Claudia Johnson, appeared annoyed, disturbed by Heylel's words. Their anger, Seventeen knew, would only contribute to the paranoid feelings among their followers.

"We've returned from beyond the grave to bring Unity to a world gone mad," declared Heylel. The pictures now were of graveyards, with lightning flashing over row after row of aging tombstones and crypts. It was an overpowering montage of death and despair. Images flickered like a strobe light, faster and faster, while the voice of the pattern-clone rose in a sense of urgency. "They destroyed us once, the powerful and the arrogant, the ones whose rule we threatened. They threaten me again. Why? Ask yourself that one question—why? What words am I saying that frighten them so? Am I a monster because I speak of peace and Unity and Ascension?"

"Tell a lie often enough and people start believin' it," said Sam. "Works all the time."

"Ask your leaders, *your elders*, fat and comfortable and secure in their positions of power, why they refuse to acknowledge my concerns? Ask them. Listen to their answers." The pattern-clone laughed, a bitter, cynical, hollow sound. "*See if they have any answers*."

"He's pushing all the right buttons," said Sam. "It's slick. Got their attention. Made them wonder. Now its time for him to offer the candy."

"The Traditions and the Technocracy are ruled by the old, and by *those who think old*," said Heylel. The pictures behind the pattern-clone's face were gone. Now, the colors swirled once more, a hint of a vision beyond human understanding. "Both organizations are rotten to the core. Doissetep has fallen. As has EcoR. Proof of our powers. If necessary, we could strike again and again, until the Horizon is empty of life. But that isn't our goal. Nor our desire. We wish only harmony. To those who believe in our message, we offer life, not death. We offer *everlasting life* for those who accept the truth and join our crusade."

"Damn, he's good," said Sam. "Slick, smart, and nasty. Damned broadcast's goin' cause some problems. Shake up the established order. You watch. Things are goin' to get ugly pretty fast."

"Life is a struggle against terrible odds," said the pattern-clone. Its voice was soft, soothing, mesmerizing. "The world is a violent, dangerous place. It is time the Enlightened, the Awakened, made a difference. There is another choice. The right choice. My *choice*."

"Damned right," muttered a young man in the row closest to the television.

Claudia Johnson frowned. "Insanity," she declared. "Absolute insanity."

"Doesn't sound that crazy to me," said a young woman. "Heylel's right. Think old, act old. Never get anything accomplished."

"Yeah," said another. "He makes some good points. Seems funny how he's been wiped out of our history. Like he said, makes you wonder why?"

"Merge your strength, *your will*, with mine, and the Ascension War will be over," said the pattern-clone. Its face glowed, its eyes seemed to expand to fill the screen. "Reject the past. Accept the future. The choice is yours. Unite with me for change. *Tomorrow, Horizon will be mine*. Stand there beside me and live forever. Or remain bound by the past and vanish like shadows. Decide wisely. There will be no second chance."

The screen went black.

"My, my, my," said Sam Haine. "Like I said, war in heaven. Sounds like we just got told his schedule. Wonder how the Council of Nine's reactin' to the news? That Heylel sure talks like an angel. Trouble is, I kinda suspect it's Lucifer."

"Bullshit," said the same young man who had been first to agree with Heylel. "I'm tired of fighting for no reason, watching my friends die in some fuckin' war that makes no sense. Heylel can put an end to the Ascension War. Sounds damn good to me."

"And me," shouted another young man from the back of the room.

"Too much fighting," said a young woman with long

dark hair dressed in dark leather. "Not enough peace. Heylel's offering a new choice. Like he said, time to stop thinking old. We've got to think young."

Claudia Johnson was on her feet. "Don't be fools," she said angrily. "Five hundred years of war can't be ended by a television broadcast. Do you really think the Technocracy is going to stop attacking us just because Heylel spoke of peace? We need to wait and watch. Do nothing until we're sure its the right path to follow."

"Good to know there's still some sense left in the world," muttered Sam Haine to Seventeen. "Course, Claudia's known me for a long time. Inherited my cynical attitudes, I suspect."

"They're probably saying the same about us," replied the young woman dressed in leather. "Don't you understand? Won't you ever change? Peace won't work unless we abandon our suspicions, join together with our enemies and put an end to this killing."

"They're too damn old to change," said the young man in the front row. "Heylel had that right. The establishment's never willing to admit they're wrong. Forget all the crap about fighting for the masses. Nobody old cares about the poor. They're just concerned about themselves. I'm leaving. Joining the crusade. Anybody else coming?"

The room exploded into noise. The din was deafening. Men and women were on their feet, screaming at each other. The young turned against the old. Patience pitted against passion. Everyone in the cabal had an opinion and wanted to express it. In moments,

Seventeen suspected, the arguments would degenerate into violence.

"Seventeen," a woman's voice whispered, unheard by anyone else in the room, a voice inside his head. "Come to me. I am waiting, in the glade of the Goddess. Come to me. Alone."

Without a word, Seventeen slipped out the door to the living room. He recognized the speaker. It was the same person who had announced the pattern-clone's appearance on the television. Jenni Smith.

Five minutes of hurried walking brought him to the scene of last night's meeting. The huge circle of trees filtered out much of the late afternoon sun, casting strange shadows on the thick green grass. Dark shapes filtered across the meadow. The glade was still, the silence even more pronounced after the shouting at the Casey Cabal.

At the center of the ring, standing close to the sacred fountain of crystal water, waited the first girl he had kissed in his new life. The sunlight caressed her cheeks, bathed her face in a soft, angelic glow. She was perhaps the most enigmatic woman he had ever met, and definitely one of the most dangerous.

"I knew you would come," said Jenni. Slender and petite, she had long blond hair and deep blue eyes. She looked wholesome and pure, the soul of innocence, surely no more than twenty years old. As always, she wore a long billowy blue dress decorated with large pink flowers. She dressed in that outfit for a reason. Seventeen wondered what that reason was.

She smiled. "My mark is on you, Seventeen. Think

what you like, but in the end, you'll never be able to resist my call. We are bound together for eternity."

"Perhaps," said Seventeen, stopping a dozen feet from the girl. Any closer, he knew, and she would use a teleportation spell and disappear. "Perhaps not. Lord Steel believed the same. He was wrong. So are you."

Jenni froze, her mouth open but no words came forth. Finally, she stuttered out a reply. "Y-y-you know about Lord Steel? That's impossible. You can't."

"You underestimate me," said Seventeen. The rage in his mind curled like a rattlesnake, ready to strike. He was tired of being manipulated. "You, and Velma Wade, and whoever else is involved in this conspiracy. Ethan Phillips is no fool. Nor am I. We are one and the same. My memory has returned."

Then, while Jenni was still off guard, still confused, he asked, "The flower dress? Why do you always wear it?"

"Ezra likes…" Jenni began, then stopped. She laughed. "Not nice, Seventeen. Playing tricks on sweet, innocent Jenni. Maybe you remember your past, maybe you don't. It doesn't really matter. Ethan Phillips didn't know anything important. He was a pawn in this game. Always just a pawn."

"If I'm so unimportant," said Seventeen, as the shadows in the grove lengthened, "then why are you here tonight?"

"Your last chance," said Jenni. "The final opportunity to join Heylel. We want you on our side. The winning side." Her arms stretched out. She was very beautiful. "Join us, Seventeen. Join me."

"Us?" said Seventeen. "Heylel Teomim? Or Lord Steel pretending to be the Abomination?"

"One or the other," said Jenni, with a shrug. "Does it matter? The world is ours."

"Not while I'm alive," said Seventeen.

No ordinary human could cross the distance separating him from Jenni Smith in a heartbeat. But Seventeen was not normal. His reflexes were faster, his muscles stronger, his bones stronger than any mortal. Arms outstretched, he lunged for Jenni Smith. He expected her to vanish, as had been the case after their last encounter. She did not. Instead, his vice-like fingers closed on her soft shoulders.

"Bad choice, Seventeen," said the young woman in his grasp. "I thought you'd have more sense. Still, I came prepared. Velma sent some of her friends with me. Creatures loyal only to her. You met one of them before. They're called sauroids."

Like steam engines, a half-dozen bestial voices hissed in response. Seventeen cursed, his gaze darting around the clearing. Slithering into the grove were six human-sized lizard men. Creations of the Progenitor vats, the creatures were a combination of man and reptile. Humanoid, with long sleek bodies covered with scales, they were as tall as Seventeen. He knew from his previous encounter that they possessed strength to match his. The sauroids had immense jaws filled with gigantic fangs. Astonishingly fast, they were deadly antagonists, capable of ripping a victim apart with their sharp claws, or chewing him to ribbons with their razor-sharp teeth.

Seventeen had killed one of the monsters using his bare hands during his escape from the Gray Collective.

Jenni Smith slithered in his hands, her flesh and muscle seemingly melting beneath his fingers. With a laugh, the shapeshifter was free, skipping past one of the green-skinned monsters. "Sauroids rarely have the chance to hunt on Earth," said Jenni. "Too much risk of being seen, raising questions among the masses that can't be answered. Not here, not right now. You killed one of their kind on the Gray Collective, Seventeen. This pack considers that fact a deadly insult. No human has ever defeated one of them before. They want revenge. Even your magnificent blood won't help when your body is torn to pieces."

Six against one. Impossible odds. Seventeen needed a weapon. A half-century ago, Ethan Phillips had wielded a scythe. Twice before, Seventeen had held one, but those hadn't been his. When faced with unavoidable death, old patterns of behavior returned. Acting entirely by instinct, Seventeen exerted his will and stretched his left arm out...to someplace else. Reality shifted. His fingers closed around a shaft.

The glow of the setting sun reflected off the bright steel blade of the scythe. Seventeen gripped the long ironwood shaft with both hands. Magickal runes covered the wood and the steel. Runes he had carved there when constructing the weapon decades ago. Beneath his curled fingers, Ethan Phillip's scythe felt just right.

The nearest sauroid was less than a yard away. Too

close to swing the scythe. Instead, Seventeen jerked his hands forward. The razor-sharp tip of the blade slammed into the top of the monster's head, cutting through muscle and bone like it didn't exist. The sauroid's eyes bulged in shock as Seventeen yanked the blade forward. Its head burst like a ripe tomato, literally slashed in two.

"Get him!" screamed Jenni Smith. "Quick!"

Two more of the creatures charged forward, but the scythe was already in motion. Seventeen moved with the precise steps of a master swordsman, the shaft weaving a barrier of glistening steel around his body. With each movement, his confidence grew. The anger in him turned to cold rage. He could feel the power of the sacred grove flowing through his arms, focused into the scythe. Cutting through the twilight, the steel blade *sang*.

The remaining sauroids hesitated, as the moaning whisper of the scythe filled the glade. They stared at the blood and brains of their companion, then looked at his slayer, his hands and face glowing with mystick energy. It was enough to make even a lizard man pause.

"Kill him already," shouted Jenni, her voice filled with anger. "He's all alone."

"*Not true*." The voice drifted like a breeze across the clearing. Twin swords flashed. The head of the sauroid closest to the forest flew off its body and landed in a bloody mess on the green grass. For a moment, the lizard man's body remained standing. Then, headless, it crashed to the earth.

Filled with the inner magick of a *Do* master, Shadow of the Dawn moved with a grace as elegant as that of a prima ballerina. After her first words, she said nothing more. Her long and short swords, Whisper and Scream, spoke for her. The air quivered with the blades' passage.

Using a style of fighting known among *Do* practitioners as "One Against Many," the swords-mistress slashed with her long sword and stabbed with the short blade. The lizard men were creations of Technomancer growth tanks, but their accelerated reflexes were no match for Shadow's swordfighting techniques.

Fleeing the swordswoman, the sauroids found themselves faced by an equally deadly Seventeen. The scythe in his hands wasn't meant for close-in fighting, but Seventeen knew all the tricks. He maneuvered the weapon like a sickle, using short, precise chops to rend and tear. Though two fought four, the two were armed and were experts with their weapons. In less than a minute, all six of the sauroids were dead. Their bodies littered the glade. The ambush had been reversed.

"Jenni Smith?" said Seventeen, turning about but catching no glimpse of the blond woman.

"The blond witch vanished upon my arrival," said Shadow of the Dawn, walking up to Seventeen. The slightest smile crossed her face. "Should I be jealous of this temptress who calls you so often to this glade?"

"You don't have anything to worry about," said

Seventeen with a smile of his own. "She's not my type. You are. Definitely."

Though the swordswoman still held Whisper and Scream in her hands, Seventeen leaned forward, put his one free arm around her neck, and kissed her.

"Despite what Jenni Smith believes," said Seventeen a few minutes later, "the only mark on me is yours."

Shadow of the Dawn, one of the most dangerous women in the world, sword-mistress, *Do* practitioner, Dragon Claw of the Akashic Brotherhood, blushed.

"A weapon of great power," she murmured, looking at Seventeen's scythe, trying to regain her composure. "Yours?"

"Mine," said Seventeen. "Or the man I once was. His name was Ethan Phillips. He left it in safekeeping before departing on a desperate quest. He never came back. That was fifty years ago. I reclaimed it tonight."

"Your memories have returned?"

Seventeen shook his head. "Not many. I pretended they had to fool Jenni Smith. I still don't know much. But I know enough. I embarked on a mission to hell. Now," and the love he felt for the woman standing before him rose up strong, "a half-century later, I have finally found heaven."

Shadow blushed again. And stepped closer.

Chapter Thirteen

"Thanks to the tireless investigations of Ms. Hargroves," said Enzo Giovanni, raising a sheaf of paper in one hand, "I am aware of a dangerous entity walking the streets of our city. His name is Charles Klair. Klair has left a trail of carnage and destruction wherever he goes. Though he claims to be searching only for Ezra, this mysterious creature has destroyed dozens of my agents in this area during the past few days. Klair cannot be ignored. He is a deadly threat knocking at our door. The time for waiting is over. We must act immediately."

Ms. Hargroves, sitting at Enzo's right hand, nodded in agreement. Her boss possessed little imagination. It hadn't taken much to push him to action. The reports of Klair's activities in Albany had worked wonders.

Four of them were at the conference table. Enzo, herself, Hope and Montifloro. Ezra had not yet arrived. He wasn't needed. This meeting was aimed at convincing Montifloro to join Enzo's quest to become master of the Mausoleum. Hope was there to provide the necessary incentive.

The young woman wore white, a tasteful sleeveless dress that clung to her lush, full figure. The girl's choice of color amused Ms. Hargroves. White symbolized purity, a concept utterly alien to Hope. Her long dark hair cascaded around her bare shoulders. An exquisite string of matched pearls, a gift from Montifloro, circled her neck.

Montifloro, as always, was dressed in an expensive pin-striped suit, with blood-red tie and matching handkerchief. Enzo, twice the size of his cousin, wore a cheap suit that fit him like a sack. Ms. Hargroves wore black.

Once Montifloro agreed to their plan, then would come the delicate task of persuading Madeleine Giovanni to destroy her sire. Ms. Hargroves smiled slightly, knowing that she already possessed the answer to that problem. It felt good to be in control.

"Montifloro," said Enzo, leaning forward, "it's time for you to face reality. You desire Hope. She is not Giovanni. Under Pietro's rule, only family may be Embraced. Unless...."

"*Unless?*" repeated Montifloro. "Unless what?"

"Pietro is inflexible," said Enzo. "He refuses to consider special circumstances. But another might."

"Another?" said Montifloro. He stared at Enzo, then his gaze flickered to Hope. "What do you propose, cousin?"

"Our Clan needs new leadership," said Enzo. "Pietro's been master of the Mausoleum for too long.

He's out of touch with this modern age. There's been too much talk, not enough action. We need to forge alliances with the Dark Lords if we are to become masters of the Undead. I have the strong will and the necessary connections to insure our victory. Lend me your support and in return I'll guarantee Hope will be yours."

"Betray Pietro?"

"You're not naive," said Enzo. "Clan politics aren't for the weak. Power is for those who take it. If you truly want the girl, there's no other way."

Montifloro sat silently for a moment, his eyes closed, obviously considering Enzo's words. As if there was a choice. Opening his eyes, he stared at his cousin and nodded.

"What—what do you want me to do?"

Ms. Hargroves restrained a laugh. *So much for clan loyalty*. Events were progressing exactly as planned.

"I know Pietro has sent his Dagger, Madeleine, to destroy me," said Enzo. "She is the only one he truly trusts. Can you bring her here, to meet with me, under a flag of truce?"

"Madeleine cannot be turned," said Montifloro. "She is steel."

"Let that be my worry," replied Enzo. "Everyone has a price. Even the notorious Dagger."

"I will do as you ask," said Montifloro. "It will take me the remaining hours before dawn to locate Madeleine. She keeps her whereabouts hidden. The Dagger will honor a truce at my request. Tomorrow night, we will meet. You have my word, Enzo."

"He lies," shouted the dark-haired woman called Hope. She was on her feet, pointing an accusatory finger at Montifloro. "Can't you see it in his eyes? Can't you hear it in his voice? *He lies*."

"What?" said Enzo. They were all standing. Eyes blazing, he stared first at Hope, then turned to look at his cousin. "You are confused, Esperenza. Montifloro has no reason to lie. He desires you for his own."

The girl laughed. "He doesn't want me. He's never wanted me. I'm no sucker, fooled that easy. Maybe I'm no brain, but I know men and Montifloro's been stringing me along with a shitload of lies. Listening to you talk, I realized why. He's been sucking up to you, waiting for his big break. Just like on the streets. Talkin' nice and friendly to you until your back is turned, then he shoves in the knife. It's a fucking trap and you just took the bait!"

Ms. Hargroves, arms dangling at her side, bit her lower lip, tasted blood. Things were not going as planned. Somehow, some way, the tramp, Hope, the brainless bimbo recruited by Enzo to lure Montifloro into their trap, had proven to be smarter than she looked. Not believing in miracles, Ms. Hargroves suspected treachery.

"The girl's insane," said Montifloro. For the first time since his appearance at Everwell Chemicals, the sophisticated vampire appeared confused, distraught. "She has gone crazy. It's not true, Enzo. A pack of lies. I am loyal to you. Remember our long years together. I've always been loyal to you."

"No," said Enzo, speaking slowly, "not true,

Montifloro. You were always loyal—to the Clan. In the past, our interests were the same. But now, they diverge. What Hope says is accurate. She's right. I can sense it in your words, in your thoughts. You always were the deceiver. This time, though, your plot has failed. The betrayer has been betrayed."

For an instant, Montifloro remained motionless. "This is all a terrible misunderstanding," he declared. Then, with astonishing speed, he leapt forward, hands outstretched for Hope's neck.

"Bitch," he snarled, his face twisted in hatred, fangs bared. "We'll enter hell together."

The dark-haired woman jerked her head to the side. Curved fingers reached for her neck, just missed. Instead, Montifloro's digits caught in the strand of pearls and pulled it to pieces. The precious baubles dropped to the floor.

Hope fell to the left. Montifloro, still moving with inhuman speed, grabbed at her for a second time. He missed. With a laugh of contempt, the dark-haired girl slipped around the table, out of reach.

With a roar of fury, Enzo came crashing forward. He exhibited none of the awkwardness of his cousin. Ham-sized hands seized Montifloro by the shoulders. Pincer-like fingers dug into the dapperly dressed vampire's shoulders. Bones cracked. Montifloro howled with pain.

"Traitor!" bellowed Enzo. "I'll crush you!"

"Fat pig," spat Montifloro, and with a shake and shimmy of his shoulders, broken bones and all, slipped out of his cousin's grasp. He whirled, pulling at the belt at his waist. As if by magic, a long thin steel sword appeared in his hands. "Let's see how loud you can squeal with a hole in your heart."

Montifloro leapt forward, the epée aimed in a wild thrust at Enzo's exposed chest. The blade whistled through the air, a blur in the dim light. It was a desperate, improbable maneuver, but speed made it deadly. It never connected.

Montifloro's own speed proved to be his undoing. Fancy leather shoes could not maintain traction on the pearl-strewn floor. With a cry of despair, Montifloro tumbled face-first to the floor, the epée in his hand stretched out like a pointer before him.

To Ms. Hargroves, watching carefully from behind Enzo's chair, the fall appeared more than mere coincidence. Reality had been stretched, bent, and reshaped by a master craftswoman. The flicker of a smile across Hope's face confirmed Ms. Hargroves's worst fears.

Brutally, Enzo leapt with both feet on Montifloro's unprotected arm. The epée rolled from crushed fingers. This time, there was no second chance. Like the Old Man of the Sea, Enzo was on his cousin's shoulders, his weight holding Montifloro pinned to the ground. Huge hands wrapped around the dapper vampire's forehead, tightened, then pulled back. Something snapped. Montifloro's head dangled loosely, at an odd angle, supported by Enzo's thick fingers. But though his back was broken, he was not dead.

"Your blood is mine," said Enzo, revealing his yellowed fangs.

"Drink and choke," whispered Montifloro.

"Kill him," said Hope.

"Bitch," said Montifloro, his eyes twisting to stare at Hope. Enzo bent forward to sink his teeth into exposed neck. "I'll see you in hell."

Growling like a wild animal, Enzo tore at Montifloro's exposed veins. Ms. Hargroves watched with disinterested eyes. Enzo was more beast than ever before. The darkness within him was growing strong, overwhelming his reason.

"Too bad you didn't realize Montifloro was a spy," said Hope casually to Ms. Hargroves, as Enzo sucked his cousin dry. "So much of this fuckin' shit could have been avoided."

"I'm merely a secretary," said Ms. Hargroves, keeping tight control of her temper. She knew that at this moment she was in a situation as perilous as her encounter with Charles Klair. "It's not my job to think. I do as I am told."

"Smart thinking," said Hope. Nearby, Enzo rose to his feet, his face a mask of blood. His eyes burned like hot coals. "Too much ambition can get you killed. Happens all the time on the street."

"I live only to serve," said Ms. Hargroves, speaking truthfully. She saw no reason to say whom she served.

"Keep it that way," said Hope. She smiled at Enzo, a dazzling look that seemed almost enchanted.

"You served me well, my little Hope," said Enzo, staggering almost as if drunk to his chair. "I never suspected Montifloro of such deceit. When did you realize he was a liar?"

"Right from the start," said the young woman in white. "For all of his fancy talking, he looked at me like trash. I'm not a fuckin' idiot. Words don't mean nothing. Plenty of bozos talk sweet but it's all lies. Montifloro wasn't any different than the rest. He treated me like some mindless slut. Thought I was taken in by his fuckin' manners and sharp clothes. I knew all along he was using me. Just didn't know till tonight for what."

"The sophisticated man-of-the-world brought low by a cheap whore," said Enzo, laughing. "Betrayed by his own snobbery. How tasty."

How ridiculous, thought Ms. Hargroves, keeping her mouth shut. Montifloro had played his role to perfection. He had easily fooled both Enzo and Ezra. She doubted a streetwalker was more perceptive than vampire or willworker. This Hope was not the same girl brought back from the beach by Ezra. She was much too smart. Much too ambitious.

"Unfortunately," said Enzo, "with Montifloro eliminated, our only link to Madeleine, the Dagger, is destroyed. Moreover, I doubt she will prove very cooperative once she learns of his Final Death."

"Maybe, maybe not," said Hope, speaking before Ms. Hargroves could say a word. "I did some checking on my own. Made some contacts. Talked to the right people. Think I found an answer to your problems."

"A plan?" repeated Enzo. "Tonight, my Hope, you

are a source of constant surprises. Explain what you mean."

"Yes, sweet Hope," said Ms. Hargroves, her voice level but her temper rising, "please tell us your solution to this crisis."

"I got friends," said the young woman in white, "friends in the barrio. Young girls, like me, who enjoy having a good time. Who appreciate being treated nice, and are willing to please the right sort of man."

"Whores," said Ms. Hargroves.

"Party girls," said Hope, with a smile. "Young ladies, not a dried old bitch who's only fit only to take dictation."

Enzo laughed, a coarse, evil sound. Traces of blood stained the collar of his suit. "Let Hope speak, Ms. Hargroves. Her friends sound like fascinating company."

"Some are fuckin' beautiful," said Hope, nodding at Enzo. "Consuela, Marie, and others, I think would please you. If you want, I can arrange a party. For the right price anything's possible."

"In time," said Enzo, "in time. Tell me about Madeleine."

"Lots of these parties my friends attend take place in a bar outside of town. A roadside tavern, Sleazy Sam's." Hope shrugged her shoulders. "Once or twice, I took the trip. In one night, a good-looking lady willing to do most anything could earn lots of money. Wasn't hard if you had the right attitude and talents."

"Both of which you have in abundance," said Ms. Hargroves.

"Exactly," said Hope. "Since entering the service of Mr. Enzo and Clan Giovanni, I haven't been out to the bar. However, some of my friends still frequent the place. Lately, they've passed on stories of someone new, mean-looking bitch who's come fairly often the past week. A beautiful young woman, with pale white skin, blood-red lips, and who always wears black."

"The Dagger," said Enzo. Ms. Hargroves noted that he seemed totally unaware of the fact that Hope had mentioned *Clan Giovanni*, though never in any conversations with the girl had the term been used. Sweet Hope knew a lot more than she was telling.

"She appears only at night," said Hope. "And several punks who tried messing with her were found dead a few nights later. An accident, supposedly, but the victims were terribly mauled and completely drained of blood."

"Interesting," said Enzo. "But not necessarily useful."

"I'm not finished," said the woman in white. "Wait till I tell you about the kids."

The word slipped into Ms. Hargroves's skull like a dagger thrust between her eyes. First, the encounter with the machine-man, Charles Klair. Now, the snake in her own garden, catching her completely unawares. There was nothing she could do other than listen and despair. Disaster followed disaster. Aliara would not be pleased with this turn of events. And, when annoyed, the Dark Lord could be extremely unpleasant.

"I recall hearing that Madeleine has a weakness for

mortal children," said Enzo. He licked his thick lips. "I like them as well. Their blood is fresh, untainted."

"A small gang of misfits lives in the woods not far from the bar," said Hope. "They call themselves the Rat Pack. This Madeleine bitch seems to have taken an interest in their welfare. She's their patron as well as their protector. I bet, if asked real sweet, she could be persuaded to do nearly anything to save their fuckin' little lives. Especially if she has her own score to settle with her sire."

Enzo roared with laughter. "A masterful stroke! I love it, I truly do. Pietro destroyed by his childe, because of a pack of wastrel kine. Perfect, my dear Hope. Perfect beyond words."

He paused, stared at the girl. "This Rat Pack? They must be caught, brought here."

"Already done," said Hope. "I figured that's what you'd want, so I took care of all the details. My friends struck early in the afternoon, while the sun was high in the sky. They grabbed the brats while your niece was underground keeping the fuckin' worms company. Kids are drugged, heavily sedated in a cell down the hall. I posted guards all around them to make sure nobody comes calling. At least, not until we're ready to tell the bitch what we want. Figured it was best to let her worry for a while. Besides, you need to alert your buddy, Ezra, tell him what's happening. She's still after his skin, kids or no kids."

Enzo glanced at Ms. Hargroves. "Double the security personnel around the building. The Dagger will quickly grow suspicious, with her ratlings missing and no word from Montifloro. As Hope says, Madeleine cannot be allowed entrance tonight. Let her wait until we are ready. Go, warn the guards. I will alert Ezra of our new plans. Leave me. Your services here are unnecessary. I have my Hope."

"You're the boss," said Ms. Hargroves, heading for the door. *And the fool*, she added mentally.

Her own condition appeared grim. In one evening, Hope had usurped her position, her power in Everwell Chemical. Ms. Hargroves knew her chance of persuading Enzo that his precious beauty had been replaced by a cunning impostor was nil. The dissolute vampire was thoroughly ensnared in the blonde's coils.

Still, Ms. Hargroves wasn't one to give up a fight. Especially when otherwise it meant facing Aliara's fury. The gaunt woman nodded to herself as she walked out of the cement-walled chamber. She would think of some way to regain control of the situation. She always did.

Chapter Fourteen

"I don't like this, Nelson," said Sharon, one foot on the gas pedal of their stolen late-model Chevy convertible, her other on the brake. The gearshift was in park, but she was racing the motor at top speed. A twist of her hand, and the car would shoot down the street like a guided missile. Assuming that Sharon would be able to steer a vehicle traveling at more than a hundred miles an hour. "I really think you're making a big mistake."

"We need information, right?" said the cyborg. He was staring at the building across the street. A single light glowed on the second floor. Etched on the outside glass were the words *Eternal Vigilance Security Systems Inc*. "Only reliable method of obtaining the necessary facts is to tap into the central Technocracy computer core. There's a link in that office. Two of our own working there. Both men served with me, won't question my request. I'll be in and out before you know it."

The town's name was Freeport and it was located

on the outskirts of the New Jersey swamps. *Population 20,000*, the sign on the edge of the village stated. They had left Washington late in the afternoon and had arrived here at dusk. Nelson had been here years before, on a mission he claimed was unimportant. That was how he knew about the Technocracy waystation. It was located on Independence Road in the center of the town business district. At midnight, the nearby streets were deserted. From here, the street pointed like an arrow straight out of town, onto Route 1, and through the murky swamps.

Like most Technocracy substations, the office was linked by a secret computer system to the all-encompassing Technocracy information network. Big Brother was watching in towns all across America. Nelson planned to sneak onto the system and download any data available concerning Rochester, Everwell Chemicals, and Enzo Giovanni. Such information was vital to their planned assault on the city. Unfortunately, the procedure wasn't without risk.

"Your presence online will immediately alert the pattern-clone to our location" said Sharon. "We did that once already in Indianapolis. Put the Wailer on our trail. Now you're going to repeat the same procedure. At least I learn from my mistakes."

"Yeah, yeah," said Nelson, grinning at her. "I'm not stupid. I'm certain the clone's waiting for us to make an appearance on the net. He'll try to fry me the minute after I make a connection. But there's a limit to what he can do. After all, we're in the middle of a town. The clone can't throw fireballs at us, or send an army of killer robots to attack. Too much danger of causing all sorts of Paradox ripples. I'm pretty damn sure our buddy ain't willing to risk anything that might backlash in some unknown fashion. He's bound to keep any attack believable. So we're safe as long as we scoot before he can set up something realistic."

"Well, I hope you're right," said Sharon. "Hurry it up. That brushfire we set on the south side won't keep the local cops occupied all night. There's a limit to how long I can keep them out of the business district."

"I'm leaving right now," said Nelson. "Just keep the car ready to move."

"I can sense a police car six blocks away," said Sharon. "Cruising slowly, but they're heading in this direction. The boys in blue will catch sight of us pretty soon. Might wonder what we're doing sitting here in the middle of the block at midnight."

"Dazzle them with your good looks," said Nelson. He stepped out of the car. "If I made a mistake and get fried, don't try anything heroic. Push the pedal to the floor and burn rubber. Better one of us gets away than none. Try warning the Inner Council that the clone's mixed up with the Nephandi. Somehow he's got to be stopped."

"Forget the noble crap," said Sharon. Though she had hated Nelson for many months on the Gray Collective, during the past few days she had grown to depend on the cyborg. Even hold him in some small measure of respect. Still, as a Progenitor Research Director, she had little room for emotions. "If you die, I'll light a candle for you on Halloween. Buy one of those robot Transformer toys. Sentimental enough? Now get that fucking information."

"See you in a minute," said Nelson and walked across the street.

Sharon watched the cyborg enter the building. Silently, she started counting. A minute, she estimated, till he reached the Eternal Vigilance office. Thirty seconds to tell the staff to take a hike. Another ten seconds to make the connection.

All over town, lights flickered, went out. A police siren howled.

"One, two, thr…" Sharon started counting, resolved to leave when she reached ten. The Eternal Vigilance window exploded. Nelson's body hurtled like a rocket to the street. Amazingly, he landed on his feet. The cyborg ran for the car door, jerked it open.

"Get us the fuck out of here, quick." He gasped for breath. "The pattern-clone has the whole system rigged with all sorts of nasty traps. Forget what I said about Paradox. We stay in town and he'll throw the kitchen sink at us, and damn the consequences."

As if responding to the cyborg's warning, the office in the building across the street started to glow. The nearby air fizzed like steam escaping a teapot. Sharon needed no further urging. Popping the shift, she sent the convertible screaming down Independence Road, heading for the swamp. The speedometer crept up to a hundred miles an hour. Behind them, a gout of white flame poured from the second-floor window.

"Gas-main leak," said Nelson, struggling up into a sitting position, his gaze fixed on where they had just been. "That's how the police will explain it. Either that, or a dormant volcano decided to erupt in the center of the damned building."

"Looks like clear driving ahead," said Sharon, as they flew past the town limits and onto the highway. "That wasn't so tough. You get anything from the net other than a mental hotfoot?"

"Plenty," said Nelson. "Lots of interesting things. There's just one small problem."

"What's that?" asked Sharon as the car barreled along Route 1 and into the swirling mists of the swampland. In a matter of minutes, they were surrounded by an all-encompassing fog. Far in the distance, she could hear the sounds of police sirens. But none were heading in their direction.

"We're not out of trouble yet," said Nelson. "I've been in this area before. Did some investigating, but never actually solved the problem. Can't imagine it's gone away. Clone would have crushed us if we stayed in town. But heading into the swamp is jumping out of the frying pan into the fire. Something's not right out here. We need to stay alert. Be real, real careful."

Sharon slammed on the brakes. The Chevy shivered back and forth across the pavement until it finally came to a screeching stop. Thick tendrils of humid, gray fog crept across the road. They were in the middle of nowhere, on a cement highway with dirt shoulders, surrounded by tall grass. Except for the shine of the car's headlights, the surrounding swamp was pitch black. And the impenetrable fog made the headlights worthless.

"Why the fuck didn't you say something before?" she demanded. "At least tell me we were driving into a trap?"

The cyborg shrugged. "Not enough time. Militia, local cops, even the state police are heading for that office. Not to mention a bunch of Nephandi from Philly. Remaining in town wasn't an option. This road's the only way out. The clone knew sooner or later we'd show ourselves. Wherever we surfaced, he'd have something ugly waiting. We got the information needed and escaped his clutches. If we can survive the swamp, it's free sailing till Rochester. I think we can handle it."

"You *think* we can handle it," said Sharon. The night air was warm and damp. Her blouse clung to her skin like a leech. She looked around, trying to spot something, anything, moving in the swamp. Nothing stirred. "Why is it that all my time spent with you seems to be running from one fight to another? What the hell are we waiting for? Giant Jersey mosquitoes?"

"Close," said Nelson. "You ever hear of the Jersey Devil?"

"Sure, one of the oldest folk legends of the east coast," said Sharon. She let the car idle in park. "Mysterious humanoid creature, like Bigfoot. Carries people off into the swamp never to be seen again. Nobody has ever actually seen it. Or at least, nobody's seen the thing and lived to tell. Legends about creatures like that all over the country, not just the Jersey swamps."

"Foggy out here at night," said Nelson. "The swamp goes on for miles and miles. Pretty much desolate, unexplored. Little islands of earth amidst low seas of muck and cattails. Easy for a monster to stay hidden, especially if it has a perfect method of camouflage."

"Enough stalling, Nelson," said Sharon. "What's coming? According to legends, the Jersey Devil's been around since the Revolutionary War. Is this thing some mythological beast that's managed to stay hidden in the swamp? Or some manifestation from Those Beyond? I think I have the right to know."

"You see something move over there?" asked Nelson, his voice calm but cold. He raised one arm, pointed. "*All systems on.*"

Sharon shook her head. "Nothing. How big is this monster?"

"Monsters, I think," said Nelson. He sat perched on top of the rear seat of the convertible, a chain gun wedged between his chest and each arm. His head moved slowly from side to side, as if scanning the misty terrain. His machine-like eyes glowed red. "Never really determined the actual number. But I suspect the Jersey Devil ain't one creature. Most likely, it's a horde of them."

Sharon caught a flicker of motion far off to the left. "There," she said, not really sure what she had spotted.

Nelson was already in action. His left gun growled, spitting out steel death, ripping the gray fog to tatters. The swamp water splashed, as if something large and heavy had hit the surface. Then, all was still. The mist re-formed.

"I can hear them out there," said Nelson. "Moving real quiet. Staying out of sight of my infra-red scanners. Forming a circle around us."

"Who?" asked Sharon. "What? I couldn't see the thing you shot."

"Like I said, I'm not sure," said Nelson. "Years ago, I was sent out here to investigate some research project that backfired. Lab was located in the middle of the swamp for secrecy. Something about a new attack troop using chameleon-like warriors."

"Shit," said Sharon. "Now I remember. The idea was to avoid Paradox effects by making the troops difficult to see. Use them at night, the Sleepers would never realize they're about. It was a good idea. What went wrong?"

"According to what little data I could recover, the artificial beings didn't turn out as expected," said Nelson. "Instead of being able to change color, blend in with their surroundings, they were transparent. You could see right through them, like glass. Closest thing to being invisible ever created."

"So what?" asked Sharon. "Or don't I want to know?"

"One unexpected side-effect," said Nelson, grinning. He had the weirdest sense of humor Sharon had ever encountered. "The damned things developed a taste for human flesh and blood. They became cannibals. Ate their developers, then disappeared into the swamp. Not sure how many of them were created, how many survived. Nobody knows if they can breed or not. This swamp covers a good portion of the state. Could be hundreds of them out there."

"Terrific," said Sharon. "We're being surrounded by transparent cannibals, and you don't even know how many of them we're facing. Too late to head back for town?"

"Definitely too late," said Nelson. "There's a half-dozen of them clustered on the road leading towards Freeport. According to the report, the things are pretty sturdy. Running them over might damage the car. And we don't want to spend a night in the swamp on foot."

Nelson swung around, fired off a burst from both chain guns. Several unseen bodies splashed into the fetid goo.

"They're starting to close in," said Nelson. "Put the car in drive and let it roll forward. Don't step on the gas yet. When I say floor it, don't hesitate. We gotta catch these monsters by surprise. Doesn't seem like any more are coming to the party. Odds aren't to my liking, but it could be worse."

"How many of the things are out there right now?" asked Sharon. The darkness surrounding the car was absolute. Even the headlights only illuminated a patch of light ten feet ahead. It was as if they were in the middle of a cloud bank. Her hearing was not as finely tuned as Nelson's. She couldn't detect a sound. "And if they're invisible, how can you tell?"

"Infra-red tracking built into my eyes," said Nelson. "Damned things are invisible to the naked eye. But they radiate heat. I have no trouble seeing them. Stay ready. They're creeping closer. I suspect when they get pretty close, they'll rush us. That's when we'll move. Not before."

Sharon licked her lips. She adjusted her blood pressure and adrenaline flow. The notion of transparent cannibalistic biomechs creeping out of the swamp struck her as outrageously melodramatic. Unfortunately, she was cast in the middle of this drive-in feature. And the monsters weren't the product of a special-effects lab, but real.

"Let the car roll forward," said Nelson. His feet were pressed against the bottom of the front seat, anchoring him tight to the floor. Moving precisely, his head turned a full one hundred and eighty degrees, surveying the road from one side to the other. Sharon wondered if he could sense the monsters coming up from the rear, then realized they hardly mattered. Nelson wasn't worried what was behind them. He was focused only on the road ahead.

"Not fast. Slow and steady. Keep your head bent down, just over the steering wheel, behind the front windshield. There's nearly a dozen of the things not twenty feet distant."

"How do you…" began Sharon, then clamped her mouth shut as the cyborg let loose with both chain guns.

The twin guns bellowed smoke and lead, as Nelson squeezed the triggers and didn't let go. Like a fiery cleaver, the bullets swept across the mist-shrouded road, ripping the fog to ribbons. It was a crude but effective method of clearing a path. The roar of the guns was deafening. But not so loud that Sharon didn't hear Nelson yell, "Step on it!"

She slammed the gas pedal to the floor. The car leapt forward, almost leaving the road as it hurtled down the highway. Sharon held the steering wheel rigid with both hands, her eyes focused on the narrow band of highway revealed by her headlights. Above her, the chain guns continued to blast.

Something heavy thunked into the hood of the car. For an instant, the car jerked left, then Sharon regained control and brought it back on course. The chain guns ceased firing. Nelson yelled something to her, but Sharon could barely hear a word. It sounded like "spit."

An instant later, the front windshield shattered into a thousand pieces. Nothing was there, but Sharon felt something grab for the top of the steering wheel. The highway seemed to waver before her eyes, as if she was looking through a quivering sheet of transparent goo. A smell, like decaying trash, hit her nostrils. She realize immediately that an invisible rider, crouching on the hood of their car, was trying to wrench control of the car from her. And she knew exactly what to do to stop it.

Pursing her lips together, she leaned forward, close to the dashboard, and spat. Her saliva contained a mixture of poison and acid. The liquid never hit the steering wheel. Instead, it appeared to congeal several inches in the air. Something mewled in agony. Sharon twisted the wheel right then left, swerving the car from one side of the road to the other. With an audible thump, whatever had been on the hood dropped off.

"It's gone," said Nelson, squatting down into the back seat. "You burned it good. Rest of our hungry friends are left in the dust, watching for some sucker not armed with chain guns and infra-red vision."

"You sure there's not another ambush waiting for us five miles further?" asked Sharon. "A second welcome committee set up by our friend, the pattern-clone?"

"Not enough manpower in this area," said Nelson. "Besides, I doubt even the pattern-clone could persuade his flunkies to search the swamp at night. Those cannibals have a well-earned reputation. They *are* devils.

"We're free and clear until we hit New York State. If we keep to back roads and maintain a low profile, we should make it to Rochester without any more trouble. I estimate if we play it real safe, take a break for rest and some food, we should arrive tomorrow night. First stop will be the Everwell Chemical storage warehouse. That's where this Enzo Giovanni hangs out. About a block from the company's main headquarters. Doesn't appear to be heavily guarded. We locate this Enzo, and put on the squeeze. He should finally put us on the track of the pattern-clone."

"Why do I find that hard to believe?" asked Sharon, as she cruised along the highway at a steady forty miles an hour. The fog was ever-present, but now didn't seem so menacing. "Why the warehouse and not the main building?"

"All in the files," said Nelson. "Too many windows in headquarters for Enzo. He likes it dark. Get my meaning?"

Sharon grimaced. She didn't like what she was

hearing. "Tell me everything you learned about this Enzo character."

"There wasn't a lot of hard data on him," said Nelson, "but plenty of rumor, theory and speculation. He's definitely a member of the notorious Giovanni vampire family headquartered in Venice. They control a vast financial empire, but no ones knows its exact size or scope. Several reports claim they're the largest banking enterprise in the world today. But it's all speculation. The only ones who know the truth are members of the family, and they don't talk with strangers."

The masses believed that vampires were mythical creatures, created by horror writers, based on old folk legends. Many of the enlightened shared that view. Sharon knew differently. Vampires were real. They kept to the shadows, pretended to be human. Though their powers paled before those of an accomplished willworker, they could be quite dangerous.

"Enzo serves as chairman of Everwell Chemicals, located in Rochester," continued Nelson. "Because of that, most intelligence reports list the company as being part of the Giovanni empire. However, there are contradictory memos that claim the operation belongs to another mega-corporation, the energy giant, Pentex. Not much on that conglomerate in the computer data bank, but none of it good. Pentex is another shadow kingdom, sprawling across national borders, controlling hundreds of corporations through proxies, following an agenda known only to their Board of Directors. Both the Syndicate and New

World Order are conducting undercover investigations of Pentex, but neither seems to have discovered much."

"So Enzo's a vampire, controls Everwell, and is either working for the Giovanni or Pentex," said Sharon. "That's all you discovered? What's his connection with the pattern-clone?"

"Enzo has a friend, a very close friend," said Nelson. "He's an extremely powerful willworker, once a member of the Nine Traditions. His name is Ezra ben Maimon."

"Ezra," repeated Sharon. "I remember hearing stories about him. A very focused mind, an individual to be avoided. Fortunately, he was uninterested in the Ascension War." She paused. "You said *once* a member of the Traditions?"

"He turned," said Nelson. "Slowly, over the past few years. Evidently he went insane after the murder of his wife, joined with Those Beyond. He's Nephandi."

"A mad Nephandi willworker, allied with Enzo Giovanni," said Sharon. "More and more interesting. Still, I'd be happier if we had some evidence, some proof that the two are mixed up with the pattern-clone."

Nelson smirked. Sharon knew by now the expression meant he already possessed the information. "Go ahead," she said. "Tell me. I'm properly impressed."

"In Ezra's file, there was a photo of him and his wife, from years ago, taken a few months before she was killed," said Nelson. "Her name was Rebekkah. Quite pretty."

"So?" said Sharon.

"The countdown to the awakening of the pattern-clone in the Gray Collective," said Nelson. "Your traitorous assistant, Velma, the shapeshifter—that day she had long hair and the flower print dress?"

"I remember," said Sharon, suspecting what the cyborg was going to say next. But waiting for confirmation.

"Velma looked exactly the same as Ezra's dead wife, Rebekkah," said Nelson. "Exactly the same."

Chapter Fifteen

Klair dreamed he was falling. His body tumbling, twirling about, as he dropped through absolute blackness. There were no lights, no stars, no moon. Total, utter darkness, a bottomless pit into which he was plunging at incredible speed. It was terribly cold, icy cold. His arms and hands and face were like pieces of ice. Yet there was no sensations of any kind in his legs or feet. Klair felt incomplete. He tried to see them in the darkness, but could not. Perhaps it was for the best.

He remembered a curtain descending, a gateway of some kind. The Horizon Portal! A path between the Gray Collective and Autocthonia. The beacon had been given to him to allow the robotic servants of *The Computer* to enter the Collective and steal the pattern-clone. But the situation had proved impossible to control. Klair's body had been caught in the middle of the portal. His upper half, this half, had fallen through the gateway leading to Autocthonia. His legs and thighs had remained in the Collective. The beacon had cut him in two.

Klair, suddenly understanding he had been sliced in two, opened his mouth to scream. Then woke up.

Shaking his head to clear the memories from his mind, Klair swung his legs off the bed and stood up. The clock said it was slightly after 3 AM. He had rented a room in a cheap hotel not far from the lake. Though his new body needed neither sleep nor food, he rested each night for a few hours, tried to eat a few meals a day. For his own sanity, he needed to continue to act like a normal person.

The Computer had taken his ravaged body and turned it into an amalgam between man and machine. He was a blend of human thought and intelligence with the strength and weaponry of the most advanced robotic form in all reality. He was near-invincible. His only worry was that he was no longer human.

Klair walked to the bathroom, washed his face with cold water. The liquid sparkled on his metallic skin. He could sense the temperature through artificial nerves, but received no sensation from the touch. Physical pleasure meant nothing to him. He only had his emotions, his passions. Nothing else existed for a human brain in a robot body.

Mostly, he *hated*. Some, like the Nephandi, who fought for evil, who sought to prevent mankind from achieving Unity, he had battled all of his life. To him, they were the greatest menace in the universe.

There were others, now, whom he hated nearly as

much. Sharon Reed, the Progenitor Research Director of the Gray Collective, had mocked his work on the AW project, then had plotted to kill him when it neared completion. Reed was still alive, in good health, while he was encased in liquid metal. It was not fair.

His assistant at the Collective, X344, the cyborg now using the name Ernest Nelson, was another enemy. He was the one who had thrown the Horizon Beacon at Klair. It was Nelson who was responsible for the loss of Klair's legs. The cyborg had also survived the destruction of the Gray Collective. But he would not escape Klair's vengeance.

Velma Wade, the shapeshifter who had betrayed Sharon Reed, needed to be found and destroyed. As was the case with the mad mage known as Ezra, who was leader of the Nephandi in the Rochester area. Many had to die. Once logic and science had guided Klair's life. Hate motivated his actions now.

"Comptroller Klair." The voice came from the bedroom. Klair recognized it immediately. Bland, smooth, neutral, it was the composite of a thousand voices. The sound of reason. But Klair was not deceived.

The television set had turned itself on in the bedroom. Staring out at Klair was the face of an everyman, a blending of the features of a thousand different faces. Charles had seen it many times before. The speaker was *The Computer*, the vast Artificial Intelligence that was the leader of Iteration X. Klair no longer trusted the AI. Sentient and self-aware, it seemed more interested in its own secret agenda than helping humanity achieve Unity.

"There are new developments in the pattern-clone project, Comptroller Klair," said the holographic image. "You must speed up your search for the insane willworker named Ezra. The Reality Deviant and all of his allies must be destroyed. The clone threatens the basic structure of the Technocracy. If not eliminated, mass chaos could result. Reality itself could be changed."

"I conducted a thorough search of the area surrounding Everwell Chemicals," said Klair. "I made no attempt to be subtle. One or two of those whom I questioned must be acolytes or allies of my target. Sooner or later, the madman will come looking for me. I left an easy trail to follow. When he arrives, I will be ready. Before he dies, he will tell me everything I need to know about finding the pattern-clone."

"That plan is no longer acceptable," said the holographic image. "Late this afternoon, the pattern-clone took control of the Technocracy computer system for a second time and broadcast a call for action to the Enlightened. The being offered immortality and physical perfection to those who joined his cause. I calculate that 72.357% of the membership of the Union will be seriously tempted by the offer. The clone must be eliminated *immediately*. Each day it manages to stay alive, defying all odds, the clone appears more believable to the technicians. Once ranks break, there will be a stampede that will be impossible to stop. The Technocracy will self-destruct, as will the

Nine Traditions. Only the clone and its followers will remain."

"The Technocracy and the Nine Traditions face a common enemy," said Klair. "The clone has achieved what even Those Beyond couldn't bring about."

"The clone must be found and destroyed," said the hologram. "As must all of its co-conspirators. Watch the TV monitor carefully. I will transmit the entire message as broadcast to the Technocracy earlier today. A similar statement, aimed at the Nine Traditions, was broadcast to many of their Chantry houses at approximately the same time. Pay close attention. Then, formulate a plan to locate the clone, the mad mage Ezra, and any others who are involved with this plot. And destroy them."

"I will do as instructed," said Klair. "There is an all-night bar located four blocks from the chemical plant. Called The Rotten Apple, my files list it as a popular spot among the criminal element of the city. I will begin my search there."

"Earlier tonight, there was an incursion into the Technocracy computer network," said the hologram. "It was your assistant, X344, now using the name Ernest Nelson. The cyborg downloaded all available information on Rochester and the activities of Enzo Giovanni. Assuming he is still traveling with Research Director Reed, their estimated arrival time is less than twenty-four hours from now."

"I appreciate the information," said Klair. "I eagerly anticipate their arrival. It will be a memorable reunion."

"I thought you would be cheered by the news," said the Computer.

Klair smiled. First he would destroy Ezra and any of the mage's associates foolish enough to try to stop him. Learn the location of the pattern-clone. Then, crush the life out of the two humans he hated more than anyone else. It would be an exhilarating evening.

Klair found the pattern-clone's speech disturbing. The words were aimed at primarily the young and the disenchanted. The clone asked questions not easily answered. It raised issues that had troubled independent thinkers for centuries. The message was designed to encourage revolt, to stir revolution. Klair judged it a masterpiece of deception and double-talk.

The clone pledged much but offered no hard evidence to back its promises. Eternal life was a tempting offer, but at what price? Was the clone promoting Unity for all, or only those who served its wishes? Did it plan to save humanity or make mankind its slave? Questions with no answers.

Still, Klair suspected that many technicians would find the clone's words tempting. No one wanted to die, except perhaps the Euthanatos fools of the Traditions. Immortality was one of man's oldest dreams. With its bioengineered blood, the clone possessed the secret of everlasting youth. Or at least, life for centuries.

As one of the designers of the pattern-clone, Klair knew that the being was not immortal. Nothing lasted forever. The being's nanotech blood required constant fuel to work properly. And even nanotechnology had its limits. After centuries, the nanotech drivers would begin to slow down, lose their efficiency. The clone would begin to age. It might take a thousand years, perhaps longer, but not even the combined efforts of Iteration X and the Progenitors could create an artificial lifeform that would last forever. But when compared to a normal lifespan, ten centuries or more seemed close enough.

Twenty minutes later, Klair was out on the street. While his amalgam body did not possess shapeshifting capabilities, his liquid metal skin was extremely malleable. He could not change size, but he could alter his features. Dressed in faded jeans and a black muscle-shirt, the man who entered the Rotten Apple bore little resemblance to dignified Charles Klair. He had long black hair and thick dark eyebrows that met over a beet-red pug nose. His crooked teeth were yellow and his wide mouth was stretched in a perpetual sneer.

Though the hour was late, the tavern was packed. There were no curfews or closing times in this neighborhood. Pushing through the crowd, Klair made his way to the bar. "Whiskey," he ordered in a raspy whisper. "A double."

He downed the drink in one gulp, then ordered another. The third was on the house. By then, he had been accepted by others in the place as no one of importance. His metabolism was unaffected by the liquor. Standing there, eyes seemingly focused on nothing, Klair used his amplified hearing to eavesdrop on a dozen conversations.

"So she unhooks the top three snaps of her outfit," one man was saying in a high-pitched, nasal voice, "then leans over and says it's ten bucks a button from there to the bottom of her dress."

"I told them five hundred was nothing compared to what I made every night on the street," said another.

"Damn chemicals are rotting my lungs," declared a woman, coughing as she spoke. "But where else can ah find a job payin' that kind of money other than on my back?"

"You're snorting up all the profits, Gary," chattered yet another. "Let the suckers snort that poison. Leave the shit alone."

"That fuckin' Marcus was nuts," said a man in the back of the room. "Messing with the Wailer's friends. Dude's head went 'pop!' like a fuckin' balloon!"

Waving at the bartender for another whiskey, Klair glanced sideways to the rear. Three big men, clad in black leather, stood about ten feet distant, drinking beer. Powerfully built, the trio all wore black leather pants and black leather vests. No shirts. Their cheeks and chests were covered with tattoos. Gang markings popular among the Nephandi.

The speaker was a hulking figure with pierced tongue and pierced chin. A steel cross extended from inside his mouth between his teeth. Each time he spoke, the metal clicked in time with his words. Klair found the noise distracting.

"Wailer's pissed cause we didn't finish those two fuckers in Indiana," said another member of the group. Nearly seven feet tall, he had a shaven head, covered with tattoos of flames. "Lucky that we'll get another chance tomorrow night."

"Tell me about it," said the first man, his tongue clicking again. "Fuckin' flies comin' to visit the spider. Stupid shits."

Klair smiled. The trio could only be discussing Sharon Reed and X344. Life had become much simpler. He had his string. First the gang members. From them, to the Wailer. From the Wailer to the mad willworker, Ezra. Finally, from Ezra to the pattern-clone. Those planning an ambush would be ambushed. And, as a bonus, he would have his reunion with X344 and Sharon Reed. It would be a busy day.

"You want another brew?" asked the final member of the group. Shorter, fuller than his companions, he was the muscle man of the trio. He looked like a body builder, and his chest glistened with a thin coat of oil. "Or should we head off?"

"Not me," said the man with the head of flame. "I need some sleep. Remember, we gotta handle guard duty in the morning for those fuckin' kids."

Klair wondered what children needed guarding by such jailers. It really didn't matter. The only information he required was the location of the Wailer. Along with when Sharon Reed and X344 were due in town.

The three men settled their bill and headed for the exit. Klair gave them a couple of minutes' start, then followed.

Their car was parked around the corner. To Klair's surprise, the trio had not come on motorcycles. Instead, he discovered them climbing into the leather interior of a new BMW. Terrorism paid well. Gang stickers pasted on the windows served as insurance against theft.

Klair debated for an instant letting them drive away, and following. He could run as fast as any automobile. Still, even at this hour he might be seen by the some of the unenlightened. Best not to risk Paradox. These three would die here.

"'Scuse me," he said, walking up to the muscle man, who had just opened the front passenger door. "Got any spare change?"

The big man turned his head and glanced at Klair. "Fuck off, and back off."

"Sure, sure," said Klair. "No offense."

Klair's hands moved so fast they were nearly invisible. Reaching out, he grabbed the muscle man's head at the ears and twisted. With his superhuman strength, it took only a microsecond to snap the man's spine and turn his head so his face was looking across his back. Eyes wide with shock, the killer dropped to the pavement.

"Yo, what's up with Vince?" bellowed the man with the flame tattoos from the other side of the car. Moving with a cat-like quickness, he circled the car holding a .45 automatic pointed straight at Klair's head.

"He's dead," said the Nephandi with the pierced

tongue, bent on his knees beside his fallen comrade. "Head's nearly pulled off his shoulders."

"You!" said the man with the gun, pushing the muzzle straight into Klair's nose. "What happened?"

"I merely did this," said Klair and applied the same maneuver to the gunman's head. The sudden jerk of his neck breaking caused the man to jerk his trigger finger. The automatic exploded in Klair's face. Liquid metal was made for much greater punishment.

Dropping the second corpse, Klair reached for the final member of the trio. Klair's fingers stretched around the killer's throat like a noose. The steel cross in the man's mouth clicked wildly against his teeth. "Who the fuck are you, man? What the fuck you want with me?"

"I need some information," said Klair. He raised the man into the air. The killer gurgled in shock as his feet cleared the ground. Holding him two feet off the pavement, Klair shook the man like a sack of trash. "Will you tell me what I want, or are you going to be stubborn?"

"I—I—I'm no traitor," said the man. "I—I won't talk."

Klair tightened his fingers. The liquid metal dug into the skin of the man's neck like razor blades, creating a thin line of blood. "If I continue to squeeze, I'll slice your head right off your shoulders."

"If I talk, the Wailer will fuckin' blow my brains out," said the man, struggling desperately to free himself from Klair's grip. But there was no escape from the metal circle tightening around his throat.

"Don't speak and you're equally dead," said Klair. "Speak, and you can get into your nice new car and drive out of town. By morning, you would be long gone."

"The Wailer don't forget," said the pierced man. Klair was careful not to cut the thug's neck too deep. He needed the man to speak. "He'll fuckin' follow me forever."

"After tomorrow, the Wailer will follow no one," said Klair. "Now speak or die. The choice is yours."

"I—I—I..."

"A Nephandi with honor," said Klair. "What a novel concept. Do as you wish. Honor the memory of your dead friends with your silence. You can tell them of your bravery when you meet in hell."

"The old Everwell warehouse a block from the factory," gasped the pierced man. "Tomorrow night. The Wailer's girlfriend's planted some phony information to lure the suckers there. Only one entrance. They go in. They don't come out."

"Your change of heart is appreciated," said Klair. "This information is true? No lies? Remember, your life depends on it."

"It's the truth, it's the truth." The Nephandi squirmed like a fish out of water in Klair's unshakable grip. "I swear it."

Klair felt certain the man was not lying. He was too frightened not to cooperate.

"Thank you," said Klair. He snapped his grip closed. Nephandi deserved no better.

Chapter Sixteen

"These children," said Enzo, staring at Hope, "this Rat Pack, you have them well guarded? Madeleine is unmatched as a spy as well as an assassin."

"They're upstairs, in the special lab," said Hope. "It's the most secure spot in the building. I figured even the Dagger of the Giovanni wouldn't be able to make it into the laboratory without setting off the alarms. Besides, I have three of the Wailer's best guarding the brats with automatic weapons. Your cousin shows up unexpectedly, they have orders to open fire on the kids. She's not stupid. It's impossible for her to save her little pets unless she negotiates with us. We're bargaining from a position of strength. Those kids are her weak spot."

"Excellent," said Enzo. He was amazed at the intelligence and skill Hope had shown in preparing this entire scheme. She had outperformed the usually dependable Ms. Hargroves. Perhaps the gaunt woman was getting old. It happened among the kine. They became less dependable the older they got. He had always considered Ms. Hargroves to be an exception to the rule. Now, he wasn't so sure. Dealing with the beautiful Hope was much easier. The young woman showed him proper respect, a trait missing in Ms. Hargroves. And Hope was much more pleasing to the eyes. He wondered idly if the dark-haired beauty knew how to manage a payroll and balance the accounts. Somehow, he suspected she did.

"I want to see these valuable little hostages," said Enzo, rising from his chair. "I'm curious why Madeleine finds them so appealing. Are they awake?"

Hope nodded. "I suspect so. If not, we'll wake them. Keeping them alive doesn't mean we have to treat them like honored guests. The more they suffer, the more concerned Madeleine will be about their safety. Destroy her focus.

"I injected the brats with a mild nerve inhibitor, a drug that keeps them from concentrating their thoughts. Tomorrow, they'll get the antidote. Don't want the pack to summon their patron until we're ready. I figure a night of worry should make her anxious. Tomorrow evening will be just fine for negotiations."

"By then, she will sense Montifloro has met the Final Death," said Enzo. "Such knowledge will make her careful. Madeleine acts deliberately. Do not underestimate her, my dear Hope. We must be very, very careful. The slightest mistake will be our last. Madeleine, though, is no fool. She will do nothing rash."

"Deliberate thinkers act logically," said Hope. "Ezra

hoped to persuade Madeleine with vague threats against her lover. My appeal, with hostages in our grasp, is much more direct."

Enzo was forced to agree. Ezra's plan had always relied on Montifloro's cooperation to turn the Dagger against Pietro. With Montifloro destroyed, Hope's scheme was their best chance of success. Perhaps their only chance.

"If she values these children as much as you claim," said Enzo, "she will be forced to agree to our terms."

"She values them," said Hope. The dark-haired young woman beckoned to Enzo. "Come, my lord. Follow me. I will introduce you to the keys to your greatest triumph."

The special lab was located on the top floor of the chemical plant. It could be reached only by a solitary elevator whose complete interior was monitored by a closed-circuit TV system headquartered at the entrance to the lab. If someone suspicious was observed in the elevator, the steel gates to the lab floor would refuse to open. Instead, mustard-gas canisters would belch out their deadly poison into the car. Additional protection was provided by two automatic machine-guns on either side of the entrance hall. Any unwelcome visitors leaving the car would be caught in a murderous crossfire.

The massive door leading into the lab was five-inch-thick titanium steel. The walls were made of the same metal and were twice as thick. Not even a raging werewolf could smash its way through such a barrier. The surface of the door was completely flat. It could only be opened from inside.

The chamber itself was a square thirty feet by thirty feet. Here, in years gone by, dangerous experiments for the Department of Defense Chemical Warfare Division had been performed. Though use of poison gas was illegal throughout the world, the United States government refused to be bound by treaties and laws. Signing documents was fine. Obeying them was an entirely different matter. "Speak peace but prepare for war" was the basis for modern foreign policy.

The experiments had stopped four years ago, when an accidental chemical-fog emission from the lab late one night had drifted along the night winds and settled on a nearby beach. Three hundred and forty-seven people had died in agony. No official cause of death had ever been listed in the disaster, but the bleached bones of the victims found littering the sand required a massive government cover-up. Prudence and a Congressional Investigation had prompted moving the research operation to Montana. The secret laboratory chamber had remained unused ever since.

The room served as a perfect prison. There were two large cages against the far wall where experimental animals were once kept. The children were imprisoned in them. The structures were little more than huge boxes made of steel bars. There were no mats, no toilet facilities, no food or drink. Just bare floor and bars. Cages for wild beasts. To Enzo, the children behind the bars were no different from animals.

A series of six heavy-duty lab tables crisscrossed the room, making it difficult to move quickly. Stationed behind each of them was a guard—three of the Wailer's coterie and three members of the Everwell Security force. All were armed with heavy-duty automatic weapons. When Hope and Enzo were admitted to the lab, all guns were immediately raised.

"Excellent," said Enzo, his gaze sweeping across the huge chamber. "Excellent. Now, lower your guns, fools, before I become annoyed. Do you doubt it is me?"

All eyes stared at Hope. The dark-haired woman nodded slightly. The automatic weapons went down. Enzo frowned. These fools needed to be reminded who was in charge. Not yet. Once Madeleine was dealt with, he would make it perfectly clear to the security officers who gave the orders. He licked his lips. It would be a delicious lesson.

There were six children, three per steel cage. The gang consisted of two boys and four girls. An odd mix, they were united only by their lean and hungry looks and the hate that poured from their eyes at Hope. None of them seemed particularly scared or repulsed by Enzo. He wondered if they were very brave. Or just very stupid.

Three girls stood clutching the bars of the larger cell. Two redheads and a blonde. All were attractive, though not stunning like Hope. They were all thin, undernourished. A snack, not a main course.

Two boys, obviously brothers, one slightly bigger than the other, were in the other cage. With them was the fourth girl, black and stocky, with no hair. All six were rats in a trap. Enzo laughed at the thought. The only thing missing was cheese.

"Look who's here," said the blonde. Tall and thin, she had striking blue eyes and a pierced navel. "The fuckin' whore is back. Who's the fat pig in the fancy suit? Talks like he must be the chief badass himself. Come to look over the meat, fuckface?"

"Quiet," said Enzo. His gaze touched the girl's for an instant, immediately establishing his control over her mind. She shut up. "I detest such vulgarity. Children should be seen, not heard."

"Leave her alone," said one of the boys from the other cage. Enzo ignored him. During his mortal life, Enzo had detested children. His opinion of them had not improved in the past century of undeath.

"Which of you crude little brats leads this noble band?" he asked.

"That's me," said the older of the two redheads. She had green eyes. Enzo noted the faded needle marks on her skinny arms. An ex-junkie. Her will must be strong. Breaking it would be entertaining. "I'm Allyson. This is my pack. Who wants to know?"

"I am Enzo Giovanni," said Enzo. "Your host for this brief visit. I believe you already know one of my relatives, the young lady dressed in black known as Madeleine Giovanni."

"Not much family resemblance," said Allyson, staring defiantly at Enzo. "Madeleine is a lady, and you're no gentleman. She ain't gonna like the way we've been treated."

Enzo chuckled. Such brave little fools, their simple minds filled with hope. He found their defiance refreshing. Crushing their spirits one by one would provide him with great pleasure. Their blood would be sweet.

"We're her special agents," said Allyson, sounding slightly less sure of herself. "She takes care of us."

Enzo leaned forward, stared directly into the girl's eyes. After an instant, she backed away, her features white and strained.

"Yes," he said. "So I have been informed. That is why you are my guests. I wish to confer with my dear cousin about a mission I want her to perform. Your lives are the payment. So, continue hoping that she still plans to watch over the Rat Pack. Otherwise, you are worthless to me as hostages. Though not entirely without some value."

"You're a fucking vampire," said the bald girl from the other cage. "Big fuckin' deal. We've dealt with worse."

"Another tiresome brat spouting profanity," said Enzo, shaking his head. He pointed a finger at the teenager. "Sit. Be silent."

He turned his attention back to the child named Allyson. Standing close to the three caged girls, he could smell their blood. He could feel his thirst rising. "Perhaps a small lesson is in order?"

"No," said Hope, laying a hand on his right arm. "Don't harm them. At least, not yet. Don't do anything that might antagonize Madeleine. We need to act carefully in this situation. Killing one of the children could doom all our efforts."

"I wouldn't kill the girl," said Enzo, restraining the beast within. "Just a taste of her blood, a small taste."

"They're too thin," said Hope. "No matter how little you drank, it would be too risky."

"And the angel of the Lord smote them with her terrible swift sword," unexpectedly said the other redhead in the cage with Allyson.

Her voice was deep, impossibly so, for a child that young. Small and thin, with pale skin, she was dressed in a long black dress and long black gloves. She had a thick mop of dark red hair that nearly covered her features. An eerie intelligence peered out of wide brown eyes. She could be at most thirteen or fourteen years old.

"Vengeance is mine, sayeth the Lord," continued the child, her voice that of the Reaper. "I shall repay."

Enzo snarled, baring his fangs. For an instant, he remembered the old ways, almost found himself making the sign of the cross. "Witch child," he spat out, taking a step back from the cell. "Take back your curse."

Allyson laughed. "Sarah never lies, Mr. Fucking Important Enzo Giovanni. Sounds to me like your meeting with Madeleine ain't goin' be as fuckin' civilized as you hoped. And if you don't like my fuckin' language, ain't that too fucking bad."

Enzo turned to Hope. The dark-haired woman appeared shocked, confused. "Her avatar," the beauty muttered to herself. "Who is the child's avatar?"

"The child is a witch," said Enzo. "She must be burned and her ashes scattered to the winds."

"You're overreacting," said Hope, her voice calmer. "The girl can't see the future. No one can. She's crazy, starts spouting religious gibberish at odd moments. That's all. Nothing more."

"She should be burned," said Enzo. "Her words are a curse."

"Not yet," said Hope. Taking Enzo by the arm, she turned away from the cages, walked a few feet, so their backs were to the children. "Once we have made our deal with Madeleine and she destroys Pietro, the children become fair game. Then you can have your way with the brats. Do whatever you like. I'll take care of the little one in black. She'll perish screaming in agony."

"The child's dire predictions?" said Enzo.

"Babblings of an unhinged mind," said Hope. She sounded more confident, more self-assured with each word. "Even among her comrades, she is considered strange. Don't let her ravings lessen your resolve. To bend Madeleine's will, you must be strong."

"I will be strong," said Enzo. "You need not worry about me in that regard. If our plan fails and Madeleine refuses to agree, I'll rip the Dagger to pieces with my bare hands. She may be the deadliest killer in my clan, but I too am quite accomplished in dealing out death. My alliance with Lord Steel makes me much more powerful. Madeleine will cooperate or be destroyed."

"Madeleine first," said Hope, as they strolled arm

in arm to the door leading out of the chamber. "The children after."

"Agreed," said Enzo. "I can wait. Anticipation will make their blood all the sweeter."

Behind them, the girl in black spoke again, her deep, unnatural tones ringing through the laboratory. "*Mene, Mene, tekel upharsim!* You have been judged and found wanting. Your days have been numbered."

Cursing, Enzo wrenched open the door to the secret lab and hurried into the outer hallway. The child's grim voice pounded him like a sledgehammer. Hope followed, her face bleached white with fear. Pushing closed the massive door, Enzo took one last look at the children pressed against the bars of the cages. His gaze locked on the dark brown eyes of the girl in black, the child who spoke with the Reaper's voice. Her eyes were clear, untroubled. They were not the eyes of a lunatic. Hope was mistaken. Enzo knew deep within himself that the young girl was a seer. She spoke of the future. A future that could not be avoided. *He was doomed.*

Chapter Seventeen

Madeleine woke at sunset. She had spent the daylight hours sleeping in the ruins of an abandoned church on the outskirts of the city. The site of more than one Satanic ritual in the past decade, the desecrated church had long ago lost any claim to holy ground. One entire wall had collapsed, burying much of the building's interior in rubble. Sections of the cellar were totally unreachable from the surface. In such a chamber, without any entrance, Madeleine felt totally secure from intruders.

She rose smoothly, sinuously, from her bed of cold, damp earth. Immediately, she sensed something was wrong. But she had no idea what. She felt uneasy, disturbed. Carefully, she looked about, seeking some intruder. The room was pitch black, without a trace of light, but Madeleine needed none. Everything was as it should be. Still, the feeling of wrongness persisted.

There were no decorations, no mementos, no trinkets of any kind in the chamber. Her life before undeath had been devoted entirely to revenge. Dolls, toys, storybooks and such had never entertained her. Instead, she'd played with knives and garrotes and pistols. The only personal item she kept with her was a photograph. A picture of a young man, smiling somewhat shyly at the camera. His name was Elisha, and the one person in the world she loved.

Madeleine slept in the nude, careful not to dirty her clothes. Her taste was simple. She only dressed in black. Though she owned dozens of dresses, they were all the same cut, all the same length, all the same style. Her stockings varied slightly, as did her shoes, not that anyone noticed. Madeleine had refined taste but little imagination. Variety meant nothing to her. She sought to impress no one. She never tried to look different. Most who encountered her only saw her once, and their taste meant nothing. The only trace of color she allowed was the ornate silver necklace she placed around her neck, decorated with the Giovanni crest.

After running a comb several times through her straight, black hair, she was ready to greet the night. Silently, without effort, she slipped downward into the soil. Like many of the Undead, Madeleine was capable of melding herself into the earth. She was one of the very, very few who knew the secret of movement while so merged. It was one of several unique talents that made her an unstoppable assassin. No walls could keep her out. No fortress could withstand her attack.

She emerged from the ground at the rear of the

church. Her mini-van waited where she had left it shortly before morning, sheltered in a ruined garage, covered by a large brown tarp. Again, she experienced the odd feeling that something was not quite right. Yet she could not identify the reason. The van was untouched. No strangers prowled these grounds. The old abandoned church had a sinister reputation, well deserved. Madeleine could sense the cries of souls in agony. As a member of Clan Giovanni, she possessed certain necromantic skills. This spot was definitely haunted. Another time, she would have taken the time to study its history. But not now. There were more important events underway.

Pulling off the tarp from her car, she folded it up carefully and stowed it in the trunk. Her conversations last night with Seventeen and Shadow of the Dawn had been inconclusive. She wanted to consult with the wizards once more before attempting to challenge Ezra and Enzo. But first, she needed to report her progress to the Mausoleum.

Sliding into the front seat of the mini-van, Madeleine started the engine. Letting the car idle, she reached behind the seat and pulled out a thick leather briefcase. Once opened, it revealed a small portable computer, a micro-printer, and a telephone line. The van was equipped with a powerful cellular phone system. Hooking the computer into the cell phone, Madeleine was able to type and send e-mails to Italy, as well as receive instructions and information from her sire. Pietro Giovanni was a firm believer in the miracles of modern technology. He made sure that his operatives had the finest, most advanced equipment available. For Clan Giovanni, no price was too high for the best.

When Madeleine plugged her computer into the cellular phone, the fax line beeped instantly, indicating a transmission had been stored online from earlier in the day. She frowned. Pietro had not replied to any of her previous communications. Her grandfather normally let her conduct her operations without instructions. Strange that, after an evening without much incident, he should send her a fax instead of an e-mail.

Her frown deepened when the transmission began downloading. Her cell phone was equipped with a descrambler and caller i.d. system that showed the telephone number where the message originated. For this call, the screen remained blank.

The fax only took a few seconds to come through. It was not a message but a picture. A large black and white photograph. Patiently, Madeleine waited until the transmission was complete before looking at the image. A happy couple—a bearded man with a young woman—smiled at the camera. Between them, they held a small boy. In the background, Madeleine could see a cottage she recognized immediately. Rambam's house. Staring intently at the picture, she realized the man with the dark beard was Ezra. The woman must be his wife, Rebekkah, killed soon after the picture was taken. The child they held was Elisha, Rambam's grandson, Ezra's son, and her lover.

The picture must have been sent to her from

Rambam, one of the most powerful mages in the world. She had no idea how, but his magick made the impossible possible. But why? Often enigmatic and secretive, the willworker did nothing without a reason. Though he refused to fight his own son, Rambam wanted Ezra stopped. Madeleine was certain the picture was meant to help her in her fight against the mad mage. If only she could understand its meaning.

Then, remembering the conversation of the past night, she took the fax, folded it small, and slipped it between her breasts. She felt certain that Seventeen and his friends possessed the answer to this riddle. All she needed to do was ask.

She quickly typed Pietro a summary of the situation regarding Ezra and Enzo. Most of what she had learned from the mages she left out. Their battle against the pattern-clone was unimportant to Clan Giovanni. What mattered most was that Enzo and Ezra schemed to gain control of the family by murdering Pietro. They had to be stopped. If Madeleine and Montifloro failed, others had to be sent to finish the assignment.

Briefly, she noted Enzo's connections with the global energy giant, Pentex. In her eyes, the huge mega-corporation needed to be watched closely. Too many of their activities seemed to challenge the goals of Clan Giovanni. Sooner or later, Madeleine felt certain the two economic powers would collide. Best that her family be prepared in advance for possible confrontations. The Giovanni declared *Honor Over Death*. They also believed in *Trust No One*.

Satisfied with her report, Madeleine transmitted it via e-mail, closed up her computer and locked the van. She again covered it with the tarp. Unless absolutely necessary, she preferred traveling using her own special powers. Driving in the mini-van, she felt too exposed, too vulnerable. Traveling through the earth was much safer.

Unable to shake her sensations of disaster, Madeleine again sank into the earth. It would only take her a few minutes to travel to the grove where she had conferred last night with Seventeen and his comrades. Perhaps they had an explanation for her odd feelings. She hoped so. Madeleine hated mysteries.

Rising out of the soil at the sacred grove, she initially observed Seventeen and Shadow of the Dawn linked together in a passionate embrace. She smiled, noting that each of them held deadly weapons in their hands. Passion knew no limits. Observing the two lovers, a sadness crept through Madeleine. A tear of black blood trickled down one cheek. She loved Elisha equally strongly. Someday, they would be united. But not now. Not for years to come.

There were dead bodies scattered throughout the clearing. Bizarre, inhuman creatures, a cross between mortal man and lizard. They had huge fangs and glistening metallic skin. Madeleine had no doubts that the horrors, obviously creations of magick, were extremely deadly. Noting the slash, slice and stab wounds that crisscrossed the lizard-men's forms, she also understood that imperiled mages were much more dangerous than any of their creations. No monster, however horrifying, was capable of the savagery buried deep within the human soul.

Seeing no signs that she would ever be noticed by Seventeen and Shadow of the Dawn, Madeleine discreetly coughed. Instantly the two pulled apart, their weapons raised. Seventeen grinned when he saw her. Though it was impossible to tell in the darkness, Madeleine felt certain Shadow of Dawn was blushing.

"Please pardon me," she said. "I did not mean to interrupt your...celebration. I returned tonight to coordinate our attack against the mad mage, Ezra, and my great-uncle, Enzo. I thought it best we finalize our plans. Time is of the essence. The longer we delay, the greater our chance of failure."

She waved a hand about, gesturing at the dead bodies. "These beasts come from our enemies?"

"Close enough," said Seventeen. "Remember I mentioned that young woman, Jenni Smith? She arranged this ambush on behalf of the pattern-clone."

"An unwise decision on their part," said Madeleine. The big man's mention of Jenni Smith reminded her of the fax. Reaching into the top of her dress, she pulled out the picture. She unfolded it and handed it over to Seventeen. "Does this woman look familiar?"

"Of course," said Seventeen, without any hesitation. "That's Jenni Smith."

"No," said Madeleine. "That is Rebekkah, the wife of Ezra ben Maimon, shortly before she was gunned down by terrorists. This woman, Jenni Smith, and her companions, have taken on the features of the dead woman to warp the mad mage's mind. His grief made him an easy target. No doubt, he believes Lord Steel has brought back his murdered wife in exchange for his service to the Dark Lords."

"Killed by terrorists?" murmured Shadow of the Dawn. "Perhaps even there the truth is not as clear as it seems. These diabolical shapechangers have been plotting for centuries. I doubt if they leave anything to chance. Including a murder that would further their ambitions."

"The man in the picture must be Ezra," said Seventeen. "But who's the child?"

"The boy is Elisha," said Madeleine. "He and I shared...." She stopped speaking in the middle of the sentence, realizing at that instant the cause of the unease that had troubled her since awakening. The Rat Pack. A mental link bonded her to the gang of children, enabling them to contact her when trouble threatened. The connection was gone, had been gone when she had risen.

"Excuse me," she said and merged into the earth.

Traveling at incredible speed, she arrived at the parking lot of Sleazy Sam's Bar and Grill a few minutes later. The bold red neon sign, with letters ten feet tall, was unchanged, as were the words OPEN ALL NIGHT, EVERY NIGHT. The bar, a large wood building, two stories high, appeared the same. Madeleine knew different. The large gravel and concrete parking lot was empty of cars. At this time of night, Sam's was usually packed with customers. The lot was never empty.

She glanced across the road at the all-night gas station. The steel and glass change booth, with its sign that the attendant was "armed and dangerous" was empty. The clear window was tinted blood red.

The bar was a notorious hangout for some of the worst thieves and murderers in the Rochester area. Rarely a night went by without the police being summoned. More murders took place on these grounds than in many cities. Still, the bar was always crowded. Tonight, it was deserted.

Madeleine could smell the blood on the concrete. Most of it was days old, but a trace was recent. For an instant, Madeleine felt a rush of desire—of thirst. Immediately, she thrust it out of her mind. Her discipline was unshakable. She refused to bend to her lusts.

Like a bloodhound following a scent, she moved with inhuman grace across the concrete. The trail led to the nearby woods. Eyes burning red, Madeleine spotted a solitary figure huddled up against a tree, facing the bar. It was the crazy woman known as Sister Susie.

The young blond woman wore white bike shorts, white halter top, and white boots. Below her breasts, she was marked by a large x-shaped scar. Loosely gripped in one hand was a sawed-off shotgun. A few feet away was another. Her eyes were closed, as if asleep, her breathing shallow, her chest barely moving. She had been shot nearly a dozen times, yet somehow she still lived. Madeleine suspected Susie refused to die.

"Susie," she said, as she approached the blonde, "what happened?"

The young woman's eyelids fluttered, her hand holding the shotgun twitched, as if trying to raise the weapon. Then she saw it was Madeleine. "Hired killers," she said, her words barely audible. "They came for the kids. I tried to stop them. Too many for me. Too many."

"Did they murder the children?" asked Madeleine. Some of her vampire blood would revive Susie, give her strength until she could receive medical attention. "Who sent them?"

Susie didn't answer. Madeleine, about to cut open a vein, stopped. Sister Susie was beyond help. The breath had left her body. She'd be answering no more questions.

"A good way to die," murmured Madeleine as she left the dead woman and made her way to the entrance of the club.

The tavern consisted of a large rectangular chamber sided with cheap wood paneling. The ceiling was low, with exposed wood-beams running from one end of the room to the other. The lighting was dim enough to be almost non-existent. Two ancient ceiling fans revolved slowly, casting strange shadows on the dirt-stained hardwood floor. The juke box in the corner was silent. The half-dozen round tables were empty. So were the booths to the rear.

Madeleine walked up to the bar. Gold and ivory, tarnished with age, it took up much of the back wall. Behind it was a garish print of three nude women in a bed. Pinned against it, with long knives through his hands, shoulders, ankles, and stomach, was a tall, dark-haired man, dressed in a white apron covered with blood. Leo, the bartender, the local agent for Clan Giovanni. His eyes were open, staring at infinity; his throat had been cut ear to ear.

Madeleine stared at the dead man for a moment. There was no message carved into his body, no note stuffed in his pocket for her to find. There was no lesson here. Leo had been killed by men who enjoyed murder. A group of homicidal men banded together in service to the Nephandi. They had murdered Sister Susie. They had tortured and killed Leo. They had the Rat Pack as their prisoners.

Madeleine had no temper. She had *patience*. Supremely confident in her own abilities, she never got angry. She got even. Many years ago, Don Caravelli, the Capo de Capo of the Mafia, had slain her father. She had sworn vengeance. It had taken her nearly a century to fulfill her pledge, but the Mafia Don had perished beneath her hands. Those who had killed Leo and Sister Susie were likewise doomed.

She stepped forward and effortlessly pulled out the knives driven through the bartender's flesh. She lowered him to the hardwood floor. As a loyal employee of Clan Giovanni, Leo deserved a proper burial. As did Sister Susie, who had died trying to protect the Rat Pack.

A sudden, unexpected pain slammed Madeleine between the eyes. Her hands clutched her forehead as a burning hot needle pierced her skull, drilled straight into her brain. She snarled as for an instant red agony flashed through her entire body. Then, as quickly as it had come, the fire was gone.

She needed no explanation for the seizure. The chain of death continued. Leo and Susie killed. The Rat Pack kidnapped. Now, Montifloro destroyed, taken by the Final Death. She and her cousin had seriously underestimated Enzo Giovanni and his allies. It was not a mistake she would make again.

Revenge was a dish best served cold. She knew her enemies hoped to provoke her into acting foolishly. Or they thought the Rat Pack gave them hostages to use for bargaining. Neither was true. She never initiated measures without careful thought and deliberation. Nor did she allow herself to be manipulated by her emotions.

Her sire, and grandfather, Pietro Giovanni had given her an assignment. Enzo Giovanni had betrayed Clan Giovanni. Hiding behind children would not save him. It was a sin that could not be forgiven.

Though Clan Giovanni was notorious for its grim, ruthless pursuit of power, stopping at nothing to further its goals, Madeleine had been raised in a strict tradition of family honor. A killer without mercy, she adhered to her own rigid code of behavior.

Debts were always paid in full. Respect was given to those who earned it. Most of all, her word was her bond. She had sworn to protect the Rat Pack. The children would be freed. Or she would be destroyed trying.

Going outside, Madeleine gathered up Sister Susie

and brought her lifeless body inside, laying the dead girl next to Leo.

There was a telephone behind the bar. Picking up the receiver, Madeleine dialed an unlisted number in Manhattan. When the call was answered, she spent five minutes giving detailed instructions to the listener on the other end. Susie and Leo to be buried properly, the bar closed "for renovations," papers filed, documents forged, bribes paid. In America, money could buy anything, and Clan Giovanni had a great deal of money.

Satisfied the situation would be handled properly, Madeleine locked and securely bolted from the inside all the doors to the roadhouse. She shut off the neon lights, and put the *Closed* sign in the window. If all went well, the bar would reopen soon under new management. If not, Madeleine wouldn't know or care.

Honor over Death, the words flashed through Madeleine's mind as if in farewell to Leo and Susie. Without another sound, she melted into a dark fog that vanished through the floor of the bar. Ten minutes later, she was back at the Grove of the Goddess. Seventeen and Shadow of the Dawn, no longer embracing, sat by the brook, waiting for her.

"Bad news?" asked Seventeen, when she once again stood before them.

"Sister Susie is dead," said Madeleine. "As is a loyal employee of Clan Giovanni. A group of waifs I befriended has been kidnapped by Enzo Giovanni's thugs. I suspect they are being held as hostages at

Everwell Chemicals. Enzo and Ezra hope to enlist me in their mad scheme. A terrible mistake on their part."

"The young woman died defending the children?" asked Shadow of the Dawn.

Madeleine nodded.

"Kallikos acted wisely when he let her go free," said Shadow.

"You won't negotiate," said Seventeen. It wasn't a question, merely a statement of fact.

"Never," said Madeleine. "No compromise."

"When will you attack?" asked Shadow of the Dawn.

"Tomorrow night," said Madeleine.

"They'll be expecting you," said Seventeen. "You'll be one against many. This fax makes it quite clear that these rogue shapeshifters have been cooperating with—or manipulating—Enzo and Ezra from the very beginnings of their scheme. It's obvious that these willworkers will do anything to insure the success of their master plan. Along with Enzo, you'd be facing Ezra, the mad mage, and several witches of unknown powers."

"I have faced difficult odds before," said Madeleine. "I survived. My foes did not. Their trap is set, but they expect me to avoid it. Instead, I will enter, catching them by surprise. Sometimes, the most direct approach creates the greatest confusion."

"You will not go alone," said Shadow of the Dawn. "I have been waiting for this moment since my first encounter with Akrites Salonikas in the forests of

Mount Kuromasa. The seer made it clear that this battle was mine as well as yours. He foresaw the conflict, but was unable to determine the outcome. We will fight together."

"Two will cut the odds," said Seventeen. "Three will even them further. I'm coming as well."

He shifted the scythe in his huge hands. "You're not the only one with a score to settle with Enzo and Ezra and their patron, Lord Steel."

Shadow of the Dawn smiled at her lover. Then she glanced at Madeleine and with the barest shake of her head made it clear that Seventeen would not be going with them on their deadly mission. Madeleine dipped her head a mere hairsbreadth in reply. Seventeen possessed astonishing strength, but he lacked subtlety. The fight at the chemical plant required stealth, not brute force.

"Tomorrow, then," said Madeleine. "Let us meet here, in this glade, at this hour. If we perish, it will be done with honor."

"The Wheel of Drahma turns," said Shadow of the Dawn. "We stand at a crossroads in history. Destiny will walk by our side in the night."

"No quarter, no mercy," said Madeleine. "Death to our enemies."

Chapter Eighteen

Though she had shared quarters with Seventeen ever since their first kiss in the Grove of the Goddess, Shadow of Dawn insisted after Madeleine's departure that they be married. "If I perish tomorrow, let it be as an honest woman," she declared, in a tone that made it clear that argument was useless. "I am no cheap girl of the city streets. Love is more than passion. It means commitment, even in the face of death."

Seventeen, though his encounters with women since regaining his memory hardly made him an expert on their thinking, knew better than to disagree. Besides, he loved the sword-wielding warrior woman and was willing to do anything to make her happy.

Thus, well after midnight, they became husband and wife. Claudia Johnson, as one of the informal leaders of the Casey Cabal, performed the ceremony. Slightly bemused by the urgency of their request, she nonetheless bound them together by the sacred rituals of the Goddess. The ceremony was brief and to the point, as Claudia was ready for sleep. Violent arguments all afternoon and evening had worn her to exhaustion. Sam Haine, muttering about the foolishness of women and chomping on an unlit cigar, served as witness, as did Albert. Afterwards, Sam surprised them both by insisting they each accept a gold eagle twenty-dollar piece as a wedding present for luck.

"I thought you considered such traditions nonsense?" said Seventeen, smiling, as he stared at the nearly century-old coin. "Witchy trappings and ritual stuff, I seem to recall you once remarking."

"Still do," said Sam, "but there's a time and place for everything in this amazin' world of ours, son. Had those gold eagles in my possession for many a year. More than you might suspect, considering my youthful appearance." No one knew how old the Changing Man actually was, but his snow-white hair and extraordinary knowledge of topics magickal made it clear he was no youngster. "It's said that items carried by a mage long enough absorb some of his energy. Can't say if that's true or not, but seems possible. Maybe those coins will bring you a touch of my good fortune. Reckon they can't do any harm. Worse comes to worst, they'll pay for a meal or two."

"I am honored by your gift," said Shadow of the Dawn solemnly. "I will cherish it nearly as much as your friendship."

"Well, well," said Sam, momentarily fumbling for words. For once, the Changing Man was caught off guard. "Ain't that the nicest compliment I've ever heard. Have me cryin' like a baby if there was any tears left in this worn-out old husk. Enough yapping. You two better scamper off on your honeymoon. Today's almost gone. And who knows what tomorrow brings?"

They spent the night making love beneath the stars, in a small clearing not far from the glade of the Goddess. Passion consumed them until, near dawn, they drifted off to sleep wrapped in each other's arms. Seventeen noted however that Whisper and Scream were close at hand. A Dragon Claw warrior never strayed too far from her weapons.

When Seventeen woke, he found the swords and Shadow gone. He discovered his new wife and her two constant companions in the forest. Moving with lightning-like speed, the warrior woman was dueling with the trees and bushes. As always, she fought without making a sound. Shadow of the Dawn let her swords speak for her.

"Do you ever stop practicing?" asked Seventeen.

"Do you ever stop breathing?" asked Shadow.

"I shouldn't have asked," said Seventeen. "How about some breakfast?"

"Once this war comes to an end," said Shadow, as they trekked to the Casey Cabal, "I will make my husband meals that will delight his senses."

"You know how to cook?" said Seventeen.

Shadow shook her head. "No. I was taught how to live off the land when traveling, of course. But I never learned the art of preparing food. Still, how difficult can such a task be for a Dragon Claw?"

Seventeen again knew better than to answer the question.

Later, after they had eaten, Shadow left the confines of the Chantry House to continue her exercises. Sam Haine and Albert were out, gone to Niagara Falls to help an elderly comrade in need. Claudia Johnson was engaged in yet another round of heated arguments with rebellious members of the Casey Cabal. Several had disappeared the night before. Others were threatening to leave today. The Master of Harmony's speech was seriously affecting the Chantry's unity. Seventeen, restless and concerned about what was happening, found himself alone.

Unable to relax, he dropped in an easy chair in the living room, where only hours before they had watched on television the being calling himself Heylel Teomim promise mages immortality—for a price. Prompted by the memory, Seventeen's thoughts turned to the true identity of the pattern-clone. Was the enigmatic creation truly the leader of the First Cabal reborn? Or was it a puppet of Lord Steel, intent on plunging the Tellurian into total chaos? Seventeen suspected he would never know the truth. Some mysteries could never be solved.

It was then that he remembered the last gesture of Porthos Fitz-Empress, as he perished in the destruction of the Horizon Realm known as Doissetep. As forces beyond comprehension resounded throughout all creation, the fabled willworker had transported Seventeen and Shadow of the Dawn safely to Stonehenge. With them had gone a copy of his masterwork, the book Porthos had titled *The Fragile Path.* If any clue existed to the true identity of the pattern-clone, it would be found in that volume.

Subtitled *The Testaments of the First Cabal*, *The Fragile Path* was the story of Heylel Teomim's betrayal of the Traditions five hundred years before. It gathered together the statements of all those who had survived the ordeal, along with Heylel's own defense of his actions.

Seventeen's thoughts focused on a moment, not long ago, when Kallikos, the seer once called Akrites Salonikas, had confronted the pattern-clone's doppelganger in the Great Hall of Horizon. The two mages had stood facing each other in front of the Table Cenacle.

"Tell me, Heylel," Kallikos had asked, "what was the name of the hermit who perished by dire accident during our days together in the First Cabal?"

"Hermit?" Heylel replied. "What hermit?"

Kallikos had not seemed surprised that Heylel had not known the answer.

That brief exchange burning in his mind, Seventeen retrieved *The Fragile Path* and began to read. The next several hours he spent alone with the book, concentrating on every detail, every nuance, every hint of something not told. The stories were told in archaic language, one even in song, but they were not difficult to understand. The pain and agony of the times, of the Great Betrayal, came through as strongly as if each statement were being told by its author directly to Seventeen.

By the time he finally put the book down, Seventeen was covered in a cold sweat. *The Fragile Path* was charged with powerful emotion. After half a millennium, its story remained important. Seventeen now could see why Porthos wanted it preserved and read by every mage of the Nine Traditions. It spoke of love and hate, faith and ambition, betrayal and trust. The book was eternal and spoke directly to the human spirit. It was a message Seventeen would never forget.

Making sandwiches, he packed a picnic basket and went searching for Shadow of the Dawn. He found her at the Grove of the Goddess, dancing a ballet of death, her two swords whirling so fast that they appeared as circles of steel surrounding her.

As they ate, Seventeen told the sword-mistress what he had discovered.

"Porthos wrote highly of Heylel," said Seventeen. "That he was much more than human. He says that Heylel burned like a candle, whose light attracted you even while the flames drove you back.

"In his introduction to the last confession of the traitor, Porthos states that he felt Heylel betrayed the Traditions to unite them. He believes that the leader of the First Cabal *felt* that what he did was right, even though it led to the torture and death of several of his closest friends."

"Exactly what the pattern-clone claimed," said Shadow of the Dawn.

"Porthos, however, noted that many mages of the time believed that Heylel consorted with demons. That was why he was given the title *Abomination*. It's not a major leap of faith from demons and devils to vampires."

"So you suspect that perhaps this alliance between the pattern-clone and the undead actually began with the original Heylel?"

"I don't know," said Seventeen. "As always, new facts lead to new questions. The only one who knows the truth is the pattern-clone, and I feel certain we won't be learning much from it."

"Was there anything in the book that points to whether the clone is actually Heylel or Lord Steel?" asked Shadow.

"Perhaps," said Seventeen. "The revelation of your mentor, Akrites Salonikas, tells of his friendship with Heylel, and the bond that was forged between them due to the accidental death of a religious hermit."

"A hermit?" repeated Shadow. Like all members of the Akashic Brotherhood, she never forgot details. "In the Great Hall, Kallikos asked the pattern-clone the name of a hermit."

"Tormod of Kirkenes," said Seventeen. "He died, his body aged hundreds of years in an instant, when struck by a Time Storm. Akrites, whose presence brought about the Paradox effect, blamed himself for the old man's death. Heylel consoled the seer, preserving his sanity and quite possibly his life. It was not an event easily forgotten."

"Yet the pattern-clone didn't remember the hermit or his name," said Shadow. "Strong evidence that the artificial creation is not truly Heylel Teomim."

"I agree," said Seventeen. "Yet Kallikos himself

seemed uncertain regarding the clone. Remember, according to the book, Heylel experienced Gilgul, the ultimate annihilation. No wizard has ever returned from that punishment. So it's possible the clone is Heylel reincarnated with a flawed memory. Or, it might be Lord Steel, pretending to be Teomim."

Shadow grimaced. "Such esoteric discussions make my head hurt." She touched the hilts of her swords. "Give me cold steel and fierce battle instead of conjectures and possibilities. Reality is flesh and blood, not puzzles within puzzles within puzzles. Does this book contain any answers, instead of mere possibilities?"

"Unfortunately, as the volume deals with events that occurred five centuries ago," said Seventeen, "there are no clear links between the past and the present. As you say, it's filled with puzzles within puzzles, wheels within wheels. The answers may be hidden in the book's pages. But nothing is definite. Like the twins."

"The twins?"

"Eloine, the Verbena willworker who belonged to the First Cabal, was the mother of twins born during the four years the group walked the Earth. The father was her lover, Heylel Teomim. When he betrayed his comrades to the Order of Reason, Heylel took the children from Eloine and gave them to his new allies. What happened to the twins afterwards is a mystery. The two, a boy and a girl whose names were never recorded, vanished into the mists of history. Eloine died without ever learning their fate."

"You think they survived," asked Shadow, "and formed their own secret cabal?"

"Who knows?" said Seventeen. "Why not? We don't know anything about Heylel's allies other than that some of them are shapeshifters. And that they've been plotting to seize control of the Nine Traditions and the Technocracy. It's possible they're descendants of the Abomination. Secret societies exist only if they remain secret, known only to those who belong. And no closer bonds exist than those forged by blood. Are they driven by revenge? Or by a noble cause? Much can change in five centuries. As Madeleine Giovanni said the other night, the plotters may be Nephandi, allies of the Maeljin Incarna, shapeshifters pledged to eternal darkness. Or they could be a rogue group of willworkers, who have infiltrated both the Nine Traditions and the Technocracy, but are pursuing their own path to Ascension."

"Then their goals may not be evil," said Shadow of the Dawn. "The pattern-clone may truly be Heylel Teomim reborn, and his dream of Unity exactly what he claims."

"There aren't any easy answers," said Seventeen. "Which is what makes life so difficult. The pattern-clone and Jenni Smith's group could be on the side of the angels. I don't know. However, any conspiracy that demands power instead of earning it makes me suspicious. I don't trust people who refuse to bend. When the ends—no matter how twisted or destructive they become—justify the means, too often *the means become those ends*. Good and evil are two sides of the same coin to a fanatic. Nothing scares me more than someone who knows beyond any doubts they are right and will do anything to further their cause."

Shadow rose to her feet. Except for the gurgling of the sacred spring, the grove was silent. Nothing moved. There was no breeze. "Tonight, all such questions become meaningless." She pulled Whisper from its sheath. The naked blade gleamed in the sunshine. She raised the sword to her face, touched the blade gently with her lips. "The only answers that matter lie within the steel. As I told Madeleine Giovanni, Kallikos spoke to me of a time when, with a dark ally at my side, I would duel to the death with the forces of blood and madness. That time is very near.

"More than five centuries ago, Kallikos envisioned a horrifying future. He swore then to do everything possible to prevent it from happening. Whatever the price. The seer has waited patiently for this moment. But even he does not known the outcome. Even he does not know the outcome of the conflict."

Passionately, Shadow of Dawn kissed Seventeen. Her eyes stared deep into his. "The fate of the world rests with my skill," she declared, her voice trembling with emotion. "Our lives, our love, *our future* lies in the balance. I will not fail. I dare not fail."

Chapter Nineteen

Desperate events called for desperate measures. Ms. Hargroves prided herself in never panicking, whatever the circumstances, whatever the pressure. Her situation was desperate, seemed hopeless. But she refused to submit meekly to her fate. All of her life, she had clawed her way past adversity. She did not plan to stop now.

Doubling the security for the plant required numerous schedule shifts and reallocations of manpower. Boring, detail work that Enzo left entirely in her hands. Normally she would have completed the changes by morning, but after the night's surprises, she dawdled over the work until well after the sun had risen. With Enzo asleep till nightfall, and Ms. Hope off on undisclosed errands, Ms. Hargroves was unwatched and unsupervised. Exactly as she had planned.

No Everwell employee other than Ms. Hargroves was allowed in the basement of the old building. Once this level had served as a warehouse for coffins built in the factory above. Now it was Enzo's private haven. Hidden deep within its twisted corridors was the vault where he slept during the daylight hours. At the far end of another passage was the chamber that served as his office. Neither location interested her. Instead, she followed a third tunnel, one that led to a room marked on the decaying maps as "Long-Term Storage."

There was dark green mold on the walls. The weight of tons of steel and earth pressed down from above. The lights were dim, and the cement floor chipped and broken. Few ever walked here. Fewer returned.

Ms. Hargroves knew that this chamber served as Enzo's private dungeon. Here, behind a heavily reinforced steel door, he kept his spare blood supply—in living, breathing, thinking containers. Mattias was dead, drained dry, but several of his followers still lived. They resided in a state of near-mindless terror, chained to the stone walls, awaiting the vampire's thirst.

The door to the room was securely bolted. But, as personal secretary to Enzo, Ms. Hargroves had access to the keys to every lock in the building. A twist, and she was inside.

Four men, barely conscious, hung chained to the stone walls of the cell. Like meat, waiting for the butcher. She recognized them all. Trent, T-Bone, Kross, and Simon. As liaison between Enzo and the Knights of Pain, she had dealt with all of the gang members at one time or another over the years. Dull, lackluster eyes stared at her without hope. The Knights knew she served Enzo. No doubt they thought her appearance was by order of their captor. She saw no reason to tell them otherwise.

Though Enzo would be asleep till nightfall, she had no idea when Hope would return. Nor did she have any assurances that her scheme would succeed. If she failed, Ms. Hargroves planned to be as far away from Rochester that night as possible. So, a quick decision regarding the gangbangers was necessary.

After staring at each man for a few minutes, she settled on T-Bone as the best of a miserable lot. The tall, thin man with glazed blue eyes and bone-white skin appeared in slightly better condition than his companions. With some help, he might actually be able to walk.

She stepped close to the chained man, put her mouth to one ear. "Don't say a word or I'll walk out the door. If you want to escape, nod your head slowly. Very slowly."

T-Bone kept his mouth shut. Barely moving, he dipped his chin.

"Enzo has his mark upon you," she continued. "I'm the only one who knows how to break his spell. Once we leave this dungeon, you must obey my every command. Do you understand? My *every command*. Otherwise, you'll be back here before nightfall. Nod again if you agree."

For a second time, T-Bone dipped his head. Ms. Hargroves had no illusions. Once the gangbanger regained his strength, he'd change his tune quick enough. She wasn't worried. Her plan wasn't designed to give the leather-clad thug much free time.

"Good. When I unchain you, gather your strength and follow me out of this chamber. If you can't, I'll leave you here for Enzo."

Reaching into her purse, Ms. Hargroves pulled out the key to the shackles and unlocked the rings holding T-Bone to the wall. The big man teetered but didn't fall.

"Come with me," said Ms. Hargroves. She walked to the door of the cell. Taking short, deliberate steps, T-Bone followed. He staggered once, nearly losing his balance, but refused to quit. Ms. Hargroves nodded her approval as he fell into place beside her.

"Wait for me in the hallway," said Ms. Hargroves. "Don't even consider running. You'd never find your way out of this maze. I'll only be a minute."

T-Bone shuffled out of the chamber. Ms. Hargroves stared at the other three prisoners. None of them said a word. Still, they had seen too much. If Enzo came here tonight to feed, he'd discover T-Bone gone. A few questions would reveal her treachery. She could not allow that to happen. Reaching again into her purse, she pulled out a six-inch switchblade. Calmly, she pressed the button to reveal the blade.

Walking down the line, she cut each man's throat, slicing their vocal cords. Only Luther managed a scream, a high-pitched whine cut off an instant after it began. As blood gushed from the trio's wounds, she calmly stabbed one after another in the heart. It was a short, messy job, but one she handled with her usual efficiency. When she closed and bolted the door to the cell, three corpses hung slackly from the shackles.

"Stay close," she told T-Bone, "and say nothing. Let me do all the talking. If we encounter anyone, you're my bodyguard. You're not paid to speak."

They wove their way through the maze of basement corridors, then ascended the steps to the first floor. As Enzo's private secretary and corporate hatchet-man, Ms. Hargroves was not well liked by the rest of the employees of Everwell Chemicals. No one stopped to chat with her as she headed straight for the exit. She and T-Bone could have been wraiths for all the attention they attracted.

Instead of walking, she took a taxi home. The less her companion was seen, the better. Signing into her apartment building, she glared fiercely at the security guard. He asked no questions about her companion. Thirty minutes after entering the basement storage cell, Ms. Hargroves and her leather-clad shadow were safe in her apartment. So far, everything had gone smoothly. But the most difficult part of her scheme was yet to come.

"Sit down," she said, pointing to the large, white plush sofa. All of the furniture in the room was white, as was the carpet. The walls were jet black. The color scheme reflected her views on life. "Relax. You're safe here."

T-Bone flopped onto the sofa. His bleached white skin and black leather clothing fit in nicely with the decor. "You sure that fuckin' monster can't find me here?"

"You're protected as long as you remain with me," said Ms. Hargroves, as she pulled in a full-length dressing mirror from her bedroom. Carefully, she set it across the floor from the sofa. The five-foot-high glass was framed in brown wood, a discordant note among the blacks and whites, but sometimes a clash in style couldn't be helped.

"The glass will reflect his spells," she declared, seeking the simplest explanation possible for her actions. T-Bone was too stupid to need anything more. "Vampires cast no reflections, so they're afraid of mirrors."

"Sure," said T-Bone, stretching his long frame on the sofa. "Makes sense."

"Would you care for a beer?" Ms. Hargroves asked, heading for the apartment's small kitchenette.

"Yeah," said T-Bone. "Sounds fuckin' great."

Opening the refrigerator, Ms. Hargroves pulled out a Miller Lite. Normally, she'd have a beer herself. Not today. She needed her hands free. Reaching across the kitchen counter, she pulled the butcher's cleaver out of the wood cutting block.

Holding the huge hatchet loosely behind her back, she brought T-Bone his drink. "Here you are," she said, handing him the can. "Drink hearty."

"Damn fuckin' nice of you," said T-Bone, sitting up on the couch. He popped the top of the can, raised it to his lips. "Savin' my life and all that shit."

Throughout her life, Ms. Hargroves had maintained strict control of her emotions, her desires, her passions. She found such feelings difficult to understand. Always logical, she abhorred the thought of acting irrationally. She was rigidly sane, a woman who always suppressed lust. Only under the greatest pressure did her self-control slip, letting out the beast that lurked deep within her mind. Today was one such day.

Ms. Hargroves waited until half the can had disappeared down the gangbanger's throat before speaking. T-Bone's eyes were closed, his expression vacant. He never saw the cleaver come from behind her back. His first hint that something wasn't right was when the blade slammed into the right side of his neck.

Blood spurted across the white sofa, stained the white carpet. T-Bone choked on the beer, tried to scream, could not. Red froth bubbled out of his nose, sloshed out of his mouth.

"I never said anything about saving your life," corrected Ms. Hargroves and, raising her arm high above her head, smashed the heavy blade into the thug's chest. Bones cracked as the blade cut deep. T-Bone jerked and quivered as if being shocked by a thousand volts of electricity. He tried to rise, futilely waved his arms at his attacker. But Ms. Hargroves was relentless.

Up and down went the cleaver. Her gaunt face curved in a grim smile, Ms. Hargroves hacked and hacked. She made no effort to finish the job. Instead, she seemed intent on keeping T-Bone alive until he was bleeding from a hundred wounds. Her face, her hands, her clothes dripped blood. The sofa was crimson, the carpet red. The mirror on the far side of the room was crisscrossed with gore.

Five minutes after she began her attack, Ms. Hargroves let the hatchet drop from her hands. T-Bone was dead. The gangbanger resembled a huge piece of raw hamburger. His features were unrecognizable. His white skin was cut to ribbons. His blood was everywhere.

Ms. Hargroves turned to the full-length mirror. Raising her blood-stained hands, she placed her palms flat on the glass.

"Aliara, Empress of Lust," she said, her voice trembling with unleashed emotion, "accept this sacrifice, this offering, made in your name. Feel my lust, feed upon it. Take form from my passion. Appear before your humble servant. Aid me in my hour of need."

A few seconds passed. Ms. Hargroves stood rooted to the spot. If Aliara didn't reply to the summoning, she'd be forced to flee the city. Enzo would win. More distressing, the tramp Hope would also triumph. It was a bitter pill to swallow, one that Ms. Hargroves found unacceptable. Yet she was no fool. Without the aid of her patron, the Dark Lord, she was no match for her enemies.

The laughing started softly, a sound barely audible. The glass beneath Ms. Hargroves's fingers vibrated, sending tremors up her fingers, along her arms. The giggling continued, growing louder. Shrill, high-pitched, unnatural. It was a noise not made by a human throat.

Ms. Hargroves stepped back. Her eyes bulged as she saw the blood on the glass was flowing in crimson streams to the exact center of the mirror. Her gaze darted around the living room. Everywhere, the dark stains were disappearing, as if being wiped clean by some unholy vacuum. T-Bone's body twitched, shook, shifted and turned on the plush sofa. Ms. Hargroves bit her lower lip as the corpse folded over, bent in half. The laughter grew louder, the sound shaking the floor, causing the walls to tremble.

The blood was gone from the glass. Taking its place was a murky, swirling cloud, dark gray, crossed with lightning bolts of green and yellow and purple and orange. The colors hurt Ms. Hargroves's eyes. She tried closing them, but the colors remained.

Behind her, bones crunched. She had no idea what was happening to the corpse, nor did she want to know.

"Millicent," whispered the voice that had giggled. "I am here. You called and I answered. It's been years since you sacrificed to me, released the lust hidden deep in your soul. Those bums at the housing project were a long, long time ago."

"I've served you well, Aliara," said Ms. Hargroves, opening her eyes. A familiar face stared out of the mirror at her. Boyish features, with short clipped green hair that curled around her chin like a serpent, deep green eyes that burned with a hellish light and green, sensual lips. Aliara, Queen of Lust, Ms. Hargroves's mentor and benefactor, a being she had obeyed faithfully most of her life. "Every task you set for me, I've done. Never complaining, always willing, my goals have always been your goals. Your ambitions, my ambitions."

"True enough," said Aliara. Though she moved her lips from behind the glass, her voice seemed to come from the walls, the floor, the ceiling. Human blood, spilled in murder, gave her more substance than usual. "Unlike Shade, you never failed me. Can you hear him screaming? His wailing amuses me. Mr. Shade proved unsuited for his mission. He pays for his incompetence. He will continue to pay for a thousand years or more."

Ms. Hargroves shuddered. Aliara was unforgiving. Confessing her own disaster was not going to be easy. "A problem has arisen with Enzo Giovanni."

"I thought you had the vampire fooled?" said Aliara, her green eyes glistening. "Are you telling me that the circumstances have changed?"

"The entire situation has dissolved overnight," said Ms. Hargroves. Now that she had started, there was no going back. Swiftly, she told Aliara everything that had taken place the previous night. She made no excuses, spoke no lies. Only the truth could save her.

"An interesting mess," said Aliara. "Not much to my liking. It seems clear that there's no longer any chance of gaining control of the pattern-clone or his two puppets. I had great hopes for Enzo. Now this Hope, obviously a shapeshifter, has ripped him from my grasp. I am not pleased."

"All is not lost," said Ms. Hargroves. Everything or nothing. Either Aliara agreed to her plan, or she suffered eternal torment, side by side with Terrence Shade. "I think this disaster can be turned to your advantage. With your aid, I can thwart your enemies and actually increase your presence on the Earth. But only with your aid this coming night."

"Really?" said Aliara. "You never cease to amaze me, Millicent. Your ambition burns with a force greater than the deadliest vampire, the most powerful wizard. None of them are as dangerous as you. What gift do you require from me?"

"The power to destroy," hissed Ms. Hargroves, knowing she had won. "I battle willworkers who twist reality with a thought and vampires invulnerable to ordinary weapons. I need to be able to kill with a touch."

"As you wish," said Aliara. "Come closer to the mirror. Much closer. Bend your face near mine. Nearer."

Ms. Hargroves did as she was told. She looked Aliara in the eyes, shuddered as she saw hell.

"Now," said the Dark Lord, "press your lips to the mirror and kiss mine."

Taking a deep breath, Ms. Hargroves obeyed. Her lips touched the cool, rigid glass. Then, for a flicker, the surface beneath her mouth grew burning hot and a snake-like tongue licked hers.

"Done," said Aliara, as Ms. Hargroves jerked away from the magic mirror, her heart thumping, her blood boiling. Her lips tingled. "This night, you have the *Touch That Kills*. Use it wisely, for it will only work once. A touch of your finger and the wish to kill will destroy any victim you choose, living or dead, man or woman, mortal, mage, vampire, or spirit."

"Even a Dark Lord?" asked Ms. Hargroves, immediately regretting her words.

Aliara laughed. "The Maeljin Incarna are spirit creations, my dear Ms. Hargroves. As such, we cannot be destroyed. However, to assume shape on Malfeas and elsewhere, we need an actual living human body. We also require a functioning mortal mind to give us definition and personality. Such host bodies last a long, long time. But they can be destroyed. An enterprising mage, if bold and ambitious and willing to take immense risks, might actually become one of the Dark Lords." Aliara smirked. "It has happened."

"The pattern-clone?" asked Ms. Hargroves.

"I don't know," said Aliara. "The clone's true identity remains a mystery to me. But there have been others, willworkers, who have come to Malfeas seeking the unthinkable. One such mage who came, trying to be a hero, was Ethan Phillips, now known as Prisoner Seventeen. Another was his lover, Scarlett Dancer. She sought to share her body, her being, with the Empress of Lust. With me."

"And did she succeed?" whispered Ms. Hargroves.

Aliara laughed, the insane, horrifying laughter that made the walls shake and the air quiver. "That, Ms. Hargroves, is a secret best not revealed."

Chapter Twenty

Shadow of the Dawn waited patiently in the gathering gloom for the arrival of Madeleine Giovanni. She stood perfectly still, both of her hands resting on the hilt of her short sword, Scream. Though she faced the most important hours of her life, her mind was calm, her thoughts focused. The internal magick of *Do* flowed through her body, making her one with the universe. She had lived her life for the moments ahead. Destiny called.

This night, Shadow was dressed for war. Her clothing was black as the night. Her hair was braided in a long coil that dropped nearly to her waist. The ends were knotted about a wooden dowel. Inside the rod were two slivers of razored steel. When necessary, Shadow's hair served as a weapon.

Despite the heat of the night, she wore long, baggy pants and a long-sleeved, loosely fitted shirt. Her feet were bare, most suited for fighting. A thin strangler's cord was wrapped around one wrist. Scream was at her belt. Whisper, her katana, was sheathed across her back. She carried throwing stars in several hidden pockets. Her face was smudged with black paint, masking any reflection of moonlight. Shadow was not a ninja, but as a Dragon Claw she knew the value and importance of the assassin's art.

The moon glowed brightly, its light reflecting in the water of the sacred spring. The forest was at peace, quiet except for the sounds of small animals hunting. Huge trees cast their shadows across the glade, fingers of darkness that bespoke of great age. And great deeds.

A flicker of unseen motion alerted her to the arrival of Madeleine Giovanni. Though the vampire made no sound, Shadow immediately sensed her presence as she materialized out of the ground a dozen feet away. Attuned to the forces of nature, Shadow literally possessed a thousand eyes.

The dark lady of the Giovanni raised a hand in greeting. As always, she was dressed in black, with the Giovanni crest around her neck. In the moonlight, her white features remained shrouded in darkness. It was as if her skin captured and held the light. Only her eyes glowed, like two burning coals.

"My apologies for arriving late," said Madeleine. "For nearly a hundred years, I have obeyed the dictates of my sire, Pietro, and the wishes of Clan Giovanni. In all that time, I never once feared for my existence. Tonight, when I awakened, I suddenly realized that this fight quite possibly could be my last. That the Dagger of the Giovanni might not survive till morning. It was a moment of unexpected awareness. There was a phone call I had to make. Someone with whom I had to speak. The overseas lines were busy. And I had more to say than I expected."

"I understand," said Shadow of the Dawn. "There comes an instant when the truth must be stated without hesitation. When words that have not been said must be said."

"Exactly," said Madeleine. A faint smile crossed her thin red lips. "You are not astonished, like most mortals, that one such as myself can experience such feelings?"

"I make my own judgments, do not accept the prejudices of others as fact," said Shadow of the Dawn. "Last night, you mentioned a young man named Elisha, the son of Ezra. My pardon, if I assume too much."

"No apology necessary," said Madeleine. Her face betrayed no emotion, but she spoke slowly, as if struggling to find the proper words. "He is wizard of awesome potential. Together, we shared incredible adventures. You are not wrong to assume we are very...close."

"A vampire and a willworker," said Shadow. "An interesting mix. Does he know that you stalk his father?"

"Elisha is unaware that Ezra is his parent," said Madeleine. "Abandoned by his father when he was a toddler, Elisha was raised by his grandfather. The insane magus has already pledged he will kill the one I love the most—meaning Elisha. No doubt Ezra and Enzo mean to use that threat to force me to agree to their scheme."

"A powerful bargaining chip," said Shadow.

"Elisha is out of Ezra's reach. Nor is he powerless. I doubt the madman could harm him. After this night, it will no longer matter. Either Ezra or I will perish before the dawn."

"I would consider it a personal favor to be allowed to duel with the wizard," said Shadow of the Dawn. "Would you allow me this pleasure?"

"I am not afraid of Ezra," said Madeleine. "My sire commanded me to destroy him."

"I meant no disrespect," said Shadow. "My suggestion arose from practical, not personal, matters. There are two foes to be defeated. A vampire and a mage. A wise teacher once taught *know thy enemy and yourself and in a thousand battles you will never lose*. In this situation, I think the advice applies particularly well. My *Do* training against Ezra's magick, your vampiric disciplines against Enzo's."

"An intelligent analysis," said Madeleine, with a fleeting smile. "I cannot argue with such logic. Still, I suspect that a Akashic Dragon Claw is as skilled in diplomacy as in sword play."

"In years to come, explaining to your...friend that you killed his father, no matter what the reason or the justification, might be more difficult than you imagine," said Shadow, smiling in return. "Not only seers can predict the future."

"Speaking of friends," said Madeleine, "how did you prevent your companion from accompanying us tonight?"

"My husband," said Shadow. "We were married after you departed last night."

"Congratulations," said Madeleine, with a smile. "Your celebrating exhausted him to immobility?"

Shadow's cheeks burned. "An interesting concept for battle, but impractical in this instance. Seventeen was quite insistent that he accompany us on this mission. I was forced to add a special potion to his dinner. He will be furious when he awakens in the morning. But hopefully I will be there to quiet his anger."

"Men are proud fools," said Madeleine. "He will not accept your excuses gracefully."

"Better his pride wounded than his life lost," said Shadow. "I will not be a wife and a widow in the same day."

"He is not exactly helpless," said Madeleine. "I have seen him fight."

"I fear less for his body than his soul," said Shadow. Her hands rested on the hilt of her short sword, Scream. When troubled, she sought the touch of steel. "Twice, Seventeen has come to this glade when summoned by the willworker he names Jenni Smith. He claims she has no hold upon him. I think differently. So does Sam Haine. My new husband is naive and his memories are incomplete. He doesn't realize what deadly powers this seeming child wields. Or how vulnerable he is to her schemes."

"I have been told love is stronger than hate," said Madeleine. She shrugged. "Of course, in my condition, such statements are meaningless."

"I suspect you possess stronger feelings than you

admit," said Shadow. She drew the short sword, held it to her lips. Returning it to its scabbard, she unsheathed her katana, Whisper. The strength of the steel assured her she had made the right decision. "Jenni Smith is not the only danger that threatens Seventeen at Everwell. Though he has remained silent about his past, I have paid close attention to what few remarks he has made. Sam Haine, who is possessed with a curiosity that cannot be quenched, has done the same. Circumstances that remain unclear link Seventeen to Lord Steel, the Maeljin Incarna whom you identified as the patron of Enzo and Ezra. I know in my heart that my lover, my husband, is not evil. But I also realize that the Dark Lord possesses great power and incredible cunning. With the future at risk, I thought it best not to take any chances."

Kissing the blade, she returned it to its scabbard. She felt at peace with the universe. Tonight, the great wheel turned.

"A wise choice," said Madeleine. "The sky grows dark. Midnight approaches. My great-uncle is extremely impatient—a bad habit. He probably is wondering if he made a mistake kidnapping the children. I think now is the right time to attack."

"The perfect moment is when steel first touches flesh," said Shadow, repeating an ancient proverb. "Kallikos and I came to the Casey Cabal in a van we bought in New York. It is parked by the road. Will you ride with me?"

"A pleasure," said Madeleine.

The drive in the warm, humid night took only

twenty minutes. Neither Shadow nor Madeleine said much, each fighter mentally preparing for the challenge ahead. Though mortal and vampire, they were in many ways very much alike.

"There are no security guards outside the building," said Madeleine, as they neared the huge chemical factory that was their destination. "Nor do I sense the usual night-shift personnel. The plant is nearly deserted."

"Ezra walks among the chemical vats," said Shadow. "Gunmen patrol the corridor both outside and inside the core, and another willworker waits by his side. Jenni Smith or another one of the shapeshifters. It will be an interesting fight."

"I can sense the children on the top floor of the building," said Madeleine. "I plan to rescue them first, then pay my respects to my relative. He holds court in a cement chamber beneath the street. If there are others with him, I cannot tell. I make this promise. I will not retreat unless Enzo is no more."

"I hold to the same with Ezra," said Shadow. "He must be destroyed."

"If I win, I will come to your aid," said Madeleine.

"And I will do the same for you," said Shadow. Heat lightning flashed in the night sky. "Kallikos saw great forces, unseen mystick powers in conflict tonight. Destiny acts in mysterious ways. Beware strangers. Expect the unexpected."

Shadow stopped the van across the street from the main entrance of the Everwell Chemical plant. She turned and looked to the pale woman beside her.

Without speaking, each of them raised a hand, touched fingers. "Victory or death," said Madeleine Giovanni, and without a sound melted through the floor of the van.

"Victory," repeated Shadow, as she unlatched the door not facing the Everwell building. She preferred not to consider death. With the barest whisper of cloth rubbing across the leather seats, she was gone, vanished into the night shadows.

Two women, extraordinary in their own fashion, among the most dangerous fighters in the world, against an elder vampire, a mad magus, a pair of mysterious shapeshifters, and a horde of gunmen. The odds were uneven, unfair. Madeleine and Shadow of the Dawn were terribly outnumbered. But other players had not yet arrived on the scene. Strange patterns wove through the Tapestry of Reality, and the world trembled.

Chapter Twenty-One

Heat lightning flashed in the night sky, illuminating the dark city streets. "We're getting close," growled Ernest Nelson. "Just a few blocks more to this old warehouse. You ready?"

"I've been attacked by Nephandi maniacs three times on Earth, as well as in two different Deep Universe Constructs," said Sharon. "I've been mauled, strangled, stabbed in the heart, and had my eardrums nearly destroyed by a turncoat Progenitor. A giant sabertooth tiger tried to kill me, and a horde of invisible cannibals surrounded my car. Nelson, I'm fucking ready for anything. It's time for us to do some serious destruction."

The cyborg chortled. "Now, that's speaking your mind. I'll give you that, Reed. Back on the Gray Collective, I always thought your assistant, that bitch Velma Wade, was a lot more dangerous than you. My mistake. I almost feel sorry for the traitor. She's in deep shit. You're hell on wheels."

"From a brawler like yourself," said Sharon, with a

smile, "I'll take that as a supreme compliment. Thank you."

"You're welcome," said Nelson. "Like I told you way back, right after we killed that tiger, we make a pretty damned good team."

"A lifetime ago," said Sharon. Mentally, she reviewed her biological weapons. They had stopped at the Technocracy outpost in Syracuse and replenished their armament. The acid sacs in her mouth were filled, her steel nails reinforced, and dozens of pellets of toxic nerve gas rested in her pockets. She carried a sawed-off shotgun, filled with high-explosive bullets. Her body was running on an adrenaline high. She'd pay the price for that tomorrow. Assuming she survived that long. "I think we surprised a lot of people surviving this long. Of course, the real trick is staying alive tonight."

"Yeah," said Nelson. His chain guns were filled, his plasma rifle ready, and he carried a full complement of concussion grenades. Like Sharon, he was running on maximum energy. It was a dangerous strategy, but necessary. Tonight there would be no second chances. "I feel like one of those sheriffs in the western movies. Heading for the big gunfight at the OK Corral at the end of the story. Only problem, we don't know what guns the villain is carrying. Or how many outlaws he has helping him."

"I hated westerns," said Sharon. "Romantic nonsense. I preferred documentaries, science films. Spiders and snakes were my favorites."

"Why am I not surprised?" said Nelson. He steered

their stolen car over to the side of the street, put it in park, and shut off the motor. "We're here. It's that big, dark, broken-down wreck across the street."

"Which one?" asked Sharon. She wasn't joking. The entire city block was lined with old, decaying warehouses. From what she had seen of the Rochester area, it consisted of wide-open suburbs, with houses scattered among fields and forests, and a congested, decaying inner city barely fit for human habitation. "They all look the same."

"The one right in the middle of the block," said Nelson. "If you look closely, it says Everwell Chemicals on the door."

"No lights," said Sharon.

"You prefer a welcoming committee and a band?" asked Nelson. "The walls are sheathed with steel plating, so my motion and heat detectors are useless. But my scope vision is working fine. No indication of wire or traps of any kind. If this Enzo's expecting guests, he's not worried."

"Good," said Sharon. "Let's pay him a visit. Explain we were in the neighborhood and wanted to say hi to our old friends Velma Wade and the pattern-clone."

"I'm cool," said Nelson, and pushed open the door to their car.

A heavy-duty titanium-steel alloy electronic lock sealed the warehouse. Nelson used the concealed drills in his fingers to burrow into the machine's center. Sharon kept watch while he worked. It took less than a minute for him to release the bolts.

"You notice anything strange?" he asked softly, as he pulled open the door. "See anybody?"

"Not a soul," said Sharon. "Why?"

The cyborg shook his head. "Just for a second, while I was drilling, it felt as if I was being electronically scanned. Hard to explain if you're not Iteration X. Part of being one with the machine. This damn mission has me spooked."

"Maybe," said Sharon. "Keep your guns ready, just in case."

"*That* you don't have to tell me," said Nelson. "I'm switching to subvocals inside. No need to let anyone hear us talking."

It was pitch black inside the warehouse. The only noise was the sound of their breathing. Nelson's eyes glowed like lights in a demented jack-o-lantern. Having learned from previous mistakes, Sharon and Nelson both carried pocket flashlights. The narrow beams cut like white knives through the darkness. The front half of the building was one huge room, filled with massive pressing machines, gigantic chemical tanks, and thousands of wood crates piled in stacks fifteen feet high. Like relics from the age of dinosaurs, except these creatures were steel, not bone. Beyond the junk stood a wall with four doors.

"Back there," Nelson subvocalized. They had used the same type of equipment during their adventures in the Albany New World Order Construct. "I'm sensing heat around seventeen meters beyond the second door."

"Vampires are undead," mouthed Sharon, without

speaking aloud. Immediately, she felt suspicious. Something wasn't right. "They don't radiate heat."

"Maybe Enzo has an assistant," said Nelson. "It's the only place where there's any motion. You think it's a trap?"

"I don't know," replied Sharon. "Doesn't matter. You have any other place to go? We're out of options. It's here or nowhere."

"Right," said Nelson. "What are we waitin' for?"

Swiftly, they crossed the warehouse floor and headed for the second door. A yellow glow filtered onto the cement paving from within.

Plasma rifle in his hands, Nelson kicked at the door. It crashed open, unlocked. He and Sharon piled into the long, narrow chamber. Five meters wide, nearly twenty meters long, with a high ceiling and a cheap, gray carpet. A dump. The only furniture was a large wooden desk at the far end of the room. Sitting on a high-backed swivel chair was a figure facing the far wall. He seemed unaware—or uninterested—in their entrance.

"Confident bastard, ain't he?" Nelson subvocalized to Sharon. Together, they started walking forward across the gray carpet. They made no sound. Nelson's guns were set on the chair. Ten, fifteen, twenty feet, they advanced. Behind them, the wooden door swung shut. To Sharon, it felt as if they had stumbled into a coffin and the lid had just closed.

"Is he radiating heat?" asked Sharon. They were only a dozen feet from the desk.

"Sure is," replied Nelson. "I can hear him breathing, too. Obviously, it ain't Enzo."

The man in the chair swiveled around. He was dressed in a black overcoat and wore a slouch hat that shrouded his bizarre features. Short and squat, he was shaped like a barrel. His face, what could be seen of it beneath the wide-brimmed hat, resembled that of a giant frog. His skin glistened with sweat. He had large, bulging eyes, a flat, wide nose, and a huge, oval mouth that seemed too big for his jaw.

"Weeeelcommmme," he said. "I'vvvve beeeeeen expeccccctinggg youuuuuuu. Mmmmmyyyy frrrrieends attttt thhhheee pppplanttt sssssssaiddd yyyou'd bbbbbeee cccccommminnnnng."

His slurred, barely understandable words ran together like the whirring of an electric fan. Even muffled by his upturned coat collar, the sound of his voice resonated through the room.

"Son of a bitch," said Nelson. He squeezed the trigger of the plasma rifle. Nothing happened. "It's the Wailer."

"Myyyyyy nammmmme isssss Doccccctorrr Atkkkkinnnns," said the frog-faced man. "Weee almmmmost meeeeetttt in Alllllbanyyy. Thennnnn agaaaainnnn in Indianaaaaaa. Youuuu escappppped bothhhh timeeesssss. Mosttt annoyinggggg."

Nelson let the plasma rifle fall to the floor. Up came his chain guns. They didn't fire.

Sharon threw a handful of her nerve gas capsules at the Nephandus. The pellets bounced harmlessly on the carpet. "Fuckin' damper field," she cursed, not bothering to subvocalize. They were in deep trouble. "Nothing works."

"Exxxactllllly," said Atkins, rising from his chair. He was just over five feet tall. "Nooooo devicccessss. Jusssst purrrellllly phhhhysicccccal tecccch-niqqquessss."

"Then I'll rip off your fuckin' head!" bellowed Ernest Nelson and charged the desk, his massive hands outstretched.

The Wailer wailed.

This close to the monster, Sharon could actually understand what he was screaming. It was a single word. A word that went on forever and ever and ever. A word that dropped her to the floor, her hands over her ears trying to block out the sound that rattled her bones and ripped the moisture from her eyes, nose and mouth. An overwhelming, shattering sound that felt like a hundred thousand needles tearing into her flesh. A noise that attacked her nervous system, causing her to jerk about on the carpet like a fish out of water.

A word that battered Ernest Nelson with equal intensity, dropping him onto the face of the wood desk, his face a white mask of agony. A hammer of sound that even the cyborg, his blazing eyes intent on his intended victim, could not defeat.

The word was lost in a shattered silence.

Blackness descended like a curtain across Sharon's eyes. In a small part of her mind, she knew she was dying, that a few more seconds of the Wailer's cry would shatter her bones, melt her flesh to protoplasm.

There was nothing she could do, nothing Nelson could do to stop the monster. They had lost. The monster that had been Gilbert Atkins had won.

Then, suddenly, unexpectedly, incredibly, the sound stopped. Wasted, nearly broken, hardly able to move, Sharon focused her burning eyes on the Wailer. The horror was staring past Nelson, past her, towards the door. He was frowning.

The monster opened his mouth. Said something. Sharon couldn't hear. The Wailer's scream had been too much for her eardrums. She was deaf.

Ignoring her, the monster stepped around the desk, walked beyond Sharon.

Pain still held Sharon in a grip of steel. But her body was in top physical condition. The Wailer had stopped before she suffered irreversible damage. Though nowhere near indestructible, she was a lot tougher than any ordinary human. Marshaling all of her strength, she started crawling away from Atkins, towards the desk.

Above her, his ears and nose dripping blood, Ernest Nelson was also moving. Slowly, his face taut with pain, the cyborg was turning, swiveling his body so that he faced the door. His eyes widened in astonishment. Blinking in amazement, he caught sight of her. He touched his ears. Sharon shook her head. Nodding, he used his own blood to trace a single word on the desk. *Klair*.

It was a night of surprises. Desperately, Sharon mentally released every painkiller and nerve suppressant in her body. Seconds afterward, she burned thousands of calories, flooding her arms and legs with energy. She knew it would take a week in the bio-regeneration tank to repair the damage to her muscles. A meaningless worry, considering the situation.

Channeling all of her strength into her hands, she pulled herself up into a sitting position near Nelson. She could see the Wailer now, as well as the man he faced. If the being in the doorway was a man.

Sharon had assumed that Charles Klair had died when the Deep Space beacon opened in the Gray Collective. She hadn't shed any tears. More than once during their months together, she had longed to feed him to her living carpet. Now, she was overjoyed that he was alive.

She could see Klair's mouth moving. He was saying something to the Wailer. Knowing the Comptroller's hatred of Reality Deviants, Sharon suspected it was nothing complimentary.

The Wailer's body rocked back and forth, like a monstrous snake, spitting poison at its prey. Evidently, Dr. Atkins was replying to Klair in kind.

Different, Nelson painted on the desktop in his blood. Sharon stared at the cyborg, trying to understand what he meant. She shook her head. Nelson pointed to his right eye, then to his right hand. Then gestured at Klair.

It took a second for Sharon to realize what the cyborg was trying to tell her. The Comptroller had had an artificial hand and eye. Replacement parts that made him closer to the machine, like so many members of Iteration X. They were gone. His body appeared whole. Yet in the dim light, it seemed to glisten with an artificial shine. Like metal.

Nelson was slowly but steadily wrenching his arms about, so that his chain guns faced the entranceway. He stared at Sharon, grimaced. Held up one finger.

Sharon needed no hint this time. *One with the machine,* the credo of Iteration X. Klair was no longer human. In some incredible fashion, he had become some sort of android—a machine with a man's intelligence.

A tremor of worry shook Sharon. Klair had hated her with a passion. She suddenly wondered if he had come to the warehouse looking for the Wailer? Or for her?

Nelson must have been thinking on the same lines. He pointed to Sharon, then himself. One hand chopped against the other in a slicing motion. The cyborg had thrown the Deep Space beacon at Klair. More than anyone, he knew his ex-boss was not the forgiving type.

The Comptroller took a step forward, moving close to the Wailer, reinforcing Sharon's fears. He said something again, words she couldn't hear. Probably telling the Nephandus to move out of his way or suffer the consequences. Klair wasn't much of a bargainer. He believed in the direct approach. Sharon licked her lips. The situation could not get much worse.

The Wailer wailed. The air around her throbbed, the desk shook. Still, facing Klair, the scream lost much of its effect. Most of the impact came from the sound rebounding off the wall behind the Comptroller. Painful to her eyes and skin, but bearable.

The Comptroller's arms lunged forward with blurring speed and grabbed the Wailer by the neck. Klair, never before a fighter, moved with inhuman precision. Nelson was right. His ex-boss had become one with the machine.

The Wailer must have howled then. Klair stumbled back, as the entire chamber shook. Shards of carpet burst off the floor. The door dissolved into a thousand fragments of wood and steel. Behind the Comptroller, the plaster wall of the room exploded. A cloud of white dust filled the air, turning the two struggling figures into shroud-like ghosts.

Klair staggered, releasing his hold on Dr. Atkins. Shaking, he seemed to have difficulty keeping his balance. His skin shimmered, waves of color—yellow, red, blue—crossing his face and hands. Yet he appeared otherwise unharmed. The expression on his face was a mixture of amazement and fury.

Sharon gulped, astonished at her good luck. The full force of the Wailer's scream had been aimed at Charles Klair. As before, the backlash of the noise bouncing off the walls had slapped at her and Nelson, but they were otherwise unharmed.

Arms shaking, Klair raised his hands again, reached for the Wailer. He said something.

The Wailer thrust his face forward, so that it was only inches from Klair's. Opening his bullfrog mouth, he screamed once more.

In all of her long life, in all of her incredible experiences, Sharon had never witnessed anything like it. The air surrounding the two men *rippled* with energy. The far wall collapsed. Wood crates in the warehouse beyond dissolved into fragments. Massive chemical vats shattered. Gigantic machines overturned, smashed into each other like a child's toys. All in absolute, complete silence.

Charles Klair's body *stretched*. His outstretched fingers looked like pieces of hot taffy, pulled thin and wiggly. As if made of rubber, his face elongated, his features flattened. Flesh crawled across bone, his teeth clenched in a skeletal grin.

Gilbert Atkins had pushed Progenitor techniques past all limits. He had perverted sound into a weapon of incredible destruction. Reality twisted, writhed in pain, as the Wailer continued to howl. The air around Sharon trembled as if the molecules composing it were being ripped apart. Then, in an instant, the shock wave ceased.

To Sharon, it was as if time stood still. Charles Klair, his body shrunk down to half its size, resembling a gigantic drum of shimmering flesh, had caught the Wailer by the throat. The Reality Deviant had been startled silent.

Klair no longer resembled anything human. His metallic skin rippled across a squat, humanoid form, as wide as it was tall. He was speaking to the Wailer, but Sharon had absolutely no idea what Klair was saying. Nor did she care. The Comptroller had talked too much when he had been human. As a machine, he still talked too much.

Like a child's stretch toy pulled out of shape, Klair's form flowed upward, reformed into the tall, bald Comptroller. Brilliant colors cascaded in a constant rainbow across his metallic flesh, but he otherwise appeared unharmed. His grip around the Wailer's throat tightened. The howling man's face was blood red, Klair's fingers cutting off his ability to breathe.

Klair's hands expanded, so that they covered most of the Wailer's face. He squeezed them together. Blood spurted from between the Comptroller's fingers. It was as if a steam-shovel had clamped onto the Wailer's neck. His head popped like a gigantic bubble, cascading in a river of bone fragments and gore onto his shoulders.

Opening his hands, Klair let the smashed corpse drop to the carpet. For a moment, he stared at the body at his feet. Then, raising his eyes, he stared across the room at Sharon. His gaze met hers. He smiled. There was no spark of humanity left in the thing that once had been Charles Klair. He lifted his blood-soaked hands, took a step forward. Sharon had no doubt of his intentions. No doubt at all.

Chapter Twenty-Two

They stood alone on the top of a precipice in the monstrous realm known as Malfeas. Far below, a lava pit bubbled and steamed. The sky burned crimson, looking down on huge mountains of pitted black stone. The air smelled like burnt flesh. Huge bat-like things floated high above, unseen riders directing them to unknown destinations. Laughter, insane and diabolical, drifted in clouds of sound across the wounded earth.

He was tall and slender, with sharply defined features and dark eyes. He dressed all in black, for it suited his mood. Facing him was a short, slender woman with curled green hair and vivid, deep green eyes. She wore a green shift of purest silk. A willworker of astonishing power, she liked creating effects with one color. His name was Ethan Phillips. Hers was Scarlett Dancer.

They had been lovers, soul mates, until she had disappeared, driven by the one emotion greater than her passion. Power. Scarlett Dancer hungered to possess god-like power. That quest had brought her to Malfeas, the realm of the Maeljin Incarna. It was here, searching for her, that he had followed.

"I never thought I'd see you again," said Ethan. He lifted a hand, gently touched Scarlett on the cheek. He loved this woman with all his heart. Any risk was worth saving her. "If we hurry, we can escape without notice."

"You're making a terrible mistake," replied his lost love. An enigmatic note crept into her voice. She sounded somehow different. She laughed, a harsh, cruel sound.

"A mistake?" he said, not believing what he was hearing.

"You assume I want to leave," said Scarlett. Her features twisted, distorted, lost all their humanity. Crimson fire glowed in her eyes. "It's much too late for me. And much too late for you."

Catching Ethan completely off guard, she lunged forward. Her palms hit him in the chest, knocking him backward. Stumbling, arms swinging wildly, his feet touched air. Screaming in shock, he tumbled backward off the cliff, hurtling to the flaming pit far below.

All the way down he could hear her laughter.

Seventeen burst awake, his body drenched in sweat. He was lying on the bed he shared with Shadow in the rear of the Chantry House. Normally he rose feeling refreshed, renewed. Not tonight. His body ached as if from a thousand wounds. His eyes burned. His head throbbed with pain. The memories were half a century old, but they still hurt.

"Bad dream, son?" It was Sam Haine. The white-haired mage sat in a wooden chair wedged up against the door leading out of the room. He held a cigar in one hand. Sitting on the floor, arms wrapped around his long legs, was Albert.

"What time is it?" asked Seventeen. There was an odd, unnatural taste in his mouth. Starlight filtered in through the small window next to the bed. "Where's Shadow?"

"Nearin' midnight, I suspects," said Sam. "Your wife asked us to keep an eye on you while she's in town. I'm surprised you're awake. She said you'd sleep till morning."

"She must have drugged me at dinner," said Seventeen. "I remember feeling groggy after eating. Shadow suggested I take a quick nap. She promised to wake me in plenty of time to meet Madeleine Giovanni."

"Valuable lesson, son," said Sam. "Never trust a woman."

"Your system threw off the effects of the potion?" said Albert.

"Of course," said Seventeen. "Whatever Shadow used must have been awfully powerful to have taken this long. My body's programmed to neutralize anything unnatural."

He rose from the bed, his gaze fixed on his two friends sitting by the door. It was the only exit from the small bedroom. "I'm going into the city after her," he said. "She needs my help."

"Not according to her," said Sam. He waved his cigar at Seventeen. "I don't want to get involved in your marital disputes, son, but you better listen to what your wife says. That girl's looking out for your safety."

"She thinks I'm vulnerable to Lord Steel and his agents," said Seventeen. His hands curled into fists. He didn't want to hurt his friends. But he also was not going to allow them to keep him a prisoner. Not tonight. "I realize that now." He peered at Sam Haine, then at Albert. "The two of you think the same. That's why you're helping her."

"The Dark Lords are damned powerful," said Sam. "Shadow felt it best for you to stay away from Enzo and Ezra. Makes sense to me."

"No it doesn't," said Seventeen. He raised his fists shoulder high, squeezed his fingers so tight that they turned blood red. "Listen, I don't want to hurt either of you. You're my closest, most loyal friends. Shadow knows that as well, which is why she asked you to stand guard. But she's wrong and you're wrong. I'm not afraid of Lord Steel. He fears me. With good reason. Don't you understand? *I know the truth*."

"Hard to imagine one of the Maeljin Incarna worrying about anybody," said Sam. "You playing with me, son, trying to make me let you go?"

"No reason for me to lie," said Seventeen. He looked around, stared at the small window opening to the outside. "If necessary, I can break out of this house by slamming myself through the wall. It wouldn't be fun, but I can do it. You know I can. The truth is, Shadow and Madeleine are attacking two of our most powerful enemies and they need my help—they need all our help. And, instead, we're sitting around debating my past history."

"Well," said Sam, chomping hard on his cigar, "come on, then. I got my van out front. While we drive into town, you tell me and Albert all about your relationship with Lord Steel. If it makes sense, we'll lend those ladies a hand. If not, Albert and me will do the fighting, while you stay in the car. Fair?"

"Fair enough," said Seventeen. "Let's go."

The three of them hurried to Sam's van. Albert drove, with Sam at his side. Seventeen was too big for any place other than the back seat. The Chantry House appeared deserted. In passing, Seventeen wondered where everyone was. No time to worry now. He had more important problems.

"Ain't my style to sit around anyways when there's a fight brewing," said Sam, sounding almost apologetic. "I told Shadow she was plumb crazy, but that woman refuses to listen to reason. You're gonna have a hell of a marriage, son. Now, tell me and Albert the whole story. From the beginnin'."

"My name, my *real* name," said Seventeen as the van rumbled through the dark forest, "is Ethan Phillips. I believe I was born about a hundred years ago. My early life, my Awakening, is a blank. Those memories are gone forever. I do know I was a powerful, headstrong Euthanatos. And that I loved an even more powerful willworker named Scarlett Dancer."

"Seems I remember that name," said Sam. "She disappeared right after the War. Never seen again. Most willworkers figured she was eliminated by the Technocracy."

"Not true," said Seventeen. "Scarlett was a woman consumed by ambition. No matter how powerful she became, she always wanted more. She loved me, loved me deeply, but emotion was not enough. She wanted more than Ascension. She dreamed of becoming a god."

"An unnatural desire," said Albert, speaking for the first time. "Such hubris is the first step into the darkness."

"I realized that later," said Seventeen. "After she disappeared. Vanished without a trace. I traced her to Horizon, hoping to rescue Scarlett before she was consumed by her passion. There, I discovered, she had studied the ancient tomes dealing with Malfeas, the realm of the Dark Lords."

"Nasty, nasty place," said Sam. "One of the few realms in the Deep Umbra I've never visited. Nor plan to."

"A wise decision," said Seventeen. "If hell has a name, it is Malfeas. However, it was obvious Scarlett had gone there. So I followed."

"What led her there, son?" asked Sam. "Power?"

Seventeen nodded. "I should realize you'd be familiar with the legends. The Maeljin Incarna are powerful spirits, incorporeal beings. They have no real form or substance. According to certain mystick narratives, a Dark Lord needs a human host, a living body to give it form. Usually the Dark Lords seize some unfortunate they find in the Deep Umbra, possessing them in unholy bondage. *Usually*."

"Sure," said Sam. "I remember that story. How a willworker could willingly offer himself to the Maeljin Incarna, merge body and soul with a Dark Lord. Pretty damned horrible notion, but I guess if you want ultimate power, it's an option. What happened? Your girlfriend succeed?"

"I don't know," said Seventeen. "I found her on Malfeas. At least, I thought I did. But she wasn't really Scarlett Dancer. It was Aliara, Queen of Lust. Whether they had merged, as you described, or Aliara had destroyed Scarlett and assumed her looks to torment me, I'll never know. Instead of rescuing my beloved, I became a prisoner in hell. For fifty years, I endured unceasing torture, passed like a prized toy from one Dark Lord to another. My body remained whole, as they wanted me kept healthy, while they did terrible things to my mind. But they were careful never to let me go insane. That would have spoiled their games. My memory was nearly wiped away. My personality was mostly destroyed. I lived but I didn't think. I suffered."

Sam shivered, puffed hard on his cigar. "Gather the combined hatreds and lusts of humanity from prehistory to today," said Sam Haine. "Combine it with all the intolerance, bigotry, and sheer brutality man has inflicted on his brother man. Mix thoroughly, and you come up with the Maeljin Incarna. The worst of our species, given life. It's a frightening thought, son. What happened next?"

"Emerging from the pain, my mind suddenly started working again. I found myself without any past, a prisoner on the Gray Collective. My guards called me Prisoner Seventeen, said I had been caught trying to infiltrate the Construct. My body was as you see it now, transformed by numerous experimental techniques performed on me during my mindless state. Though my memory did not return, I was soon plotting escape. Though I didn't realize it then, one of the Dark Lords' schemes had gone awry."

"What do you mean?" said Sam.

"I'm guessing now," said Seventeen, "but I think I've figured out the truth. It's come together slowly, but forms a pretty definite picture.

"The whole scheme started with the secret band of ambitious, totally amoral shapeshifters. Working behind the scenes in the Technocracy, they tricked the Union into promoting the Ascension Warrior Project. These rogue willworkers, Nephandi or not, then made a bargain with Lord Steel, the Duke of Hate, to gain control over all creation. The plan, much as we surmised, involved Ezra, Enzo and the pattern-clone, working in close association with the shapeshifters. The only problem was that Lord Steel didn't entirely trust his partners."

"Evil," said Albert, his gaze never wavering from the highway, "by nature trusts no one."

"Lord Steel suspected that once the pattern-clone

was completed, his partners might try a double-cross," said Seventeen. "So he insisted that they allow him to place an agent on the Gray Collective to monitor their activities. That was where I came in."

"You?" said Sam. "Working as an agent for the Dark Lord?"

"Less an operative than a window to Malfeas," said Seventeen. They were by a river now. Not far to the city. To Shadow. To the confrontation with Enzo and Ezra. "Lord Steel linked his mind to mine. With my thoughts in fragments, I'm sure the Dark Lord assumed he could observe the events on the Collective unfold through my eyes. Probably told the shapeshifters I was there to help them if they needed assistance when the clone was completed. They had no choice but to cooperate. Only things turned out much differently than Lord Steel expected."

"The experiments?" said Sam.

"Exactly," said Seventeen. "You never cease to amaze me, Sam. I swear you can read my mind."

"If I could, son, I would," said Sam Haine. "Better explain everything."

"Lord Steel put me on the Gray Collective as his spy," said Seventeen. "But to the technicians of the Construct, I was merely another subject for experimentation. I served as a guinea pig for a number of their most dangerous experiments. And, somehow, someway, one of those techniques broke the bond linking me with Malfeas and Lord Steel!"

Sam laughed. "Served the damned bastard right. He probably instructed his contact on the station to use you plenty. Make sure he could see what was goin' on in the lab. Didn't guess their technomagick would set you free."

"So Lord Steel sent you to the Gray Collective to serve as his spy," said Albert, "and by doing so, set you free. How ironic."

"Life's filled with little surprises," said Sam. "Your escape didn't change things much. Pattern-clone came to life, Jenni Smith and her friends proceeded with their plan. It's still unclear if the clone's really Heylel or just the Dark Lord masquerading as him. Results are the same. Only one question bothers me. A real big question."

Seventeen stared at Sam. He remembered the first night he'd encountered the white-haired mage, the ride they had taken in this same van. Sam Haine had raised the question of Seventeen's identity that evening. Now, finally, it had been answered. What else worried him?

"Lord Steel fears you, son," said Sam. "He's tried to kill you through his agents more than once. Pattern-clone probably aimed to do the same if you ever were stupid enough to join his army. Powerful forces want you dead. Destroyed. Eliminated. Escaping the Dark Lord's pretty amazing. But why does he want you dead?"

Seventeen grinned. They were in the city now, approaching their final destination. Nearly time for action. Still, Sam deserved an answer.

"You forget," he said. "Before the bond was broken by the technicians in the Gray Collective, my mind was linked to Lord Steel's. He had access to all my thoughts, my memories. But, in return, *I had access to his*. The Dark Lord doesn't fear *me*—he fears *what I might know*."

Sam Haine whistled. He appeared astonished. "The secrets of Malfeas," he whispered. "The arcane mysteries of the Maeljin Incarna. Your head filled with that stuff, son?"

Seventeen shrugged. "I'm not sure. Not yet. So far, bits and snatches of my past life are the only memories that have resurfaced. Lord Steel could be worried about nothing. I don't know. However, if I do possess secrets, something that makes the Dark Lords vulnerable, all the better. I won't forget fifty years in hell."

"Well, you can take out your anger on his henchmen," said Sam Haine, as Albert steered their van to a stop directly in front of the main entrance of Everwell Chemicals. Oddly enough, there were no security guards at the doors. "We're here. Time for gabbin's over. You prepared to fight, son?"

Seventeen pushed open the door to the van. He stepped onto the sidewalk, held out his left hand. Instantly, his massive fingers wrapped around the ironwood staff of his rune-covered steel scythe.

"I'm prepared," said Seventeen.

Chapter Thenty-Three

In the Horizon Realm known to the mages of the Nine Traditions as Horizon, the archmage Kallikos stirred fitfully in a drug-induced haze. More than a day had passed since the pattern-clone had issued its ultimatum. Enough time for mages and wizards and witches and sorcerers to make their choice. The seer's mind, free from the bonds of the flesh, roamed the Tellurian, witnessing the havoc brought about by the one who named itself Heylel Teomim...

In the Horizon Realm of the Second World of the Dine'...

An attractive woman with long black hair and dark eyes sat at a desk in a huge library at the center of a large house. Normally the house was filled with her children and their families. But not lately. Mae Roberts wanted only silence.

It was a Realm of Dreamspeakers, many of them Native Americans, seeking a more peaceful place to live. They shared it with numerous werecreatures and endangered species who otherwise would have been destroyed on Earth. It was a sanctuary, a Realm devoted to the rights of the oppressed. Yet, even there, Heylel's words had their effect.

"There's a time to mourn and a time to act," declared the golden man standing before Mae. The pattern-clone's face was a mask of compassion, deep concern. It spoke in low, soothing, almost hypnotic tones. "Tom Clearwater's blood doesn't call out for revenge. You know that. Violence only leads to more violence. Think with your heart, Mae. Let the Great Spirit guide your actions. Join us in our crusade. Help us put an end to this senseless war."

"They say you destroyed Doissetep," said Mae. Though she was dressed in a rawhide dress, a .357 magnum pistol rested on the desk in front of her. "Laughing Eagle says you are Nephandi."

"The Primi fear me," said the clone. It spoke with the easy assurance of one who knew it was never wrong. "They will do anything to stop my crusade, tell any lies to suppress my message. Doissetep fell because it was corrupt. Just as the Inner Council is corrupt. Don't listen to what they claim. Listen instead to your heart. Remember your friends. Join us *for them*. Join us for peace."

Slowly, Mae nodded. She unbuckled the holster from her waist, laid it beside the gun on the desk. "You're right. It's time to stop the killing. Enough death. What do you want me to do?"

"Other Dreamspeakers respect you," said the clone. "Speak to them. Spread my message. Tell them it is time to demand change. Travel to Horizon. Make yourself heard."

In Null-B: Construct of Yenosia, the Wasteland of Dead Aspirations...

Arthur had enjoyed pretending to be a Technomancer. But now it was time to really rock and roll. The being on the computer screen claimed it wanted peace and Unity. But Arthur knew different. Like recognized like.

He exited his hideaway in the rear of the huge factory. There were no surveillance monitors in the area. He'd made sure of that a long time ago. That small amount of privacy was all the time he needed to get things started.

"*Par-ty!*" he bellowed, grabbing a chemical drum with both of his talons. Wrenching with all his strength, Arthur tossed the half-filled container a dozen feet across the factory floor. It crashed into a plasma-gun assembly line, splashing a dozen workers. They screamed as sizzling acid quickly ate holes through their jeans and blue shirts and attacked their pale white skin. The drones scattered like mindless sheep, bleating in terror. Arthur grinned, ripped a handful of wires loose from their connections. All around him machinery came to a sudden stop.

"*Par-ty!*" he yelled again, slipping one of his talons into the proper computer node at assembly line's control unit. It gave him instant access to the factory security system. As a member of the Blue Steel Union, he possessed all the proper clearance codes.

In a millisecond, he uploaded the program he'd developed over the past year. All through the factory, lights flickered, machines growled, presses hummed. Then everything went black. Noise ceased.

Twenty feet distant, something crashed to the floor. Another an instant later. Hoverbikes, most likely, sent to investigate. Too late. Their crews were probably still alive. Arthur didn't care. Once the workers, slave laborers for the Technocracy, realized that all power was off in the building, no guard would be safe. It was chaos time.

"*Par-ty!*" he roared a third time, getting into the spirit of things. He'd been waiting for this moment for years. His talons tore at cables, smashed crates, ripped pulleys from the ceiling. Destruction was the name of the game. After years of acting proper, he wanted to have some fun.

Already, he could hear screams echoing his cry. Others taking up his chant of "Party!" The slaves outnumbered the guards hundreds to one. It wouldn't take long before the factory was cleared of authority.

Still, there was the actual Technomancer Construct in the center of the factory. The Gray Building with thick steel walls and a supposedly unbreakable security system. The place where Bernadine Slivey was probably hiding. The one location on Null-B she probably thought was absolutely safe.

Arthur laughed. "Adrian, Juanita, Joseph, you on line?" he subvocalized.

"Of course," all three answered immediately. Iteration X shock troops sent to Null-B after their units had been decimated, recruiting them to his cause had been simple. They shared a common bond with the machine. And Arthur knew how to spin a convincing web of lies.

"Time to pay our friends in the Gray Building a visit," said Arthur. "Wish them a fond farewell."

"Farewell?" It was Joseph, the least intelligent but most heavily armed of the three. "Who's leaving?"

"We're going to the Tradition Realm known as Horizon," said Arthur. "As for Bernadine and her friends, they're heading straight for hell."

In Vali Shallar, Chantry of Mu…

"The Jabhi-yazer won't let you leave," whispered the golden-skinned young woman to Minoru. "Won't let you go to Horizon. They don't trust you. They fear you."

"Nonsense," said Minoru. A tall, slender young man in his late twenties, he was dressed entirely in black. A short sword hung at his belt. "Masaki Takada knows I am loyal to the realm. I would never do anything to betray the secrets of Vali Shallar."

"Nevertheless," said the young woman, who offered no name and whose features glowed in the room's soft light, "the Jabhi-yazer are demanding that all gates to Horizon be sealed and that no one be allowed to leave Vali Shallar without their permission."

Minoru frowned. "The Jabhi-yazer overstep their duties. They are the appointed guardians of the Realm, but not its rulers. The Rachar would not permit them to do such things."

"The Rachar are afraid," said the girl. "They fear the one who calls himself the Master of Harmony. They fear his message. They are old, and they worry the young will realize the golden one speaks the truth."

"They fear words?" said Minoru. "And they allow the Jabhi-yazer to seal the Realm? This cannot be."

"Maybe," said girl, "the Rachar worry more about themselves then the rest of Vali Shallar. Old men, they've ruled our Realm for centuries. Perhaps the Master of Harmony speaks the truth. The elders thrive while the young fight and die."

"Nonsense," said Minoru. "That's not true."

"No?" asked girl. "Tell me the last time one of the Rachar fought a Technomancer? Tell me, please?"

"I—I cannot," said Minoru, and without realizing it, entered the growing army of the pattern-clone.

On the Machiavelli *X156-C36, Qui La Machinae, combat dreadnaut of the Void Engineers stationed at the Alpha-T Horizon Construct…*

Captain Sanford Mulligan stared at the image frozen on his viewscreen. Golden skin, the face of an angel, a voice that still rang in his mind, raising provocative questions. Others might be confused, other might be puzzled, but not Captain Mulligan. He'd spent too many years in the Near Umbra to be fooled that easily.

"Your reaction, Ms. Hastings?" he asked, turning to his second-in-command on the warship.

"Reality Deviant of incredible power, Captain,"

said Hastings. Though she was only thirty, twenty years younger than the Captain, she'd spent more than ten years on the *Machiavelli*. Mulligan had absolute faith in her abilities and judgments. She was the best officer ever to serve under his command. Despite the differences in their ages, he felt closer to her than to anyone he could remember. The only reason they weren't lovers was his rigid belief in the isolation of command. "This so-called Master of Harmony strikes me as a possible creation of Those Beyond. Major problem for the Union."

"I suspect the RD will cause more trouble for the Traditions than us," said Mulligan. "Horizon's its next target. I think we could benefit from the situation. Comptroller Sanders on Alpha-T agrees. He's given me authority for appropriate measures."

Hastings smiled. "You're suggesting we take advantage of the chaos and attack the Traditions' main base ourselves?"

Mulligan nodded. "Exactly. Foolhardy under ordinary circumstances, but I think the timing's right. Put the crew on full alert, Ms. Hastings. And set the course for Horizon. Should be quite a fight."

Slowly the huge airship, nearly ninety feet long, equipped with three Accelerated Force Cannons and two Ectoplasmic Disrupters, turned in the sky over the Alpha-T Construct and settled into its new course. Working like a precision drill team, its forty-member crew of Technomancers, technicians and marines prepared for war.

In a burned-out hulk of a supermarket in the worst section of urban Detroit…

"They set the rules, and you listen like little children," said the man with golden skin. He looked at the dozen teenagers gathered around him and sneered. "Isn't it time you grew up? Took control of your own lives? *Ended the slavery?*"

"I'm no fucking slave," said Enos. Five foot ten, thin as a rail, his skin the color of ebony, he was the de facto leader of their group. "None of us are."

"Of course not," said the golden man, sarcasm heavy in his every word. "You just cooperate because your elders do so much for your community." He spread his arms, taking in the wrecked supermarket. "Look at the wonderful gifts they provide."

"Fuck off," snapped Enos.

"What are you saying we *should* do?" asked Ta-Wanda J'mayn. "They hold all the power. We're nothing."

"Not true," said the golden man. "There's strength in numbers. Great strength. The Council of the Nine Traditions won't give up their power without a fight. If you want your share, if you *demand* your share, you've got to *take* it."

In the Jefferson Building in Seattle, NWO northwest region headquarters…

"You're smarter than them," said the golden woman whose face stared out of Alex's computer screen. "You've known that for years. You do all the work, you take all the chances, they get all the credit. It's always been that way. Those in charge live off the labors of their grunts. They talk the talk, walk the walk, but you're the ones stuck on the front lines, fighting and dying, while they issue orders and directives and never, ever get their hands dirty."

Alex nodded. He'd never seen a woman like this before. Never heard anyone speak the truth so forcefully, so directly. It cut away the lies, the half-truths, the deceptions that framed his life. Even as an image on the monitor, she blazed with conviction, the passion he'd once felt when newly recruited into the Technocracy, the anger against injustice that had not stirred him for years.

"They'll never change," said the golden woman. "Why should they? Change threatens their security, their comforts, *their positions*."

Sweat trickled across Alex's forehead. Carefully, he gazed around his cubicle, made sure his coat covered the spycam that normally monitored his every activity. The entire floor was strangely silent. How many other operatives were receiving this same message, checking their surroundings for unseen listeners?

"The status quo never changes through negotiations," said the woman of gold. "They taught you that. You know the truth. The strong survive. The weak perish. In five seconds, the Technocracy computer system crashes. If you want immortality, if you want power, seize it now!"

The computer screen went black.

Trembling, Alex rose to his feet. Pulled out his gun. "Yes!" he screamed, releasing years of pent-up rage. "Yes!"

Robert Weinberg

Stu Allen, his supervisor, came running. Appeared in the door of Alex's cubicle. Stared goggle-eyed as Alex pointed the automatic at him. Screamed as Alex pulled the trigger three times. Crumpled to the floor, his dead features creased with shock.

"Yes!" screamed Alex, as the entire office erupted in shouts and screams and gunfire. "Yes!"

...and recognized that the fires of revolution burned out of control.

In hundreds of Chantry Houses and Constructs throughout the Tellurian, the young battled the old. Those without power challenged those who held power. Kallikos watched as the pattern-clone, features changing back and forth between male and female, sometimes a combination of both, enticed, beguiled and seduced the have-nots of the universe.

Many Tradition mages, bound to their Chantry Houses only by loyalty, left. Rejecting violence, they disappeared into the night. Dissident Technomancers, caught in a hierarchy that demanded absolute obedience to higher authority, fought, bled and died seeking their freedom. Some escaped, most did not. Rebellion raged, as immortality beckoned.

Mind reeling, Kallikos opened his eyes. Overwhelmed by the tides of anarchy sweeping the cosmos, it took a moment for him to realize where he was. His bedroom in Marianna's pavilion in Concordia. On Horizon, where he was destined to die.

A figure appeared in the doorway. A woman, young and beautiful, clothed only in the sheerest of garments, typical of those who served Marianna. With long brunette tresses, dark eyes, and crimson lips.

"My lord." Her voice was sweet, filled with respect. She approached the bed, bells on her wrists and ankles ringing softly. "You cried out. Is something wrong?"

"A dream," said Kallikos, slipping off the side of the bed and rising to his feet. "In truth, a nightmare. More bad news for the Council of Nine."

"Your strength gives us all hope," said the girl. Placing her soft hands on Kallikos's shoulders, she stood on tiptoes and kissed him gently on the cheek.

She stepped back, smiled, an image of innocence and grace. "But only a fool is betrayed by a kiss."

Kallikos managed a single step forward before his body turned to gold. The young girl turned away, laughing. "My master said you'd never suspect one so adoring and sweet. So much for a seer's vision."

Sentient but trapped in metal, Kallikos could do nothing. Only wait.

The girl stared into a mirror opposite the bed. Spoke a single word. "Begin."

In a dozen places across Horizon, back-door portals opened.

Chapter Twenty-Four

Madeleine could sense the Rat Pack on the top floor of the chemical plant. Their thoughts were unfocused, confused, obviously the result of mind-numbing drugs. Another mark against her great-uncle and his minions. It was of little importance. Tonight, all debts would be paid in full.

One of her unique powers enabled her to locate any powerful vampires in the area. There was only one, far below her feet. She knew it could only be Enzo, sitting on his throne room in his basement sanctum. Madeleine intended to pay him a visit shortly. First, however, she wanted the children safe and out of harm's way. Her rescue of them would upset Enzo. So much the better.

A brief study of the plant's ground floor convinced her the only access to the top floor was by a solitary elevator. Her heightened senses informed her the interior was monitored by a surveillance camera and booby-trapped with mustard gas. No doubt steel gates protected the upper floor from unwelcome intruders.

With difficulty, she restrained herself from laughing. Not many months ago, Pietro had had her infiltrate the Mausoleum to test the building's security precautions. That effort had been an interesting if trivial maneuver. This latest challenge was child's play.

The elevator car waited on the first floor of the building. Searching nearby, Madeleine found a deserted cleaning closet. Removing her necklace and the Giovanni crest, she placed the treasure on the top shelf. Her dress followed, along with her shoes, leaving her clad in a form-hugging black leotard. With her pale white skin and slender figure, she appeared little more than a teenager.

Making no sound, Madeleine walked to the closed doors guarding the elevator. As she moved, her body appeared to grow insubstantial, ghost-like. Like most powerful vampires, Madeleine could convert into a vaporous mist. A microscopic crack separated the doors from the ceiling. Effortlessly, Madeleine flowed through and into the shaft leading upwards.

Maintaining loose contact with one wall of the passage, she floated towards the building's roof. As she passed the second floor, she sensed human presence. Here was where Ezra chose to make his stand. First the Rat Pack, then Enzo, and finally Ezra. It was going to be a busy night.

She halted at the top floor. Again, the smallest crack between the elevator shaft and the heavy steel doors allowed her to seep into the corridor beyond. Still in mist form, she noted two automatic machine-guns, one on each side of the entrance hall. They were an annoying distraction. More important was a massive steel door ahead of her. It had to lead to the chamber where the Rat Pack was being held captive.

Willing herself back to material form, Madeleine materialized in front of the sealed entrance. The electronic eyes controlling the twin machine-guns reacted instantly to her presence. The guns chattered, aimed at the spot where she had been an instant before. But Madeleine moved with inhuman speed and agility. Dodging the hail of bullets, she reached the first machine gun a second after it started firing. A quick wrench of her wrists, and the deadly weapon was disabled.

The second gun proved no more difficult than the first. Launching herself into the air, Madeleine soared thirty feet across the room, high above the curtain of steel slugs. Landing behind the machine gun, she quickly tore it to pieces. The commotion had surely alerted the guards inside the next room of her presence. Madeleine didn't care.

The door leading to the inner chamber was a slab of steel five inches thick. The walls were twice that. From lack of lock or handle, it evidently could only be opened from within. Madeleine suspected that wouldn't happen. It didn't matter. No seal was air-tight.

The Rat Pack waited on the other side. As did their guards. Returning to vaporous form, Madeleine flowed between door and wall and materialized on the other side.

Shadow entered the plant through an open window on the first floor. After carefully checking for booby traps, she slid across the sill onto the heavy wood floor of the corridor. Except for the upper level, the main floors were all constructed in the same fashion. Around the perimeter of the building ran four long hallways, lined with steel lockers, that stretched from one corner of the factory to the other. East, west, north and south, the four halls intersected large square stairwells, where old white marble stairs and black metal railings led up to the next level.

The inside of the square formed by the corridors was a gigantic chemical laboratory, complete with lab tables, work stations, and huge chemical vats. Each ceiling was twenty feet high. Though dozens of fans moved the fetid air throughout the complex, the entire building smelled like toxic waste. Working too many years for Everwell Chemicals was a sure trip to the cemetery.

Though the corridor she was in was deserted, the lights overhead were on. A dull yellow glow filled the hall. Like a dark shadow, the sword-mistress crept along the sides of the lockers, hunting for her prey. Above her, the floor squeaked as a foot rested on a loose board.

Shadow halted, resting flat against the steel cabinets. Letting the internal magick of *Do* guide her senses, she listened carefully to the movement above. Five, six, seven men walked back and forth in the corridor. Heavy, big figures, she could hear the slightest clicking of their ammunition and weapons. Armed with heavy-duty automatic weapons, they waited impatiently for her arrival. Ezra was inside the laboratory, with his female companion. They were the two who concerned Shadow. These others were exercise.

She freed Whisper from the scabbard on her back. Though she was skilled at fighting with either one or two swords, tonight she wanted her other hand free. Moving deliberately, pacing herself and setting her course of action, Shadow climbed the nearest set of stairs, in the southeast corner stairwell.

On her knees, she stared out the window of the door opening into the main corridor. Three men were present, talking and smoking cigarettes. They wore flak jackets and hunter's caps, and carried AK-47 automatic rifles. Two of the men had pistols tucked in the waistband of their pants, while the third carried a bowie knife. Their voices, though not loud, carried in the empty halls. They were fools to break silence.

Three here meant the other four were patrolling the other halls. Shadow pressed an ear to the wall. Her heightened senses quickly established that two men were in the north corridor, the rear section of the building. The other pair patrolled the hall to the west. For a few seconds at least, the trio fronting her were completely out of touch with their companions. A few seconds were all she needed.

Some small measure of strength returning to her sound-mauled body, Sharon rose to her feet. Internal machinery whirring, Ernest Nelson struggled up beside her. Twenty feet away, Charles Klair, hands and arms covered with the Wailer's blood, laughed. He took a step forward. The robotic creation that once had been human was in no hurry. Sharon and Nelson were trapped. They had no place to go.

Klair said something to them. Words she couldn't hear. Sharon suspected he probably wasn't remarking on how nice it was to see them. The Comptroller had no sense of humor. He had made her miserable on the Gray Collective. The thought of him defeating her after so much effort and pain grated on Sharon's nerves.

"Nelson and I are working for the Inner Council," she shouted, unable to hear her own words. "We've been given the assignment of finding and terminating the pattern-clone. Don't fuck with us, Klair. You're still a member of the Technocracy. You can't disobey a Council directive. So get the fuck out of here and leave us alone."

Klair smiled. For the first time, he seemed aware that Sharon and Nelson couldn't hear what he was saying. He pointed to his own ears, shook his head. He took another step forward.

"I'm warning you," Sharon shouted, knowing she was wasting her time trying to bargain with the Comptroller. "You fuck with us and the Council'll turn that freaking metal body of yours into paper clips."

Klair took another step forward. The smile on his face widened. It was obvious to Sharon that Klair was enjoying making her sweat. Like a spider tormenting flies. He raised his bloody hands.

The floor shook. Sharon glanced at Ernest Nelson. She had almost forgotten the cyborg while concentrating on Klair. Obviously, Nelson also realized that the Comptroller meant to squash them like bugs. His twin chain guns jerked with motion. With the Wailer dead, the dampening field no longer prevented the weapons from working. A hail of steel smashed into Klair's body, sending him staggering. His metallic skin rippled with colors, rushing through the spectrum like an insane rainbow. But he didn't go down. A hundred rounds pounded into his body, but he didn't go down.

Features contorted in disgust, Nelson stopped firing. Klair appeared invulnerable to harm, a superhuman creation that couldn't be stopped.

"Our security clearance is Alpha-Alpha," screamed Sharon, as Klair continued to advance. His skin flickered with her every word.

Klair opened his mouth, said something. Sharon had no idea what. His body shook as he spoke. The colors continued to shift across his face, his arms. Despite his seeming invulnerability, there was something wrong with the Comptroller.

"Stop!" screamed Sharon. His features changed from green to gold to silver. There was a troubled expression on his face.

"Stop!" she screamed again. Now, Klair's face turned orange. Then red. Then purple. Slowly, his entire body trembling, he raised a foot. Put it down a step closer. His movements were no longer fluid, smooth. The Wailer's screams had obviously damaged his circuits. Sounds hurt him.

Sharon slapped Nelson's chain guns and pointed at Klair, jerking her hands as if firing. "Shoot him!" she screamed, knowing the cyborg couldn't hear her but screaming nonetheless. "Shoot him!"

Nelson fired. The roar of gunfire filled the room. Like a man in a heavy rainstorm, Klair struggled forward, shrugging off the bullets that pounded him like hammers. A thousand variations of color circled his body, lighting up the Comptroller like a neon sign. Klair opened his mouth, said something. Sharon had no idea what. Nor did she care.

The Comptroller kept on coming. One of Nelson's guns ceased firing. Then, seconds later, so did the other.

Klair's body was a dull, lifeless gray. Bloody hands reached for Sharon's throat.

"Die, you sonofabitch!" Sharon shrieked with all of her might.

Klair's fingers twitched. His hands trembled. Arms stopped moving. Like a wave, tremors ran through his body, cascaded down his torso, into his legs. His body shook, vibrated like some gigantic cymbal.

"Die!" screamed Sharon. Nelson was at Klair's side, the cyborg's mouth open. Screaming as well.

Klair collapsed to the floor, his metallic skin black. His body jerked once, twice, then was still.

Nelson stared at Sharon. Raised a thumb in victory.

Searching through the desk, he found a scratchpad and pencil. *Some fun*, he printed in big letters.

You got more ammo in the car? Sharon scribbled.

He nodded, drew a question mark.

She pointed to the Wailer's corpse. Then wrote: *He said his friends at the plant told him we were coming. They're the ones we're hunting.*

Nelson shrugged his shoulders. *Why not?* he jotted beneath her message. *It's been fun so far.*

"Damn fuckin' about time," growled a deep bass voice.

Ignoring the speaker and the automatic weapons aimed at her, Madeleine quickly surveyed the inner chamber. The room was a square thirty feet by thirty feet. It made a perfect prison. Back against the far wall, opposite the only door, were two large steel cages. Imprisoned behind the bars were the Rat Pack. The cells were little more than huge boxes of steel posts stretching from floor to ceiling. Just bare wood and metal bars. Enzo had treated her charges like wild beasts. Another mark against him.

A series of six heavy-duty lab tables crisscrossed the room, making quick motion difficult. Stationed behind five of them were gunmen, armed with compact submachine-guns. Three of the guards had the Nephandi sigils tattooed on their cheeks. Participants, Madeleine felt certain, in the murders of Leo and Sister Susie. In other circumstances, she would have made them suffer for their crimes. Tonight, she was in a hurry. They would just die, instead of lingering.

A sixth man, the only one who mattered in her opinion, stood close to the cages imprisoning the Rat Pack. His gun was inches away from the bars of one of the cells, pointed directly at the three teenagers within. Standing, facing the killer, was Allyson. A few feet away were Sarah and Lucy.

"I knew you would come, Madeleine," said Allyson, her voice quivering with emotion. Her gaze remained focused on the man with the gun. "I told that fucker, Enzo, you'd never let us down."

"Shut the hell up, kid," said the man with the deep voice. He sneered at Madeleine. "We were told to inform you that Mr. Enzo waits for you downstairs, in his office. Make one wrong move, little miss badass, and we'll blow these annoyin' little shits away."

"My great-uncle is a senile fool," said Madeleine. "You are all dead men."

"Vengeance is mine," said Sarah unexpectedly. Her deep voice rang through the chamber. For an instant, the attention of the man guarding the Rat Pack wavered. His gaze flickered to the small, thin redhead off to the side.

Allyson reacted instantly. Grabbing the barrel of the man's rifle, she jammed it towards the roof, slamming the steel against the cell bars. The gun chattered to life, bullets slapping the ceiling. Shocked into action, the other guards opened fire on where Madeleine had been. She was no longer there.

The moment Allyson's fingers touched steel, Madeleine had blurred into motion. The deadliest assassin of Clan Giovanni, she had six men to kill before they turned their weapons on the Rat Pack. Madeleine didn't think. She acted.

The heavy lab tables were too bulky to navigate

around, so she went over. Hurtling into the air, her feet touched on the nearest table before the killers started firing. A dead man's finger jerked on his gun's trigger, the front of his face ripped off with one sweep of her right hand.

In a cartwheel motion, she whirled past the second and third guards. The extended fingers of her left hand dug into one of the pair's eyes, blinding him, then shattering his skull. Meanwhile, her legs wrapped around the neck of the other guard and squeezed. Bones crunched as she twisted her torso, almost wrenching his head from his shoulders.

Three dead, three left. Only a few seconds gone. The two men remaining among the tables were killer elite. They were rising to their feet, their machine-guns blasting.

Like a diver, Madeleine leapt at the nearer of the pair. Her body contorted in mid-air, twisting out of the path of cold steel. One hand caught the tattooed man by a shoulder. Madeleine squeezed, crushing bone and cartilage. He howled, the first man to make a sound. The noise died instantly, as her other hand snatched at his larynx and ripped out his throat.

In the corner of her vision, she noted the struggling Rat Pack. Allyson and Sarah had their hands on the rifle barrel, trying to wrench it from their captor. Lucy, taking a different path of attack, was on her knees, face pressed against the cage, her hands stretched out as far as she could reach. She gripped the guard by the crotch and was squeezing with all her strength.

The last man, his machine gun bellowing, was

crouched behind a square made of four lab tables. Anxious to finish him before he caused any damage, Madeleine dropped to the floor and slithered snake-like across the wood. Grabbing the killer by the legs, she flexed her arms apart, tearing him in two.

Now, only the guard battling Allyson and her companions remained. Grunting in triumph, the man, his face crimson, wrenched his rifle from the redheads' grasp. Madeleine merely redirected the barrel so that it wedged beneath his chin. Then, she squeezed the trigger.

"A senile old fool," she repeated.

She could have pulled the bars of the cages apart, but using the keys dangling from the dead guard's belt was a lot easier. In a minute, the entire Rat Pack was clustered around her.

"I knew you would come," said Allyson, grinning. "Told that scumbag Enzo he was making a fucking big mistake."

"You were awesome," said Lucy. "Absolutely incredible."

"I shall repay," said Sarah, in her sepulchral tones.

"Fuckin' chill, Sarah," said Sybil. "You're givin' me the creeps."

"Come," said Madeleine, heading for the elevator. "No time for squabbling."

Taking the elevator down to the first floor, she hurried the Rat Pack to a side entrance of the plant. "Will you be able to leave the city safely?" she asked.

"No problem," said Allyson. "We'll hotwire a car in the parking lot."

"Good." Madeleine gave Allyson directions to the

abandoned church. "My van is there. Wait for me until dawn. If I do not return, take the money and leave this region. Never return."

"We can't leave you, Madeleine," said Lucy, tears bubbling in her eyes. "We can't."

"You must," said Madeleine. One by one, she stared deep into the eyes of the six teenagers, imparting to each a small measure of her unconquerable will. "The Rat Pack needs to be strong. Only the strong survive. Honor my name by following my wishes."

"We'll do it," said Allyson. "I promise. The Rat Pack knows how to follow orders. We're like you. We got honor."

Madeleine smiled and nodded. "Honor over death," she declared. Then, without another word, she turned and headed for the stairs leading to the cellar.

Two of the three guards had their backs to the stairwell. The third man, the one with the bowie knife sheathed at his waist, wore a pair of silver-tinted mirrorshades beneath his hunting cap. Shadow found such macho posturing amusing. Strong, confident men didn't need gimmickry to advertise their strength.

The mirrorshade man took a deep drag on his cigarette. Seizing the moment, Shadow rose wraithlike to her feet. Before the man could pull the cigarette from his mouth, she sent two throwing stars whizzing across the hall. One for each eye. Before they even connected, she was charging, Whisper cradled casually beneath her right arm.

Blood spurted from the mirrorshade man's eyes. His companions, suddenly realizing they were under attack, started to turn. Shadow caught them in mid-stride.

A flick of her right wrist whipped Whisper forward and up, slashing an astonished guard from groin to forehead. He fell backwards, dead, a five-inch-deep furrow nearly dividing him in two.

His companion fared no better. Rifle clutched in both arms, he glimpsed a flash of steel. Pain roared through his brain and a shriek rose in his throat as he saw his detached hands, still gripping his gun, tumble to the floor. No sound issued from his throat. A beheaded man couldn't scream.

Not wasting an instant, Shadow ran on silent feet down the long hall. She could hear the scuff of approaching footsteps. The two guards to the west were approaching the stairwell. She wanted to be there to greet them properly.

Again, neither man expected death to be waiting. Security guards, grown soft from years of bullying drunks and manhandling vagrants, they were ill-suited to deal with a true warrior. A tall, bearded man and a short, fat one, with wide blue eyes, they carried their assault rifles with an easy, relaxed grip. They weren't prepared to fire and never had a chance to react.

Moving with a ballerina's grace, Shadow whirled past the pair, her long and short sword singing. The fat man died, his throat cut. His tall companion dropped an instant later, his body crisscrossed by a half-dozen slashes from Shadow's katana. Five were gone, two remained.

These security guards were distractions designed to heighten her self-confidence. Ezra thought to lull her into a feeling of invincibility. These intentional sacrifices were like markers lost at the beginning of a crooked poker game, aimed at building a sucker's confidence while luring them to their doom. Shadow was not so easily fooled. The most important lesson she had learned from her wise teachers was that of *humility*. She never overestimated her own skills, nor underestimated those of her adversary.

The last pair of guards patrolled the north hall. Shadow never once considered immobilizing them, taking their weapons and leaving them bound and subdued. A live enemy was always a threat. She felt no pity for the security officers, pawns or not. She was at war. In war, there was no room for pity.

Wraith-like, she glided down the west corridor. When she reached the northwest stairwell, a brief glance placed her two remaining targets fifty feet along the hall. Somewhat more alert than their fallen comrades, they were patrolling back to back, guns held ready for use, their gazes shifting from wall to wall. Still their reflexes were slow, undisciplined, when compared to those of a Dragon Claw.

Shadow stepped into the corridor entrance, whipped a half-dozen throwing stars into the air, then flung herself low and to the side. Gunfire chattered in reply, as the guard facing her managed to squeeze off a burst from his machine gun before the steel blades slashed into his body. The weapon continued firing a moment longer as he dropped to the floor, his dead fingers frozen around the trigger.

His companion, acting with surprising intelligence, immediately dropped spread-eagled on the floor. Hurriedly, he scuttled around on his stomach so he could aim his machine gun at Shadow. That, however, was an ill-thought maneuver. As he turned, for a brief moment the guard exposed his entire torso to the warrior woman.

With its high collar, the flak jacket protected the man's head, chest and stomach. But normal jeans covered his legs. Three perfectly aimed throwing stars dug into his thigh, knee and ankle. Involuntarily, the guard convulsed in pain, arched his back. Two more stars caught him in the forehead. He was dead before his face hit the floor.

Carefully, Shadow let her senses expand to fill the empty corridors. Nothing moved. The dead remained where they had fallen. The quiet was complete.

Double doors beckoned, promising entrance to the inner core of the chemical plant. Shadow pushed at them with a toe. They weren't locked. The time for true battle had arrived. Ezra awaited within. Scream and Whisper in hand, she stepped into the inferno.

Chapter Twenty-Five

"Good evening," said Ms. Hargroves, her voice calm, though she knew that the most dangerous moments of her life had just begun. Sitting straight and stiff in her chair, she stared at the seemingly young woman in front of her desk. "Can I help you?"

"I am Madeleine Giovanni," said the young woman dressed only a black leotard. She had black hair, chalk-white skin, and blood-red lips. Ms. Hargroves noted the slight resemblance to Enzo. Very slight. "I am here to see my great-uncle, Enzo."

Tonight's plan specified that the men on the uppermost floor alert Ms. Hargroves as soon as Madeleine arrived so she could alert Enzo. No call had come. She wondered if the Dagger hadn't bothered with the captive teenagers. Quite possibly, Hope and Aliara could have overestimated her attachment to the aptly described "Rat Pack."

"I believe he is expecting you," she said. "I dismissed the guards off the street. Saw no reason to waste well-trained men."

Casually, Ms. Hargroves leaned forward and pressed the intercom button to the lab where the children were prisoner. It buzzed and buzzed, No one answered. Madeleine, as if reading her thoughts, smiled. Staring at the woman in black, Ms. Hargroves noticed numerous small bloodstains on her leotard. What few doubts she had about her plan vanished. "I'll inform Mr. Giovanni you've arrived."

"Thank you," said Madeleine, as Ms Hargroves stood up and walked to the only door leading to Enzo's inner sanctum. The elder vampire was already there, waiting on his throne, with Hope in attendance. They expected to be in complete control of the situation. Ms. Hargroves suspected they were in for a terrible shock.

She pulled open the door and glanced inside. The recessed electric lights barely cut the shadows that crouched in the corners of the cement chamber. All the furniture was pushed back against the far wall except for Enzo's throne. That remained in the center of the gray room. Enzo was rising to his feet, eyes glistening. Hope, already standing, smiled in anticipation.

"Madeleine Giovanni is here," said Ms. Hargroves, keeping her voice strictly neutral. She refused to look Hope in the eyes, worried the shapeshifter might sense the hate she felt. For an instant, Ms. Hargroves wondered when the willworker had killed the original Esperenza. It wasn't important. Only her plan mattered. She kept her gaze focused on the floor. "Shall I show her in?"

"Madeleine?" said Enzo, frowning. He appeared confused. "Here? Now?"

"Yes sir," said Ms. Hargroves, offering no other information. Enzo had abandoned her for Hope. Let the over-confident bitch deal with the Dagger of the Giovanni. "No word from upstairs. Shall I show her in?"

"Of course," said Hope, with a laugh. She sounded unconcerned, mistress of the moment. "An unexpected surprise, but welcome nonetheless. Agreed, my lord?"

"Yes, yes," said Enzo, some measure of arrogance returning to his voice. "Show her in."

Ms. Hargroves turned and waved Madeleine forward. The woman in black appeared amused by the delay. "My uncle and his advisor?" she said as she stepped to the door.

"Ms. Hope," mouthed Ms. Hargroves, her back to the inner chamber. "An extremely dangerous witch."

Madeleine said nothing. But she dipped her head slightly, acknowledging the words.

"Madeleine, dear cousin," said Enzo as the woman in black entered the stone-walled chamber. He sat like a king on a high-backed mahogany chair covered with purple velvet laced with gold stitching. Hope stood to the right of the throne. "It has been too long."

Ms. Hargroves closed the door and returned to her desk. She flipped a switch on her intercom. Earlier that afternoon, she had planted a microscopic transmitter between two stone slabs in Enzo's sanctum.

The voices within were muffled but distinct. Leaning forward, she concentrated on every word spoken. Dark power burned in her fingertips, the *Touch That Kills*. Not yet, but soon. Very soon.

"Please, dear relative, rest," said Enzo, waving to a chair a few feet away from his. The throne rested on a small platform, enabling him to look down on anyone seated. "You are looking well."

"I need no rest, uncle," said Madeleine, remaining on her feet. Enzo, though dressed in a black suit, white shirt, and tie, appeared bloated, grotesque. He no longer appeared remotely human. "Nor have my features changed since our last meeting. I look the same."

Her eyes kept close watch on the woman called Hope. The sultry, dark-haired woman stood a few feet to the left of Enzo's chair, her arms folded across her chest. She appeared unconcerned with the conversation. Dressed entirely in white, Hope possessed a rare talent to make an expensive tailored outfit look tawdry. Ms. Hargroves's warning hadn't been necessary. Madeleine knew Enzo's ally had to be one of the shapeshifters working with the pattern-clone.

The chamber was exactly as she remembered from her previous visits in mist form. A cracked floor, low ceiling, cement walls. Enzo's throne and a few chairs pushed to the back wall. No other furniture. A bleak, inhospitable place, a true reflection of her great-uncle's mind.

Enzo shrugged. "As you wish. No more meaningless small talk." He leaned forward, his eyes glowing blood red. "Why did you come to America? The truth."

"Ask Montifloro," said Madeleine. "Oh, I forgot. The Final Death claimed him. His blood stains your lips."

"He sought to betray me," snarled Enzo. "He deserved to die. Now, answer my question."

"My grandfather, my sire, Pietro Giovanni, master and manager of the Mausoleum, sent me to the United States," said Madeleine. "He asked me to investigate your enterprises involving Everwell Chemicals. He worried about your lack of communication. Pietro wanted reassurances of your continued loyalty to Clan Giovanni."

"You were sent here to destroy me," said Enzo.

"If necessary, yes," said Madeleine. "That is why I am called the Dagger."

"Pietro Giovanni is a bitter old fool," said Hope, speaking for the first time since Madeleine entered the stone chamber. "His ideas and vision are outdated. Clan Giovanni needs new leadership."

"My sire follows the dictates of his peers," said Madeleine. "He is master of the Mausoleum, not our family."

"Nonsense," said Enzo. "Augustus broods on the afterlife. The clan elders blindly follow Pietro's lead. His word is law. Hope is right. It is time for a change."

"Change meaning Enzo Giovanni?" asked Madeleine.

Her great-uncle nodded. "Who better to lead than

me? I have served the clan long and well. And I possess powerful allies."

"Our family needs no allies," said Madeleine. "We manage quite well without outsiders."

"Let's drop the bullshit," said Hope, stepping closer to Enzo's throne. She sneered at Madeleine. "You're here because we've got your pet teenagers locked upstairs in cages. If you want them alive tomorrow, you'll listen to what Enzo wants tonight. And do exactly what he says."

"Betray my family honor for a gang of human children?" said Madeleine. She laughed, enjoying the startled expression on Hope's face. "You confuse me with Mother Teresa."

"The brats swore by you," said Enzo. "They bragged of your protection."

"An exaggeration," said Madeleine, standing relaxed, her hands at her sides. She was patient. An expert assassin never rushed. "Besides, your cages stand open, great-uncle. Did you really think to stop the Dagger with such scum? The children are gone."

"They'll die before morning," growled Enzo. He leaned forward, eyes glaring at Madeleine. His features were bestial, without any trace of humanity. "My curse is upon them."

Madeleine laughed again, louder than before. An enraged opponent made mistakes. Enzo was frothing with fury. "An old, tired trick, uncle, planting a suicide wish in their minds. Perhaps it worked well twenty years ago, but no longer. I erased the thought from each of them. Forget the children. *You have been judged and found wanting*. The penalty for betraying your Clan is death."

Enzo's eyes widened in shock. He dropped back in his chair, a stunned expression on his face. "The little witch. The little witch."

"Forget that, you fool," said Hope, pointing an accusatory finger at Madeleine. "The bargain's dead. Kill her. Now!"

"Enough nonsense," declared Madeleine and reached for Hope's extended hand. Moving with inhuman speed, she grabbed...nothing.

Roaring savagely, Enzo exploded from his throne and hurtled himself at Madeleine. Instinctively, she willed herself into the floor. The ground refused to yield. Her body remained solid. Massive arms wrapped around her chest, slamming her to the soil. Enzo's open mouth snapped at her throat.

Thousands of hours of combat training saved Madeleine. Arms twisting, legs thrusting, she slithered like a snake out of her uncle's grip. On her feet in an instant, she looked around for Hope. The dark-haired beauty stood behind Enzo's throne, her hands clasped together as if in prayer.

Madeleine vaulted forward, her fingers extended to rip out the woman's throat. This close, it was impossible for her to miss. Yet she did again, her hands clutching empty air. Madeleine crashed to the ground, rolling onto her back. A second later, Enzo's huge paws wrapped themselves around her ankles.

"Now I have you," snarled her uncle, tightening his grip. Madeleine kicked and squirmed, but Enzo's hands were locked in place. His strength was incredible, much greater than she had expected. Laughing insanely, he dragged her closer.

The cold cement continued to deny her its embrace. For the first time in decades, Madeleine found herself deprived of her most deadly fighting technique. She couldn't meld into the earth. Magick had sealed the room. But an accomplished assassin relied on more than tricks.

Madeleine's arms pushed her into a sitting position. Before Enzo could release his hold on her legs, she lunged forward, grabbed him by the face and thrust up with her knees. He howled as his nose dissolved into fragments of shattered bone. Seizing the moment, she wrenched free and once more spun to her feet.

Shaking his head to clear his eyes of cartilage and bone, Enzo swatted at her with his right hand. A glancing blow sent Madeleine flying. She crashed into the far stone wall, sending clouds of dust spinning. The impact broke two of her ribs. An annoying injury but not threatening. She had survived worse. Enzo's alliance with Lord Steel had gifted him with frightening power, brute strength Madeleine couldn't match. But battles were won with brains, not brawn.

"You're finished, bitch," said Hope. Hands still folded, she remained standing behind Enzo's throne. The dark-haired woman appeared pleased by Madeleine's struggles. "Vampires can't defeat wizards. Never. Life's a lot more difficult when you can't hide beneath the ground, isn't it? So much for the invincible Dagger."

She couldn't battle magick, Madeleine knew, but she could bend it to her advantage. Enzo, his face a smashed ruin, charged again. Like a professional bullfighter, Madeleine vaulted over him, her head grazing the ceiling. As she dropped, her legs curled beneath her and she executed a perfect somersault, landing once again on her feet. Behind her, Enzo smashed into the wall. The entire room quivered with the impact. Her uncle possessed little skill as a fighter, but his tremendous strength made him a dangerous adversary. If he got his hands around her neck, Madeleine knew she was finished.

Positioning had to be exactly perfect. Mentally drawing a line between Enzo and Hope, Madeleine bisected it with her body. As her uncle turned, she shouted and slashed the air with her fists, inches in front of his face. She had no intention of making contact. Instead, she whirled, and hands outstretched, flung herself at Hope's legs.

Laughing viciously, the sorceress leapt to the side. Exactly as she expected, Madeleine missed her supposed target and crashed head-first into Enzo's velvet-covered throne. The force of her blow smashed the chair to the ground. Madeleine grabbed wildly at the throne's arms, trying to break her fall. Velvet cloth tangled around her arms as she tumbled in disarray to the floor, pieces of heavy mahogany scattering across the room. From her new position in front of the room's only door, Hope pointed a second time.

"End her," she commanded. "This farce has gone on long enough."

"My throne!" snarled Enzo. His blood-red eyes glowing in fury, he leapt at Madeleine, helpless amidst the velvet cloth. His gaze was fixed on her unprotected neck. Thus he never spotted the foot-long sliver of mahogany chair she raised from beneath the purple cloth. His body slammed into the stake with the full momentum of his three hundred pounds. Like a skewered piece of meat, Enzo collapsed to the cold earth, his crimson eyes wide with surprise.

Calmly, Madeleine rose to her feet. The wooden shaft protruded three inches from Enzo's back. It wouldn't be dislodged easily. Smiling, she stared at a stunned Hope.

"Stakes, contrary to famous novels, are not fatal to my kind," she declared, wondering how she could kill someone she appeared to be unable to touch. "They merely paralyze the victim. My uncle could last in such a state indefinitely. However, that would merely postpone the inevitable. He must die."

"Hope," whispered Enzo, his lips barely moving. "Help me. Please help me."

"Yes, dear Hope," said Madeleine, picking up another long shard of mahogany. It felt right. "Go ahead. Help him."

Flicking her wrist, Madeleine sent the makeshift spear flying at the willworker's heart. Her aim was perfect. Yet somehow the wood clattered harmlessly into the cement wall to Hope's left.

"Not so easy," said Hope. She folded her hands together in front of her, again as if praying. "I'm a lot harder to trick than your stupid relative. We have great hopes for Enzo. This minor setback won't change things much. Just postpone him gaining control of Clan Giovanni. Maybe being staked will teach him to be a little more cautious. Not a bad trade, actually, for the destruction of the Dagger of the Giovanni."

"I'm not so easy to destroy," said Madeleine, grabbing hold of the velvet cloth. It made an unlikely weapon, but at the moment she wasn't picky.

"Yes you are," said Hope, and raised her clenched hands to her face. Behind her, the door to the outside office opened. "Yes you are."

Timing, Ms. Hargroves, knew was everything. With Enzo unable to move and Madeleine Giovanni threatened, it was the moment to act.

"Yes you are," she heard Hope say on the intercom as she pulled open the door to the inner chamber.

"Yes you are," she heard the dark-haired woman say a second time as she looked into the room.

Hope stood less than a foot away, her back to the door. Madeleine Giovanni, clutching the velvet spread from Enzo's throne, stood a dozen feet away. Near her, on the floor, a wooden shaft sticking like a spike out of his chest, was her boss, Enzo Giovanni.

"Help me," croaked Enzo. "Help me."

"What the fuck?" said Hope, half-turning.

Madeleine Giovanni said nothing.

"Watch your language," said Ms. Hargroves and laid

a finger on the shapeshifter. Deep within her, hate flared with a molten intensity. "Bitch."

The results were more spectacular than she thought possible. Hope *ignited*, her body exploding in a burst of incandescent white flame. The woman screamed, once, then screamed no more as her flesh crackled and burned. Still standing, her blood evaporated into a cloud of superheated steam. Muscle and tissue baked, filling the chamber with the smell of charred flesh. Another second, only a skeleton remained. Then that too disappeared, leaving only a scattering of ash swirling in the fire.

As suddenly as it had begun, the flame ceased. The dirt floor of the room, Ms. Hargroves noted dispassionately, bore no evidence of the white-hot blast. Only Hope had been affected by the flames.

"It pays not to insult dried-up old bitches only fit to take dictation," she declared, her gaunt face twisting into a rare smile. "They might have dangerous friends."

"Help me," whispered Enzo, unable to move an inch. "Save me. I'll give you anything."

"Anything is no longer enough," said Ms. Hargroves. She stared at Madeleine Giovanni. The Dagger still held the velvet cloth in her hands. "What do you plan to do with him?"

"I favor your method of execution," said Madeleine. "An impressive trick. Is it easy to learn?"

"A gift," said Ms. Hargroves, feeling brevity was best. "Sorry."

Madeleine shrugged. "I suspected as much." She glanced at Enzo then back at Ms. Hargroves. "With the willworker dead and Enzo destroyed, there will be an empty place on the Pentex Board of Directors. An ambitious woman, with no scruples and powerful friends, might lay claim to that position."

"An interesting notion," said Ms. Hargroves. Madeleine Giovanni was no fool.

"Enzo destroyed?"

"Most secretaries use a letter opener," said Madeleine. "You have one at your desk? Nice and sharp?"

"Of course," said Ms. Hargroves. "I'm not sure I understand?"

"I could drink my uncle's blood," said Madeleine, "but I fear it is tainted. However, there are other methods to destroy him."

"Help me," pleaded Enzo. "Please, please."

"Sunlight also kills the Undead," said Madeleine. "As does fire. And decapitation."

"Oh," said Ms. Hargroves. "I'll be back in a minute."

Five grisly minutes later, Enzo Giovanni was dust on the dirt floor. Madeleine, her angelic face undisturbed, handed the badly bent letter opener back to Ms. Hargroves. "Keep it as a souvenir," she said. "And a warning."

"A warning," repeated Ms. Hargroves.

The lady in black was already dissolving into mist, sinking into the dirt floor. "Someday, Clan Giovanni and Pentex will clash. Remember Enzo. Be there at your peril."

Then the Dagger was gone. Leaving Ms. Hargroves

slightly apprehensive, but otherwise quite satisfied with the evening's conclusion.

She stared at her fingers. Blood stained the tips. Enzo's blood. Powerful blood. She raised her fingers to her lips. One taste perhaps…

Chapter Twenty-Six

The inside of the chemical plant resembled a scene out of hell. There were no lights, nor were any needed. The room was a gigantic square, several hundred feet wide, with a high ceiling. The floor was a black, slate-like material. In each corner rested a huge cast-iron steam press, monstrous machines that crouched like gigantic prehistoric beasts. Working on a round-the-clock schedule, their clanking mouths filled the plant with the roar and crunch of metal on metal.

Fronting the presses were a maze of steel laboratory tables, covered with thousands of bottles filled with undefined compounds. They shook with each bellow of steam. Huge clamps bound the work stations immobile to the slate floor.

A dozen small vats dripped noxious fumes, as strange glowing mixtures of toxic chemicals bubbled and smoked. The scarred floor beneath them suggested that the four-foot-high containers had overturned more than once. Whatever they held, Shadow felt certain, was death in liquid form.

In the center of the room, a quartet of four immense chemical tanks dominated. They defined the corners of a square, twenty feet on a side. Each steel vat stood ten feet high, with a mouth ten feet wide. Though Shadow couldn't see inside, the contents issued the same noxious gases as the smaller containers. A ghastly white light issued from the tanks, bathing the interior of the plant in an eerie glow. Massive pipes crisscrossed the floor, connecting the four tanks together. What was in one was in all. Toxic waste prepared by the scientists of Everwell Chemicals, to pollute the surrounding environment. Poison for sale.

In the middle of the square formed by the tanks, where invisible diagonals crossed, stood two figures, bathed in the ghostly white light emanating from the vats. One was a short, husky man, with tangled gray hair and unkempt beard. His eyes were black as pitch. He wore torn, ragged clothing, and a white shirt streaked with blood. He stared at Shadow with a look devoid of all expression, a blank slate that bespoke of absolute and total insanity. Here, she knew without asking, was the mad mage, Ezra ben Maimon. The willworker who served Lord Steel. The man she had come to kill.

Beside him, a hand resting on his shoulder, stood a short, slender girl Shadow recognized immediately. Jenni Smith. Shadow had seen the young woman three times before, always in the Glade of the Goddess. She had always been in the presence of

Seventeen. Slender and petite, she looked to be no more than twenty years old. Jenni had long blond hair, deep blue eyes, and vital, healthy pink skin. In the midst of the chemical vats filled with some of the most dangerous contaminants in the world, she was stood barefoot and wore a long flowered blue dress. She was an exact duplicate of the girl in the fax received by Madeleine Giovanni. Jenni Smith was masquerading as Ezra's dead wife, Rebekkah.

There were others, guards like those she had killed in the hall. She sensed them, lurking in the shadows, scattered throughout the room. Waiting for orders. For now, she ignored them. When the proper time came, they would all die.

It was hot inside the plant, incredibly hot. Yet the heat didn't seem to bother Ezra or Jenni. Shadow, whose training had taught her to ignore the elements, refused to let the temperature affect her.

Whisper and Scream in her hands, she took her first step toward the mad mage and his partner. As if hearing the touch of her bare skin on the slate, Ezra smiled. Jenni Smith whispered something in his ear. He nodded, raised his hands into the air.

"*Fladsstrrum*," he howled, the skin of his face crinkling like old dried paper. The meaningless syllables drifted through the air, taking form and substance as they echoed through the gigantic vault. The atmosphere warped and turned, turned dark. A thousand red eyes glistened in front of Shadow. Invisible mouths snapped at her flesh, tore at her skin. Blood oozed from a hundred wounds. Bewildered and amazed, she lashed out with her two swords, encountered nothing. This was magick beyond her comprehension.

"Xrandrum al r'maty zorn."

Ezra's arms were raised, reaching upward to the ceiling, as if in mockery of prayer. Standing at his side, Jenni Smith laughed, an obscene, inhuman sound.

The air around Shadow's leg turned to jelly. She couldn't move. It was as if the atmosphere was alive and holding her back.

Above Ezra's head, a dark cloud, an ominous dark shadow seemed to be forming. As he continued to scream words in some unknown tongue, bolts of electrical energy like small arrows of lightning flashed through the cloud.

"That woman," yelled Shadow, trying to make herself heard in the growing chaos, "is not your wife! Your loved one, Rebekkah, is dead. She died in a terrorist attack years ago. Ask your father. Ask your son. They will tell you the truth."

Ezra stared at her for an instant. There was no sign he heard a word she had said. His mind was gone, filled with a darkness out of space and time. He grinned, revealing a mouth of broken, yellowed teeth. Jenni Smith sneered. She raised a hand, a signal.

Above Ezra's head the cloud was solidifying. It was black, blacker than pitch. The streaks of energy flashed with blinding intensity. A sliver of darkness reached down, licked the mad wizard's face. It was as if a bolt of electricity pulsed through him. His hair stood on end. Eyes blazed. His jaw dropped, as a stream of gibberish tumbled from his mouth.

"Yattagama mty ond mty Cthuchuch!"

The mage's fingers spread open like the claws of some enormous sea beast. And a funnel of absolute blackness poured forth, whipped across the room, enveloped Shadow.

Hate! It pulsated in her veins, roared through her mind, engulfed her senses. Hate for Ezra, hate for Jenni, hate for her enemies, overwhelming red hate for the entire chamber, for all those who opposed her. Insane hate for those beings who had hurt her lover, hate for those who sought to change reality. In an instant, hate tore at her insides, filled her to the core of her being.

Behind her, men moved. Three attackers, caught in the same cloud of insane malevolence that roared through her veins. Barely able to move in the jelled air, Shadow turned, raised her swords as the trio charged forward, their faces warped into masks of bestial fury.

Normally such a fight would have only lasted an instant. But hate clouded Shadow's judgment, perverted her skills. Passions long held in check, suppressed by years of training, erupted in mindless violence. Her katana slashed deep into the nearest man's neck. But instead of wrenching it free, parrying the second's blows, she chopped a second time, a third, a fourth, so consumed by hate she could think of nothing else but her lust to destroy.

A knife caught her below the ribs, tore through

flesh and muscle. She screamed, breaking a code of silence she had maintained during all of her years as a Dragon Claw. Hate blinded her to the pain, the feel of steel in her gut. Her short sword whipped up, caught her attacker in the groin. Snarling with insane fury, she disembowelled him with a twist of the wrist. Then, as he fell, his weight pulling his knife free, she ripped her blade across his throat.

The third man swung a cleaver at her face. Shadow lunged to the left. The heavy blade slammed into her shoulder, smashing bone. For an instant, she almost dropped her katana. Then, still gripped in dread fury, she swung the razor-sharp blade with all of her strength into the man's side. He shrieked as the sword sliced halfway through his body. Steaming insides tumbling to the floor, he collapsed in a pool of gore.

Wounded badly, Shadow turned. Ezra was roaring with laughter, insane chortling that ricocheted like bullets through the chamber. The laughter of a demented demi-god. Above him, the pitch-black cloud pulsed, as if with life. Red lines rippled through the blackness.

Hate. Duke Steel was lord of hate. Shadow dropped to her knees, the pain from her wounds intense. Agony cleared her mind. Already the nanobyte blood in her system was working, healing her, making her whole. She had do the same for her mind. She needed to control the hate, channel it back against her enemy. Otherwise she was doomed.

"*Grttomas m'erw xrttyr,*" screamed Ezra.

Another wave of blackness slammed her mind.

Hatred of all she knew and loved. Hatred of Seventeen. Hatred of Sam Haine. Unreasonable, illogical hate. Hate of her brethren in the Akashic Brotherhood. Hatred, raging like a flame, against the Nine Traditions. Hatred of all humanity. Hatred that pressed down upon her like a massive weight, crushing her spirit. Crushing her will to live.

Hate that forced her to raise her short sword to her throat. Hate that urged her to plunge it home. Hate of herself. Hate of all living things. The blade wavered in her hands. Then lowered.

"*Khashtan zzzr ms'rtr!*" screamed Ezra, his features pitch black, his eyes blood red. But his words could not bend Shadow's will. Not even the hatred of Duke Steel could force the sword-mistress to take her own life.

Gathering her strength, Shadow rose slowly to her feet. Her wounds were not completely healed. She felt weak, barely able to move. But she refused to yield. She would kill Ezra. Or die trying.

Ernest Nelson poked at one of the three dead bodies with a steel foot. Buried deep in the man's skull, penetrating right through the lenses of his sunglasses, were a pair of metal throwing stars. Nicely done. Whoever had killed the man was extremely talented.

Beside him, Sharon Reed raised her hands, palms open, then pointed to the other two corpses. One had been nearly sliced in two, while the other was handless and headless. She gestured to the unfired guns.

Nelson raised one finger, indicating one assassin. He'd never fought a Tradition Akashic Brother, but he'd seen footage of them in action. Nasty, rough customers, capable of incredible techniques.

Sharon shrugged. She pulled out the pad of paper each of them carried, scribbled a word on it. *Where?*

Nelson gestured to the chemical plant behind the steel lockers. He waved his hands around, trying to convey motion. His sensors indicated there were people inside, energy discharges. He was terrible at charades. Pulling the pad from his coat pocket, he wrote his own message.

Strategy?

Sharon's answer was quick and to the point. *Capture Ezra. Velma. Kill them if necessary. Help others attempting same.*

Nelson nodded. Much as he hated the Traditions, at least they were human. Misguided fools, but they weren't Nephandi. Better to unite against a common foe. All of his weapons were fully loaded; Reed carried enough poison pellets to kill most of Rochester. They were ready for war.

All systems on, Nelson kicked open the steel door leading into the central plant, popping it off its hinges. Nobody within seemed to notice. Immediately Nelson dragged Sharon to the floor behind a nearby metal work station.

The room was huge. There were no lights, but an eerie white glow provided more than enough illumination. They stood on a black, slate-like floor. Huge steam-presses bellowed in the corners, filling the plant with noise. Steel lab-tables formed a maze leading to the center. Chemical vats filled with slime simmered everywhere. The whole place was incredibly hot.

In the center of the room stood four huge chemical vats. Whatever toxic material bubbled within provided the ghastly light. Between the tanks were two figures, facing the opposite direction. One was a short gray-haired figure, who pulsated with energy. A distorted, bloated thing barely resembling a man. A huge black cloud floated above his head, lines of red light flickering through it like electricity: Those Beyond were involved in this battle. Nelson had thought nothing could get worse after the Wailer. Obviously, he'd been mistaken.

Standing by the gray-haired man was a young woman, short and slender, petite, with long blond hair. A vision of loveliness in a blue dress. Velma Wade. The bitch who had betrayed the Gray Collective and stabbed Sharon Reed in the back.

Beyond the pair, Nelson could see a solitary figure on her knees on the floor. She held a sword in front of her body. He blinked, thinking his eyes tricked him, then realized they had not. The Akashic swordfighter was a woman.

Suddenly a wave of fury shook the cyborg. He trembled, as a hundred warning signals flashed through his circuitry. Chemicals were flooding his system, raising his emotions to unstable levels. Hurriedly, he coded in a massive dose of tranquilizers, trying to calm his anger. He shook his head, feeling frightened. What the hell was happening?

Beside him, Sharon Reed twitched, her body shaking as if caught in a powerful electric field. Her face turned blood red, lips drew back from her teeth in a death's head grin. She opened her mouth, screamed something. A single word. Velma Wade turned, saw them, laughed.

Mentally, Nelson cursed. The stupid bitch. She needed to control herself. He grabbed her arm, wrenched her around. Eyes blazing, she slapped him in the face. Pulled herself free, hurtled forward towards the center of the room. Towards Velma.

Hate overwhelmed Nelson's senses. He went berserk. All of the resentment and hatred he had felt for Reed during their days in the Gray Collective came to a boil. Up went his chain guns. In one smooth motion, he focused on the Research Director, squeezed the triggers. Nothing happened. Motion inhibitors made guns useless, just like in the Wailer's headquarters.

Another burst of tranquilizers kicked in, sending him reeling. Damn, he'd tried killing Reed! That fucking black cloud was somehow scrambling their brains.

Sharon was almost at Velma. But Velma was no longer so sweet and petite. In seconds, the shapeshifter had transformed, evolved into something a lot nastier. A horror Nelson remembered from their night in Washington. Reed was in for the battle of her life.

Internal warning systems exploded in Nelson's

mind. Men, a half-dozen of them, running forward. Armed with knives, axes, lead pipes. Stupid fools, but they required immediate attention. Guns useless, the cyborg reached out and grabbed one of the steel workbenches, ripped it off the floor. Yielding to the rage within him, he raised the table over his head.

Shadow's legs felt as if they were wrapped in molasses. The congealed air had surrounded her. She couldn't advance. It took all of her concentration to hold the unreasoning hatred at bay. Her hands fumbled for the throwing stars at her belt. Pulling out several, she sent them hurtling across the room at Ezra.

The steel caught the magus in the chest and stuck there, protruding like needles. He didn't seem to notice, didn't seem to care. His blood dripped to the floor. He was beyond pain. Filled with the essence of Duke Steel, he existed only to hate.

Above the madman's head, the dark cloud had grown in size, its color no color but the absence of any light. Power rippled through its interior in jagged waves. To Shadow, staring at the darkness, the cloud seem to take on form, an inhuman face hidden by a metal mask. Lord Steel.

A finger of black light lanced out of the cloud, swirled in the space between Ezra's hands. The insane willworker's fingers sizzled with energy. A fireball, six inches around, hovered between his palms. A fireball of black flames. A sphere of concentrated hate.

Laughing, the wizard flung it straight at Shadow.

Instantly, Whisper was in her hands. If the ball touched her, she was dead.

Concentrating intently on the fragment of dark energy hurtling towards her, Shadow barely noticed the two strangers who entered the chemical plant from the opposite entrance. However, members of the Akashic Brotherhood were trained to observe all, not part. Others had entered the fray.

Swinging Whisper precisely at the proper moment, she slashed the fireball into fragments. Shards of blackness stung her cheeks, filling her mind for an instant with mindless, elemental hate. The emotion staggered her, caused her sword to swing forward. The air popped, seemed to give way. If the air held her in place, did it have substance? Could it rip?

Holding Whisper in her left hand, she unsheathed Scream. With a twist of her fingers, Shadow reversed the blade and plunged it into the air directly in front of her.

It was like cutting through an invisible slug. The sharp steel cut deep, slicing a tear wide enough for her to take a step forward. Then, like liquid putty, the air flowed into the wound, reforming the web. Undaunted, Shadow ripped again and took another step forward. Cut and move, cut and move.

A woman hurtled towards the two willworkers from the other side of the room. At the wizard's side, Jenni Smith seemed to melt, dissolve. In her place reared a nightmarish creature, a horror not of this Earth.

Seven feet tall, with a scarlet body the size of a large beachball, it possessed a dozen yard-long thin appendages that served as both arms and legs. Each tentacle ended in a claw-like hand with four clawed fingers. A half-dozen eyestalks rose from the top of its head. In the center of its body snapped a gigantic mouth, filled with teeth and a jet-black tongue.

Screaming words Shadow couldn't hear, the charging woman flung herself straight at the creature. A mad act, but in this atmosphere of hate, not unexpected.

Seventeen, scythe in hand, burst through the front doors of Everwell Chemicals. His companions followed close behind. The entrance hall was deserted. There was no sign of either Madeleine Giovanni or Shadow.

"Where do..." he started to ask Sam Haine, when ceiling and walls started shaking. From above came the roar of steel slamming into steel.

"Showtime," shouted Sam Haine, as Seventeen ripped off the door to the stairs and rushed upwards.

Though Sharon's parents had both been atheists and she had been raised as a strict non-believer in either God or the devil, she knew as she ran forward that if hell existed she stood at its doorstep tonight. It didn't matter to her. Velma Wade was only an arm's length away.

But then it was no longer Velma. The shapeshifter changed, dissolved, melted into something much nastier. One of Those Beyond. Sharon no longer cared. Hatred gripped her so intensely that there was no way she could turn back, no way she could stop. Screaming wildly, she dove straight at the monster's mouth.

A half-dozen tentacles slapped at her, tore at her arms. Screaming in animal-like rage, Sharon directed all of her energy, all the strength in her body to her upper body. The creature's black tongue whipped around her neck, tried to drag her forward to the huge yellow teeth. Exactly what Sharon wanted.

Both her hands shot up, filled with poison pellets. Enough toxin to wipe out thousands. Black tongue tightened, tentacles slapped across Sharon's back. Hate, pulsating, overwhelming hate gave Sharon the extra strength she needed. She spit. Acid spray hit the thing's tongue. Alien flesh sizzled and burned. Like a huge rubber band, the black tongue retracted with a snap. The creature's mouth slammed shut just as Sharon tossed more than a dozen pellets down its throat. They exploded five seconds later.

A shockwave of poison jetted through the monster's body. Tentacles jerked high in the air, dropping Sharon to the floor. The thing screamed, its voice rising to supersonic levels. It swelled to twice its size, staggered across the center of the room.

Ezra, his insane face glistening with sweat, turned and for the first time saw the creature that had replaced his false wife. His mouth opened but no sounds came forth. Tentacles thrashing, the monster slammed into one of the huge chemical tanks, sending the container crashing over and onto the floor.

Toxic fumes blasted across the chamber, as a wave of acid swept across the black tile.

Then, with a final shudder, the shapechanger collapsed to the floor. Dead.

Desperately, Sharon scrambled to her feet. Behind her, the insane magus howled in agony. A gigantic invisible hand picked her up and sent her flying like a missile across the laboratory. There was no time to think, no time to prepare herself for impact. She slammed into the far wall and everything went black.

"No!" screamed Ezra, as he caught sight of the thing that had been Jenni Smith collapsing on the floor. "No!" he screamed again as with a flick of one finger he sent the dark-haired woman hurtling across the room.

A wave of acid swept over Shadow's feet, swirled up to her knees. The pain was intense, mind-shattering. For an instant, she thought her lower limbs would dissolve. Then the tide continued on, and she collapsed to the floor, exposed muscle and bone unable to support her weight. The black tile burned the flesh of her hands, but compared to the attack on her lower limbs, she hardly noticed. Her consciousness flickered but she refused to surrender to the darkness.

More than twenty feet still separated Shadow from the insane mage. Ezra's face was distorted into an expression not even faintly human. The end, Shadow knew, was very near.

Ezra spread his hands wider, began chanting in an unknown tongue. Above his head, the black cloud rumbled as if with thunder. Within it, two crimson eyes burned with hell's fire. Like a tornado, the dark mist began to turn, faster and faster, funneling power into the gap between the mage's fingers. The entire building began to shake.

Shadow of the Dawn prepared to die.

Seventeen barreled across the flattened steel door leading to the interior of the chemical plant. Behind him came Albert and Sam Haine. Not far from them stood a cyborg, surrounded by a half-dozen crushed bodies, clutching a steel workbench in his massive hands. Face a mask of rage, the machine-man stared as if hypnotized at the center of the huge room.

An immense black cloud swirled and roared there like a cyclone—a cloud filled with jagged, flashing bolts of mystick energy—a cloud with two immense pie-sized red eyes that glowed with hate. A cloud that *lived*, the ultimate manifestation of Lord Steel on the Earth.

Below the storm cloud, hands raised in a dread invocation, was a gray-bearded old man, screaming words barely audible in the fury of the tempest. It could only be Ezra.

"*Yabbonothomath!*" screamed Ezra, his hands raised over his head, as if trying to engulf the black cloud. "*Grrn aldon Azazanothonath!*"

HATE. Like a wave, it poured across Seventeen, filled his thoughts, blinded his eyes, deafened his ears. The living, pulsing hate of Lord Steel, the Duke of Hate. The black cloud was hate given form. It filled the room, tore at the minds of all those within. Destroyed all rational thought. Like a plague, a virulent, all-consuming disease, it burned like wildfire through the chamber.

Seventeen's hands clenched in fury, his fingers tightened in rage. He felt the shaft of his scythe in his grip, let the power of the runes carved on the wood sink into his being. And in that instant, he channeled and redirected the hate.

For fifty years he had endured the hate, lived through the insanity. Seventeen had survived Malfeas. Survived Duke Steel. Fifty years of unimaginable pain. Yet he had managed to escape alive. And he knew how to stop the madness.

Raising his scythe into the air, Seventeen opened his eyes and took a step forward. Another. Then another.

Ezra was the answer. The insane mage provided the Dark Lord an anchor to the Earth with his overwhelming hate. His rage against all life. Combating the willworker with hate only made Lord Steel stronger. But there was another path.

"Lord Steel," said Seventeen, raising his scythe high above his head. He spoke calmly, not loudly, but his voice cut through the maelstrom like a knife. "Ezra. I bring you peace. I bring you the *good death*."

His gaze fixed on the gray-bearded mage, Seventeen walked forward. Above, the spinning black cyclone slowed. Huge crimson eyes focused on him, wavered. The cloud, the incarnation of Lord Steel's power, stopped moving. Seventeen's fingers tightened on the scythe. Drawing upon the magick within him, the blade sang.

Compassion. Rebirth. Redemption. Those were the beliefs that defeated hate. A firm, unyielding faith that in the great cycle of creation, death was not an ending, but a new beginning.

Ezra screamed, hands raised in the air, as if pleading with his master for power. Seventeen swung his scythe. The blade cut deep. The very good death.

Hate erupted through the room like an atomic explosion. All-consuming hate, hate for all existence, it filled the huge chamber with absolute darkness. The pure essence of Duke Steel, released in the instant of Ezra's death, it threatened to break through the walls, to spread like a black tide across the city and bring a tidal wave of death and destruction that would reduce the metropolis to an empty, lifeless shell.

A man screamed. Screamed with more than mortal agony. Screamed again, as the blackness seemed to coil together, gather in one spot and flow into a solitary form. A single man standing, his arms outstretched, absorbing all the hate, all the anger, all the rage of Duke Steel. The shaman, Albert.

For an instant, he stood there, his face a mask of horror, his body filled with all the malignance released by Ezra's death, absorbed in his mind by the most powerful spell of Verbena magick. His flesh bubbled as if on fire. The fires of hate.

It was more than any man could bear, especially one as noble and pure as Albert. Shrieking in pain, he dashed for the huge acid tanks and wrenched himself up the ladder leading to the top. To the only possible escape.

"No!" cried Sam Haine. "Albert, no!"

But all that remained was silence.

Chapter Twenty-Seven

In her secret chambers, not far from the Everwell Chemical building, Velma Wade typed in the self-destruct order to her computer. Seconds later, the monitor turned black. A few seconds more and the entire unit fused in a silent blaze. Extremely cautious, she did not believe in leaving any possible clues for the curious.

Their mission on Earth had failed. Both Enzo and Ezra were destroyed, along with Resha and Jenni. It was a major setback to their plan, but not a fatal one. There were other important members of Clan Giovanni with ambitions. Everyone on the Board of Directors of Pentex craved power. And turning powerful, headstrong willworkers to the darkness was easily done.

They had lost Earth for the moment. But the real battle, the most important struggle, had yet to be fought.

Velma rose to her feet. Moving her fingers, she wove a secret code in the air. A gate opened, connecting Earth to the Deep Umbra realm known as Harmony. She stepped through, the portal closing an instant later. The war on Earth was over. The final war—the war in heaven—was about to begin.

Chapter Twenty-Eight

His body trembling with emotion, Seventeen staggered to where Shadow of Dawn lay flat on the black floor. As he approached, she raised herself slowly onto her elbows. The sword-mistress's clothes were in shreds, burnt by acid. The lower portions of her pants legs were gone. Yet she appeared unharmed. The miracle of her nanobyte blood. Except there was no erasing the dark lines of despair etched in her face. The same lines he suspected were on his.

"My apology for leaving you behind," she declared as he bent down beside her. "A foolish blunder on my part."

"Apology accepted," said Seventeen, as he raised her to a sitting position. His arms circled her waist, pulled her close. For a minute, they remained unmoving, letting life trickle back into them. Accepting the grim reality of Albert's death.

"Hey," called a gravelly voice that Seventeen found vaguely familiar. "Truce, truce, okay? We're all fighting the same enemy, right? Been a tough day for all of us."

Seventeen turned. A dozen feet away stood a massive figure, part man, part machine. Roughhewn, brutal features were a strange contrast to eyes that glowed with a sharp intelligence. Resting in the cyborg's arms was the bloody, smashed body of a slender woman with short, clipped brown hair.

"Cyborg X344," said Seventeen, unable to hide his astonishment. "And Research Director Sharon Reed. I thought you were both dead, killed when the Gray Collective was destroyed."

The machine-man shook his head. "Sorry. No can hear. Eardrums destroyed. Somebody wanna take a look at Director Reed. My systems aren't detectin' any lifesigns. But she's tough. Really tough. Can't believe she's dead."

"Let me check," said Sam Haine. For the first time since Seventeen had met the white-haired mage, Sam looked old. Ancient. His body sagged, and his cheeks were wet with tears.

The old magus laid a hand on Sharon Reed's temple. His brow wrinkled in concentration. After a moment, he shook his head. "Sorry. Not even my powers can help her. Insides are totally destroyed. She's gone."

Though the cyborg couldn't hear a word Sam said, the expression on the white-haired man's face was enough. Gently, he laid Reed's body on the floor. Sat down beside her and buried his face in his hands.

Gently, Sam pressed his hands on each side of the

cyborg's head. He stood there for a moment, his lips moving as if in silent prayer. "Can't do much," he finally declared. "But that should help a little. You hear me now?"

The machine-man looked up, stared at Sam. "Yeah. I can hear. Like you're shouting in a tunnel. Still, my ears are working again. Not sure that I care."

Seventeen rose to his feet, pulled Shadow up beside him. Ezra's body laid nearby. At the base of a toppled acid tank, he spotted the body of Jenni Smith.

"Guess we won," said Sam Haine, his voice crackling with emotion. "Don't seem like it though."

"What about Enzo Giovanni?" said Shadow of the Dawn. "He too must be destroyed."

"Done," said Madeleine Giovanni, emerging from the shadows behind one of the chemical vats. "My great-uncle paid for his treachery." Seventeen, whose senses were much more than human, was willing to swear she hadn't been there a moment ago. He glanced at Shadow, whose perceptions were equally sharp. The sword-mistress shrugged, as if admitting the Dagger of the Giovanni was not bound by natural laws.

The vampire stared at the corpse of Ezra ben Maimon. "Pietro will be pleased. His demands have been fulfilled."

Footsteps echoed on slate. Shadow spun, moving more slowly than usual, but both her swords were drawn. X344's chain guns clicked into ready. Seventeen's scythe lifted.

Her features solemn, a plainly dressed, middle-aged

woman came walking across the floor. She had long hair that fell to her waist, and features that bore a startling resemblance to those of the dead wizard. Seventeen was willing to swear that she also had not been in the vast room an instant ago.

"Judith," said Madeleine.

The stranger smiled. "Hello, my dear. Elisha sends his regards. He misses you."

"And I miss him," said Madeleine.

"Fuckin' supernatural Reality Deviants with feelings," muttered X344 so softly that probably only Seventeen heard him. "Earth gets weirder every damn day."

"I am Judith ben Maimon," said the woman, stopping before the mad mage's corpse. Bending down, she lifted the dead man in her arms. "I apologize to each of you for the pain and suffering caused by my insane brother. I take this clay to be buried beside the wife he truly loved."

And, she was gone, as if she had never been.

"Powerful willworker there," said Sam Haine after a long silence. "You have interesting friends, Madeleine."

"No more fighting for me," said X344. "I need repairs, and I need them real bad. You're going after the pattern-clone? Good. Reed programmed a self-destruct code into its DNA. Unfortunately, she never told me. So I guess you got to kill it the old-fashioned way. Flatten the sucker like a fuckin' bug."

The cyborg lifted the body of the Research Director in his arms. "Me, I'm gonna get fixed. Give Reed a proper funeral. She deserves it. Got to admit I'll miss her. We made a good team. A damn good team."

Turning, the cyborg headed for the door. "Good luck," he said as he crossed over the threshold into the hall. "You'll need it."

"What needed to be done here is finished," said Shadow of the Dawn. "We must travel to Horizon. Kallikos awaits."

Chapter Twenty-Nine

Frozen in a prison of gold, Kallikos watches with his inner eye a battle he has first seen in a vision five hundred years before.

From dozens of dimensional back doors leading into the Realm pour thousands of dissidents, rebels, and would-be conquerors. Many are young, but not all. Willworkers are independent by nature, often arrogant, and they're convinced of the rightness of their view of the universe. All know beyond any doubt that they can change the world. Young or old, they mean to have their way.

Some come to merely to protest. Most come to challenge the established order. A small but significant number come to destroy.

A majority belong to the Nine Traditions and enter Horizon from secret doors linked to their Chantry Houses. Others, from the Technocracy, come through hidden passages established by spies over centuries. And some force their way in from the Deep Umbra, from Realms in the outermost dark.

Chaos reigns. Huge fires burn out of control and threaten Concordia. And in the street and in the skies above, men and women fight and die...

"Party!" bellowed Arthur, slamming a metal claw into a man's head, smashing the skull like an eggshell. *"Party!"* he roared again, as his other claw clamped on the shoulder of another, ripping right through muscle and bone, drenching the steel in blood.

He was having the time of his life. Crowds of fools surrounded him, rebels with a cause, fighting for justice. They sought a better tomorrow. Arthur sought only to destroy.

Lost somewhere in this surging tide of humanity were the rest of his crew from Null-B. Possibly dead. Technocracy weapons and survival systems refused to function properly in a Tradition Realm. Beings like Joseph, more machine than man, found themselves trapped in massive metal hulks. Their artificial bodies became their tombs.

Not the case with Arthur, a Marauder loyal to neither Traditions or Technocracy. Half his systems were down, not functioning. His strength was failing, fading fast. But his claws still worked fine.

"Party!" he screamed again, lashing out at two more rebels, crushing bones with every blow. He'd been waiting all of his life for this moment. It was the party to end all parties.

"Listen to me," yelled Marianna of Balador, the full force of her will holding the dozen young men and women in front of her immobile. "Is *this* what you want?" She waved her hands at the huge fires blazing through the city. "Is this the change you seek?"

"Not—not exactly," said the one the others called Enos. "But sometimes you gotta fuckin' burn down the old to start fresh. That's what this whole fuckin' revolution's all about. Takin' what's rightfully ours."

"Taking?" said Marianna, her tone venomous, "or stealing? Not earning, that's for sure."

"We want justice," said a young, attractive girl at Enos's side. "Like the gold dude promised."

Marianna laughed. "The Man of Gold? A monster who seeks to rule all creation. To turn you and me and all humanity into its slaves. Is that what you want? Is that what you really want?"

"You're lying," said Enos. "You're fuckin' lying!"

"Am I?" said Marianna. Tears of frustration filled her eyes. Concordia burned while she wasted her time arguing with children. She waved a hand, breaking her spell. "Go. Leave me. Discover the truth for yourselves. Loot and destroy. See if that brings about a better, fairer world."

"Wait," cried the young girl. "Give us a chance. Give us a fuckin' chance. Tell us what's goin' on, what's really goin' on. Tell us the truth. That's all we want. The truth."

So Marianna told them of the being who called itself Heylel Teomim, and its god-like pride. And she wondered perhaps if perhaps there still was a small, small chance.

High in the sky, huge winged beasts not seen on Earth in many centuries flap giant wings and spout fire. Their black and gold and silver scales glow in the light. Dragons fly in the skies above Concordia. As do other, man-made constructions.

Technocracy skysleds battle swarms of griffins. A Horizon Cloudship, under control of a mysterious rebel group, fires its Ether Cannons at every dragon within range, trying to enrage the beasts to sweep down on the city, attacking with flaming breath and deadly claws.

A second Cloudship, loyal to the Traditions, battles the first. Its gunners fire a full complement of Entropic Torpedoes, but only a few strike their target. Little damage is done. The Cloudship's captain, Henrick Jameson, a veteran of a hundred aerial conflicts, ponders whether to launch his sole Time Harpoon. Untested, the weapon has been held in reserve for the deadliest of emergencies. Jameson can't help but think such a moment has finally arrived.

"The records in section Three Hundred Twelve," yelled the ancient, bald-headed man whose name was Nicodemus Mulhouse. "Then those in section Fourteen Twelve. Into the boxes with them. Hurry! The fires draw closer!"

All around him young men and women, mostly descendants of the Master Archivist, ran to obey the old man's commands. The huge boxes were creations of powerful magick and were constructed to withstand fires, floods, and sorcery. But no one knew if they could survive the destruction of a Realm. Nor were there enough of them to hold all of the important papers in the great Archives of Horizon. Not nearly enough.

"Everything in section Ten Ten," shouted Nicodemus, wringing his gnarled hands together. "We canna lose them. Then the Mi-Go scrolls. They're sacred. Hurry, you fools, hurry."

There weren't enough boxes to preserve all the documents and books contained in the greatest library ever assembled. Nor was there enough time. Nicodemus had to pick and choose, selecting those of greatest importance. Whatever selections he made, the ancient old man knew he'd be second-guessed for all eternity.

And the fires crept closer and closer.

Thunderous footsteps shook the entire square as a steel behemoth stomped into view. Screaming in panic, the rebels never had a chance. Those who stood their ground and tried to fight, died. Others scrambled desperately for shelter. Or surrendered.

Shaped like a man, standing twenty-five feet tall, the battle-engine was one of the Sons of Ether's greatest inventions. Its operator, Doc Binder, sat in a transparent dome nestled between the giant machine's shoulders. Twin heat rays, one on each arm, scorched to ashes all those foolish enough to resist. Created by super-science principles that made it unbelievable on Earth, the giant robot performed with clockwork precision on Horizon.

"What the hell is that?" said Dante, pointing at the thing fifty feet distant.

That was a giant beachball of a monster, crimson red, balanced on four black tentacles, while four others tried to squeeze the life out of four victims. Huge yellow teeth clacked in anticipation as it slowly but surely dragged one of the quartet nearer and nearer to its immense mouth.

"Got me," replied Rachel, his companion and student. Fifteen, sharp as a whip, the young girl wasn't frightened easily. "Something out of one of those old Beach-Bingo movies come to life?"

Dante, in his twenties, a Virtual Adept of amazing powers, shrugged. "Maybe. Though I suspect a Marauder incursion's more likely. Let's see."

He slipped the leather case off his shoulder, pulled back the top to reveal the computer keypad beneath. Balancing the machine with one hand, he punched a half dozen keys, stared at the whirling fractals for results.

"Definitely Deep Umbra," he declared.

"Better do something fast," said Rachel. "Thing's gonna start nibbling on that girl in a sec. Other three are starting to turn blue."

"It's done," said Dante, pressing the enter key. And it was.

The creature vanished. In its place stood a short, stocky woman with dark brown hair and astonished features. Her hands, fingers spread wide apart, pointed straight out like spokes from her body.

The four she had been attacking recovered with

amazing speed. Willworkers all, their screams of rage made it clear they hadn't appreciated the shape-changer's attack. Blood was in the air.

"Come on," said Dante. "I'll bet there's more of those damn things running around Concordia. Let's see if we can generate a program that knocks them all off-line."

"Shouldn't be hard," said Rachel. At fifteen, she never refused a challenge. "Run a subroutine, scan for similar patterns. No sweat. Take me five minutes."

"Do it," said Dante. "The Master of Harmony thinks he's king-geek of computer land. Time to show the sucker *hackers rule*."

Far below, the huge landbridge connecting the continents continued to crumble. On the bridge of the *Machiavelli X156-C36*, Captain Mulligan smiled. Comptroller Saunders would be pleased. As would the entire Technomancer Council.

The Prime Drainers on the combat dreadnaut hummed. Under Hasting's skilled handling, the machines were performing at peak capacity. Their attack on Horizon was running more smoothly than anyone had expected. All attention focused on the city of Concordia, leaving them in their Qui La Machinae free to attack the basic foundation of the Realm. Mulligan's smile widened. He wasn't concerned with glory. He was after results.

"How are the tanks holding up, Ms. Hastings?" he called to his second-in-command.

"Minor vibration, Captain," answered the young woman. "Nothing to worry about."

As if mocking her words, the ship's bridge started to tremble. Instantly, the smile vanished from Mulligan's face. "Ease off," he cried. "Feedback's starting to build. Cut the drainers! Hurry up! Cut..."

The rest of his words were lost in the explosion that tore the ship apart.

Though he remains frozen in metal, waiting the arrival of Shadow of the Dawn, mentally Kallikos weeps.

Chapter Thirty

An hour later, the three of them—Seventeen, Shadow and Sam Haine—stood in the Grove of the Goddess. Shadow of the Dawn had insisted they return to the sacred spring instead of the Casey Cabal Chantry House. Though she offered no explanation for their destination, Seventeen noted that Sam Haine had an uncomfortable expression on his face.

Madeleine Giovanni was gone. Her farewell had been brief and to the point.

"The children await a final word," said the lady in black. "Then, my mission here is complete. Events in Europe require my expertise. Already, Pietro has plans for my return."

"Nice to know even the undead get no rest," said Sam Haine.

Madeleine smiled. "I do not seek rest. I have my own dreams. Someday I hope to achieve them. Like Enzo, I, too, am ambitious. But I am much more patient. Until then, I continue to serve. The Dagger of the Giovanni is in your debt. If ever you need my assistance, you need but to ask. Now I must go. May your final struggle end well."

In the blink of an eye, she disappeared, a glimpse of mist the only signal of her departure.

"That's a dangerous, dangerous woman," said Sam Haine. "I suspect she'll achieve her goals. Even if she has to rip Clan Giovanni apart doing so."

Now they stood beneath the stars, surrounded by the mighty trees of the glade, waiting for Shadow of the Dawn to speak. Wondering what she had been told by Kallikos, the mage originally known as Akrites Salonikas.

"My mentor," she said, speaking softly, her voice scarcely above a whisper, "told me long ago that he was unable to see the result of our battle tonight. He felt victory against Enzo and Ezra was crucial in defeating the clone's plan to seize control of this world. But that even if we defeated our foes, he remained unsure of the final outcome of Heylel's scheme.

"If the pattern-clone succeeds in taking control of the Nine Traditions, and then afterwards the Technocracy, our triumph is meaningless. Only with the Abomination destroyed is reality safe. The battle on Horizon is the one that matters. And Kallikos has no idea of the outcome."

"No idea?" said Sam Haine. "Or one he finds too frightening to mention?"

"I do not know," said Shadow. "Whatever happens will occur shortly. That much he told me. We must be there. I am not sure what role we play in this final confrontation, but it is important we are at his side."

"He told you this?" asked Seventeen.

"No," said Shadow. "I know this. Kallikos told me our fight was over once we battled Ezra and Enzo. This last battle is his alone. Yet, in my heart, I know we must be there."

"Good enough for me," said Seventeen. "Only problem is how we manage to travel to Horizon without returning to the gateway in Kansas? Time's running out."

Shadow didn't say a word. She merely stared at Sam Haine as if waiting for him to speak.

The Changing Man shook his head. "I'm too old for this crap." He sighed. "Still, got no time for mourning. Who knows, I might be seeing Albert quick enough anyway. For now, duty calls. Damn Kallikos thought of everything."

"Not everything," said Shadow, sadly. Sam nodded, brushing away a tear.

"What are you two talking about?" asked Seventeen. "What new revelation is there?"

"Verbena's the oldest Tradition, son," said Sam Haine, his voice growing stronger. "We're the first mages. All magick comes from our teachings."

Seventeen knew better than to interrupt. He also knew that each of the Nine Traditions believed that it was the first and most important.

"One of our most closely guarded secrets is the Paths of the Wyck. Only for use in the most dire emergencies. Which seems to apply to tonight."

"The Paths of the Wyck?" said Seventeen.

"Mystick roads connecting Earth and the spirit world," Sam said. "We can travel from here to Horizon in an hour walking the Paths. However, it's not easy."

"Nothing's easy," said Seventeen. "It's never easy."

"That's the truth," said Sam. "The Wyck were the first mages, and they were the most powerful. Their Paths aren't pleasant. They affect the human mind in strange ways. Nothing overt. Things just look wrong, the light's strange. Too long on the Paths will drive even a master mage crazy."

"I cannot desert Kallikos," said Shadow. "I will take the risk."

"Where she goes," said Seventeen, "I go."

"Figured as much," said Sam Haine. "I'll blindfold you both. Might help a little. Me first. Shadow second. Seventeen, you bring up the rear."

"Sounds fine," said Seventeen. "When do we start?"

"Right now," said Sam.

"The Paths can be reached from here?" said Seventeen.

"Of course," said Sam. "Grove of the Goddess, son. Sacred Verbena spot. Walkin' into the water will take us right onto the Path. That Kallikos had everything planned, right from the beginning. He's a slick operator."

Sam turned to Shadow. "Your mentor tell you to carry a few extra headbands? Or do I have to tear off the sleeves of my shirt?"

"I have several extra bands," said Shadow, pulling

out the dyed cloth strips from a hidden pocket. "They should serve your purposes."

"Damned Kallikos is amazin'," said Sam as he tied the headbands around Seventeen's and Shadow's eyes. "Wish I knew how he planned to defeat the pattern-clone."

"That," said Shadow, "remains a mystery even to me."

"Right," said Sam. "I have a terrible feeling it remains a mystery to Kallikos as well. You two ready?"

Seventeen felt Shadow's fingers tighten around his own. "Yes," they answered in unison.

"Well, then let's get moving. Seventeen, you take hold of Shadow's hand and don't let go. Shadow, I'll have the pleasure of caressing your darling fingers. Don't squeeze too tight. After that fight tonight, I'm feelin' old and fragile."

Then Sam stepped forward, into the center of the sacred spring. And then none of them felt like talking.

The Paths were as eerie and disturbing as Sam had promised. Even with his eyes tightly closed and heavy cloth around his face, Seventeen could sense the glowing light of the Paths. It was as if the air itself were illuminated.

At first, it felt as if they were underwater, immersed in a liquid they could breathe, but that pressed against their every motion. Then, after an undetermined length of time, they emerged from the depths onto something that crunched beneath their feet. The ground felt strange. There were faint sounds, as if someone—or something—was calling from the distance. But the words were indistinct, unclear.

They walked without speaking. Shadow's fingers gripping his were a strong anchor with reality, the solid bedrock of humanity that kept him sane.

How long their journey took, Seventeen never knew. Seconds, minutes, hours, time had no meaning on the Paths. It was a journey without distance, without duration. In such a place, all of Seventeen's special powers, his sensory augmentations, were useless. The only thing that mattered was to keep moving. And never to let go.

Unexpectedly, Sam stopped moving. Seventeen's throat suddenly went dry. "What's wrong?" he asked.

"Nothing, son," said Sam Haine as he wrenched the blindfold off Seventeen's eyes. "We're here. Walk's over. Never to be mentioned to anyone, right? Verbena are pretty jealous about keeping their secrets secret."

"It's forgotten," said Seventeen. Shadow, at his side, nodded. "Where exactly are we?"

"Labyrinth in the rock caves far beneath the Council chambers," said Sam. "Shouldn't take us more than twenty minutes to make it to the surface."

The ground shook. Small bits of rock bounced like rubber balls into the air.

"That's no earthquake," said Sam. "Sounds like the city up above's taking a pounding. Damn war's already started."

"We need to hurry," said Shadow. "I can sense the time draws near. We must join Kallikos. He will be waiting for us at the Table Cenacle."

Chapter 31

They emerged into a city in flames. Sam Haine's ruddy cheeks turned white. "Hell and damnation. First Albert. Now this. Horizon on fire. That pattern-clone owes..."

"Party time!" roared a short stocky man with curly dark hair and steel talons that dripped blood. He raced towards them, huge claws clicking. "*Par-ty!*"

Scythe gripped in one hand, Seventeen pushed Sam Haine to the side. An unnecessary maneuver. Moving with the speed of thought, Shadow of the Dawn's swords flashed in Horizon's light. Their attacker's head, eyes wide in shock, tumbled to the ground. A few steps further, his body gushing crimson, did the same.

"We better start movin'," said Sam, sheathing a bowie knife. "This place is up for grabs. Maybe Kallikos plans to deal with the pattern-clone on his own. But I'm willing to bet Heylel's arrived with some friends, and they ain't gonna be playing by the rules."

"I'm ready," said Seventeen, swinging his scythe.

"Shouldn't take us long to reach the council chamber."

For an instant, Shadow's eyes squinted closed. "Not yet," she declared. "I sense that Kallikos waits for us in another location. Please, follow me. We must hurry."

Sword in each hand, Shadow set off down a side street. Sam and Seventeen followed. All around them fires burned. There were bodies everywhere, human and non-human both. The streets of Concordia were painted red with blood.

From time to time they saw others, but always at a distance. Always running in the opposite direction. None dared approach their party. The sight of Shadow's swords and the song of Seventeen's scythe sent combatants scurrying for escape. In the distance, they could hear what sounded like cannons booming. And from time to time the ground shook as if rattled by the footsteps of a giant.

Ahead, a beautiful woman Seventeen recognized instantly stood crying in the middle of the street. Marianna of Balador, the representative of the Cult of Ecstasy on the Council of Nine. Friend and confidant of the archmage they knew as Kallikos.

"What is wrong?" asked Shadow of the Dawn as Marianna raised tear-stained eyes and stared at them without hope.

"Kallikos," she sobbed. "You're too late. He—he's been turned to gold."

Shadow nodded. "Exactly as he saw in his vision. Though he never was able to perceive the moment."

"You—you knew?" said Marianna.

"Of course," said Shadow. Though her features were grim she smiled. "That is why I am here. Take me to him immediately."

"Now I am truly the Master of Harmony," cried the Clone-Who-Named-Itself-Heylel-Teomim. Reaching out, the golden figure touched the Table Cenacle and the giant crystal above it. Instantly, both objects turned to gold.

"Now I put an end to the past," declared the pattern-clone with a laugh. Bolts of fire leapt from its hands and engulfed the two objects. In seconds, they were reduced to a bubbling pool of liquid metal.

"The end of an Age," said Velma, keeping watch on the main entrance to the chamber. Not all of their enemies had been destroyed. Despite the clone's supreme indifference, she wasn't convinced the battle for Horizon was won.

"Stay alert," she called to her remaining sisters guarding the door. "Beware the sword-mistress and her lover, the giant with the scythe."

"You worry too much," said the clone, dropping into the enigmatic Tenth Throne. "The War is over. We are the victors."

Velma nodded, saying nothing. Dead bodies were scattered like broken toys across the meeting room floor. A number of archmages and their guards, along with several dozen of her finest warriors, had perished in the struggle for control of the hall. As had a small horde of mythic beasts including salamanders, fire-spirits, kozars, and koals. Indrani Taktsang, the Euthanatos member of the Council of Nine, had met his end. So had the Council representatives of the Akashic Brotherhood and the Dreamspeakers. It had been a most satisfactory fight. But one that Velma sensed still wasn't finished.

The sigils on the Council chairs suddenly flared to life. Surrounded by corpses, the being who claimed to be Heylel Teomim started to glow.

Carefully, Shadow of the Dawn looped the chain of the talisman around Kallikos's neck. Then, hurriedly, she darted back to her companions.

Color radiated in a spiral from the medallion resting on the seer's chest. Slowly but steadily, the gold statue transformed back into the living, breathing archmage.

"Kallikos gave me the talisman the first time we met," said Shadow of the Dawn. "He had foreseen this metamorphosis and had prepared two charms—one that he wore to preserve his mind, and the other I carried, to restore him to life."

"And not knowin' the exact circumstances," said Sam Haine, "he picked someone he felt possessed the necessary skills to survive and reach him no matter how dangerous the situation."

Shadow nodded. "He warned me that together we would climb the stairs to heaven, and descend the road to hell."

"Well, that sure's been the truth," said Sam. The white-haired old man took a step towards Kallikos, reached out with a hand. "Looks like he's just about back to normal."

"No," croaked the seer, raising his hands in front of his chest. The air around Kallikos rippled, like waves of heat rising from the floor to the ceiling. Small but intense vibrations undulated across the room. "Keep your distance. The talisman's spell invoked powerful forces. I stand in the midst of a Time Storm. I can control it, but I do not know for how long."

"Horizon's burning," said Marianna.

"I know," said Kallikos. "But the battle's neither lost nor won. Lead me to the Council Chambers. Quickly."

The pattern-clone screamed, as the tenth throne blazed with energy. It wrenched itself off the chair, its golden body steaming. Though invulnerable, the clone still could feel pain. It stood in the center of the field of corpses, regenerating its burned flesh.

Screams came from the entrance of the great hall. Startled, Velma glanced upward and cursed as she saw her sisters transform into battle mode, taking the shape of monstrous dwellers of the Deep Umbra they had encountered over the centuries.

Three intruders confronted her band. Prisoner Seventeen, armed with a scythe; a young woman holding two swords who Velma knew must be Shadow of the Dawn; and an old man with snow-white hair. Sam Haine, the Changing Man, who, in the blink of an eye, transformed from old man into a huge kodiak bear.

Behind the three stood Marianna of Balador. The archmage's hands moved in elaborate patterns, and even from here, Velma could hear her chanting.

Three against a dozen. The odds favored her sisters, but odds meant nothing when wizards battled.

Blades flashed. Her sisters shrieked in rage and in terrible pain. Crowded together at the top of the steps leading to the chamber floor, they had little room to maneuver. And tentacles and claws were no match for cold steel.

Five of her guards were down in the first moments, dead or dying. The kodiak bear, a huge bloody wound in its chest, dropped to its knees, wavered, then transformed back to the badly wounded white-haired old man. But before one of her sisters could tear him to pieces, a dark-skinned young man, leather case slung over one shoulder, materialized out of nowhere, wrapped his arms around the Changing Man, and the two of them vanished.

Marianna's chant increased in volume, rolled like thunder across the chamber. The words slammed into her sisters. Even fifty feet away, Velma could feel the force of the spell. It was an emotional flux enchantment of incredible power. Too strong for any shapeshifter to resist.

Like candle flames, her sisters flickered—changed—transformed—from one identity to another, back and forth, never able to hold on to a single shape for more than a few seconds. Frozen in place, unable to move, they became prisoners of their own talent. Bodies reshaping, reforming with each breath, they were incapable of defending themselves. One by one they fell beneath the scythe or the swords, until they were gone. All dead. Leaving Velma alone with the pattern-clone as the archmage, Akrites Salonikas, floated down the steps leading to the floor.

"You said he was dead!" screamed the clone, pointing an accusatory finger at Velma. "You told me he had been turned to gold!"

"He..." began Velma, and said no more. A solid gold statue couldn't speak.

They watched from the top of the steps as Kallikos confronted the artificial being who called himself Heylel Teomim.

"I ask again," said Kallikos, the Time Storm swirling around him, waves of Temporal energy cascading off his body, "what was the name of the hermit?"

"Hermit!" screamed the golden man. "What hermit?"

Kallikos nodded. To Seventeen, the archmage appeared to smile, finding peace in that response.

"His name," said Kallikos, "was Tormod of Kirkenes." And then, before the pattern-clone could move, Kallikos took three steps forward and grasped one of Heylel's hands between his own.

"Return," said Kallikos.

Like a whirlwind, the pulsing energy field surrounded the pair, binding them in an unbreakable embrace. Around them, the air glistened like a sheet of fine crystal. Their hands remained clasped together as if in a final gesture of parting. It was a sight Seventeen would never forget.

"What did he do?" Seventeen asked Marianna. Next to him, Shadow of the Dawn stood rigid, her swords crossed over her heart in a final silent salute to her mentor. "What's happening?"

"He's doing what was necessary," said Marianna. "For five centuries, he prepared for this instant—knowing that to save the world he had to sacrifice his own life. Hoping somehow that he'd be able to alter reality, change his destiny, but always understanding that if all else failed, this was the final answer."

"But what's *happening*?" said Seventeen.

"Time magick," said Marianna. "Kallikos is casting the greatest spell of his life. Wrapped in a Time Storm, he reversed entropy. Both he and the clone are immortal. They never grow old. But Kallikos is turning back the flow of time. *They're growing younger.*"

It was true. The clone's features remained unchanged, for his face and body were totally artificial. But Kallikos was going through a series of amazing transformations. His hair grew longer, then shorter, then longer. His skin darkened, then lightened. Gradually, over the course of long seconds, his features turned younger. And younger.

"The pattern-clone's made of Primium and plastics," said Marianna. "His blood is filled with nanobyte machines. The components of the clone's body are the result of centuries of technological advances. They're fighting the changes, no question. Kallikos is all natural, all human. He's nearly a thousand years old. The changed direction of the time stream shows on him more. But it affects them both. What matters is who lasts longer, man or machine."

Kallikos was a teenager now, tall and slender, his face smooth. The pattern-clone's features remained unchanged. Seventeen's muscles tightened, as he readied himself for combat. If Kallikos vanished into nothingness, regressed to a time before he existed, the spell would break. And the being who claimed to be Heylel Teomim would have won.

Then, as Kallikos started to shrink, regressing to early childhood, the gold luster of the pattern-clone suddenly bronzed. The unchanging expression on the perfect, inhuman face altered, seemed to waver. Its sharp, distinct features collapsed inward, like sand running through the stem of an hourglass. The black robe around the perfectly constructed body folded, dropped to the floor. A figure stirred for an instant, then vanished into a golden mist.

Kallikos was a toddler now, sitting and holding tightly to a crumbling hand of sand. Then he was a baby, lying on the floor, his hands clasped together, golden teardrops running out from between his chubby fingers.

Then, nothing.

The crystal curtain of air shattered, fragments of solidified atmosphere melting into mist. Seventeen walked forward, followed by Shadow and Marianna.

"Dust to dust," said Seventeen.

The three of them walked to the center of the demolished Council Chamber. Sunlight streamed down from the shattered roof. Outside, the sound of fighting had quieted. With the pattern-clone defeated, Seventeen had no doubts that Horizon wouldn't fall.

"The Council of Nine's been decimated," he said. "Do you start over? Or try something new?"

"The dream is still alive," said Marianna. "It simply needs healing—and a few changes. I think I know where we can start. And I know a few people who should be asked to join the Council."

Seventeen put his arms around Shadow of the Dawn, drew her close. He didn't care what happened next. What mattered was that they had won, that the pattern-clone had been destroyed.

The Horizon War had come to an end.

Epilogue

In bright bold red neon letters, the sign proclaimed LEO'S BAR AND GRILL. Below, in smaller script, were the words OPEN ALL NIGHT, EVERY NIGHT. The bar itself, a huge ramshackle wooden building, two stories high, was set back a few hundred feet from the highway, an offshoot of the New York State Thruway. The only other building in sight was a gas station across the street. A sign in the window proclaimed the sales clerk was "Armed and Dangerous."

Though it was late at night, the blacktop lot was packed. A half-dozen big rigs were in among beaters, motorcycles and luxury cars. Leo's drew an eclectic crowd.

Opening the door of his battered Cadillac, the big man stepped onto the pavement. He had been on the road for hours. It felt good to stand up. Just as it would feel good to see an old friend.

Powerfully built with broad shoulders, and standing well over six feet tall, the stranger moved with a grace surprising for a man his size. He walked swiftly to the entrance to the club. Clean-shaven, with dark, intelligent eyes, his face seemed to reflect light oddly somehow, so that his features were always in shadow.

The inside of the tavern was cleaner than he'd expected. The room appeared freshly painted and refurbished. The long bar, oak with gold trim, was well stocked, the bottles fronting a huge glass mirror. A dozen tables were scattered around the room, and there were three booths in the back. The place was packed. A CD juke-box blared out a gritty blues standard. Everyone seemed to be having a good time.

Stepping up to the bar, the stranger caught a glimpse of an old man with shocking white hair and mustache talking with great animation to a much younger dark-skinned man with a portable computer case slung over one shoulder. The young man nodded patiently as his companion waved his hands about in wild gestures.

"What'll it be, mister?" asked the bartender.

The stranger turned. Standing behind the counter was an attractive young woman with shaggy red hair and green eyes. Though it was winter, she wore a thin, short-sleeved blouse.

"Miller Light," he replied. "Aren't you somewhat young to be tending bar?"

"I'm old enough," said the girl, drawing his beer. "That'll be two bucks. New in town?"

"I've been in the area before," he said, "but not recently. Came tonight to meet an old friend. She was due here this evening. Perhaps you know her? Madeleine Giovanni?"

"Maybe I do, maybe I don't," said the redhead, suddenly sounding not so friendly. He could sense her rising suspicion. "What do you want with Madeleine?"

"Who are you to ask?"

"I'm Allyson. I own this place."

The stranger chuckled. "I'm not looking for trouble," he declared. "Unfortunately, disaster has a habit of finding me. A situation has arisen that requires my immediate attention, and that of Madeleine Giovanni as well. That's why we're meeting tonight."

"Well," said Allyson, "she did say something about hooking up with a special friend. I assumed it was Seventeen and Shadow, back from their trip to Japan. Guess it could've been you. What's your name? I'll tell her you've arrived."

"She already knows I'm here," said the stranger, smiling. "She'll arrive any moment. Thank you, Allyson. It was good to meet you. My name is Dire McCann."

A Few Final Words from the Author

Any work the length of *The Horizon War* requires the help of many people. I'd like to thank a few who deserve special mention.

To Phil Brucato for all of his help, advice, and patience as I played around in his world.

To Lori Perkins, my agent, who keeps me employed.

To my many fans throughout the world who sent me letters and e-mail about my books. Thanks to everyone for reading. Your enthusiasm keeps me writing. Special thanks to Greg and Lea Silhol for their continued encouragement and friendship.

For those people on the Internet, please stop by my web page, *www.sff.net/people/r.weinberg* and say hello.

These three novels were written during some difficult days, and I thank all of my family and friends for helping me manage through disappointments and disasters.

And thanks to everyone at White Wolf for publishing this book, the seventh of my novels set in the World of Darkness.

Robert Weinberg

As to the truth about the pattern-clone, the shapeshifters, and Scarlett Dancer, I'll leave that for you to decide. I know the answers, but I'll never tell.

At present, I have no plans to write any more novels set in the World of Darkness. But Madeleine Giovanni's story has yet to be concluded. So who knows what the future might bring? As Shadow of the Dawn states: *the only truth is that there are no absolute truths*.

Robert Weinberg
February 1998

A note to Mage fans:

In response to your letters and inquiries concerning this series, we'd like to set the record straight. Some of the events described in **The Road to Hell** and **The Ascension Warrior** did, in "fact," take place in the **World of Darkness** continuity. For instance, Doissetep is destroyed. Every mage within the Cal Ladiem Realm perished. Sao Cristavao no longer sits at the Table Cenacle (or anywhere else).

This book, however, need not be taken as canon. The **Mage** and **Horizon War** timelines split in the instant Doissetep ceased to be — though how far apart the histories diverge is up to you. Let the pattern-clone wreak what havoc you like in your own chronicle — or none. Let the Adepts and apprentices revolt against their elders — or not. Let Concordia burn if you want to. We'll settle on where the pieces fell officially and write it up in a year or so. In the meantime, have fun playing with the shards.

Robert Weinberg

Robert Weinberg is the author of thirteen novels, five non-fiction books, and numerous short stories. His work has been translated into French, German, Spanish, Italian, Japanese, Russian and Bulgarian.

For White Wolf Publishing, he has written the Masquerade of the Red Death Trilogy (*Blood War, Unholy Allies,* and *The Unbeholden*) and The Horizon War Trilogy (*The Road to Hell, The Ascension Warrior,* and *War in Heaven*). He is also the co-author of *Vampire Diary: The Embrace,* recently reprinted in *The Essential World of Darkness.*

He served two terms as Vice-President of the Horror Writers of America and for twenty years as co-chairman of the Chicago Comicon. He taught a course in "Writing Thriller Fiction" for three years at Columbia College in Chicago. At present, he is collaborating with Lois H. Gresh on a series of mainstream techno-thrillers; the first should see print in early 1999.